What Just Landed in The Villages?
and Other Short Fiction

Lawrence Martin

Lakeside Press, The Villages, FL
www.lakesidepress.com

<u>Art Work</u>

Drawings in *What Just Landed in The Villages?* and *The Boy Who Dreamed Mount Everest* are by Dan Traynor.

Drawing in *The Wall: Chronicle of a Scuba Trial* is by Evangenlinemarie.

In "My Deal With The You Know Who," music from Beethoven's *Für Elise* and Mozart's *Sonata No 3* are from musopen.org. The composer of *London Bridge is Falling Down* is unknown and the music is in the public domain.

<u>Book Covers</u>

The cover for this book and for *The Boy Who Dreamed Mount Everest* are by Dan Traynor,
    danieltraynor66@yahoo.com

All other book covers in the excerpted novels are by Judy Bullard,
    https://www.customebookcovers.com/.

ISBN: 978-0-9978959-6-4

Dedication

To the critique clubs of The Villages, Florida, which provided first the inspiration, and then the feedback, to make this book possible.

Preface

This is a collection of short fiction I have written over the past several years: one novella titled *What Just Landed in The Villages?* and eleven short stories. This collection also includes excerpts from six self-published novels.

Two of the novels and several short stories have won awards in the prestigious Royal Palm Literary Awards (RPLA) competition, sponsored annually by the Florida Writers Association (https://floridawriters.net).

- *The Boy Who Dreamed Mount Everest* won 2nd place in 2016, category of Unpublished Middle-grade Fiction.
- *Liberty Street: A Novel of Late Civil War Savannah* won 2nd Place in 2018, category of Published Historical Fiction.
- Three short stories won in RPLA competition, and two other stories have been finalists for these awards.
- The short story "Robert and His Muse – Writer(s) at Work," won a competition for publication in FWA's annual Collection Series of short fiction (Volume 11). (https://floridawriters.net/competitions-awards/collection/writers-at-work/)

You'll note my name with and without M.D. on the covers of the excerpted novels. I am a retired physician, but only use M.D. when the novel deals with medical issues and characters in the medical profession (*Consenting Adults Only* and *The Wall: Chronicle of a Scuba Trial*).

Lawrence Martin
The Villages, FL
April, 2020

Table of Contents

What Just Landed in The Villages?

Chapter 1

The whole house shook.

"Did you feel that?" George Singleton asked his wife, Martha.

"Do they have earthquakes in The Villages?"

"Not that I've heard of. This is central Florida."

George turned on the light and they got out of bed.

"What time is it?" she asked.

"Three-thirty."

"I thought I heard some dishes rattle," said Martha.

They went into the kitchen and she turned on the light. Two wine glasses left on the counter now lay on the floor, shattered. "Watch your step," his wife cautioned. "I'll clean up the glass."

"Could have been an explosion of some sort," he said. "I'll turn on the lanai lights."

The night was particularly dark, no moon. With lights on, he saw nothing on the fairway. Their ranch home bordered one of the golf fairways coursing through Hillsborough, a "village" in The Villages, the nation's largest retirement community. Over sixty of these villages, each with a couple thousand residents, more or less, made up the fifty-square-mile community.

Fairway houses sell at a premium in The Villages, since they offer nice vistas from the lanai. Sometimes golf balls rolled into the Singletons' small backyard, which for the fairway was out of bounds, separated from the rough by white stakes. An occasional golfer would walk on the lawn to retrieve his errant shot, but the rules of golf forbid him to hit it.

George knew the golf rules since he played regularly. About which, he often remarked "Not well," qualified by, "Hey, I didn't take up the game 'til I was fifty. Give me a break." Now sixty-eight and retired for two years, he was enjoying life. He and Martha, a year younger, hailed from the Cleveland area, where they both had worked as accountants. His mantra was, "No snow, no state income tax, golf year round–what's not to like?"

Martha came out to the lanai. "The glass is cleaned up. Turn off the lights. They make it more difficult to see the fairway."

"Can't see anything. No moon tonight."

"Then turn on the TV."

George did as told.

"Nothing but old movies and infomercials in the middle of the night," he said.

"CNN?"

"Nothing. Same news as yesterday."

"Let's go back to sleep. If it's anything, we'll read about it in *The Daily Sun*."

They returned to bed, and the phone rang. Half asleep, George picked up. "Hello?"

"George, this is Gladys."

"Who?"

"Gladys, your neighbor. I saw your lights go on, so I knew you were up. Did you feel that shock?"

"Oh, yes, Gladys. Of course, of course. Sorry, just waking up. Yes, we felt it. What was it?"

"I don't know. Harry went out to investigate."

"He's walking out to the fairway?"

"Yeah, he took a flashlight. You want to join him?"

"No, we'll stay here. Call us if he finds anything. Or if he doesn't return."

"George," admonished Martha, in a whisper. "Don't joke about that to Gladys."

"Sorry, Gladys," repented George. "That was just a joke. Call us if anything changes."

George said goodbye, and for the next five minutes he and Martha lay in bed, trying to find sleep.

"Hear that?" asked Martha.

"It's a siren. Maybe the sheriffs. Or perhaps EMS?"

"See? Must have been an explosion. Somebody's gas exploded."

4

"There is no gas in this neighborhood. All electric," said George.

"Right. I forgot. Well, something else."

They got up and went out to the lanai.

"Look," said Martha. "There are two sheriff's cars on the fairway. Their roof lights are flashing. What are they looking for?"

"I don't know, but I'm going out there. I'll find Harry. You wait here."

"George, I just realized what it might be."

"Oh, what?"

"A giant sink-hole. Must have just dropped down, causing the boom."

"Do sink-holes cause booms?"

"Not sure. Why don't you go see, but be careful."

George dressed and found his heavy-duty flashlight. He unlocked the lanai door and walked past the cart path toward the flashing car lights. The April night air was warm, temperature in the low seventies. In addition to the two sheriff's cars and several deputies in uniform, there were nine or ten Hillsborough homeowners milling around. He found Harry.

"Hey, Harry. What the hell's going on? Was there an explosion?"

"Apparently not."

"What then?"

"Look. They won't let us get closer. Those car lights show something's there."

"It's a blur," said George. "What are they seeing?"

"Here, let me shine my flashlight." Harry aimed it at an object about thirty yards distant.

"I don't see anything," said George. "What are you shining your light at?"

"It's over there. I'll wave the light back and forth. See?"

"What? A rock? What is it?"

"Exactly. A rock or object of some kind. But it's tall, goes way up. I heard one officer say it could be a meteor."

"A meteor?" asked George. "On our golf course? Just my luck. Are others coming this way? I don't have meteor insurance. And I have a tee time here tomorrow."

"Don't worry," said Harry, "the rules of golf give you a free drop near all meteors."

"Ha, ha," said George. "You're not funny."

More people came out of their homes, walking from backyards to the fairway. Two more sheriff's cars arrived. George wasn't sure how they reached the fairway from the street, but assumed they just crossed the curb, the cart path, and anything else in their way.

A tall man in uniform exited one car and began giving orders. "You people will have to return to your homes. We need to secure a perimeter. The golf course is now off limits pending further investigation." Then he spoke into his two way radio.

"Yes, sir, it's being secured. Five minutes? Okay, will do."

Turning to the residents, the sheriff spoke. "I'm sorry, folks, but I've got to ask you to leave now. Anyone still on the fairway will be detained. Do I make myself clear?"

The homeowners were all law-abiding retirees, none interested in seeing the inside of a squad car. Harry and George walked back to their homes, each house situated just across the cart path about 150 yards from all the activity.

"Well," said George, "they can't arrest us for sitting on our own property. I'm going to bring out a lawn chair, sit right in front of my lanai."

"Mind if I join you?" Harry asked.

"Not at all. We'll have a party. Ask Gladys to come, too. Good thing it's warm tonight."

George grabbed four chairs from the lanai and positioned them close together on the lawn. Gladys came out. The four friends sat and waited.

"I bet on a sinkhole," said Martha.

"The sheriffs think it may be a meteor," said Harry.

"I bet it's an explosion, set off by some kids on the golf course," said Gladys.

"There are no kids in The Villages," said George. "Unless they're visiting."

"It could be a terrorist attack," offered Harry.

"Why would terrorists attack the seventh fairway?" asked George.

"Ever play this hole?" asked Harry.

"Several times."

"What was your score?"

"Funny. Someone's going to blow up the fairway because of a high golf score?"

"Golfers are nuts. What can I say?"

They heard the sound of a helicopter and looked in that direction. They could see its powerful searchlight scanning the ground.

"There it is, over by the clubhouse, coming this way."

"Well, that will shine some light on this thing," said Harry.

"Yeah, literally," said George. "It doesn't seem to be coming down to land. Wonder why?"

"It's circling the sheriff's cars," said Harry. "I guess they need it just to see what caused the boom."

While the helicopter hovered at a fixed altitude, several hundred feet above the fairway, its search beam traced the ground back and forth. The beam's arc gradually diminished, finally settling on the object that had been only dimly visible from the ground when Harry and George inspected it. The powerful light then traced the object from ground to helicopter level and higher. Much higher.

"What the hell?" said George, as he rose from his chair.

"I'll be goddamned," said Harry.

Martha moved over to George and grabbed his hand. "What *is* that?" she asked.

"It's the end of the world," said Gladys.

Chapter 2

The helicopter beam revealed the object's immensity—a domino-shaped structure situated with its long axis perpendicular to the length of the fairway, an estimated 200 feet by 30 feet at the base, and of enormous height. Its angles were sharp and pure, its surface an unblemished bronze sheen when illuminated. Definitely not a meteor. And just as definitely, given its instant arrival, not of the earth.

"It's not the end of the world," said George. "But it sure as hell is the end of *our* world."

"It's got to be a mirage," offered Harry. "An optical illusion. We can't be seeing what we're seeing."

"I don't know what it is," said Martha, "and right now I'm too tired to care. I'm going back to bed, see what's on CNN. Maybe this is all a bad dream we're having."

Gladys nodded agreement. "Harry and I are going to do the same. No point in staying out here. Let the authorities handle it."

The two couples retreated to their respective homes. It was now almost 4:30 a.m. Martha turned on the bedroom TV. Sure enough, CNN had breaking news. "Unidentified Flying Object lands in Florida."

"It's not a UFO," said George. "It's a giant slab. Any moron can see that. And it's certainly not flying."

"Oh, that's really helpful," deadpanned Martha.

There were no visuals of the object on the TV, just the CNN anchor on the phone with Sheriff Brad Smith.

"We understand something strange has landed in Florida, Sheriff. In a large retirement area about an hour northwest of Orlando. Can you tell us what it is?"

"So far all we have are images from the helicopter. With sunrise we'll have a full view. It appears to be a large rectangular object and very, very tall."

"Sir, do we have any idea where this object came from?"

"None whatsoever. I am not even going to speculate. Right now we are securing the area and waiting on federal officials. Also, the governor is sending out National Guard troops to help if needed. We'll hopefully know more with sunrise."

"There's always something going on in The Villages," said George.

Martha nodded in agreement. "Can't we just go to sleep and deal with this in the morning? I have tai chi at nine o'clock."

She turned off the lights and they quickly fell asleep.

George woke a few hours later and noted the time. "Are you up?"

"Yes. What time is it?"

"Seven-thirty. I'm getting up. See what's going on."

"Wait, I'm coming too." The view from the lanai showed the security perimeter now extended to the out-of-bound stakes just yards from their home, and up and down the fairway. Surrounding the object were half a dozen law enforcement vehicles and a small army of National Guard troops. Some of the soldiers were busy erecting tents.

"Well, we're not going out there," said Martha. "Turn on CNN."

George pushed the remote control's TV button. The same CNN anchor from a few hours earlier appeared, and at the bottom of the screen in bold letters were the words: **Breaking News.**

"...Our correspondent Winston Clarke is in The Villages, a large retirement community an hour northwest of Orlando. As you can see from this map, the object sits about in the middle of one of The Villages' golf fairways. Winston, what do we know at this point?"

Winston stood outside the CNN truck parked close to the fairway. He and his crew had arrived from Orlando only a half hour earlier.

"Not much. As you can see, the object is huge, estimated to be about half a mile high. It does not appear to taper, either. Since its arrival, the sheriff's deputies have cordoned off the area, and the governor has ordered out National Guard troops, anticipating a huge crowd of gawkers. Homes line the fairway, and many of the inhabitants are camped out on lawn chairs, waiting like the rest of us to see what happens next."

"Okay, Winston. We'll be back to you in a few minutes. Right now we have Dr. Cornelius Goodman on a phone line. He is head of civil engineering at the University of Florida, in Gainesville. Let's hear what he has to say."

"Dr. Goodman, are you there?"

"Yes, I'm here."

"Professor, what can you tell us about this object?"

The professor's still photo filled half the screen. The other half showed streaming video of the object taken from a helicopter.

"Not much, only what I can see on TV, of course. But the size of the object, to stand as erect as it is, would require an in-ground section at least 200 feet deep. Otherwise it would be very unstable. It is hard to see how something could impact the ground to that depth and not disintegrate or collapse. So its arrival, at least, appears to employ an advanced technology. This is all speculation, mind you, and I'm using civil engineering principles based on Earth's gravity. But for this thing to land without disintegrating, or without creating a crater ten miles wide, to me indicates a *very* advanced technology. That's all I can say."

"So you're saying this object is definitely from outer space?"

"No, it's too soon to say where it came from. All I'm saying is, I am not aware of any technology to construct such an object and have it land overnight on a golf course, or anywhere else, with no apparent impact zone or widespread destruction. And it's my understanding, the surrounding homes were minimally damaged, if at all, and that no one was injured."

"Do we know what the object is made of?"

"I'm afraid I don't know any more than you. It appears to be some type of smooth metal. Here's another thing I should mention. I understand that some officials on the ground have touched it and the object is not hot. If it came in fast through our atmosphere, like a missile, it should be super-hot. The fact that it's not suggests the object was guided in at a very slow speed during the night, so it didn't just fall from the sky."

"Thank you, Professor Goodman. This just in. The president will be addressing the nation at ten a.m. today. We will show his address live, so stay tuned."

George looked at his wife. "You still going to tai chi at 9 o'clock?"

"Yes, unless they've canceled it. And I won't know 'til I get there. I called, and there's only an answering machine."

"What about the president's speech?"

"You can tell me what he says. I need my exercise."

***

At 7:50 a.m., a neighborhood foursome arrived in golf carts for their scheduled tee time on the Evans Prairie Golf course. Much to their annoyance, the clubhouse was closed. They met a clubhouse representative outside.

"What's going on?" asked one of the foursome. "We have a tee time in twenty minutes."

"Have you been watching the news?"

"Yes, but the news said it landed on the seventh fairway of the Egret nine. You can see that monstrosity from anywhere in The Villages, but it's just one object and one fairway. Why can't we play the Killdeer and Osprey nines? That hunk of metal won't bother us, and we certainly won't bother it. Promise."

"Sorry," said the hapless golf shop employee. "I'm afraid the whole course is closed."

"You mean you really closed all twenty-seven holes because of one fairway on one nine?"

"We had no choice."

"Damn. Do you know how hard it is to get an early tee time? Do you think you'll reopen this afternoon?"

"We have no idea. Check with CNN."

"I just called the Bonifay course," said one of the men to his golfing buddies. "No answer."

"Well, it's close enough," said one of the cart drivers. "Let's ride over there."

The men grumbled, got back into their carts and sped off to see if Bonifay was open.

***

Martha traveled via golf cart to the Village of Collier Recreation Center, for her tai chi class. Ordinarily, on a golf cart you can bypass the village gates, which are only for cars and trucks. She was annoyed to find the golf cart path blocked by horseshoe barricades and an armed soldier. As she approached, the soldier directed her to get in line to go through the car/truck gate, which was also manned by a soldier. Ahead of her were two cars and five golf carts.

What a pain. I've never seen this before.

It took several minutes to reach the gate guard. He was cordial but direct. "Need to see your Villages ID and one other piece of identification, ma'am."

"What? Just to go to tai chi?" As soon as she spoke, Martha realized the guy was serious and any obstinacy would only delay her passage.

"Yes. We have to make sure all of you are Villages residents, ma'am. It's orders."

"You don't work for The Villages?"

"No, ma'am. National Guard."

"Is that why you're carrying a rifle?"

"Yes, ma'am."

She fished in her pocketbook for her resident ID and driver's license.

"Here you go." Under her breath, she muttered, "What next?"

"Thank you, ma'am." He returned the cards, pressed a red button and the gate opened.

She made it to her tai chi class at the last minute. Only half the usual crowd was there, but a few came late, all annoyed at being detained at the gate. One woman quipped, "All of a sudden they have guarded gates to get in here. Used to get in just by using your gate card. Who sent that stupid slab anyway?"

Chapter 3

Although Martha Singleton missed the president's 10 a.m. speech, most Villages residents did tune in, including the Singletons' next door neighbors, Gladys and Harry Farnsworth. Back home in Pennsylvania, Harry owned a print shop and employed twenty people. Gladys was one of them, working as a secretary. Five years earlier they had both turned sixty-five and Medicare kicked in. That was when Harry sold the shop and they moved to The Villages.

Now the Farnsworths were watching the president give a speech that sounded like it could have come from a B-grade science fiction movie.

"Good morning. My fellow Americans, by now you have all seen images from The Villages, Florida, where an object landed that our experts feel certain is not part of a meteor and is not human-made. The Villages is a retirement community in north central Florida, with a population of over 125,000.

"I have been informed by my national security team that no country – not the United States, China, Russia nor any other – has the capability to make such a massive object and land it on a golf course, or anywhere else. At the moment we don't have any recording of its trajectory through the atmosphere. However, data from satellite and ground tracking stations all over the world are being thoroughly examined.

"All reports to date are that the object landed safely and no one was injured, but a few homes were rattled by the landing. I have been in touch with Florida's governor, who is on his way to The Villages. At the present time we are treating this as a national emergency and are sending scientists and engineers to investigate. We will keep you, the American public, as well as the international community, updated with our investigation and any new developments.

"Unfortunately, as you can understand, rumors are easily generated when there is no hard information. I have authorized a website, which is now live. It will give hourly updates on what we know and what is happening at the landing site. The website is at the bottom of your screen. If you hear a rumor, and it's not confirmed on the website, consider it likely false."

"It'll probably crash," said Harry.

"What? That slab thingy?"

"No, no, the government's website. Remember the Obamacare website when it first came out?"

Gladys just nodded as she continued to look at the TV. The president was not finished.

"It is now approximately ten a.m. Eastern Standard Time, and best estimates are that the object landed at three-thirty this morning. We know from reports that many people are in the process of traveling to The Villages so they can view it. The area immediately surrounding the fairway is secured by the Florida National Guard. The Governor has asked me to urge you *not* to come. The Villages is a gated community, and you will not be allowed to enter under any circumstances unless you live there or are a registered guest with a picture ID. Again, this is being treated as a national emergency, so we must keep the area as secure as possible."

The doorbell rang in the Farnsworth home.

"I'll get it," Gladys said. "I've heard enough. The president doesn't know any more than we do."

She left Harry watching the TV, and went to open the front door. Before her stood a young man in uniform, carrying some type of fancy rifle. He did not appear older than twenty.

"Yes? Can I help you?" she asked.

"Ma'am, sorry to bother you. I'm with the National Guard, and we are asking all homeowners in the vicinity of the object to move out in case there is any danger. We are prepared to assist you any way possible."

"Danger, what kind of danger?"

"We don't know, ma'am. We are strongly advising homeowners in the vicinity to move to a safer location, with relatives or friends, either to another village far from this location, or outside The Villages altogether. We will guard any vacated house, so your property will remain secure. We are concerned about your personal safety."

"You're kicking me out of my house? Harry! Harry!"

Harry came quickly. "What's going on, young man?"

The guardsman, erect and deferential, repeated his request.

"Looky here, sonny boy. I am three times your age, and I fought in Viet Nam. If you think you're going to come here and kick us out of our home, let me set you straight. Leave us alone. And take that goddamn slab with you." Harry slammed the door.

"A nice young boy, Harry, just doing his job."

Harry didn't reply. He went to peer through the living room blinds to see if the young man was leaving. "He's walking over to George's house."

Gladys walked up behind Harry to take a peek. "Do you think George and Martha will move out?"

Harry turned to look at his wife. "Do you think the Dodgers will ever move back to Brooklyn? Same answer."

Gladys did not follow baseball. "You and your baseball analogies. How am I supposed to know?"

"Okay, sorry. I meant, not a chance."

"Good. Hate to lose them at a time like this."

"Me too," said Harry. "This is getting ridiculous. You get a piece of metal in your backyard, and they send out the National Guard."

"Well," said Gladys, "it is a big piece of metal."

***

Marlene Bean lived on the other side of the fairway, alone. Mr. Bean died two years ago, and Marlene's closest family was in Maine. She loved The Villages, the friendship, the activities, and the fairway view from her lanai. She had slept through the boom and the sirens and the helicopter and didn't know anything was amiss until awakening around 7 a.m., when she looked out back. Now her view was disrupted by something very tall, not to mention squad cars and many men in uniform. All this made her unhappy. She knew Gladys Farnsworth from her mahjong club, and called.

"Gladys, do you see what's in our backyard?"

"Honey, we almost saw the damn thing land."

"I paid extra for golf course views," said Marlene. "Who can I call?"

"Well, honey, try the president. Didn't you just hear him on TV?"

"No, what'd he say?"

"Outer space."

"Who's out of space?"

"No, no, the thing's from outer space."

"What do I care where it's from? It's blocking my view. I'm really upset."

"Well, we have bigger problems, Marlene."

"Like what?"

"Suppose they're hostile?"

"Who?"

"Whoever sent that thing."

"I just want it moved."

"Don't we all. Marlene, you still drive your golf cart, don't you?"

"Sure, why?"

"Why don't you get in it and drive over here? People are still moving around this place, so you should get here in about ten minutes. We need to have a little talk."

***

The 9 a.m. Writers of The Villages club met on time, in Bradenton Recreation Center. The club consisted of a dozen retired men and women devoted to the writing craft, several of whom had already published at least one novel. Chatter began as soon as the members assembled around the card tables.

"You couldn't craft better fiction than this."

"You mean science fiction."

"Say, Richard, didn't you write something like this last year?"

"Similar, yeah. In my piece aliens landed in Europe and left Stonehenge-like structures in various places, but not a single monolith like this slab. So yeah, I guess I thought of the general idea first."

"Do you think they read your piece?"

"Who?"

"Whoever sent that slab."

"Could be."

"Okay, let's start the meeting," said James Howard, the group's leader. "Given that we have now been invaded, I think it appropriate our next writing assignment be based on this incident. So for the time being, let's put aside whatever we're working on. For next week each of us should prepare a short fiction on *what happens next*. Two thousand words max. Are little green men going to come out of the object? Will it start playing music from another galaxy? Is it going to fall over and kill somebody, smash the clubhouse?"

"You mean two clubhouses," interjected Horace, one of the regulars. "This thing is big enough to pick off two at once."

"Okay, good point," said Johnson. "Anything is possible. So next week, assuming we're all still around, we'll critique the pieces. Make sure to email your work so we have a chance to review it before the meeting. As usual, the best one will win a free lunch at TooJays."

"What do you mean by best?" asked another member. "Best writing or best prediction?"

"Good question. I think best writing," said Johnson. "The best story. This is the Writers of The Villages Club, not the Crystal Ball Club."

"I have a question," said another member, who was known for starting many stories and never finishing any. "I had a tee time this afternoon at Evans Prairie. Now I understand it's closed. Anybody have a game this afternoon with an open spot?"

Chapter 4

The migrations began early, almost as soon as the news hit the airwaves. Tens of thousands of people started pilgrimages toward Mecca, Jerusalem, Amritsar, Rome, Salt Lake City and Malibu. The driving force was similar for all groups: End of Days.

Pleas went out over the airways from mayors, governors, presidents: stay home. They were largely ignored. The slab was a sign, an absolute sign, of intelligent life elsewhere. A sign that God not only exists, but was taking charge. If this was going to be the end, people wanted to be in the religious centers, spiritually closer to heaven, if not geographically. Malibu was an aberration. The California destination began with a Twitter message that rapidly metastasized in the Los Angeles area. "They are coming by land *and* by sea. Get to Malibu Beach if you want to survive the apocalypse." The message made little sense but did result in mobs descending on the beach.

TV evangelists also lost no time offering their own interpretation. Their messages were eerily similar.

"God is punishing us for our sins."

"God has sent a message. It is time to repent."

"What is the meaning of the slab? There can be only one meaning, and it is this: 'Earthlings, you are sinners. We have come to teach you the ways of the Lord.' "

At least one evangelist affirmed personal contact.

"I have been in touch, yes I have. Yes I have! The slab's inhabitants have communicated with me, told me their plans. They want you to know this. They will spare the good people. The bad they will abandon. The bad they will abandon to a fiery hell. It is now up to you. Are you good or bad? You know in your heart. Be prepared to repent, to become good, so the slab will rescue you from the hell that will become Earth when they are done with the sinners!"

Why the aliens chose him as their conduit, to the exclusion of seven billion other earthlings, he did not say.

***

By 1 p.m. on Arrival Day, as the landing day became known, traffic on U.S. 441, the main highway to The Villages, had slowed to a crawl. By 2 p.m. it stopped. People got out to walk. National Guardsmen patrolled every entrance and all the bordering streets. Outside the retirement community's gates people stood and gawked at the distant slab, aching to get in, to see it up close, to touch it.

At first, businesses outside The Villages relished the influx of tourists, until they realized that the influx couldn't efflux. Then they closed. At 3 p.m. Florida's governor, now at an undisclosed location inside The Villages, declared a state of emergency. A thousand more guardsmen were called up, to help unfreeze the tri-county area over which the Villages spread. Tow trucks were recruited from outlying communities to move empty vehicles off the roads. Once a single lane was cleared, pedestrians not living in the area were bussed to Orlando or Gainesville, far away from The Villages.

Inside the gates, Villages residents were annoyed for different reasons. Scooter the DJ couldn't make it to Lake Sumter Town Square, where he was to provide the evening's free entertainment: songs from the 50s and 60s that brought out hundreds to line dance. Two other town squares – Brownwood and Spanish Springs – also lost their nightly entertainment. And kitchen and wait staff couldn't get in to service several popular restaurants, including TooJays Deli and Cody's, so they closed early in the evening. Even more bothersome, Villages residents missed flights out of Orlando International Airport because of the bottlenecks on the Florida Turnpike and other north-south routes.

Some, however, felt blessed.

"So much less traffic," said one resident.

"At least we can still play golf on the other courses," offered an avid golfer. "Evans Prairie was too tough a course anyway."

"My grandkids think this is a hoot" was oft repeated, along with "I emailed pictures of me with the slab in the background." And several residents "enjoyed having all the young guardsmen around. Livens up the place, makes me feel younger."

Real estate agents also chimed in. "Once this slab is gone, we should sell a lot more houses. Now the whole world knows about us. I couldn't imagine a better publicity campaign."

***

The day after Arrival Day the Villages Civil Discourse Club met in Colony Recreation Center. The scheduled topic was *Inequality in America: Is it a necessary evil?* One member was to argue 'yes', another 'no'. Over fifty people showed up, a good turnout.

"In view of the event of yesterday morning," began the club president, Bryan Dickinson, "I've decided to postpone the scheduled topic. Today's discussion will be a bit more timely. The new topic will be *What is it, and what does it mean?* Does anyone want me to define *it*?"

There was laughter, then someone said, "Its purpose is to disrupt the Civil Discourse meeting and make us change the subject." More laughter.

"Now, I've thought a lot about this since yesterday," said Dickinson. "It would be foolish to speculate on where it comes from, or its purpose. I thought it would be more productive to discuss how we, the people who live in The Villages, should respond. I know residents bordering the Evans Prairie fairway were asked to leave their homes, and I understand all have resisted, so that's one answer right there. The government has wisely decided against any forced evacuation. Creating a central Florida refugee population of over 125,000 senior citizens would be a political disaster, so we are all free to stay or leave as we wish."

"I'm going, right after this meeting," yelled out a retiree.

"That's fine, Nick," replied the club president. "As I said, it's up to each of us individually. Not sure it's better outside, though. There are hordes out there wanting to get in, touch the thing, pray to it, or whatever. Thankfully, the governor has secured the site, and gawkers can't get in, so for now I think we are safe here. Although, to be honest, I shudder to think what would happen if the world started trampling through our backyards. So, who wants to start?"

The "Professor" raised his hand. His real name was William Mishkin, but many members simply called him Professor because of his always thoughtful and instructive commentary. Mishkin was to be the "no" side of the club's postponed topic.

"Yes, Professor?"

"At least for now, the threat to The Villages is not from this object, which likely does come from another star system but instead, as you pointed out, from fellow earthlings who would storm our gates and destroy our neighborhoods. For the moment, we are protected by an ever-increasing army of National Guardsmen. But if the world decides to beat a path here, let's face it, there is no army on earth to stop them. So the basic issue, for all us residents, seems to be this. Do we stay and hope for a happy ending, or get the hell out? Is Nick the only one leaving? Let me see a show of hands. How many plan to leave because of this object?"

A few hands went up.

"Let me add," said Mishkin, "this is not something that can be decided in Civil Discourse. As the Music Man remarked, we can talk, talk, talk, but we don't know the territory." He sat down.

"Well said, Professor. Okay, who's next?"

Several people raised a hand to speak. Dickinson called on Katy.

"It's hard to argue with the Professor, but we can't say this object poses no threat. Any intelligence that can bring this thing to a golf course can certainly destroy us. It's all just a great unknown. Civil Discourse isn't going to answer anything. My husband and I are leaving this afternoon. I understand they are letting all traffic move away from The Villages, and we're going to take advantage of the opportunity. Before it's too late, I might add."

"Thanks, Katy."

Several hands went up. The club president called on Garland, who stood to speak.

"I'm just the opposite. We came here to retire, not flee. As long as the place is open, with activities ongoing, we're staying. Let the government deal with it. It's a national issue, not a Villages issue."

There followed applause from several club members.

Nick stood to speak without being called on. "You can applaud Mike's decision, but the real question is how long our amenities can be maintained. We've already lost one golf course. The gates are now like border-crossing checkpoints, with guards and delays getting through. Who wants to stay if the place degenerates into an armed camp? I, for one, don't."

In response, comments came randomly from around the room.

Let's wait and see."

"How long?"

"Until the shooting starts."

"You have a gun?"

"Everyone in Florida has a gun."

"Well, I for one, don't."

"You should get one."

Just then the door burst open. In the doorway stood Gerald, the Recreation Center manager. "Hate to interrupt, guys, but you'll want to see this. The TV is in the next room."

You don't interrupt Civil Discourse unless the building's on fire, so the members knew it must be important. They followed Gerald into another room. The TV was tuned to a cable news channel.

"We are broadcasting live from The Villages, Florida. What you see on your screen is happening now. All law enforcement vehicles have been moved away from the object, as it appears to be morphing into a different shape. This change began about five minutes ago. At the left of your screen is a view of the object from ground level; at the right, the view from a government

24

helicopter, which is hovering about 2500 feet above ground, near the top of the structure."

Most Civil Discourse members watched in silence, but a few could not resist commenting.
"Look at that."
"I'll be damned."
"Wow!"

"As you can see, the rectangular shape is changing into a narrow shaft, with a large flare at the bottom and an even larger, rounded-ball shape at the top. There is nothing outside molding the slab, so it all appears to be happening from within. Silently, I might add. From our distance there is no sound of any motor or engine."

The object was indeed changing before their eyes, and the eyes of the world. Several club members considered driving over in their golf carts to see the change in person, but stayed put when they realized the show might be over before they got there.

The morphing was complete in another ten minutes. The skin color was the same, a dull bronze, and it seemed to be the same height as before, but the slab was now a different shape entirely: a slender, round tower, wide at the base, narrow in the middle, and with a large bulbous top.

"It's a water tower," said one club member. "A super-tall Villages water tower."

Chapter 5

Until Arrival Day, The Villages had five water towers, each about 250 feet tall; now it had six, with the latest addition ten times taller. Its shape was exactly proportional to the much shorter towers, but its function? If the slab could morph into a different shape, could it also add water? And pipes in the ground? Or was there a different function for this new shape?

The day after the morphing, Marshall Dodson, a retired biologist, ate lunch with three buddies in the recently-reopened TooJay's Deli, Lake Sumter Town Center. All four were in their 60s, retired and happy with their post-work lifestyle. Marshall, the youngest at 63, lived in Charlotte, a Villages neighborhood about a mile from the anointed fairway. Before moving to The Villages, he taught biology at Savannah State College. Among other activities, he ran a popular birding club.

Naturally, conversation focused on the object. "It's mimicry," said Marshall. "We see this all the time in nature. Creatures adopt colors, shapes, scents, behavior, in order not to get eaten."

"What creatures?" asked Mel Vincent, a retired plumber.

"Lots of examples. Praying mantises, grasshoppers, moth caterpillars – they can change to resemble twigs, bark, or leaves to avoid detection."

"Who's going to eat the slab?" asked Gabriel White, a retired school principal, while munching on his pastrami sandwich dripping with mustard.

"Well, look, guys," said Marshall, "just suppose you landed on Earth from another star system. The shape you land with is a Lego brick or a mahjong tile. You look around, don't see any other Lego bricks or mahjong tiles. All the really tall objects you see are water towers. You don't want to be eaten by one, so you adopt their shape. It's quite understandable, really."

"Wait a minute," interjected Mel. "Don't insects adopt mimicry so *they* can prey on *other* creatures, to be the eaters, not the eaten?"

27

"Well, that too, Mel. They try to fit in to their environment, for whatever reason. To avoid being attacked or to become more efficient attackers."

Mel was unconvinced by Marshall's explanation. "So is our neighborhood slab trying to avoid getting eaten, or is it hiding so we won't notice it's different from the other water towers?"

"I admit it's got a height problem there," agreed the biologist. "But suppose it's in the learning mode. I wouldn't be surprised if by tomorrow we see the same shape but much shorter."

"Yeah? What's it going to do with all the extra metal? Send it back into outer space?"

"Possibly," said Marshall. "Possibly."

"Really?" snapped Gabriel, as he took another bite of pastrami. "If you believe all this, I have shares of a bridge in Brooklyn I'd like to sell you."

"Can't you think of something more original, Gabe? I'll buy the Verrazano. Do you own that?"

"Funny," retorted Gabriel. "Like your ideas."

"Look, guys," continued Marshall, "it's just a theory. Who's to prove I'm wrong?"

"Well, if you're so smart, what's it going to do next?" asked the heretofore silent fourth diner, Frank Baumgartner.

"Interesting you should ask, Frank. My writing group has challenged us to come up with the answer to that question. Everyone's writing a short story on what they think. It's due next week."

"Oh, and what is your conclusion?"

"I'm positing the slab was sent on autopilot, and the beings who sent it here are not inside. Sort of like our Mars rovers."

"We have rovers on Mars?" asked Mel.

"For years," replied Gabriel. "If you kept your head out of comic books, you'd know what was going on in the world."

The plumber shot back. "In the world? I thought Mars was another planet."

"Touché," said Frank. "Mel got you there, Gabe."

Marshall ignored the banter between Mel and Gabe, preferring to continue with his idea. "Suppose you were a

28

Martian, and one of our rovers lands on your planet. You might think the rover itself is an intelligent creature from outer space, even though it's just a machine."

"Why on earth would you think that?" asked Gabriel.

"No, Gabe," replied Mel, "it's 'Why on *Mars* would you think that?'"

"Two in a row, Mel. Not bad," said Frank.

Gabriel glowered but said nothing.

Marshall continued with his explanation. "Okay, guys, let's get serious. If the rover is something far beyond Martian technology, as that giant hunk of metal is for our own technology, there's probably no way for the poor Martian to tell if the rover *is* the species, in this case *Homo sapiens,* or just made by the species."

"Makes sense," said Gabriel.

"You're a biologist, Marshall, not a rocket scientist," offered Frank, who was a NASA scientist before moving to The Villages. "The slab could have all the intelligence of its creators and still be a machine. Aliens who could send this thing to our golf course don't have to be inside."

"That's just what I said, Mr. NASA. If you'd been listening. The slab was sent on autopilot, and whoever sent it to Earth is not inside."

"I heard you what you said, Marshall, but there's a not-so-subtle distinction between my point and the Mars rover."

"Which is?"

Gabriel gave Mel a knowing smile, which Mel acknowledged with a subtle here-we-go-again nod. They enjoyed moments like this, when their two 'scientific' friends got into a pissing match. Which happened not infrequently.

"Artificial intelligence, robots if you will, can do all the thinking and maneuvering necessary," explained Frank. "Machines in this advanced technology likely can replicate, and do anything their creators can do. So it's possible, indeed probable, that whatever or whoever created this slab endowed it with decision-making intelligence. I doubt it's a Mars rover situation at all, but more like what our Mars rovers will be like in a hundred or a thousand years. Zero dependency on humans."

"So no remote control?" asked Gabriel.

Though Gabe's question was directed to Mr. NASA, Marshall answered first. "That's pretty much what I said to begin with, if you guys had been listening. The Mars rover is just an example of a machine sent by intelligent beings. Like this slab."

"That's right, Gabe," replied Frank, ignoring Marshall's comment. "No remote control if the laws of physics hold throughout the universe. The closest star to Earth is four-point-three lights years away. Any messages traveling the speed of light would take that many years to reach us."

"Why can't they – whoever they are, of course – be orbiting the earth, unseen, and sending messages from, say, a thousand miles away?"

"Possible, I suppose," said Frank, "but I think something big enough to control the slab and remain in our orbit would likely be picked up by Earth's satellites. We're way out on a limb here. My point is, you don't have to have organic creatures inside or even nearby to control this thing. It could all be done by intelligent machines, robots. Just more metal."

"Sounds logical," said Gabriel, who now had a question for the biologist. "Marshall, you never said what was going to happen next. Which is the point of your fiction, is it not?"

30

At this critical juncture in the TooJays' conversation, a comely twenty-something waitress stopped by to ask if anyone wanted more coffee. They all said no thank you, and she walked to another table.

"If you want to see young people around here, you have to go to a restaurant," mused Mel.

"Nah, you can find them at Walmart, too," said Gabriel.

"Don't you guys have grandkids?" asked Frank. "The Villages offers Grandkids Camps a couple of times a year. You'll see lots of kids there."

"My grandkids are in college," said Mel. "Do they have a camp for college kids?"

Mel raised his forearm, palm outward: his stop sign. "Hey, guys, we're getting off subject here. Gabe, you asked me a question. Let me answer it. The first half of my story is what I already told you. An exploratory machine sent on autopilot, like a Mars rover. That takes 750 words. The second 750 explain what I think will happen next."

"And you're not telling us so we'll buy your book?" asked Gabriel.

"Hey, it's just 1,500 words, Gabe. Hardly a chapter, let alone a book."

"No," said Frank, continuing his dig, "he's not telling us because he doesn't know."

"Maybe not. We'll see." Marshall paused to build suspense, to make them ask.

Gabriel called for the bill.

Mel excused himself to the bathroom.

Frank checked his cell phone for messages.

No one asked for his story's ending, which annoyed Marshall not a little.

***

That same afternoon the phone rang in George Singleton's house.

"Hello."

"Mr. Singleton?"

"Yes."

"My name is Vince Doolittle, a reporter with *The Villages Daily Sun*. I'm calling because I understand you live on the seventh fairway at Evans Prairie, is that correct?"

"Yes, what of it?"

"I heard you and some neighbors felt the impact when the object landed. If you don't mind, I would like to ask you a few questions. We're doing another story for tomorrow's paper and want to interview people who live on the fairway. I'll be brief if you don't mind answering a few questions."

George did and didn't mind. Two days in, his and Martha's lifestyle was already disrupted. Now a nosy reporter.

"You sound very young. How old are you, if I may ask?"

"Me? I'm twenty-two, sir."

"Been with the paper long?"

"About six months. Did you actually see the object land on the fairway? I know it was in the middle of the night."

The reporter was persistent. No reason to antagonize him, look bad in the paper, thought George. He decided to cooperate.

"No, we heard and felt a thud, then when we got outside, it was already there. I'm afraid I don't know much more than anyone else, and probably a whole lot less, so don't think I'm going to be much help to your story."

"I understand. We're more interested in the effect on Villages residents. How has it affected you personally?"

"Like everyone else. People's reactions to it are what affects us. The gate business, the masses outside The Villages, the restrictions on our freedom of movement compared to before. This thing doesn't seem to be bothering anyone, and if there was no reaction to it, we'd be fine. But I understand, it is one of those earth-shattering events, and we just happen to live at ground zero."

"So no ill effects that you attribute to the object, sir? Like headaches, dizziness, anything like that?"

George assumed the reporter was fishing for good copy. *Villages resident claims his body invaded by backyard aliens.*

"Nah, nothing really."

There was more fishing, and George's responses were mostly no's and negatives. Just a big hulking piece of metal. Leave us alone and we'll be fine.

"Thank you, sir," said the reporter. "The article will be in tomorrow's paper."

The article did indeed appear the next day, under the headline:

While the world gawks, Villages residents mostly unfazed by giant object in their backyard

Chapter 6

By day four after Arrival Day, the local situation seemed under control. Crowds were content to gawk from numerous viewing points outside The Villages, using telescopes or binoculars. Farmers within a mile or two rented their land for people to park. The more crowded farms attracted food and portable-toilet vendors. Airspace over The Villages was closed except to government helicopters. There were now 2,000 national guardsmen in place, most of them camped out on three golf courses. The other courses remained open for play. An estimated ten percent of the residents had already left their homes, content to watch the news from far away.

The president gave a nationally-televised press conference. Questions came fast.

Q: Mr. President, are we making any attempt to get inside the tower?

A: There is no entrance point our scientists can see, so the answer is no.

Q: Have we taken any of the metal for analysis?

A: We are avoiding anything that might affect the structure's integrity, lest it affect homes and people who are still living in the area. Our scientists have produced a spectral analysis of the metal, which has been published in the newspapers and on the internet. They have found at least one element not of this earth. Further analysis is underway.

Q: Has there been any digging around the base, to see what it's standing on?

A: Again, our scientists and engineers have cautioned against any measure that might affect the structure's integrity. So the answer is no, no digging. All examination has essentially been without trying to undermine, invade or damage the structure.

Q: How about landing on the top? Before it changed shape, it appeared to have a flat surface on the top.

A: Yes, that was considered. However, it was a relatively small area, and given the winds up that high, and total uncertainty about the object itself, the military decided not to risk landing a helicopter or putting soldiers on the top.

Q: How about airwaves? Is it broadcasting anything we can pick up?

A: Nothing that we've found. And we have very sophisticated monitoring around the object.

Q: Why haven't you ordered an evacuation of the surrounding area?

A: There's no basis, really. One hundred and thirty thousand citizens live in that retirement community, and for the vast majority it's their only home. Right now there is no reason to order an evacuation.

Q: Mr. President, there are rumors that a similar object has landed in Area 51 in Nevada. Can you confirm or deny that rumor?

The president hesitated before answering, and turned to look at his press secretary, Charlie. They whispered a few words to each other, while mumbling increased audibly among the press corps. The mumbling stopped abruptly when the president began to speak.

A: Sorry for the diversion, but this was a new rumor to me, and I wanted to check with Charlie. We don't have that rumor on the website yet, but it will be up there within the hour. There are so many rumors out there. Is Jimmy Hoffa hiding in the object?

"Hoffa" elicited laughter. Except from the reporter who asked the question, Bill of Vanity Fair; he stood stiff, waiting for an answer.

A: To answer your question, Bill, there's no truth to the rumor at all. Now let me repeat – there are many rumors out there, and I'm not going to waste your time, or mine, trying to answer each one. We will keep our website as up to date as possible. If you hear a new rumor, check it out there. And one more thing, which I shouldn't have to emphasize, but will. We are not hiding anything. This is not some Hollywood stunt, some publicity gig. The thing is real, and we are working as hard as possible to keep you and the world abreast of any developments.

A *New York Times* reporter raised her hand and was called on.

Q: Mr. President, if I may veer away from the object and focus on the larger picture. What are foreign leaders telling you, or asking you, if you can share that with us?

A: Sure, Sally. I've been communicating with half a dozen foreign leaders, and we've had some good discussions. I've invited them to send scientists to The Villages, to make their own examinations, and as of now, teams from Russia, Japan, and England are on their way. Every leader I've talked to understands the slab – tower – is extraterrestrial. They are as concerned as we are. Clearly, whoever sent this object has tremendous technological prowess and could be a threat to all mankind. We're all aware of that possibility…

***

Marshall Dodson was not worried. He had already been in contact. Via email. His email came from 01001110 01101111 00100000 01010010 01100101 01110000 01101100 01111001. Had he bothered to investigate the sender's IP address, he would have found it untraceable, a feature of the Tor network that can hide the identity of the sender.

The body of the message read:

01001000 01101001 00101100 00100000 01001101 01100001 01110010 01110011 01101000 01100001 01101100 01101100…

Ones and zeros continued for several more lines. He entered the code into a web translator and asked for an English translation. The sender was "No reply." The message: "Hi, Marshall. Come at 0330 next. Bring another species with you. Knock three times."

Certainly the message was from the tower. He assumed binary code was the universal method of communication by aliens, so it all made sense. And 0330 must mean 3:30 a.m. If it was p.m., the message would have decoded as "1530 next."

Bring another species? Of course! The object had only encountered humans so far, he realized, and now sought contact with other Earth creatures. With great glee Marshall looked up at his window sill. There, curled into a ball sat his beautiful, black-and-white-furred Siberian cat, Fluffy. Ever since his wife died the year before, Fluffy had been his one true companion. He had no use for dogs or goldfish or parrots, and could never understand why other people bothered with those creatures. The *cat* was his best friend. He knew the aliens would love Fluffy. *But what if they abduct her? Or both of us? Take us back to their galaxy?*

The thought truly excited him. Something told Marshall they were not hostile. As a scientist he knew this thought was somewhat irrational, but felt strongly it was also true. He would bring Fluffy with him.

At 3 a.m. on day five Marshall took Fluffy – comfortably ensconced in a cat carrier – and drove his golf cart as close as possible to the Evans Prairie fairway. He parked behind a TV truck and carried Fluffy to the perimeter set up around the tower. There he was promptly halted by two young, rifle-toting male guards, one of whom spoke.

"Sir, you can't go any further."

"You don't understand," retorted Marshall. "The slab – uh, tower – has contacted me. Asked me to come." He showed a printing of the email and its decoded message.

"Yeah, we know. How do you think it got your name?"

"It's smart. Probably knows everyone's name."

"Sorry, bud, but it's a hoax. Check with your friends. Go to the government website. Someone's got your goat."

"You've seen other invitations?"

"Yeah, couple of others. Always to come in the middle of the night, it seems."

Marshall looked around. He found the area was reasonably well-lighted. He didn't see any other residents, just a group of men in uniform, sitting or standing. *Couple of others came here also, with invitations?*

"Say, you wouldn't happen to know the names of others who showed up with invites, would you?"

"No, we don't take names, just like we're not taking yours. Don't mean to be disrespectful, sir, but there are a lot of nutty people in this here place. You should be thankful we're guarding it now. That slab is weird, but where it landed is kinda weird also."

Assholes. Young punks. They are *being disrespectful. But no point trying to push in. I bet they wouldn't hesitate to shoot.*

"I suppose you young boys would think that. You may think we're weird, but there are a lot of smart people who've retired here. You think all we do is play shuffleboard?"

"You best go home, sir. You don't want to be arrested for trespassing."

Marshall stood before the soldiers for half a minute and pondered his options, which came down to only one. "Let's go, Fluffy. We're not wanted here."

He drove home in his golf cart and went back to bed. But first he gave Fluffy a bowl of tuna-flavored cat food.

***

Marshall awoke at 10 a.m. and checked the government's new website. The link BE ON GUARD FOR HOAXES brought him to a web page of short paragraphs, each a warning. The paragraph headings were: "Overnight home rentals on the landing fairway"; "Helicopter rides over the slab-tower"; "Play golf where it landed"; and "Coded email invitations to visit the slab-tower." Only the last item interested him, and he read it slowly.

> The email invitation is in binary code, a series of ones and zeros. The recipient may assume this is the way aliens communicate with humans, since it is a "universal code." Decoding is easily done in one of several websites, e.g. http://binarytranslator.com/. The server sending these messages has not yet been located, possibly due to use of the Tor network. We are continuing to investigate. At this time there is no evidence of any communication from the slab-tower. If you receive one of these emails, ignore it. It is most certainly a hoax.

Marshall pondered the warning. *How can they be so sure?*

Chapter 7

The slab-water tower did not move or morph any further. Still, day and night, multitudes maintained vigil outside The Villages, waiting on who knows what. The end-of-days crowd filled religious centers for prayers, incantations, sermons. The White House continued to give daily updates based on information from on-site scientists and engineers, but that wasn't much. In some ways the lack of news was reassuring. The object wasn't harming anyone, at least not yet, though a few people did imagine a *War of the Worlds* scenario: giant aliens intent on destroying mankind.

The majority of Villages residents did not seem overly concerned. Except for the fact of its physical presence, the object itself wasn't threatening or disrupting. It didn't smell, made no noise, emitted no radiation; in all ways the slab-tower was a 'good neighbor'. But its sheer size and improbable manner of arrival meant it could never be ignored. If it did not leave, then neither would the mass of people surrounding The Villages, aching to get in. And that meant the lifestyle once enjoyed by Villages residents now came encumbered with the ever-vigilant National Guard, television cameras, and enterprising reporters.

Fortunately for the residents, most activities were in play. The Mavens of Mahjong club was particularly active. Only one or two members had moved away, the rest preferring to live with the object rather than miss any games. They met twice a week. Women sat four to a table. At one of the tables, three of the women chatted about the event. Knowing just who said what was not material to the conversation at hand.

"That slab is just a giant mahjong tile."

"It was a slab. Now it's a tower."

"Well, when it landed it was a slab. And not very pretty. Look how pretty our tiles are. Nice designs. The slab was drab."

"You think they play mahjong?"

"Who?"

"The people in the slab."

"There's no people in the slab."

"How'd it get here, then?"

"The same way one of our rovers got to Mars."

"Who's been to Mars? Do we have people on Mars?"

"We have rovers on Mars. They're little mechanical trucks, sent through space. Takes seven or eight months to get there."

"That's a long trip."

"It's just a machine. The long trip doesn't bother them."

"Who drives them on Mars?"

"No one. They're like robots on wheels."

"I have no interest in going to Mars."

"It's a one-way trip."

"To Mars?"

"To Mars. Did you know that the first people who go will be pioneers, with no plans to return? My grandson says he wants to go. He's only twelve. Mishugenah, that kid."

"Well, I'm not interested. No Costco on Mars."

"No Costco in The Villages either."

"Yeah, but we have Sam's Club and Target."

"Hey, girls, we're off track here," said the fourth tablemate, heretofore silent. "No one's going to Mars. And the slab is not a mahjong tile. Can we just play?"

"Okay. It's just conversation."

"Mishugenah, that kid."

***

That night, at the weekly Folk Music Club, two dozen string players were about to start their performance of popular folk ditties. Villagers in the audience, usually at least forty in number, had access to printed lyrics so they could sing along.

The Folk Music leader addressed the group. "In honor of our visitor from outer space, we're going to start with *I'll Fly Away*." There was brief applause. "As in, we hope they will fly away soon."

I'll Fly Away was a familiar tune to those assembled, but this night it was special; the singing was loud and robust. Never mind that there was no real connection between the lyrics and what stood on the Evans Prairie golf course.

41

I'll fly away, oh glory, I'll fly away.
When I die, hallelujah by and by, I'll fly away.

***

Homes on the landing fairway went up in value overnight. Not that anyone was selling. The problem was that offers to buy one came with a demand for immediate possession. Typically a closing takes weeks or months after an offer is accepted, but buyers wanted to move in right away, as any delay and the object might be gone. To facilitate the deal they were willing to "rent to buy." No homeowners were willing to move out that quickly.

By necessity Villages residents learned to adapt, to accept this gigantic, extraterrestrial structure in their midst, while many parts of the world convulsed over it. Malibu Beach was a near disaster. Thousands of people showed up, prepared to camp out. With no sanitation facilities and limited provisions, the invaders threatened nearby homes, including some belonging to Hollywood stars. The rich and famous evacuated pronto, trusting the police to protect their property. The governor had to call out the National Guard. It took twenty-four hours and a fleet of school buses to effect a beach evacuation. Three people were killed in one of several clashes with the authorities.

***

At the very moment Malibu was being evacuated, Gladys, her friend Mildred from across the fairway, and two other women – Hilda and Samantha – lunched at the Bonifay Country Club restaurant. As soon as the waitress left with their orders, the conversation turned topical.

"It's all much ado about nothing," said Hilda. "I mean I see the thing. I can see it from my front yard in Duval. So what? It just sits there, blocks the sun. Doesn't move. You know, a couple of our water towers are in people's backyards, and they live with it. Just because this thing is five times taller, so what?"

"Ten times taller," said Samantha. "Ten times."

"Ten times, twenty times, I say leave it alone. The National Guard should get out of The Villages. What are they waiting for?"

"Armageddon," said Gladys.

"Who is Armageddon?" asked Mildred.

***

There were many requests to interview residents living "on the fairway." And not just by the local newspapers and cable networks. *The New York Times*, *The Washington Post*, *The Wall Street Journal* and *Time Magazine* all sent reporters to mingle with the residents and report back. The *New York Sophisticate*, an east coast online weekly with the tagline "For sophisticates wherever they live," and famous for its first-person features on current events, also sent a journalist.

On day five, George and Martha were among several couples interviewed on CNN. They stood with the reporter and cameraman in their tiny backyard.

"I'm here with George and Martha Singleton, who live on the seventh fairway," the interviewer, a young man about thirty, began. "The Singletons are from Cleveland Heights, Ohio and have lived here for two years."

One of the TV cameras panned from George to Martha, neither one smiling.

"How are you two holding up?" asked the reporter. Behind him another camera showed the looming structure, now in the shape of an overgrown Villages water tower.

"As well as can be expected," said Martha, turning her head toward the tower.

"Did either of you see the slab land?"

"No. We were sleeping. But we felt the house shake, and that woke us up."

"I know you must get this question often, but have your lives been disrupted by this object, which as I stand here is almost in your backyard?"

"Not much. Takes a lot more time to get through the gates, of course. And now we can't play several of the golf courses. Stuff like that," said George.

"Well, our tai chi club still meets," chimed in Martha.

"Yes," added her husband, "and my bowling league."

"That's good, that's good," opined the reporter, in a manner to suggest he might be thinking the opposite.

***

Somehow, the tabloid *National Investigator* was able to find stories totally missed by CNN and other major news media. Starting on day two after the landing, the *Investigator* printed one amazing story after another.

Day 2: Two Villages residents visit inside the Space Slab, find no life forms. See pictures on page 8.

Day 3: Villages resident sees aliens leave Slab-Tower, has video. "I was almost abducted," he says.

Day 4: "I fought off one of the aliens."

The "pictures on page 8" looked like sets from a space movie – sterile rooms with fluorescent lighting. The "video" on

YouTube was a blur of someone running across a golf course. The poor gentleman who claimed he fought off the aliens was too busy to take any pictures, but he did provide a description. Something like the movie character ET, he said, but with sharp teeth.

The *Investigator* story on Day 5 came from "unnamed sources high up in the Administration." Its headline read:

President meets with aliens, negotiates peace instead of war.

***

And so it went, for two more days. A week post-arrival, the Writers of The Villages club met again.

"Okay, we're all still here," said James Howard, the club leader. "That's encouraging. Last week we were challenged to write a short piece, the theme being 'What Will Happen Next?' Two thousand word limit. So far, the big change is the slab's morphing into a slender tower on day two. We don't know what the hell that means. I've read all your emailed pieces, some of which are very interesting. Who wants to go first?"

Marshall Dodson raised his hand.

"Okay, Marshall, go ahead and read."

***

On day eight post-arrival, *The New York Sophisticate* published online its first-person report from The Villages.

Chapter 8

The New York Sophisticate
The online magazine for sophisticates wherever they live
***
Report from The Villages, FL
By Lawrence M. Abraham

PART 1, posted April 15, 2---
My first view of the tower comes while driving up the Florida Turnpike from the Orlando Airport, about twenty miles south of The Villages. Not knowing anything about events of the past week, one might think it just another tourist attraction, with perhaps a Ferris wheel and roller coasters and all the other trappings of an amusement park. Why else would anyone build such a tall structure in the middle of nowhere?

A few miles out and it's apparent this is something different. Every acre of farmland – and there are many such acres surrounding The Villages – seems covered by cars, RVs, and tents. There are telescopes set up beside vehicles, and many people with binoculars and cameras. You don't see that three miles from Disney World.

A further distinction from Central Florida's amusement kitsch comes at The Villages entrance gate: National Guardsmen toting scary-looking rifles. If you are not authorized, you won't get in. I squeeze my press pass in one hand, lest some zombie smash the car window and steal it. I've hardly arrived, and I'm already thinking about aliens.

"Driver's license and one other piece of photo identification, sir," a young guard demands. With those and the pass, I am let through. I notice the gate camera that takes a picture of every vehicle's license plate. I ride slowly to the Lakefront Hotel in Lake Sumter Town Center, one of three commercial districts inside the massive retirement community.

After checking in and taking an extended walk around the town center – which is full of small shops, restaurants and parked golf carts – I ask myself why this magazine hasn't been here before. Why did it take the landing of an extraterrestrial object, perhaps the most culture-changing event in world history, to have a New York reporter *show up*? (A colleague from *The New York Times* is staying in the same hotel.)

I mean, The Villages is the largest retirement community in the country – currently clocked at about 125,000 residents -- with enough Florida history, anecdotes and unique demographics to certainly warrant a feature story or two *sans* the alien angle. Did you know the place began as a small trailer park in the 1970s and now sprawls over fifty square miles, three times the size of Manhattan? Me either. Did you know The Villages has the largest concentration of both married *and* single seniors in the country? Ditto.

The day after the object's landing – which, if you have to ask what I refer to, suggests you may be living in a cave and some hiker dropped a printout of this story nearby – my editor said, "Get down there and find out what the hell's going on." And he didn't mean in a scientific way, either.

Unless something's changed since this article was posted, no one knows what the hell is going on, where the object is from, or how long it plans to stay. Will it kill us all or leave peacefully? Don't know, but I met someone who does. At least that's what he says.

Marshall Dodson is one person I met who feels certain there are life forms in the object, and that "they" (he does not use the word aliens) have communicated with him. Never mind there is no "they" anyone can discern. Just a hunk of metal, 2,750 ft. high. No one knows how much of it is below ground.

Dodson denies alien abduction, claiming just benign (and rather mundane) email communication from the slab.

"Ones and zeros," he says.

"That's binary code, isn't it? That's how they communicate?"

"Yeah, binary code, the universal language."

"What did the message state?"

"To come visit."

"Did you?"

"Tried. The guards wouldn't let me even get close. The government says the email's a hoax, but we have no proof of that."

I decide to change the subject. "You're retired?"

"For two years. I was a biology professor."

Unlike Marshall, who is from Georgia, most residents came from the Northeast and Midwest, although a great many first set up home elsewhere in Florida, before moving to The Villages. And just about everyone here is retired, though a few still work part-time to supplement their social security and pensions. The fully-retired majority is content to live out their remaining years in a place they lovingly refer to as "Disneyland for Adults." Now their days are disrupted, and they all wish *it* would just go away.

Before the object landed, The Villages was a fairly open community. The gates to some sixty different residential neighborhoods were used mainly to slow traffic and let golf carts cross the neighborhood entrance roads. Unlike a truly gated community, as you might encounter in posh areas of Orlando, Tampa or South Florida, here the roads are county owned, which meant any non-resident could get in.

Not anymore. Now you better live here or have a *bona fide* guest pass. My *New York Sophisticate* press pass – obtained not without some bureaucratic haggling – is only good for one week. If I don't leave at expiration, the National Guard, which are all over the place, will escort me out. Sort of like a country that only gives short-term visas and god help you if you overstay. Still, once here, everyone is friendly, cordial. I like the vibe of the place. *Why haven't I been here before?*

The world – starting with our president, Florida's governor and hundreds of scientists studying the object – wants desperately to know what it is, where it's from and what it plans to do: with Earth, with Earth's people, with Earth's solar system, for God sakes. But there is another question seldom asked. Why did the half-mile-high metal slab land here, on a Villages golf fairway? If it's so smart, wouldn't it have picked someplace more relevant to Earth's power centers? Manhattan's Central Park, say, or the Washington Mall or Moscow's Red Square? Didn't it Google "Open spaces in major cities"?

For Gladys and Harry Farnsworth, whose backyard abuts the anointed fairway, the question isn't worth asking.

"Who cares? Why do you care?" Harry challenges.

These are nice people, who agreed to meet me on condition I "don't ask dumb questions like the others." I flunk that condition in the first few minutes, and quickly apologize. They are annoyed with outsiders, or rather "inquisitive boobs who want to make us look like local yokels."

"Our readers want to know what it's like to live so close," I explain. The Farnsworths' home is one of a dozen ranch homes backing to the fairway, and there are another dozen on the other side. (Almost all homes in The Villages are single-family, ranch-style – only one small apartment complex, and that one recently built).

"At first, it was Wow!" says Gladys, a diminutive woman the same age as her husband, 70. "We were as awe-struck as anyone when the thing landed. We were never afraid, though, and when the National Guard suggested we leave our home, Harry went ballistic. Fortunately, no one's forcing us out."

"Well," chimes in Harry. "When the thing changed to look like a water tower, that was a bit scary, I must admit. It could just as well change into a giant missile or bomb. You never know."

"I think it's done changing," says Gladys. "Just hope it stays erect. If the thing falls over and crushes us, we hope it's quick. But we're not leaving. Wish everyone else would, though. Don't mean to be rude, mind you, but all the attention is just a nuisance."

(NOTE TO *SOPHISTICATE* READERS: We will post Part 2 of Mr. Abraham's article tomorrow, 8 a.m. E.S.T.]

***

"Well, what'dya know," exclaimed Harry, upon finishing Part One of Abraham's article, "at least he quoted us correctly."

"Does he say anything we don't already know?" asked Gladys.

"Nah, same old rehash. But he's not writing the thing for us. It's for the great unwashed who have no idea about The Villages or the people who live here. I'll give this to him – he's a darn good writer. It's a long piece, second part to be posted tomorrow. I imagine everyone in The Villages will be looking forward to Part Two."

"Oh, what the hell, Harry, let me read it. You got me curious."

Harry didn't want to get up from his comfortable desk chair, so he moved aside to let her read the screen. After a few "scroll downs" she was done, but had one question.

"Who's this guy Marshall Dodson? Ever hear of him?"

"Nah, but if you look hard enough, you can find all kinds of kooks in The Villages. Ones and zeros. What a hoot."

"I suppose they could also say that about you, when people read this. 'Who's that crazy guy Harry Farnsworth, who acts like this is an everyday event?'"

"I didn't say it was an everyday event."

"No, just…let me see." She leaned over again and read the screen. "You said, 'Who cares?' and 'Why do you care?'"

49

"My comments clearly show that I'm annoyed with the media, not that I'm blasé about the event. Compared to that guy Dodson, I come across like…like…a sophisticate."

Gladys laughed. "Now that's funny. My Harry, *The Villages Sophisticate*."

Chapter 9

The New York Sophisticate
The online magazine for sophisticates
wherever they live
***
Report from The Villages, FL
By Lawrence M. Abraham

PART 2, posted April 15, 2---

On the second day of my visit I meet with Melissa Bosley, The Villages' Director of Recreation, and apparently the go-to person for official interviews with national reporters. She agrees to give me "fifteen minutes" in her office in Sumter Landing Town Center.

"My job is to support the lifestyle everyone came here for," she says. "We have about 125,000 residents, average age about 66. Let's face it, they're not interested in waiting out this thing months or even weeks. They want to keep doing what they came here to do, stay active and healthy and involved in activities. Do you know we have over 3,000 clubs here in The Villages?"

These are talking points, intended to be quoted, though stated with some conviction. "What about safety?" I ask.

"If the government determines we are unsafe, obviously we have to comply with that. But you heard the president; no one's being forced out."

"So, do you welcome all the publicity?"

"It's one of those two-edged swords," she offers. "Puts us on the national map, but interferes with our lifestyle. And since non-Villages residents can't get to our town centers, the commercial activity is way down. If the thing left today without causing any harm, I would say it's been a plus in terms of publicity, but a short-term drain on the local economy. Of course if it causes trouble..." She does not finish the comment.

I leave her office and go to the site, the seventh fairway of one of three nines called the Evans Prairie Championship Golf Course. The National Guard has it well cordoned off, and I can't get any closer than I did at the Farnsworths' backyard. Several TV trucks are parked on the access street, along with assorted police cars and a number of Guardsmen walking up and down with rifles. Nothing you want to mess with. I arrived in The Villages after the morphing, so didn't get to see the object's slab shape (except on TV). But the water-tower shape is impressive enough. The height of two Empire State buildings, it seems to go on forever.

And here's something else: It's a piece of sculpture, a gigantic Brancusi with its bronze sheen, graceful curves and lack of a single visible seam. I feel confident that stores, in Florida if not all over the world, will soon be selling desktop replicas. I take a wide-angle selfie with the tower in the background and email it to my wife and kids.

While here I attend Writers of The Villages, one of the 3,000 clubs Ms. Bosley mentioned. Marshall invited me, said he was going to read his article based on last week's assignment, an answer to the question "What Happens Next?" The answer is anybody's guess, of course, but there is a free lunch for the author of the best story, determined by a vote among the members.

The club has some twenty registered members, although only about ten are here for this week's meeting. The number is typical, says the leader, James Howard, a retired librarian. He doesn't know of anyone who left The Villages because of the object. "Several people are away on trips, or have some other meeting at the same time."

Because of the magazine that employs me, I am an instant celebrity. A couple of people have read my columns, and ask: "Do you actually make a living writing?" I feel their awe and am, without justification, slightly embarrassed.

Apparently everyone in the group is self-published, some with over half a dozen books listed on internet sites. They meet weekly to critique each other's work, typically a book chapter or slice of a memoir, although now it is the short story on what to expect from their interstellar visitor.

I am asked to contribute to the critiques, and do my best to stay friendly and professional. The quality varies, but there is no lack of imagination in answering the question. Here are five of the scenarios:

- An ET-like alien and its extended family leave the object and take up residence in The Villages;
- The slab-tower lies down slowly to sleep, thereby crushing two hundred homes, but only after all the inhabitants escape;

- The object takes off, returns to its home galaxy and reports that there is nothing interesting to be found on our planet (this one was funny);
- It drops pieces of metal on the fairway, like apples from a tree, which then begin to grow to the size of the mommy slab;
- It disappears below ground and exits in the Pacific Ocean, where it floats like a barge to Japan and then re-erects itself.

Marshall's story, though reasonably well written, does not excite the members. In his telling, the slab ups and leaves peacefully.

"That's it?" asks one of the group, as if impugning Marshall's imagination.

"We were asked to write about what's going to happen next. That's what the email said it would do."

"Forget that prediction," says one member, dripping sarcasm. "Just tell me about the stock market."

Surprisingly, only one of the seven stories I heard posits hostile aliens, à la *War of the Worlds* or *Independence Day*. Its author is an ex-marine named Rick, who has published two Viet Nam-era war novels. In his story the tower begins emitting powerful laser beams that incinerate everything in their path. Within hours practically all of central Florida, including The Villages, is toast. The deadly beams, emanating from the tower's bulbous top and able to curve over the horizon, next home in on Tampa, Jacksonville, and Miami. Conventional firepower — aerial bombs, tanks — have no effect on the tower. By this point in the story all Villages residents are long gone and the president must decide whether to nuke or not.

After 1,500 words, Rick introduces a little bit of his own drama. "I see it's close to eleven, and we won't have time for any discussion, so I think I'll read the last few hundred words next week."

Those hungry for an early lunch are happy to wait a week to hear the ending, but others want to go over the time limit and have him finish. "Just tell us what the president decides," insists one member.

Coyly, Rick holds his ground. "Next week, guys. Then we'll see."

In addition to Rick's conclusion, there are three other stories to be read the following week, after which the club will vote on the best one. I will be gone then but, like the rest of the world, will be watching the news to see what transpires in this suddenly very interesting part of the world.

After the meeting I join several members of the writers' group for lunch at a nearby country club restaurant. There, Marshall holds forth on his belief that the morphing was the slab's attempt to mimic existing water towers in The Villages, which are a tenth the height. Mimic as in biologic adaptation, to blend in with the surroundings. Everyone at the table lets out a chuckle, including yours truly.

Other Villages residents are more down to earth. (Sometimes a cliché is quite apropos.) Separately, I meet with two of them. Frank Baumgartner is a retired NASA scientist, mentioned by several retirees as someone I should interview. It is a warm, sunny day, so we meet on a bench beside Lake Sumter. He is tall, with a full head of gray hair and, unlike anyone else I've met, is dressed in a button-down shirt and long pants. I have come to appreciate that retirement is not just a different state of mind, but for most, a different way of dressing as well. Around us, almost all the men and women are in shorts.

Baumgartner proffers a scientist's skepticism. "There's a lot of crackpot ideas floating around," he says, careful not to impugn any specific friend or neighbor. "I've heard them all. But really, people here are no different than the swarms outside. It's just that we – or at least most of us – know we have to live with it and, given the relatively few years left to us, would rather capitulate and get on with our lives than give up and leave. So that's rational. But it doesn't keep some guys from inventing stuff."

"Like what?"

"Communication with the object via email. Receiving brain wave telepathy from the slab. Alien abduction. Telekinesis in their homes."

"Telekinesis?" I ask, not exactly sure what he means.

"You know, pots and pans moving on their own, chairs floating in the air, stuff like that. They claim it's happening, all caused by the object. And it all gets reported – if that's the right word – in tabloids like the *National Investigator*. You've seen that?"

"Yes." I had seen the *Investigator's* headlines in the airport.

"They even manage to throw in a few pictures. An 'alien' running across the golf course. You have to wonder who believes this stuff."

I ask Frank if he knows Marshall Dodson, and he laughs. "Did you talk to him?"

"Yes, I did," I reply, without relating what we discussed. "What do you think of his binary email claims?" I'm hoping for some quotable fireworks but come up empty.

"Well, I'm not going to comment on specific individuals, especially people I know," he says. "Let's leave it at that." His answer reminds me of The Villages motto: "America's Friendliest Hometown." I'm beginning to see why.

So I then ask, "Well, what do *you* think about the object's origins, its purpose here?"

"Me? Haven't a clue. And I'm not going to make stuff up to explain the unknowable."

William Mishkin belongs to a club called Civil Discourse, where he recently spoke about whether residents should stay or leave. He is gnome-like, short, bearded, with an open Hawaiian-style shirt. Two people who gave me the referral called him "The Professor," because he was one before retirement and "sometimes talks like one." Over coffee at the local Starbucks, he is dispassionate, and not at all stuffy.

"Let's accept the object is from another star system. Common sense seems to dictate that if it – or whoever controls it – has hostile intent, then it probably won't matter whether you live here or at the North Pole. Some people have left, to be sure, mainly those who want to be with loved ones in case there is an apocalypse. For me and most others, the tower's not noisy or smelly or ugly even, so we'll stick around. As long as the Guard protects the place."

"Not ugly?"

"No, actually quite the opposite. Half-mile high water-tower shape. Like a beautiful, very tall lady."

"And do you think this 'very tall lady' has sent out communications to anyone in The Villages?" I am hoping for some person-specific commentary, a response to belie the "friendliest" moniker of the place. Not to be. Without identifying anyone, Mishkin says simply, "The stories you hear are completely unbelievable. Hogwash."

So there you have it. Whatever the shape, and your perception of it, some things are so far unarguable: It is silent – no sounds or electromagnetic waves any of our instruments can detect; the event is not a publicity stunt; and so far it hasn't killed anyone. But what it is and where it came from – and will it ever go away? – no one knows. Like Anna's King said, it "is a puzzlement."

***

"I think the article makes us look good," said Harry, after reading Part 2.

"Yeah, I agree," replied his wife. "He did a good job. Even handed. I wonder what this guy Dodson thinks about the piece."

At that very moment Marshall Dodson was also reading Abraham's online article. He did not find it even-handed. *Lot of crackpot ideas floating around? Completely unbelievable? Hogwash?*

"Assholes," he said to his cat. "Unmitigated assholes."

Chapter 10

On post-arrival day twelve, at 9:15 am, Harry and Gladys Farnsworth sat in their backyard, enjoying the warm spring air, for the moment uncaring about the giant thing on the fairway and the masses of troops throughout The Villages. The object itself was silent but they could hear, wafting over the fairway, a faint hum from National Guard generators near the tower's base.

Then Gladys heard another hum, lower pitched, coming from a different direction. "Hear that, Harry?"

"Hear what?"

"Do you have your hearing aid on?"

"No, but I hear you fine."

She pointed away from the tower, down the fairway. "Sounds like a plane."

"Yeah, now I hear it. Does sound like a plane. But I don't see anything. Wait, I do see something, coming in over those houses." He pointed in the direction of the sound.

Gladys followed his arm out to the sky. "Now I see it, too. It's coming right at us. You think he's going to land on the fairway?"

"Hell if I know. I don't think there's enough room. Probably a government surveillance plane. God, I hope our backyard doesn't turn into an airport."

The plane grew closer, the hum louder.

"My god, looks like he is going to land!" She pointed to the near horizon. "Look, it's coming right over the houses. Is the pilot crazy?"

They both stood, their gazes fixed on the small single-engine plane, now only a few hundred feet in the air, its direction toward the tower. In a few seconds the plane whizzed past their house, then arced slightly upward.

"Oh, no! He's going to—"

"Crash!"

A huge fireball erupted a quarter way up the tower. Within seconds, a jumble of metal and flames fell to the tower's sloping base, then slid slowly to the ground.

Gladys and Harry could only stare. There was nothing else to do.

***

National Guard troops circled the burning wreckage, unable to get close. A few minutes later sirens wailed in the distance. Fire trucks arrived with their water hoses.

"Too late for that," said Harry. "Whoever was piloting the plane, he's dead."

"Do you think it was a suicide?"

"The part of the tower where the plane hit is what, maybe forty feet in diameter, at most? The pilot took direct aim. There's no other explanation."

"Well," said Gladys, "we've been standing here like bumps on a log since the plane hit. Can't really tell what's going on out there. Maybe it's on TV already. They keep constant surveillance of the area. Let's go see."

They entered the house, but before clicking on the television, the landline rang. Harry glanced at the receiver. "It's George. I'll get it."

Harry picked up the handset. "…Yeah, Gladys and I saw the whole thing. We were outside…A small plane, like one of those Piper Cubs…Hell, what else could it be?…We'll know soon enough….Going to turn on the TV…Move out?...You really think they'll force us out now?...Over my dead body…War? Hell, George, it's not war with that tower. If anything it's war with the nut jobs who can't just live and let live…Okay, talk to you later."

"Harry, what's that about, forcing us out?"

"George is worried. Thinks they'll force everyone out, level all the houses, make this into another Area Fifty-one."

"What's Area Fifty-one?"

"You know, where all the aliens live. In Nevada."

"Why fifty-one? What are the areas one through fifty?"

"Gladys, turn on the TV."

And there it was, in bold letters at bottom of the CNN screen.

SMALL AIRCRAFT CRASHES INTO SPACE TOWER, PILOT KILLED. SUICIDE SUSPECTED.

For the first hour that was the limit of information. Gradually, over the next few hours, the story evolved on all the cable networks.

"The pilot, Timothy Mackinaw, posted a warning on Facebook just minutes before taking off from the Leesburg, Florida Airport. The airport is only fourteen air miles from the tower."

Mackinaw's Facebook posting then appeared on the screen.

"Why doesn't the government do something about this creature from outer space, set to kill us all if the government doesn't act? Doesn't anyone remember Russell in Independence Day? Are there no more heroes among us? Sadly, no. Just wimps! It is up to me to get rid of this thing. I will do it, so help me God! I love you, Mom!" Timothy

To try to make sense of it all, expert talking heads soon flooded the channels. Within four hours after the crash, a former official with the FAA opined on Fox News:

Official: "Clearly the National Guard didn't see this coming, and I don't mean the plane itself, I mean the possibility of a rogue attack."

Fox Moderator: "But it's our understanding there was a no-fly zone set up over the entire Villages area."

Official: "Yes, but that was intended, I'm sure, to keep tourists away, gawkers who wanted to fly over the area and do some sightseeing. It wasn't set up for rogue pilots bent on suicide. The National Guard never installed anti-aircraft weaponry."

Fox Moderator: "Well, what would you say should be the next step?"

Official: "The government needs to do three things. First, shut down any non-commercial flights anywhere near The Villages. Second, bring in anti-aircraft missiles and be ready and willing to shoot down anything that comes even close to where the object sits. And third, and I know this won't be popular, evacuate all the homes that could be affected by anti-aircraft fire. Treat it like a war-zone. They need to do more to secure the area, by removing all civilians."

Fox Moderator: "By 'they' you mean the federal government?"

Official: "Both the Florida state and federal government, working together, to make sure the homeowners are fairly compensated and moved safely away. While the situation is certainly unique, in war, which this is, you *can* force evacuation. The time has come, I'm afraid. I see no alternative."

"Turn off the TV, George. I can't take it anymore. Let's drive to Atlanta, stay with my sister."

"Why, just because some dumb official says what he'd do? He's no different than that National Guard brat, trying to kick us out. I'm not leaving."

"This is not some bratty soldier advising us to leave. You heard him. It's like we're in a war zone. What's the downside of driving to Atlanta until this blows over?"

"The downside is, we're over-reacting. You leave here and next thing you know the National Guard kiddies will be living in our bedroom. Or they'll use our house for target practice. I don't fear the tower. I fear the government. It's safer to stay and monitor the situation."

"Okay, if you insist. But I'm going to pack our suitcases now, just in case. If the time does come, we can leave right away, even if it's the middle of the night."

***

The president's news conference at 8 p.m. that same day included the Secretary of Defense, who outlined the military response: 1) anti-aircraft missiles were being placed around the tower; 2) all non-commercial aircraft in the three-county area of The Villages were grounded indefinitely. He took no questions. Those were left for the president.

Journalist: "Mr. President, what about the residents? They are in the line of fire if there is another rogue attack. Are you ordering evacuation?"

The President: "We have not decided. I've been in touch with Florida's governor on this issue. The problem is that suicide attacks, such as what took place this morning, could come from any direction, and anti-aircraft missiles could be fired over a potentially large area. So do we evacuate just the immediate tower area, or the entire retirement community? And it's not just The Villages. The tri-county area actually has about 700,000 people, so evacuation, if it comes to that, has to be considered carefully, and we have not made a decision at this time. Obviously, anyone who feels at risk should leave of their own accord."

Gladys pushed the mute button on the TV's remote. "That's us, George. On our own accord. Let's go."

"We're not being ordered to leave, you heard the president. They fire a missile at some other suicide plane, it could land anywhere, up or down The Villages or even in Ocala. Maybe even Orlando, for god sakes."

"You're being obstinate."

"And you're being foolish. Look, let's rethink this in the morning. I'm going to bed."

***

The next morning was completely overcast, not a peep of sun. Foreboding, perhaps, for the tower scene had changed. Now Harry and Gladys could see several missile trucks arranged around the tower, their bays pointing up at a thirty-degree angle.

And the news stream was continuous. "…The army has moved in…Any plane approaching the tower will be shot down…"

Gladys resumed her campaign for leaving. "Now, don't you think we should go?"

"Why? Nothing's really changed. It's not like another country is going to strike first. All they're trying to do is protect the thing from suicide pilots."

"It's scary. I'm scared, Harry. Do you realize any one of those missile trucks could destroy every house within sight, in minutes?"

"They're for planes, not our homes. Why don't you call Martha? See what she and George are up to."

"Up to, or up? It's only seven-thirty."

"They're always up early. Call 'em."

Gladys called.

The Singletons were indeed up. No sooner had Gladys broached the question, then Martha said, "We'll be right over."

A few minutes later the four neighbors sat in the Farnsworths' lanai, sipping coffee and discussing their immediate future. There were frequent glances to the military scene a few hundred yards distant.

"I say we leave," offered Gladys.

"Where would you go?" asked George.

"I have a sister in Atlanta. We can stay with her a few days."

"Well," said Martha, "our closest relatives are in New York, and I have no desire to go there. They still have snow on the ground. George and I are staying put."

"Your choice," replied Gladys. "Harry and I will probably leave. Maybe even later today." She looked at Harry, hoping for confirmation.

Her husband would not confirm. "Gladys is much more concerned than I am. I actually feel safer here, able to monitor the situation, than if I was hundreds of miles away. I know that may seem crazy. So no, no plans to leave, certainly not today."

Gladys began to tear up. Martha got up from her chair, walked over to Gladys and took her hand. "It'll be all right, Gladys. We're not going to leave either."

"Martha, I agree with Harry," said George. "No point in running away just yet. And we're not even being ordered to evacuate. I say we should stay, unless there's a military order that we have to obey."

"I really appreciate you guys coming over," said Harry. "Gladys will be fine. We'll just tough it out together. One day at—"

"What the hell?" interrupted George. "Look! Look at that!"

They all turned to see where George was pointing. The tower was changing—again.

Chapter 11

"Don't you see? It's changing!"

Harry nodded. "And glowing."

Thirteen days after landing, as the four retirees argued about what to do next, the tower had suddenly begun to glow *and* morph. First came a dull glow, visible to the masses miles away, who could see the tower's top half clearly with their telescopes, binoculars and cameras. At the same time, the curves gave way to lines and edges, as the object changed back to the giant slab shape.

In and around The Villages, people reacted to the sudden changes with awe and apprehension. *The Greatest Show on Earth*, some TV announcer called the display, and of course it was. No one ran, no one panicked. Instead, there was a collective resignation built around one simple question: "What next?"

People around the world saw the changes as well, perhaps even more acutely on television than one could appreciate in person. But there was no mistaking the fact that, by the minute, the tower was glowing brighter and reverting to its previous form, a gigantic domino-shape.

Within ten minutes the morphing was complete. Less than a minute later, a powerful beam shot from the top of the slab, straight up, a cylindrical streak of light perhaps five feet in diameter. Unlike any beam ever generated on Earth, this one did not appear to peter out or dissolve in the ether of space. As far as people with personal telescopes could see, there was no end to it. Two satellites in geosynchronous orbit followed the beam upward, and they too saw no end. A powerful land telescope in Chile tracked the beam as it shot above the North American horizon; no end could be seen in any of the scope's images.

Then, slowly at first, the slab took off, tracking the beam's verticality. People nearby heard a low sucking sound as the tower rose out of the ground. A little wind was generated. There was no motor noise, no sound of any rocket or engine. Fifty feet above ground it hovered, motionless, as if waiting for something. The slab's bottom showed only traces of earth that once belonged to the golf course.

More remarkably, on the ground there was no foundation, nothing visible that could have secured the erect position of a half-mile-tall structure. All that remained at the site was a twenty-foot depression, a displacement of dirt by the immense weight that once stood there.

After hovering half a minute, the slab ascended at a slow rate, perhaps a thousand feet every ten seconds, tracking the beam like some giant space elevator. It vacuumed the beam as it rose, leaving no light in its path. At five thousand feet the slab hovered again, briefly, then zoomed through the atmosphere, out of sight in less than a second. From ground level, one moment it was visible and the next it was not. The slab and the beam had simply disappeared into space.

***

"Well, Harry, that solves our little problem," said Gladys. "It's gone."

"That was an impressive exit," said George. "Very impressive."

Maybe it'll come back," Harry replied. "Maybe it just went for a stroll."

George smirked. "What, you think it's a snowbird?"

No one knew what to think. Only a few minutes earlier, the object seemed permanent, immutable, a fixture of their lives. Then, like some cosmic magic trick – now you see it, now you don't – it was gone.

***

The National Guard took much longer to leave. Guard remnants were still around a week later, but by then The Villages was almost back to normal, with the exception of many visitors previously kept out who now wanted to see "the landing site." The Villages had always welcomed visitors, to patronize its town centers and take tours in anticipation of retirement, but this was a different breed. More gawkers than spenders, they would eventually force a rethinking of what to do with the landing site. Still, while the world speculated and cogitated over this most singular event, local residents were only too happy to be free of the angst, the publicity, the feeling of *confinement.*

The next meeting of Writers of The Villages had come and gone. The winner of the "What happens next?" competition was Rick, whose doomsday scenario, though spectacularly wrong, was considered the best-written and most entertaining piece.

Marshall rationalized the result. *The contest was for the best fiction, not the best prediction. That was made clear from the beginning.* His ego was somewhat soothed by the curiosity of one club member, Justin Brown. Justin had a reputation as "the critique-curmudgeon." He found something to criticize in every member's writing, and his comments were not always well received. But he was smart and knew something about science, so Marshall was more than happy to oblige his questions.

"Hey, Marshall, how'd you know it would leave, or was that just a good guess?"

"The message I received stated it would leave peacefully."

"It told you so in binary code?"

"Indirectly. The messages were not a hoax, but sent from the tower."

"Wait. From the slab-shape or the water-tower shape?"

"Well, when I got them, the thing had already morphed, so they came from the water-tower shape."

"Okay."

"I think it was a test to see if they could communicate with life forms on Earth. They got our names and email addresses from the close-in Wi-Fi and cellular networks. Government experts assumed the messages were a hoax, and I can't blame them. Somehow the messages emitted no airwaves or radiation. But when I went to the fairway that night, I noted something odd."

"What's that?"

"A couple of uniformed guys sitting around had dogs on leashes. And they weren't guard dogs, either."

Marshall's comment about "dogs on leashes" was picked up by another club member nearby, Gregory, who now moved closer to the conversation. That suited Marshall just fine. He relished any audience.

"Are you telling a dog story?" asked Gregory.

"Get lost," said Justin. "He's explaining his ideas about the messages received from the slab. It interests me, unlike your piece of crap. Aliens with bug eyes."

"Screw you," said Gregory. "Your story wasn't so great either. The slab goes to sleep and crushes houses. Oh, how sweet."

Marshall now wished Gregory had kept his distance. "Greg," he said, "Justin is interested, even if you're not. Please, either listen and be quiet, or leave us. Okay?"

"Easy choice," said Greg, with obvious disdain. "Bye." He pivoted and walked away.

"Pain in the ass," said Justin. "Can't write worth a damn. How the hell did he get in the club?"

"You were asking?" said Marshall, hoping to bring the conversation back to his story.

"I don't know what the hell I was asking before Asshole arrived. Oh, yeah, how do you know they weren't guard dogs?"

"They were pets. I mean, one was a golden retriever, and the other looked like a beagle. And I bet if they had let me snoop around I would have come across a cat or two."

"So they took their pets with them on guard duty? So what?"

"Then I went back over all the news videos from before my binary-code message, including scenes around the slab and tower. Never saw an animal in any of it. All of a sudden they're bringing their pets? At three in the morning?"

"And from that you inferred these guys also got binary-coded messages?"

"Yes, exactly. I figured these guys must have been using their cell phones at some point, which emitted numbers for text messages to be received, or possibly even email addresses. Something that can land here from another galaxy can surely pick up our primitive airwaves."

"I suppose so. And then what?"

"Well," Marshall continued, eager to get in his story before another interruption, "when the tower communicated to them, presumably the same type of message I had received, the soldiers brought their pets. Pets being another species, of course, this is what the object was interested in. Someone playing a joke in The Villages might know my name and email, but not theirs or their cell phone numbers. Not unless they were very close to the object. Yeah, could have been some resident who sent those messages, but I figured your typical retiree is not going to be that tech- savvy. So I just put two and two together and realized this had to be communication from the object."

"But if the police or Guard soldiers did knock on the tower, as you tried to do, what happened?"

"I imagine nothing happened. Perhaps it was just a way of acknowledging the messages had been received. And if they did knock with pets in hand, there might have been enough time for the object to analyze the animals' DNA. Maybe that's all they were interested in."

"So no hidden doors opened to abduct the *Homo sapiens* and their pets?" Justin let out a little laugh.

"Apparently not. No reports of anyone missing."

"But you haven't answered my question. How'd you know the thing would leave when it did? In your story I believe you 'wrote within a month'."

"I got another binary-coded message. This one was short, almost biblical. It stated: 'An orbit round, then depart your planet.' The only problem was what was meant by a 'round.' I first thought it referred to Earth's orbit around our sun, which takes a year. But I thought a year was too long, and guessed maybe the moon's orbit around Earth, a month."

"I see," said Justin, managing to express both skepticism and anticipation in a single utterance. "Of course, the thing zoomed away in just under two weeks. So much for your orbit guess. And what if orbit meant Pluto's, which takes a couple of centuries? Frankly, Marshall, if this was fiction, we'd call it a plot hole."

"But I was right, wasn't I? I said it would be gone in less than a month. Finding intelligent life where it landed may have been a distraction, and it decided to leave early. Who knows? Anyway, with this assumption I finished my story."

Justin had found out as much as he wanted to learn about Marshall's story. He decided to ask one more question.

"Do you think it will ever return?"

"Probably not. I imagine it's got a lot of planets to visit before heading home."

***

The day after the tower flew away, George, Martha, Gladys, and Harry met for a quiet dinner in the Farnsworths' home.

"What'd you think of *The New Sophisticate* piece, Harry?" asked George. Did that fellow, Lawrence Abraham, quote you fairly?"

"Yeah, about what I expected. I thought Part One was okay, but after I finished Part Two, I came away thinking he makes

69

The Villages seem like a really weird place. You know, New York smart-ass here, reporting from Looneytuneville."

"I think he likes the place," said Martha. "At least that's my take on it. Now the thing's gone, he can return without a press pass. How old is he, anyway?"

"Oh, mid-forties, I imagine," said Gladys.

"So not ready for prime time," quipped George. "Has a few more years before he qualifies. Did you know we have more people here from New York than any other state, apart from Florida itself? And many of those moving here from within Florida started out in the Empire State?"

"Yeah, I saw that. Something like ten thousand people."

"Mildred called today," offered Gladys, hoping to change the conversation with a non-sequitur.

"Oh, what'd she want?" asked Martha.

"Nothing, just to tell me how happy she is, now that she has her view back. Don't think she has any understanding what this was all about."

"Who does?"

"I mean, the outer space part and all. She's in her own world."

"Aren't we all?"

"Let's drink to that." George raised his wine glass and clinked it against three other glasses, then looked at Harry.

"Did you hear what they're going to do with the seventh fairway?"

"No, what?"

"Cut it in half, make the area around the landing site – our backyards – a wetlands, totally off limits. No more golf course view. The rest of the fairway will be a short par three."

"Whoopy-do," replied Harry. "That might improve my score."

"Maybe that was the slab's whole point in coming to Earth," said Gladys, "to improve your golf score."

"Funny, funny."

"You know," said Martha. "Those aliens weren't so bad after all. Made us appreciate what we have here."

"I always appreciated it," said Gladys.

"I know. But it gave us a different perspective, don't you think?"

***

That night, Marshall sat at his computer. A new email message came through, again in binary code.

01000011 01101111 01101101 01100101 00100000 01110110 01101001 01110011 01101001 01110100...

He translated it rapidly using the internet decoder.

"Come visit me sometime. Your friendly alien from fairway seven, aka Frank Baumgartner. Heh, Heh, Heh, Heh, Heh!"

Chapter 12

The seventh fairway of The Evans Prairie Egret course, where the object had once stood, was not divided in half, nor made into a wetlands. That idea died quickly.

As the National Guard departed, more and more people from surrounding areas came to see where the slab landed. They crowded the bordering streets, and many did not respect private property, trampling between seventh fairway homes to "get a better view." It was soon apparent that even a wetlands reconfiguration would leave the landing site open to trespassers, and that The Villages could – no, would – become another Florida tourist attraction, albeit unplanned and undesired. Tourists would come but not retirees, at least not to live there.

Fear of plummeting property values and tax collections prompted unusually fast government action. Florida's governor convened a meeting with U.S. Department of Interior officials, the Congresswoman for Florida's 11th congressional district, the County Supervisor, and The Villages' Executive Council. The Villages EC governed the community's golf courses and common areas, essentially everything not in the name of individual homeowners.

The goal of the so-called "Villages Landing Committee" (VLC) was to come up with a better plan, one that would preserve The Villages as a desirable retirement community, while keeping gawkers away. All agreed that any solution, to be effective, would need the financial and administrative backing of the federal government.

The VLC devised a brilliant plan based on a single idea: reconfigure the landing site so people would have *no desire to come*. In a rare display of quick cooperation among disparate agencies, the plan was accepted and money appropriated. Construction began almost immediately.

First, the entire fairway was plowed under and made into a lake. The area under water was extended to include all home sites on all the bordering and nearby streets. There was little opposition because, even though the homes were taken by the government's power of eminent domain, each home was bought at almost double its pre-landing market value. To sweeten the takeover, affected homeowners were offered any new construction in The Villages at a ten percent discount. While the homes were being dismantled and removed, another fairway, a par four, was also submerged. To keep the golf course at nine holes, two other par four fairways were divided into par threes.

Next, the lake's circumference was planted with thousands of large oak and sand pine trees – an instant forest – and then fronted by a high and esthetically-pleasing wooden fence, obscuring any possible entry or view of the water. "No Trespassing" signs made it clear that anyone caught trying to climb the fence would end up in deep legal trouble.

Even before construction began, the FAA designated The Villages – some 50-square miles – a permanent no-fly zone, except for emergency transport helicopters. The first few pilots who did not heed the ban (or claimed ignorance) and took passengers up to "see the landing site" had their planes confiscated. They eventually got their planes back, but only after paying a large fine. Flyovers quickly ceased.

The lake, with landscaping, took only four months to complete. By then multiple bloggers and online chat rooms had made clear just how effective the reconfiguration was.

■ "Nothing to see – the landing site's totally cut off from the rest of The Villages."

■ "Don't bother going, it's a waste of time."

■ "Use Google Earth if you want to see where the slab landed."

The hapless visitor who came just to find the site quickly discovered the truth of these comments and left without a sighting or photo. And if she bothered to ask any resident where it was, she was apt to be told, "I have no idea myself."

The reconfiguration's success led many Villages residents to quip: "After Social Security, this is the best thing government ever did for us."

***

While the lake construction was erasing any trace of the landing site, Frank Baumgartner made an overture to Marshall Dodson. "Let's have lunch."

Marshall agreed, though still sore at his buddy for the email ruse. They met a few weeks after the slab's departure, in TooJays Deli.

"So, feeling guilty?" asked Dodson, after water and menus were delivered, but before they ordered food.

"Not at all. Just wanted to touch base, see how this all played out in your mind."

"You writing a book?"

Baumgartner laughed. "The thing was so boring, nothing to write about, really."

"Well, if you do, and you mention my name in any context, I'll sue your ass for a million bucks."

"Not to worry. No book, no mention of Marshall Dodson. Sorry, you won't be famous."

"So tell me, how did *you* know when they would leave?" asked Dodson. "Or 'it' would leave, since we never identified a 'they'."

"Oh, it communicated with me. I was their contact here, since I'm the ex-NASA guy."

"Yeah, I heard they were looking for the top bull-shitter in The Villages."

Baumgartner did not flinch at the remark. "Look, Marshall, no one made you believe my emails. You believed them because you wanted to, and because I sent binary code with no traceable address, so the idea of alien emails seemed plausible. But mainly because you wanted to believe they were communicating with *you* — had chosen *you* among billions of earthlings."

"What about the guards, some who also brought their animals?"

"Yeah, I caught a few of their email addresses in my network. They – and you – should have heeded the government's website warning. Binary coded emails *were* a hoax. I imagine others were sent out all over the country, not just by me."

"But how do you even know I believed these emails, or went to the tower in the middle of the night?"

"You talked about it. A lot, apparently. To your writing group and others. So it got back to me. The more I thought about the whole situation after the slab departed, well, that's when I decided we should have lunch."

"Yeah, I suppose I was pretty excited at one point. But still, about the slab leaving when it did. How did you know?"

"No smarter in that regard than you, or anyone else. I just figured they'd leave soon or we'd all be dead from some galactic-inspired catastrophe. My 'round of orbits' could mean anything. You interpreted it one way, which happened to fit. Lucky guess. Look at it this way, Marshall. We had a little excitement for a few days. It stretched our minds, made us think of the infinite universe."

"So, Mr. NASA is going biblical now? What's your next prediction?"

"I'm hungry. Let's order."

Epilogue

On its way home, to a star system far, far away, the slab filed a report of the mission that had brought it to The Villages, Florida. Translated, the report read as follows, with Earth terms replacing normalized galactic measurements.

Re: Monitoring Sphere Replacement Project for Star System 312879.92.

All planetary spheres that were inserted during the Project's first visit nine million years ago, to monitor this solar system's tectonic changes, were replaced with newer models.

Only Planet Number Three, at an average distance of 93 million miles from its star, showed multi-cellular, carbon-based life forms. Those life forms with the highest level of intelligence were not observed on the previous visit, when the highest level registered 0.31 on the galactic scale.

On this second visit, the highest intelligence level registered 1.06, still very primitive by galactic standards. Creatures at this level are similar to ones found on other planets with an atmosphere comprising mainly oxygen and nitrogen. Like the others, they have four appendages and a small, multi-cellular transmitter module encased in a thick material at the apex.

They also share resemblance by their custom of lying in a semi-conscious state for approximately one-third of this planet's rotation cycle.

Unique to these 1.06 creatures, compared to all others on the planet, were frequent back-and-forth movements inside slow-moving metal structures of varying sizes.

And this most peculiar -- while traveling in the smaller-sized moving metal structures, some of the creatures chased after tiny, white ball-shaped objects, which they hit with thin rods. After a few such hits, we observed the ball drop into a circular depression on the planet's surface. However, as soon as this was accomplished, the chasing creature removed the ball from the depression. Overall, this seemed to be purposeless activity.

While we were replacing the Project's planetary sub-surface monitoring spheres, one of the creatures displayed that peculiar self-destructive behavior noted in life forms around other stars (see report of Planet 8, Star System 431987.81). This creature, encased in a piece of flying metal, crashed into our vessel. Upon impact the creature's body parts were scrambled, and it had no apparent capacity to reconstitute, another sign of primitive development. The velocity on impact was insignificant and caused no damage to our vessel.

We also surveyed these creatures at other latitudes and longitudes of the planet, and secured intelligence and behavioral analysis of a large number. They all behaved similarly, except for the small-sized vehicles and the purposeless hitting of small white balls noted in our landing vicinity. Otherwise, they displayed the same level of primitive intelligence, and the same recumbent, semi-conscious periods.

As per the Project's rules, we made no attempt to communicate with any creatures, or to influence their behavior. We do believe they were aware of our presence, by the permanent confluence of creatures around our base, and the previously-described instance of self-destructive behavior.

At one point, our vessel did emulate the shape of a nearby non-organic form, in order to facilitate tracking atmospheric changes. A rounded top served our purpose better than the flat, rectangular configuration.

The Project's next visit to this star system will be in another nine million years, in order to replace the current set of spheres. Then, we will see if Planet Three's life forms have advanced to any degree. Given what we found on this visit, and our experience from visiting similar planets with carbon-based life and an oxygen-nitrogen atmosphere, we are doubtful.

- The End -

Short Stories

This section includes 11 short stories, several of which were finalists or prize winners in the Florida Writers Associations' annual Royal Palm Literary Awards competition.

"I hit a deer."

As he drove home in the late January afternoon, Harold Clarke replayed in his mind the visit with Dr. Johnson only an hour earlier. Harold didn't want to arrive home and have his wife ask a bunch of questions he couldn't answer. She always nagged him with questions after each doctor visit. She could have come with him but chose not to because of her "rheumatism."

His treatment for prostate cancer seemed to be going well, said Dr. Johnson. "The radiation treatments are doing their job. Just four more, then you'll be done."

As cancers go Harold's wasn't the worst kind, and he was glad it had been caught with a blood test, or at least suspected from that test, which led to a biopsy. He was also glad that he had turned sixty-five a year ago, so all the treatments were covered by Medicare. And one more thing to be thankful for—retirement, so he no longer had to work in the Middleburg cheese factory. He had been a foreman, true, but retirement couldn't have come too soon.

So life was good, except for the cancer. Harold didn't like the word cancer. Every time he left the doctor's office, the word resonated in his mind. They didn't speak the word at home. His wife called it "the prostate thing you have." He called it "my prostate problem." Only Dr. Johnson called it cancer, and after every visit the word lingered for a few days. Nothing he could do about that. So driving home the word kept entering his head. He would push it down, try to think of other things, like seeing his grandkids this coming weekend.

The roads were icy. Wintertime they were almost always icy in northeast Ohio's rural Geauga County, where he and his wife lived. Their home was a modest ranch, on one-half acre, and the nearest neighbor lived a quarter mile away. The drive home took him down County Road 124. All roads in this area had those "Bridge Ices Before Road" signs. There was a short bridge on his way home, and Harold always slowed going over it.

He looked at his watch. Now almost six o'clock and dark. *Gets dark so early in the winter*. He loved Geauga in the summer, warm and leafy. Winter was pretty, too, if you were inside. He had the car heater up full blast. Radio played in the background. Cancer on his mind. No, the grandkids, not the cancer. Cancer's being treated.

He made it over the bridge, slowly. Once over, he could speed up some, get home a little quicker to warmth and supper. As he turned a curve in the road, he saw a creature on the right- hand shoulder, just outside his headlight beams. He could hardly make it out. Lots of deer in the winter, he knew. They were always lurking around. He stared and for some reason, maybe ice, his car skidded off the highway, onto the shoulder.

Before he could regain control there was impact. A loud thud. The creature was pushed hard away from the road and was no longer visible as his car slid past. Did it run away into the woods? He thought it might have. Harold steered left to get back on the highway. There were no other cars about and he continued down the road. "Dammit! I must have hit a deer."

He got home and parked in the garage. Under dim light he could see a large dent in the front right fender. *Damn! That's going to be expensive to fix.*

In the house his wife's questions started right away. Maybe it wasn't fair to call this nagging; really, she was just concerned about his health. They'd been married forty years, so he figured she was entitled. After Harold answered the last question he said, calmly, "I hit a deer on County Road 124. Near the BerryHill Farm."

"You did? Were you hurt?"

"I'm okay. Don't think it was killed. Think it might have gone off into the woods."

"What was it doing on the highway in weather like this?" she asked.

"They're all over the place."

"How bad's the car?"

"Dented."

"Let me go see." They went out together. Each took a flashlight.

"That's not good," she said, rubbing her hand over the metal crater above the right front bumper. While he examined the front passenger door to look for other damage, she saw some small bits of cloth attached to the bumper. She picked them off under the flashlight beam but didn't say anything to her husband. She kept the pieces squeezed in her left hand.

"Anybody see you hit it?" she asked.

"Nah, road was empty."

"Well, you hit a deer, that's for sure. Got to be more careful on these icy roads."

Early the next morning Harold went to the mailbox to get the *Geauga Sun Press*, as was his routine, so he could read it with his coffee. There on the front page was an article, headlined: "Geauga Man Killed on Cty. Rd. 124, apparent hit-and-run fatality." The article explained that a passing motorist saw the body shortly after 6 p.m., and called the police. The dead man was identified as a local Amish named Samuel Yoder, age 36. Police were looking for the driver but had little to go by. There were some paint flecks on the deceased's clothing but so far nothing to identify the vehicle. There were no witnesses.

That's interesting, Harold thought. Same highway. And pretty much the same location, close to the BerryHill farm where he had encountered the roadside creature.

A few minutes later his wife came into the kitchen. He showed her the article but said nothing. She read it.

"So?" she asked.

"I hit a deer," he said.

"Yes. Yes, you did. You hit a deer. No doubt about it. Now, what would you like for breakfast?"

- END -

My Deal With The You Know Who

I entered Jake's Deli on Cleveland's west side and, as instructed, took a seat in one of the booths. The waitress came over and I told her I was waiting for someone, and we would order together. A minute later he walked in. From a distance, he seemed to be just another guy coming from the parking lot. Though we had never met, he seemed to recognize me right away. He walked straight to the booth, sat opposite me.

"Hello," he said, in a deep baritone voice that sounded affected. I was still skeptical at that point. We shook hands. His hand felt cool, almost clammy, and his grip quite strong.

"Hi," I said, rather meekly. "Why did you choose Jake's Deli for this meeting?"

"They have great pastrami, of course. Good enough reason."

I searched for some sign of his identity and think I found it in his face. The angles were sharper, more unnatural-looking, and his eyes were deeper into the sockets than normal, as if he was made up for some horror movie. He wore a felt hat and I am certain there were two protrusions, one on either side of his head, poking up the felt. This was no imposter, or if so, a very good one.

Our waitress returned and didn't look twice at the new arrival. "What'll it be?" she asked, after depositing two waters.

He ordered pastrami on rye. I ordered lox and a bagel.

"Are you paying?" I asked, sort of joking.

"Yes. You'll pay later." He was not joking.

I cleared my throat.

"So," he said, in a somewhat haughty manner, "what exactly do you want?"

"To play the piano. Well."

"You play now, but not well?"

"Hardly. I am a beginner. An adult beginner. Still at level one. In fact, my current instruction book says it's written for seven- and eight-year olds."

"Ummm," he said, suggesting some interest. "And how old are you?"

"Just turned fifty-five."

"And playing for how long?"

"Lessons for a year. No prior musical experience."

"But you're an accomplished writer," he said.

"Thank you. How do you know that?"

"Ah, Howard Greenleaf, New York Times best-selling author. Murder mysteries, private-detective thrillers, I believe the genre is. Yes, I read the papers. In fact I read everything that's printed anywhere, every day. I focus on the obituaries, I must admit."

"Funny."

"Death is not funny, my friend. That's my business."

"I am aware," I said.

"Just what level of piano playing do you wish to achieve?"

"A higher level," I replied. "Much higher. To play classical. Beethoven, Rachmaninoff."

"Impressive," he said. "Ludwig, I had nothing to do with, a true non-believer. But of Sergei I am familiar. Almost had him, but in the end he changed his mind. Brilliant composer, pianist. This will take some doing."

"And to play like Barenboim."

"Ah, a true prodigy. You ask a lot."

"I wouldn't ask if you couldn't deliver. Just tell me the terms."

"The usual. Your soul, plus."

"Plus? Plus what?"

"A time limit. I am patient but there are limits."

"I won't accept an early death, before I can enjoy the fruits of my new talent. We must agree on that date, and you must honor it."

"Of course. I honor all my promises. That's more than you can say for the other fellow."

"I don't want you to pull a Robert Johnson on me."

"Ah, poor man. He couldn't keep his hands off another's wife. Such talent. Only after he met me at the Crossroads, of course."

Quicker than expected, the food arrived. It looked delicious, and I felt hungry. We both began eating.

"Best pastrami in your town," he said.

"So, how much time would I have to enjoy my new talent?"

"This change will be a lot of work," he said. "First you must sustain some brain trauma, which I can arrange. Nothing serious, but it must be a medical event, or you will not be believed. There are many cases of sudden musical genius following head injury, so that will give you some cover. It also makes my job easier. Then, I think a decade would be fair."

"Just ten years? I die at sixty-five?"

"Mozart died at thirty-five, and I had nothing to do with that."

"That was over two hundred years ago," I protest.

"Just a minute ago, in my book."

"Yes, but he had a head start. Even with his early death, a thirty-year career. How about fifteen years? I could live with that." What an ironic statement, I realized.

After a brief pause while eating, he said, "I can do fifteen, with a caveat."

"Which is?"

"To the extent you are successful in your new career, you are unsuccessful in your current one."

"You mean as a writer?"

"As a writer."

"Okay, I can handle that. Writing's a chore anyway. And my agent is a pain in the ass. The publisher's no bargain either. They want my books, which are all best sellers, and they only give me fifteen percent. I've even thought of self-publishing. Everyone wants to nickel and dime you. Hey, wait a minute? What will I do for income? My wife doesn't work."

"People are always worried about the minor details," he said. "You'll still receive book royalties, at least for a while. At some point you may find your thrillers, shall we say, out of style. But you can make it with your music, that's how good you will become. Though I have a disclaimer, which I give to all talent seekers."

"Talent seekers. You make it sound like a category."

"It is. One of my largest. Second only to those seeking sudden wealth."

"All right, I'm listening."

"I will give you the talent. I will not control what you do with it. How you handle the notoriety, how it affects your personal life, will be up to you. Handle things poorly and you may come begging for less time than the allotted fifteen years. I've seen that happen before."

"Fair enough. I understand. Say, what exactly does it mean to give up one's soul?"

He looked hard at me, took one last bite of his pastrami and said, "Trade secret."

Then he let out an eerie-sounding laugh that sent a chill down my spine. I looked around and no one seemed to notice. Perhaps only I heard it.

"Do we have a deal?" he asked.

I was desperate. Tired of playing *Mary Had a Little Lamb*, *London Bridge* and *Alouette* like a kid still wetting his pants. Tired of struggling through the F and G scales with both hands, while trying to memorize their numerous chords and inversions. At my rate of progress, I would be able to play Beethoven's *Für Elise* in another fifty years.

"Yes!"

"Then we shake hands," he said, "and there is no turning back."

We shook hands. He took out a $50 bill from some pocket, placed it beside his empty dish and walked out of the deli.

***

"Call 911!" I heard someone yell, just outside Jake's Deli. "I think he's alive."

Of course I was alive. A Toyota Prius had just come over the curb, aiming right at me. Were it not for the light post between us, I would not be what the bystander said. The car wrapped around the post, hit me broadside. I fell to the pavement and conked my head. I saw stars and darkness but could hear.

Minutes later I lay in Memorial Hospital's Emergency Department. Then came the CT scan, the elevator ride to the neuro ICU, the endless stream of doctors, and explanations.

"A severe concussion, small subdural hematoma, he'll recover. He's lucky. No loss of motor function."

That's good, I thought. Wow! So quick. Didn't expect it. I began thinking of the keyboard. Do I know anything? The C-major scale, what is it? C-D-E-F-G-A-B-C. Good. I still know something. Probably no more than before.

They released me from the hospital three days later. Cynthia, my wife, drove me home. Our one son had visited me in the hospital and, assured of my full recovery, was back in college, a thousand miles away.

"Do you want to lie down?" she asked, as soon as we entered the house.

"No, I want to play the piano."

"Really? When is your next lesson?"

"I have to call to reschedule."

"Well, I hope you haven't forgot everything," she said.

Cynthia went to the kitchen to prepare dinner. I sat at my Yamaha 650DX electronic keyboard and pressed the 'on' button. Played the C scale, then the F scale and G scales. Nothing different! No more fluidity than before. Same hesitancy. I wanted to cry.

I opened up the piano book, Level 1, to *London Bridge*. Right hand treble clef, left hand base clef. I could read the simple notes, as before.

London Bridge is Falling Down

I began playing, and humming. 'London Bridge is falling down, falling down'.

"Sounds good, honey," Cynthia called out from the kitchen.

I decided to go faster. And faster.

She came in to the living room. "When did you start playing so fast?" she said. "I don't think you missed a note."

"Really? I don't know. Just tried it faster."

Could it be? I went to another piano book, with more complicated songs. Must be careful, I thought. Didn't want to alarm her. I put on earphones, so only I could hear the notes, and opened to *Scarborough Fair*. Always had trouble with that one.

I zipped through it effortlessly. Not possible! Can't be. I did it again.

I ran to my computer, printed out *Für Elise*, Beethoven's simplest melody, a piece any conservatory student could do half -awake but was forever beyond my reach. So many sixteenth notes! Impossible.

Für Elise – Beethoven

Zip! No problem. Before the accident I could read and tap out the notes but never play them with any hint of musicality.

Cynthia put a hand on my shoulder. "What are you doing with the earphones?"

"I don't want to bother you," I replied and continued playing the tune.

"You're not bothering me. I'm glad you can still play. Who knows what that injury could have done to you?"

***

With some trepidation I went for my next lesson, in the home of Mrs. Esther Marples. She is a nice middle-aged woman, always patient with my piano klutziness. I didn't know how she would adjust to what I could now do. Did she even teach at the higher levels? Most of her pupils were kids.

"I heard about your accident," she said. "I'm happy you seem fully recovered. Have you had a chance to practice?"

"Yes, and I've tried something a little harder."

"Oh? Let me hear it." She expected to hear something from the Level 1 book, but instead I removed from my folder the Beethoven sheet music, and placed it on the piano.

"*Für Elise*? Really? My, you are ambitious."

I begin playing. Flawlessly.

She let me finish, then said, "That was nice."

"Thank you."

Her smile then turned to a frown. "But that is not you. I've worked with you for some time, I know what you can and cannot do. Have you been hiding this from me?"

"No, honestly, after the accident…"

"Accidents don't make people better players," she said. "I don't understand. Why have you come here week after week, struggling with the notes, if you can really play like that? Here, play *Alouette* for me. That is so ingrained in my mind, I know how you handle it."

I could not fake my old way. I played like a virtuoso.

She closed the piano book and stood up. "Howard, I cannot instruct you. Something strange is going on, some type of change that is beyond me. I have no experience with pupils like you. I suggest, no really, I insist you find another instructor."

We were cordial. I thanked her and insisted she take the check I had in my pocket. I did not ask for the name of another instructor. If I was to find another, I would prefer they not know each other.

***

I needed validation and did find an instructor in a distant suburb, a highly recommended professional pianist. I used an alias: Howard McGuffin. I felt thankful my fame as a writer was by name only, unlike, say, a movie star whose face anyone might recognize.

I explained my playing history as starting in childhood, and that I worked as an accountant. Under this guise I progressed rapidly, and was playing Mozart and Beethoven sonatas in less than a year. My instructor said I should qualify for Juilliard except for my age, and asked if I'd ever performed in public. I said no, I didn't want to. He said I had to give a recital, and that until one performs in public, one never knows if they have the stuff to be a good pianist. He would program me into his next one, a semiannual event for his most advanced pupils.

The recital—a local for-charity concert—took place in the community's high school. I was the oldest performer, but there were several young adults and the rest teenagers. All quite talented, I must say.

The event sold out. I played a Mozart sonata: sixteenth *and* thirty-second notes! Here's a few of the opening measures.

Mozart: Sonata No 3

Someone recognized me, and afterwards a suburban newspaper reporter sought me out. I could not lie. Yes, I play under the name McGuffin. Yes, I wrote under Howard Greenleaf. Yes, *that* Howard Greenleaf. The next day, in the suburban newspaper, the headline read: **Once-famous author debuts at recital under alias.** Then the sub-headline: **Developed sudden talent after hit by car.**

The "once-famous" hurt. I had done no writing since the accident, held no book signings and given no interviews. I was beneath the literary radar. Worse, my last manuscript, submitted just before the accident, had been rejected by the publisher because "it's too much a copycat to your previous book." The editor had suggested a rewrite, which of course I could not do: too busy practicing. Actually, that's only partly true. I did try to rewrite one chapter and but had no interest in finishing it. No, that's not true either. I didn't know how to do it. I had lost my writing skill and my desire. As predicted. It was now music or…senility.

Book sales fell off and my income plummeted. Fortunately, the recital proved a success and I was approached to do piano gigs. The first and best offer came from an unexpected source: Majestic Cruise Lines. They were looking for a no-name but accomplished pianist to play in one of their ship's lounges, short classical pieces preferred. Their clientele were the ultra-rich and ultra-sophisticated. Free room and board for two weeks, for Cynthia and me, and a stipend of one grand to boot. I jumped at the chance.

The route included several ports of Asia. The cruise was exhilarating. I only had to play two hours a day, so we were able to enjoy most of the sights and shipboard activities like everyone else.

Mid-cruise, while alone on the deck looking out over the Pacific, I heard that same deep baritone voice from Jake's Deli. "Enjoying yourself?"

I turned and faced him. "What the hell are you doing here?"

"Ah, Howard, watch your language, please."

"I have many more years to go."

"Of course, of course. Just checking up. It's our first anniversary. Just making sure everything is working as promised. I have delivered, have I not?"

"Yes, now let me be, please. I want to enjoy this trip."

"As you wish," he said, and then disappeared. Not literally—he just walked through the revolving glass door leading to the starboard cabins. Strange, though, I never saw him on the ship again.

As luck would have it, one of the ship's passengers was a professor from Oberlin Conservatory of Music, only forty-five miles from our home. This professor taught music theory and played piano himself, but did not perform professionally. He came up to me one evening, praised my playing and offered some unexpected insight.

"You are very good," he said, "but if I had to guess, I would say you came to the piano late in life, probably in your twenties."

"Oh? Why is that?"

"I can tell. There is a difference between prodigies who start as kids, and those rare adults who learn to play well after full maturity. Tell me if I am wrong."

I wanted to tell him 'age fifty-five', but knew he wouldn't believe me.

"You are correct," I said. "Started in my late twenties."

"Ah, so. Once you start late, it is very difficult to acquire the skills of someone who started at five or six or seven. I believe Barenboim was six. Mozart only four."

I knew he spoke the truth. And despite my new-found ability, its limitations pained me. He must have seen the pain in my face.

"I can help you," he offered. "I think you should come to Oberlin, let me work with you to see if there isn't some room for improvement. Just a suggestion, nothing guaranteed. If you commit, there will be no fee. You will be part of my research."

I agreed instantly. Was it just a coincidence that this professor taught near the very city in which we lived?

Later, in our cabin, Cynthia had some doubts. "Are you going to commute? It's over an hour from our home, more if there's a lot of traffic. And what about your gigs?" she asked, concerned about our plummeting income.

"I can still do gigs but not as many. Maybe I can stay in Oberlin during part of the week, come home on weekends." We agreed I should give it a try.

I stayed in Oberlin Monday through Thursday, and came home for long weekends. The professor secured a dorm room for me, as a hotel was too expensive. One night, alone in bed and lonely, I called home but Cynthia did not answer. I called her cell and got a voice message. Where could she be at 10 p.m. on a Tuesday night? Obviously a concert or something, but I got worried. No, really, I got suspicious, so I drove home right then, arriving around 11:30. She was not home.

She returned to the house at midnight and was shocked to find me waiting. At first, she feigned disbelief that I would question her, but then she cried. Yes, she was with another man, she admitted. "I'm lonely," she said. "It's got to either be me or the piano."

Then I remembered the conversation in Jake's Deli. *How you handle the notoriety, how it affects your personal life, will be up to you.* I had no notoriety, but my personal life was suffering by devotion to the art.

I did not want to risk losing Cynthia. That had not been part of the bargain and did not have to happen. And I had no intention of giving up the piano.

I professed my love for her, vowed not to let her transgression interfere with our relationship (though I did think of killing the guy), and in the end convinced her we should sell the house and move to Oberlin. With the money from the sale we could easily live in an apartment, and she could enroll in college courses she'd always thought of taking, mainly art history.

And so we sold the house and relocated.

The professor turned out to be something of a taskmaster, determined to prove that late starters could learn to play as if they had begun in childhood. I was the oldest adult player in his research project. Somehow I managed to avoid discussing my "early years" of playing since, of course, they didn't exist. Later, he did hear that I became a pianist only after a car accident, at age fifty-five, but I don't think he ever believed it. In any case, it never became an issue. The important thing is that, under his tutelage I played better and better, until one day he asked me to perform with the Oberlin Symphony.

The fiend had delivered on his promise. I knew the day of reckoning would come, and I'd have to deliver on mine, but tried not to think about it.

Time passed and I became somewhat famous on the second-tier concert market. After Oberlin I played with the Toledo Symphony, then had gigs with orchestras in Columbus, Louisville, Indianapolis and Little Rock. I played mostly the easier piano concertos. Before my accident, these concertos would have been unthinkable.

Now I must fast forward. Life was good until it wasn't. I was diagnosed with prostate cancer and underwent surgery that curtailed my performing career for several months. The doctors were optimistic but I was less so. How could I live fifteen years if my life was cut short by cancer? After all, we had a bargain.

He showed up in the hospital the day after my operation. "Just want you to know, I had nothing to do with this," he said.

"What?" I was incredulous he would make an appearance at this time *and* disclaim responsibility.

"I get you at fifteen," he said. "Sooner if the other fellow chooses to interfere. So don't blame me."

As if he had a conscience.

"I don't blame you," I said. "Just make sure my talent isn't affected. It damn well better not be."

He smiled and then, as he is wont to do, exited quickly, without another word.

I did recover, and my talent wasn't affected. Still, I was living from day to day, always practicing but never making enough to get by comfortably. Meanwhile, I concentrated on Beethoven's Piano Concerto No. 5, the magnificent *Emperor*— my ultimate goal. Anyone who can play the Fifth has arrived.

The years went by, and I won't bore you with the life of a second-tier concert pianist. But Cynthia stayed with me. And never once did I think of ending my bargain earlier than the allotted fifteen years. Nor did I ever wish for the old days of writing bestsellers. I let music be my passion.

Then one day I was invited to play with the famed Cleveland Orchestra, in a children's concert at Severance Hall. Their pianist had taken ill, and I was the closest good one around. It also helped that I was available on short notice—one day. The program included brief selections from Mozart and Tchaikovsky. My playing must have impressed, because the conductor asked what I could play at full length with the orchestra. Without thinking, I said "Beethoven's Fifth."

"Let's see," he said, and arranged a rehearsal. I passed, and he programmed the piece. But not in Cleveland. In Carnegie Hall, New York City. The Cleveland Orchestra performs there every two years or so, and they were delighted to feature Ohio's 'newest musical prodigy,' as one trade publication later put it.

Cynthia and I traveled to New York two days before the concert. There would be only one rehearsal. I was so involved with preparation that only when we arrived in New York did I realize the concert night was the fifteenth anniversary of my handshake.

So the big night came. I scanned the audience and didn't see him. You may not believe me, but I did not feel nervous. I played my heart out and the audience loved it. From the opening multi-octave notes Beethoven wrote in 1811, I was transfixed, transformed, in another world. It was as if I had transcended the stage, the hall, the city, and was no longer of mortal flesh but with Beethoven. Yes, *with* Beethoven. Forty-one minutes later we were done. A moment of silence, then the audience stood, clapped and cheered. They were, it seemed, rooting for me. Not just for my musical ability but *for me.*

The performance over, the orchestra members began drifting away. Just then a tall man in tuxedo entered from the left wing. He stood out because he wore a bowler hat. Of course I knew it was him but, still elated by the performance, played dumb.

"What do you want?"

"It is time."

"I suppose so," I said, ready to meet my fate. I just didn't think the end would arrive at the very pinnacle of my career, on the threshold of becoming, if not famous, at least financially secure.

"However," he said, "I must admit, I was so impressed with your performance tonight, I am truly reluctant to call in the chit at this time."

"What?"

"If you continue to give performances like that, I am willing to extend the term, with no further conditions."

What could I say? He was giving me more time. And no conditions!

"I don't have to do anything else?"

"It would be a pity to snuff out this talent, and where you would be going, sadly, there are no pianos. Continue to play well, my friend." And with that he left, as abruptly as he had appeared. I felt excited and elated. Now I could continue playing, what I loved and wanted most.

By this time I was alone on the stage, with the vast auditorium nearly empty. I walked to the front of the stage, to take one last look at the vast space. Carnegie Hall! Magnificent. Suddenly, all the stage lights came on at once, blinding me. I lost my footing and fell forward, head first. On the way down I heard an eerie, high-pitched laugh—vindictive and horrifying in its meaning. His laugh.

I started screaming. "No! No! No! No!" Then everything went blank.

I woke up in the ambulance with a severe headache. Oh, not again, I thought.

Yes again, only this time to New York's Central Park West Hospital. Same routine as fifteen years ago: exam in the Emergency Department, followed by head CT scan and hospital admission.

"You've suffered a concussion, and because you blacked out we need to keep you overnight for observation," said the ED physician.

When I reached my private hospital room, there were already messages from the Orchestra's conductor and concertmaster, wishing me well, and stating my performance had been great. The conductor said to call him when fully recovered. Very encouraging.

Cynthia did not want to go back to the hotel alone but, being assured by the doctors that I would survive, left the hospital around one in the morning. She was told she could pick me up around noon.

So I am now sitting in bed, updating this whole saga on my portable PC. For the record, I am a fast typist.

Of course you want to know if I can still play the piano. You're perhaps thinking that with the new head banging I might have lost the ability.

Well, I wonder also. I can envision the notes for Beethoven's Fifth in my head, but can I play it?

I needed to find out, and just after Cynthia left went searching for a piano. All sizable hospitals offer music therapy and keep a keyboard that can be wheeled to patients' rooms. So I got out of bed and walked to the nurse's station, demanding access "to the hospital's keyboard."

I might as well have demanded a double dip butter pecan ice cream cone. The night nurse told me, "It's the middle of the night. Everything is locked up. I'll leave a message for the day shift to see what we can do then. Now get back to bed." Okay, she did say "please."

Rebuffed, I have just returned to my room. I want to sleep but can't, still excited by the night's events. What you are reading now I typed at two in the morning in bed, on my laptop computer.

What's this? Someone has just wheeled in a portable keyboard! My request was honored. Wait. That someone is a tall male nurse. It's him! Dressed in nurse's garb.

I must record everything, not get excited. Will type and save as long as possible.

I am typing, he is speaking. He says I asked for the keyboard, here it is, he will be happy to listen. And he has my medicine, he says.

"What if I can't play?" I just reminded him I've suffered a concussion. I want to ask if he pushed me off the stage, but sense the question would serve no purpose. Now I remember his words back at the Hall: *If you continue to give performances like that, I am willing to extend the term.*

"We have a bargain," he says.

"How did you get in? You're not really a nurse, are you?"

"We made a deal," is his reply. "Do you not want to play? Just a few opening measures of Beethoven. That will be fine. Then your medicine."

I can say no. I want to say no. I want to go to sleep. But there is the keyboard. There is my salvation. Could the concussion take away fifteen years of musicality? I am curious. I am scared.

I am getting out of bed. For the record he is dressed in a nurse's uniform and I see the Central Park West Hospital logo. So a male nurse from this hospital. He won't give his name. He just says to play. I am scared. But I want to see if I can still play.

If you don't hear from me again, goodbye.

***

EXHIBIT 15

Above certified and submitted *in toto* and without alteration, Case #27633, New York City, NY January 8, 2---

- **Cynthia Greenleaf, Executrix of the Estate of Howard Greenleaf vs. Central Park West Hospital, in the wrongful death suit of Howard Greenleaf...**

- END -

An Ordinary Patient

<u>Dr. Katz's Pulmonary Clinic, March 15, 2006</u>
Dr. Jerome Katz's last outpatient of the afternoon is Frank Reynolds, 80, a spry, alert gentleman, with crew-cut white hair, and a face wizened from years of smoking. He is short, and thin. The nurse weighed him at 130 lbs.

Mr. Reynolds was referred to the lung doctor for "evaluation of dyspnea [shortness of breath] and COPD [chronic obstructive pulmonary disease]." Almost all cases of COPD come from smoking, and Mr. Reynolds is no exception.

He is sitting on the exam table when Dr. Katz walks in. The doctor introduces himself, goes over the chief complaint and a few other items with Mr. Reynolds, then asks, "So, just how much did you smoke?"

"About one pack a day, over sixty years, I guess. Started as a kid."

"When did you quit?"

"Oh, eight years ago, right after my heart surgery. Doctor said I had no choice."

Mr. Reynold's complaint is shortness of breath climbing stairs or walking for more than a few minutes, but he feels comfortable at rest. His cardiologist asked for the pulmonary consultation, stating in his referral note, "I don't believe his dyspnea is from his heart, more likely from lung disease."

During the history Mr. Reynolds acknowledges having some "emphysema," which he matter-of-factly attributes to his occupation—laborer and jack-of-all-trades at the local electric company, 1951-1985.

"How about the cigarettes?" Dr. Katz asks.

"Nah, maybe. But the air at the plant was not good for you. Lots of guys came down with lung disease of one type or other."

Dr. Katz often hears heavy smokers blame a work environment for their disease, and usually does not try to change this perception—unless, of course, they are still smoking.

"Why did you quit using the bronchodilator?"

"Ran out."

"Did it help when you were using it?"

"Didn't really notice much difference, Doc, to tell you the truth."

Dr. Katz, fifty-four, is chairman of the Pulmonary Division in his hospital. He is well-respected by his medical peers and a consultant for many of them. He takes a good medical history and has a genuine interest in his patients, but occasionally comes across as a little brusque. Some say he does not suffer fools gladly, an ambiguous compliment. There is also about him an air of having seen it all in years of practice. He most welcomes challenging, difficult-to-diagnose patients, and confesses to be somewhat weary of run-of-the-mill smokers with their COPD. Still, every patient gets his full attention.

After a brief physical exam, Dr. Katz decides to order pulmonary function tests. He has already viewed the chest x-ray, which shows only some minor scarring from the heart surgery.

Okay, here's another old guy with smoking-related COPD. I'll prescribe a long-acting steroid inhaler, get baseline PFTs, and arrange for a three-month follow up. Need to finish here, make hospital rounds. Just a little more history and I'm done.

"What did you do before the electric company work?"

"Oh, I did a few odd jobs. Drove a milk truck for a while, then some labor work."

Standing, Dr. Katz writes quickly on his clipboard, notes scribbled for a letter to the cardiologist he will later dictate. Returning his gaze to the patient, "Over what period of time, after high school?"

"Yeah, well, I went into the army right after graduation, got out at twenty-one, then did different jobs until I began work at the electric company."

"Did you start smoking in the army?"

"Yeah, they used to give out free cigarettes. Got me hooked, I guess."

"So if I figure correctly, that was during World War Two. What did you do in the war?"

"I was in the infantry."

This bit of history interests the doctor. His parents emigrated from Europe after the war. They were survivors. He has studied the period. He once visited the Buchenwald concentration camp, near Weimar, Germany, where they were liberated by American troops. He knows the date: April 11, 1945. How had they survived? Whenever asked they always avoided any detail, saying only, "We were lucky. The Americans came just in time." His parents married in 1948. He was born four years later.

"The infantry? Where?"

"I was in Europe."

"Where in Europe?

"France. You've heard of D-Day?" Reynolds asks, with a twinkle in his eye.

"Yes, of course. June 6, 1944."

"Well, I was there."

"Where?"

"Omaha Beach."

"You landed on Omaha Beach on D-Day?" There is a childlike incredulity in Dr. Katz's question, as if he is interviewing someone who once landed on the moon.

"Yep. Part of the second wave. We hit the beach at seven a.m."

"You were what, back then, eighteen?"

"Just turned nineteen the week before. Landed with the Twenty-Ninth Infantry. Almost killed, too. But we made it past the German gunners. Got out alive. Lots of my buddies didn't."

"You killed Germans?" *What a dumb question. Sorry I asked.*

"Doc, you don't wanna know. You saw *Saving Private Ryan*?"

"Yes, I did. Seemed pretty realistic, the opening scenes."

"Sanitized." Reynolds lets out a chuckle. "Hollywood. In the movies, you don't get the smells, the smoke. You don't get the screaming of men you know, shot and dying."

"Still, realistic for a movie, don't you think?"

"Yeah, they showed some bad stuff, but then the camera moves away. Imagine eight-ten-twelve hours of those opening scenes."

"I can't. What you guys did was—"

"Look, I'm no hero. I just wanted to survive. I was damn lucky in the war. I did what I had to do."

"How long were you on the beach?"

"Two days. After we secured it, they moved us out quick."

"Well, I'm glad you got through. Where did your outfit go after Omaha?" Dr. Katz looks down at his notes, begins writing again.

"Right through Normandy, past all those hedgerows, straight to Saint-Lô. That was fierce also."

"Did you get to Paris?"

"Sure, on time off. After our boys and the French liberated it."

Omaha Beach...Saint-Lô...Paris after our boys liberated it. Dr. Katz halts his note-taking, stares at the page. His mind is no longer on the chart, but on Frank Reynolds as a nineteen-year-old infantryman. On Reynolds landing in Normandy eight years before he was born. On him running through German bullets on the beach, living by chance while many of his buddies were mowed down. On this man as a teenager fighting to save the world, his world. On Frank Reynolds just *being there*, perhaps the most pivotal moment in world history. Dr.

Katz ponders how close his parents came to not making it. *I would not be here but for…*

These thoughts crowd the doctor's brain and prevent him from writing any further. He just stares at the page, pen in hand, as if he is about to write something. But he doesn't. He pleads with himself to finish the evaluation, to break the spell cast by this elderly patient with an ordinary medical problem in an otherwise ordinary afternoon clinic. With every ounce of will, he tries to control an emotion swelling inside, but he cannot. Very soon, tears will come.

Any minute now, I feel it. I must not let him see.

He glances up, and after the briefest look at his patient, pivots so his back is to the exam table. "Excuse me, Mr. Reynolds. I'll be right back. I have to check something in your records."

Dr. Katz quickly exits the exam room and from the hallway enters the bathroom, thankful it is unoccupied. He locks the door.

He has avoided other clinic personnel. If co-workers did see him in the hallway, they might think he is anxious to use the toilet. But no, he is just anxious to be alone, to feel this overwhelming emotion— *alone.* He looks in the bathroom mirror, sees the watery flow. He makes no sound, lest someone hear him and knock on the door, to ask "Are you okay?"

He sits on the closed toilet, paper towels in hand to wipe the tears. *Wow, that was unexpected. Did not appreciate I was this vulnerable. But I am, can't help it. Mom and Dad warned me when I was growing up, "America saved us. Don't forget." I've never forgotten, so why now, why this? I want to say something, to tell him he is a hero, one of the greatest ever in my book. No, not now. Another time, another day. He is not seeking my praise, but help for his lung condition. Have to stay focused.*

Finally, the tears stop. He stands by the sink, washes his face and, after thorough drying, cups his hands and drinks some water from the faucet. Comfortable that all signs of his outburst are gone, he returns to the exam room.

Mr. Reynolds is sitting on the table as before, waiting. "Are you okay, Doc?"

He knows. "Yes, yes, I'm fine. Before I left, you were telling me about Normandy. It got me thinking, and my mind strayed a little bit. Have you been back since the war?"

"Once, in nineteen ninety-four, for the fiftieth anniversary."

"I've never been."

"You should go, Doc."

"I know. I will ... I will go."

His patient smiles. "Good. I'm glad."

Me, too. More than I can tell you, Mr. Reynolds. "Now, here's what we're going to do about your shortness of breath..."

- END

The Audition

The assistant leaned over and whispered to the conductor, "Maestro, we must move to the next venue, the candidates are waiting."

The fifty-year-old conductor, tall, handsome and urbane, nodded to his young assistant, then said to the two guests in his office, "Thank you for your contributions. They are really appreciated. I am afraid, now, I must go to an audition for a new Philharmonic violinist. My assistant keeps me on schedule. Without Robert, I would wander these halls with my head in the clouds."

The conductor's guests acknowledged the comment, and everyone stood and shook hands. Maestro and his assistant left the office and walked briskly down the hallway. His real name was Joshua Sonenschein, but he preferred Maestro and everyone called him that. The title conferred dignity and recognition in the classical music world. On a lesser man the title might seem an affectation, but on Sonenschein it fit nicely.

That he was married to the Metropolitan Opera diva, Melissa Evergreen, only enhanced his stature. They were the musical royalty of New York. Early on they had chosen career over family. They had their music, their esteemed positions, and each other. Life was good.

"Their gifts are very generous, Robert. We must always be gracious to our benefactors. How many performers today?"

"Four, sir. Two from Curtis in Philadelphia, two from Juilliard."

"They have been vetted?"

"Yes, they were chosen from a group of eight who played for the concertmaster yesterday, and each is highly recommended for your consideration. Any of them would be an excellent addition to the Philharmonic, although one is still a student."

"Should not take long. You have my Mahler score for tonight?"

"Yes, Maestro, right here." The assistant pointed to a folder under his arm.

"Good. I want to review a couple of passages during the audition."

The conductor was dressed in slacks and a shirt open at the collar. He had a full head of hair carefully coiffed, now showing some grey. Robert, about thirty, wore a business suit and tie. Except during performances, inside David Geffen Hall people rarely saw Sonenschein without his assistant. The two men entered a small auditorium beneath the main stage. The space seats about 150 people and is used for auditions and private performances. Standard audition lighting was arranged, so the performers could not make out faces in the audience. A sound engineer sat to one side of the stage, ready to record each audition.

The four candidates waited patiently in their individual practice rooms. None would hear the others' performances, as they would go on stage one at a time. All but one were seasoned violinists: Mr. B., concertmaster for the Juilliard orchestra; Ms. T., a Curtis violin instructor for ten years and a pupil of the legendary Maurice Zigismond; Mr. R., a member of the Metropolitan Opera Orchestra, who wished to move up the scale of orchestral prestige; and Ms. M., a Juilliard prodigy, now in her eighth year under the tutelage of Yvette Baromoldi. If chosen for the position Ms. M. would, at eighteen, be the youngest Philharmonic member and for this reason was considered an unlikely candidate. But it was not uncommon for Juilliard to send promising students for the experience of auditioning and, if they advanced, performing before the Maestro.

Sonenschein and his assistant sat in the third-row center; no one sat on either side or in front. A few other people were in the auditorium, hidden in rear seats; they may have been relatives or teachers of the performers. Visitors did not introduce themselves or make comments, lest they have a negative effect. In auditions like this one the conductor is God; he will listen without any external influence. Each performer's poise, stage presence, and even hygiene are important, of course; for this reason, the Philharmonic had long since abandoned the practice of final candidates playing behind a screen. Still, in the end, it is the music that matters. Even with a short audition, Maestro could tell. Yes or no.

Mr. B. gave a rousing performance of Beethoven's violin concerto, opening movement. He could not see the conductor, who was at the time closely examining the score of Mahler's First Symphony on his lap with a small flashlight and making last minute decisions on tempo. Every minute or so Maestro would lift his head, as if to show he was paying attention. Then he would return his eyes to the Mahler score. Like all great conductors, he often resorted to multi-tasking and did not consider his divided attention rude or improper. He could hear enough during those few head-raising moments to know what he liked and what he didn't. And if you asked him, he would say he was listening to *all* of the Beethoven while *also* counting out tempo for the Mahler symphony.

Each musician was limited to ten minutes, which allowed Mr. B. time to finish the first movement. At the end the conductor leaned over to Robert and said a few words. Robert then stood to address Mr. B. "Thank you, sir; we will let you know. Excellent performance, by the way."

The next performer, Ms. T., came out in a flowing white dress, seated herself in the performer's chair and began playing several of the Paganini caprices. She was superb. Robert, himself an accomplished pianist, leaned over to Maestro at one point to comment on her playing. The conductor nodded in agreement, lifted his head for a few seconds to better appreciate the music, then retreated to the Mahler score. At the end of her recital he whispered some words to Robert, who called out the same result: "Thank you, thank you very much. Wonderful performance. We will get back to you."

Mr. R. came out in a dark grey suit and stood beside the chair, preferring to play standing. He chose the opening movement of Tchaikovsky's violin concerto. His cadences were secure, the tempo just right. He had purposely studied Maestro's own orchestral rendition and gave a performance he was sure would be admired.

After a brief conversation with Maestro, Robert told the performer, "Very nice, very nice, sir. We will get back to you." In the world of classical music auditions, these words were not a rebuff; musicians are not accepted or rejected the day of the audition. That same day, a high-quality recording of each performance would be on Maestro's desk, so he could review any of the performances, and no candidate would have to wait more than a week for a response.

"One more," Robert said, "the Juilliard student."

"Yes, one of those," Sonenschein replied with an air of resignation. He would of course stay for the last audition. Virtually all orchestra members spent time in a music school or conservatory, and you don't bite the proverbial hand. If a top school like Juilliard recommends one of its students, you do not tell them no. And the fact that she survived the concertmaster's preliminary round meant she must be very talented.

Ms. M. came on the stage wearing dark blue dress pants and a white blouse. She was young and pretty. Her appearance on stage—with violin in hand—was remindful of young prodigies who are often invited for a one-time performance with a major orchestra. She stood about 5'5", of medium build, with blond hair arranged in a ponytail. As with each of the contestants, there was no introduction. Their order of appearance, along with the printed program, told Maestro what he needed to know.

Her piece was listed in the program as *Concerto No. 4 in F minor, Opus 8*, by Antonio Vivaldi, otherwise known as *Winter*, one part of Vivaldi's *Four Seasons*. Classical music lovers consider these concertos almost a musical cliché, since the recordings are played so often by the general public. Yet the melodic pull of each "Season" is powerful, and professionals know them as difficult and rewarding pieces for the violin.

She began bowing and expertly played the first movement, *Allegro non molto*. While she played, Maestro looked over the Mahler score. It was Vivaldi vs. Mahler, and Mahler won easily. Sonenschein would not be unhappy to never hear *Four Seasons* again. Like Ravel's *Bolero*, Prokofiev's *Lt. Kije* suite and Tchaikovsky's *1812 Overture*—pieces he would no longer conduct himself—he considered Vivaldi's treasure a victim of performance overkill.

Yes, Ms. M. was talented, else she would not be on this stage playing before Maestro. Robert would thank her after the recital, then call Ms. Baromoldi the next day and thank the teacher for sending such a promising student. He assumed she would not be chosen for the position, at least not this year.

The music flowed smoothly from her instrument, melodic and engaging. All too familiar, perhaps, for during the first movement the conductor did not lift his head once. Five more minutes to go, he thought, and they would be done. As soon as that wish crossed his mind she began the second movement, and something in her playing changed. The change would hardly (if at all) be noted by a non-professional, but to Maestro it was obvious. When she should have bowed up, she bowed down; when the melody slowed down (after all, it was written *largo*), she gave it a little zip. Where eighth notes should have played legato she played some of them staccato.

The change caught Maestro off guard and he lifted his head. *What's going on here?* The playing was strange yet somehow vaguely familiar. He had heard that musical style before. Not from this girl, to be sure. But her interpretation was unique, starting with the second movement. He knew the piece like any high school student knows the Gettysburg Address. The notes were there in the right order, but the dynamics, the range of crescendos and decrescendos, were not a typical Vivaldi rendition. Where had he heard this interpretation? His mind wandered back across innumerable musical encounters. Yes! Now he remembered where. And when. Long ago, before he became a famous conductor. Before he even met his wife, the opera diva.

A few minutes remained in the concerto. Sonenschein abandoned the Mahler score and fixed his eyes on the stage. During the last movement, he did not look down once. When she finished playing, he leaned over to Robert. The message to his assistant was different this time.

Surprised, Robert asked "Are you sure, Maestro?"

The conductor reaffirmed his instruction.

Robert called out, "Ms. M., could you please wait in your backstage practice room? We would like to discuss the performance with you."

Ms. M. nodded and replied, "Yes, thank you."

There was a cough somewhere in the auditorium, but no movement to talk to Maestro or ask any questions. The conductor and his assistant walked up the stage and exited to the right. They entered the practice room where Ms. M. sat alone, her violin on a table. Robert said, "Ms. Michelle

Michaux, I would like to introduce you to the Philharmonic's Maestro."

She stood and they shook hands. She had no idea what this was about and displayed an ingénue's nervousness, though there was also some relief that meeting the great conductor came after her performance, not before. As for Robert, he was both curious and puzzled. Interviewing a job applicant right after a performance was most unusual. A day, two days later, perhaps, if you planned to hire her, but not at that moment.

"Please, call me Michelle," she said.

"An interesting performance, Michelle, very interesting," said Maestro. "Who is your teacher?"

"Yvette Baromoldi," she replied.

"From Juilliard?"

"Yes."

"Did she teach you to play Vivaldi's *largo* the way you just did?"

"I'm sorry, Maestro, I am not sure what you mean."

"In the second movement, where Vivaldi slows down, or most people interpret it that way, you increased the tempo. And those staccato notes in the third movement. It was good, mind you, I am not critical, but did she teach you that phrasing?"

"I, I...I don't know. I don't know. It's the way I've always played it. Perhaps my mother taught me that way. I'm not sure."

Neither Robert nor Michelle noted the tension in Maestro's facial muscles, but it was there. Along with a quickening of his pulse.

"Your mother is a violinist?"

"Yes."

"Her name is Michaux?" Maestro knew no violin instructor of that name but hoped there was such a person.

"No, her professional name is Bennington. Amanda Bennington."

The conductor steeled himself with every bit of nerve. He did not want to face Robert directly, lest his assistant ask 'What's wrong, Maestro?' He must stay in control, in charge. Standing slightly askew of his assistant, he said, "Robert, please wait outside. I'll be out in a few minutes."

"Are you sure, Maestro?" There was disappointment in his question, for this was an unusual request to Maestro's assistant who had, after all, arranged the audition.

"Yes," the conductor replied in a low but demanding tone. "Just a couple of minutes. Please wait for me."

Robert did as asked and closed the door behind him. Maestro positioned himself near the door, a comfortable six feet from Michelle. He assumed the position of interviewer, giving her the impression that perhaps she was a serious candidate for the Philharmonic after all.

"I understand you are still a student, Michelle. May I ask when and where you were born? I hope I am not being intrusive."

"Not at all. Paris, France, November 16, 1998."

There was a pause as Maestro digested the information and did a quick calculation. "Then you are eighteen?"

"Yes."

"Your parents are French?"

"No, no, Maestro. My mother is American. My adopted father is French."

"Adopted?"

"Yes, my biological father left my mother before I was born. I never met him."

"Was he a musician?"

"Maestro, I never knew my biological father. I don't even know if he's alive. My real father, the only one who matters, is Henri Michaux. That is my name." Her response was assertive, signaling she did not wish further inquiry on this issue.

"I am so sorry. You are right. It's none of my business. But tell me about your mother's teaching. Your interpretation of the Vivaldi movement intrigues me."

She appreciated moving the discussion away from personal background and toward her violin. "I started playing at age six. My mother was with the Paris Symphony at the time. She did not trust the teachers for someone my age, so she taught me the first four years. When we moved to America I came under the teaching of Miss Baromoldi, and stayed with her when I entered Juilliard."

"Well, you speak perfect English. I assume you spoke English in Paris."

"Oh, yes, my father is French but he grew up in England, so our household was mostly English speaking."

"He is a musician?" An innocent question.

"No, a businessman. He travels back and forth to France, but we live here in Manhattan."

He studied her face and the way she responded to his questions. For her part, she could sense his eyes probing hers. His manner was not predatory, and she did not feel threatened, but there was some discomfort, this middle-aged man questioning about her violin studies and more. *Did he like her playing? What does he want?*

"You liked the piece then, Maestro?"

"Yes, yes, very much. Your style is interesting, I do admit. Your mother must be a wonderful teacher. Do you have brothers or sisters? And if so, do they play?"

"A fourteen-year-old brother, or half-brother, if you will. Andre plays the piano."

"Your mother taught him also?"

"No, she always says she's a 'one-instrument girl.'"

"Your mother says *that*?" His voice, now quivering ever so slightly, emphasized the last word, showing more surprise than warranted. He almost asked 'Still says that?' but caught himself.

"Yes. 'Michelle, I'm just a one-instrument girl.' That's my mother." She gave a little laugh, accompanied by a slight upturn of her lips to one side and then a wry smile. He stared at the confluence of upturned lips and smile. *His* smile.

116

Her mother would confirm what he knew and then his life would change. She had sent her for this purpose. Not her teacher, but her mother. *Her mother sent Michelle to me!* And—he felt certain—*Michelle does not know.*

He wanted to walk over and embrace the young violinist, but that would seem most inappropriate. He could not move. He could not embrace her, he could not flee, he could not cry out. He could only stare at the young woman and ponder. The interview was over. Maestro was no longer in control.

"Maestro, why are you crying?"

- END -

Wishful Thinking

1918

It was impossible to avoid the heavy smell of disinfectant throughout the ward, a high-vaulted space that was once the nave of the St. Quentin Cathedral. The cathedral was taken over by the Germans in 1916, during the first Somme battle, and since then used for various war functions. The stained-glass windows, still intact, did not open, but some ventilation was provided by the open front and side doors. There was a reason for the strong medicinal odor. Another smell, one hidden by the disinfectant, was that of rotting flesh, pus, and feces.

German army physician Captain Gustav Steiner and his staff ignored the smells as they made their rounds: Twenty patients in this ward, one bed at a time. In the afternoon the team would round on another twenty patients. All were men recently injured in the desperate German offensive known as the Somme battle of 1918 (German code name: Operation Michael), and what the French called the Second Battle of Picardy (the province in which the battle was fought). Before arriving to this makeshift ward, the men had received first aid or emergency surgery. Now they needed disposition: more acute care or triage.

Military authority carried over to the field hospital. Captain Steiner's triage decisions were, in effect, military orders, obeyed without question. His orders in some cases included the decision not to treat, which invariably meant death to the patient. Steiner, an Allgemeinearzt (general practice physician), joined the military in 1916 and was immediately sent to the front, or as he liked to call it, the back of the front—about fifteen miles behind the German trenches. Three field hospitals were set up to receive the wounded. Since hundreds were wounded daily, beds were kept full. Turnover on most days was more than fifty percent. From the St. Quentin wards, many men were sent back to Germany, some were fixed up and returned to the front, some were buried. None stayed longer than a few days.

Most of the nurses were women recruited from the German civilian population, and this was as close as they ever got to the trenches. It was close enough, for the distant sound of bombarding shells was a constant. On rounds with Steiner were his young assistant, Dr. Stanheuser, two nurses and a military medical clerk responsible for keeping a written record, which Steiner would later review and sign.

The medical group approached the bed of the first patient. "Dr. Steiner, this is Corporal Bughel," said Stanheuser. "He is recovering from amputation of the right leg just above the knee. He was injured two days past, exiting his trench. Surgery was yesterday." The soldier before them was a boy, not more than eighteen. His facial expression was sullen and he did not speak.

"Son," said Steiner, "are you in pain?"

"Some, sir, in my right foot." There was no right foot.

"Nurse, is this man getting his morphine?"

"Yes, Doctor Steiner, regularly."

"See to it. And as soon as the surgeon says he's ready, send him back home. He is done with this war." Duly noted by the medical clerk.

In the next bed, behind curtains, lay a man dying from influenza. He was comatose, eyes closed, breathing fast.

"Influenza, sir. We don't expect him to live through the day."

The man was a painful sight, all the more so because his dying was apparent to the surrounding patients. Except for the performance of certain procedures, curtains were only drawn around the terminally ill. Steiner bent over with his stethoscope to auscultate the man's chest. The diagnosis was apparent without this exam, but the doctor felt he should listen anyway.

"Rales. Let's move on."

The next patient was introduced as Private Rhineberger. His eyes were closed due to morphine sedation. "Gassed with phosgene, sir."

"How did that happen? Are the French using poison gas?"

"Lobbed by his own unit, sir. His sergeant reports that the shell misfired and landed five feet from where he and a comrade were standing. They were both overcome by the fumes and blinded, running in circles. His buddy ran the wrong way and was shot down by French sniper, presumed dead. Rhineberger was pulled back by our unit and survived, albeit he is blind and has facial burns."

The soldier's face was wrapped in gauze and the burns were not visible.

"What do we have for phosgene burns?"

"Not much. He's getting morphine, and the gauze is changed twice a day."

"He will stay. There is large risk of infection if we move him out too soon."

Steiner could see twenty patients in under two hours, forty patients in a day, and in between rounds the doctors and nurses worked in the intake pool, treating new arrivals. With lunch, paperwork and two short breaks, the workday lasted from 7 am to sundown. Triage rounds were perfunctory in most cases, and medical fatigue set in by the tenth or fifteenth patient. Doctors did their best to hide such feelings, since the soldiers in bed were so much worse off and deserved their attention.

A corporal lay in bed twelve. "Shot through the jaw, sir. He is unable to speak but moans and growls. His tongue was completely amputated." The young man glared back at the medical team with a look of anger and utter disbelief at his fate.

"Did the bullet exit?"

"No sir, it's lodged in his jaw, causing him some pain as can be expected. There is nothing to do surgically."

"Corporal, let me look at your throat. Please open." Steiner was handed a flashlight. The corporal stared at

Steiner and did not budge. "Can he hear, is his hearing gone too?"

"As far as we know, he can hear," said Stanheuser, "but since he cannot speak, there is no communication. We have given him a pencil and paper to write his name, but he throws them away."

"We don't know his name?"

"That's a problem, Dr. Steiner. We really don't know. There was no identification on him and he won't answer any questions. Just growls and moans. We had to tie one hand to the bedpost to keep him from leaving. His captain is due in from the front this afternoon and will identify him."

Steiner noted the left wrist restraint secured with a metal binder. The man was pitiful but not more so than most of the other patients. He would have to be stern. Facing the corporal from a foot away he yelled, "THAT IS AN ORDER, CORPORAL. OPEN YOUR MOUTH!"

Slowly, passively, the order was obeyed. Steiner's flashlight revealed a reddened palate, with fresh blood oozing slightly from the right buccal cavity. The bullet could not be seen. Nor could any tongue. After the exam the patient spit into a handkerchief held by his free right hand, the cloth already bespotted with mouth blood.

"Where did this happened?"

"Between the trench lines. Our troops were advancing over what they thought was an empty quarter. They didn't see a machine gunner to their right. Six in his platoon were shot dead, two survived. He was one of them."

"Son, we are trying to help you. We need to know your name and where you are from." Steiner handed him his pen and the chart board. "Write your name, please."

"Ahhrggghhhhh! Ahhrrrrgggghhhhhh!" Steiner reeled back, momentarily frightened by the animal response.

"I'm afraid he's not all there, sir," offered Stanheuser.

"I agree. Let's move on. We'll watch him one more day, make sure there is no infection. His captain will identify the poor soul. He'll never talk again. Send him to Berlin Heilanstalt für Geisteskranke (Berlin Mental Hospital for the Insane). They are best able to deal with him."

That afternoon Captain Hans Jurgens came to pay his respects to men of his unit. As requested, he stopped by Dr. Steiner's office.

"Ah, Captain, thank you for coming. You have some brave men. We'll get the healthier ones back to you as soon as possible. Did you see bed twelve? Who is he?"

"Yes, I heard you had no identification. He's a brash young corporal, good soldier, though he is finished, I'm afraid. From Austria, name's Adolph Hitler."

"Yes, the poor fellow is shell-shocked, in addition to losing his tongue. He'll be going to Berlin Heilanstalt für Geisteskranke. He'll die of old age there, if he doesn't commit suicide first."

- END -

The Golf Gods

The golf gods are not nice. They're not benevolent, either.

Maybe you don't believe in golf gods. Or maybe you're one of those non-golfer monotheists, and just assume there can only be one golf god. If so, doesn't really matter what you think. Most of us who play the game have enough firsthand experience to believe they're real. And there's surely a group of them, not just one. Don't think just one could cover all the courses and all the millions of golfers.

If the ancient Greeks had played golf, they would have identified the golf gods for us. They certainly knew about not-nice gods and goddesses. *Nemesis* was the Greek goddess of retribution and vengeance, and would be about right as the first golf god. But golf is a modern game, at least compared to discus throwing, so we've only learned about golf gods in modern times. Now we don't make any distinction about gender; simplifies things to just call them all gods.

And they are a mean bunch. Get on their wrong side and you are hosed. What you really want to do is: a) never ask for their help, and b) try to stay out of sight. You can learn the first part through rigid self-control but part b, well that's most difficult. They see every hole, every shot; some folks think they can even *read your mind.* I personally don't think so, but I could be wrong.

What they *can do* is make your ball curve left or right, skedaddle into the drink, bury itself in the sand, or skirt by the cup at the very last millisecond, even when the laws of physics state very plainly it should drop in. They can even alter the slope of the green just as you're putting. Say you see the green slopes left to right, so you hit your ball a foot or two to the left of the cup. On its way there's an unexplained roll, and the ball keeps going *left.* Whoa!

How'd that happen? The golf gods shifted the green a bit, that's how.

One other nefarious trick they like to play. It's called *make the ball disappear on the fairway*. You hit the ball, it lands out some 220 yards straight down the fairway, just over a slight rise —all your playing partners agree on that fact. But when you get there, the ball is nowhere to be found. That's because the golf gods quickly scooted it over to the deep rough, or maybe even buried it underneath the short grass.

One saving grace is that when you start your round you are pretty much ignored by the golf gods. At that point they just don't care about you. They see you alright but they don't notice, if you get what I mean. The best analogy is the birds—geese, herons, egrets, pelicans, storks—found on many courses. They see you but don't much care when or where you hit the ball— unless you do something to draw their attention.

Same with the golf gods. We draw their attention by doing something foolish. Like playing well when we're not supposed to. When they see you getting too uppity, you are in for a heap of trouble. They look for uppityness, yes they do. They *might* leave you alone if you are humble and shy, although I'm not sure about that, so don't quote me. But go do something uncharacteristic for your game—like shoot several pars in a row or chip in from the bunker or sink a forty-foot putt—and they will home in on you like a honeybee on a warm flower. Especially if you yell, or boast or do high fives. They hate high fives. They will get you on the next hole, or maybe the one after that.

As I said in the beginning, they are not nice. They don't ever want to help you, only to put you in *your place.* And if your place is mediocre golf, that's where you are going to stay. Try— just try—to get out of your mediocrity and they will slam you back so fast your head will spin. Three pars in a row? OK, Joe, the next hole you are in for a double bogey. No, let's make that a triple bogey, just for laughs. Oh, they do laugh, you just can't hear them.

"What about the God of Luck?" people often ask. "Doesn't that god play a role, fight off the bad golf gods, *intervene*?" Alas, there is no such god. Luck on the golf course happens when the real, actual golf gods are busy elsewhere. Your ball hits an out-of-bounds tree and bounces back onto the fairway. That's luck. The golf gods weren't watching. Or your ball heads straight for a deep bunker but is stopped by a misplaced rake and so stays on the grass. Same thing. Probably you are playing so poorly anyway, the golf gods aren't paying attention.

I have a friend who carries a handicap in the high teens. A while back we played in a foursome and after seventeen holes his score was seventy-five. One more par on the last hole and he'd have a seventy-nine, breaking eighty for the first time. For a high handicapper, that's a big deal: bragging rights, something you might tell your grandchildren.

He had just come off a birdie on number seventeen and high-fived me and two other playing partners. I didn't say anything but kind of had a premonition at that point. On the way to the eighteenth tee he was all "Wow, I've never broken eighty before." Not boasting, really, but enough to draw the golf gods' attention. They were likely busy with some other bloke, but now they for sure focused on my friend, standing there on the last tee box. Nothing draws their attention faster than a so-so golfer about to go and do something special.

Well, you can guess what happened next. He hooked his drive into a pond bordering the fairway. Now he's hitting three beside that little body of water. His next shot lands in the middle of a deep greenside bunker. His fourth shot sends the ball right up against that bunker's lip, where it gets swallowed, almost whole. It was a sight to see: a tiny portion of the white ball protruding from under the sand. My friend takes an unplayable, costing him a stroke, and is now laying five, still in the bunker.

The golf gods are laughing and my friend is on the verge of some opposite emotion. Well, his next shot gets the ball on the green, so now he's laying six. He then makes two putts for a score of eight: what golfers call a "snowman" because that's what an eight looks like. Purists call it a quadruple bogey. My friend called it a disaster. Actually, his final score of eighty-three is still a very respectable round for a high handicapper, but not what he was hoping for. The golf gods made sure of that.

OK, so maybe you think this golf god business is all poppycock. If you think that, then either you don't play the game or you are naïve. The golf gods are real and will mess with you if given an inclination. You'd best understand this aspect of the game.

Be humble, my friend. Stay quiet. And play your game.

- END -

Big John and Little John

Fredericksburg, Virginia - December 13, 1862

The Georgia Regulars were as effective a fighting force as any in the Confederate army. The men mostly came from coastal areas of the state. They were farmers, laborers, clerks, blacksmiths, teachers, dockhands. Friends and neighbors often enlisted together; in some communities, this meant every eligible man. No one thought it would be such a long and deadly war.

Once enrolled and given weapons and uniforms, the Regulars quickly formed a cohesive regiment. They did not espouse fighting for any particular principle, and certainly not to "preserve slavery"—indeed, very few came from families that even owned slaves. They had some feeling about "states' rights", meaning the North should leave Georgia alone, but that was not what made them risk their lives in every battle. The great motivator was *camaraderie*, that special bond among soldiers who shared a common geography and heritage.

Big John and Little John grew up on adjacent farms near Brunswick, Georgia. After enlisting together in late 1861, they were sent to Macon to join the Regulars, then eventually made their way to the Army of Northern Virginia—Robert E. Lee's army. Their unit, Company C, consisted of seventy-five men under the command of Major John D. Walker.

Little John was not so little, perhaps five feet four inches tall, but slim, weighing no more than 115 lbs. There were certainly other men of small size in the army. A Confederate General, William Mahone, known as "Little Bill," stood five feet five and weighed only 100 lbs.

Big John stood six feet one inch tall and weighed 220 lbs., so there was never any confusion about who was "big" and who was "little." In the early days of enlistment they related how they came to be such good friends. Big John loved to hunt and Little John was a crack shot; he could hit a possum from 100 yards. "So we were neighbors and did a lot of hunting together," Big John said. "Now we're hunting Yankees."

Big John claimed to be twenty, but his well-trimmed beard and deep-set eyes made him look a few years older. Little John offered his age as eighteen, but a clean-shaven face made him look younger, perhaps only sixteen. Age did not matter, though, as both were well respected in the Company: Big John for his strength and bravery in battle, Little John for his marksmanship. In one minor skirmish, Little John had picked off a sniper hiding in a tree; the Yankee fell dead to the ground, right in front of men who could have been his targets.

There were other buddies in Company C, but none so close, it seems, as these two. Having each other as constant companions, the pair tended to keep apart from the rest. They did not partake in the idle talk common after dinner or initiate conversation with other soldiers. Also a bit unusual—they did not complain, about anything. They were to all outward appearances model soldiers, aloof but dependable, reliable. Men occasionally asked Little John why he didn't join them in playing cards or horseshoes. He would reply, in a friendly, boyish way, he would rather "clean my gun" or "go looking for squirrels." A born hunter, his fellow soldiers said, and left him alone.

Big and Little John also did not join in spooning, the method used to stay warm while sleeping. Spooners slept chest to back, like spoons in a drawer, so that each man got some protection from the wind and cold. A typical spooning unit held four to eight men. Soldiers took turns "sleeping on the end." The fact that other men also avoided spooning, preferring to sleep alone under a thin army blanket, made Big and Little John's avoidance less suspect.

Company C's constant movement with a different camp almost every night, the exhaustion that brought sleep on quickly, and a natural incuriosity among the men whose main concern was simply surviving, all gave Big and Little John a certain amount of freedom when not in battle. A permanent army camp, far from the enemy, where gossip might gain traction, would no doubt have generated more inquiry as to the nature of their relationship. In such a setting, the soldiers might have thought more about their pairing, and concluded it was "peculiar," "strange" or simply "not natural".

Only once was there any notion of something not right. In the woods around Fredericksburg, a few days before the great battle, a corporal woke up to take a piss and wandered near where the two Brunswick buddies were sleeping, away from the camp, behind a dense clump of trees. Under the moon he could see the pair laying face to face, in full embrace, the lips of one on the neck of the other—decidedly not the posture used in spooning. The corporal did not disturb them but took his leak and returned to the camp. There was no one awake to talk to, and he wondered if he should even mention it the next day. He fell back to sleep, undecided.

Some 186,000 troops assembled at Fredericksburg on December 13, 1862, the largest concentration of men in any Civil War battle. Union General Ambrose Burnside, newly appointed commander of the Army of the Potomac, maneuvered most of his 114,000 men across the Rappahannock River to attack General Lee's 72,000-man Army of Northern Virginia.

Many of the Georgia Regulars, including Company C, were stationed atop Marye's Heights, a goal of the Yankees. Fighting was fierce. By the end of the day, results were clear: Burnside's larger army had been repulsed. To the Confederates, this seemed like sweet revenge for their defeat at Antietam just three months earlier. When the Regulars saw the Yankees retreat they began whooping and hollering.

"Hold off," said Major Walker, "they're not gone yet. We'll go down a bit, make sure no Yankees are hiding out for another assault."

Big and Little John, plus three dozen other soldiers with rifles poised, followed Major Walker. A hundred yards down the hill, they took enemy fire.

"Oh, shit!" yelled the major. "Get down." The men dropped to the ground, but not before several were wounded, and two were killed by Yankee bullets.

"I'm hit, John! I'm hit!" The words came from Little John.

Big John rushed to his side. "Where are you hit? Where?"

Little John pointed to his right thigh. Big John saw blood soaking the pants leg. He knelt down to get a closer look. "We've got to get you back up the hill." Two soldiers came to his aid. Big John handed over his rifle and asked them to cover his retreat. He then lifted Little John and carried him in both arms up to the Heights, to safety.

He tried to have Little John stand but the right leg was painful, causing him to almost faint. Big John laid him in a grassy area and placed a blanket for a head rest.

By this time, the great battle of Fredericksburg was almost over. There were dozens of other wounded lying about, and the medics were very busy.

"I need a stretcher!" yelled Big John to one of the medics. His cry instead brought a nearby surgeon, and also the attention of several other Georgia Regulars.

"What's the matter?" asked the surgeon, by rank a colonel.

"He took a bullet," said Big John. "I need to carry him to the hospital on a stretcher. These men can help, if I can get a stretcher."

The surgeon looked down at Little John. "Where are you hit, son?"

"My leg, sir." Little John pointed to his right thigh. Blood covered that side of his pants down to the boot.

"Anywhere else?"

"No."

"I've got to examine it, to see where the wound is, stop the bleeding. Then we'll get you to the hospital. Let's get the boots and pants off."

"No, I'm all right. Just can't walk."

"I know, but you can lose the leg if it's still bleeding. Don't worry, I won't do any operation here. Not taking your leg off."

"No, I...I. Please, just let me lie here. It's...I'll be cold."

"Nonsense," said the surgeon. "We'll give you a blanket as soon as I see your leg. We won't let you freeze."

"No, no. Leave me be. I'll be all right."

"Son, the pants are coming off."

Big John interjected. "Can't we just get a stretcher? I'll help carry him to the hospital."

"Is there some false modesty here?" asked the doctor. He would not tolerate any further delay and called out to two soldiers standing by. "Get the boots and pants off of this man. Now!" The soldiers moved quickly to obey.

Big John muscled in to stop the undressing but was restrained by other soldiers. On being pulled away he yelled, "Leave him alone!"

One soldier removed Little John's boots and pants as the other held his arms. In that first instant, with the pants off, Little John's underwear drew attention. The doctor pulled down the undergarment to knee level for a fuller inspection. He saw the bullet wound surrounded by dried blood, but no active bleeding. Then his eyes were drawn to another part of Little John's anatomy.

"What is this?" he asked.

No one said a word. Everyone stared at Little John's exposed pelvis.

Using both hands, the doctor pulled Little John's thighs slightly apart, looking for the thing that was not there.

131

"Jenny!" yelled Big John, still restrained by his comrades.

The doctor ignored Big John's outburst and, without moving his eyes spoke in a calm, professional manner.

"Well, well. *Now* I understand. He's a she."

- END -

The Critique Club

"Okay, Jordan," says Samantha, our Critique Club leader, "it's your turn to read."

The seven other members of our Fiction Writers of Sunnyville club all have a copy of my story, previously emailed, and will follow along as I read. FWS is an accomplished group of retirees; all have published at least one novel and are working on another or, as in my case, on short stories. We meet every Friday morning in one of Sunnyville's many club rooms, seated around two card tables.

I take a sip of coffee, then proceed with a brief introduction. "This is a rather long short story, over 7000 words. I'll keep to our limit and just read the first 1500. It's called 'A Cold, Snowy Path', about a lone hiker in the Yukon, late nineteenth century. In the dead of winter."

I begin reading. I can tell there is interest in the story and wonder what critique the members will offer. The story is in the genre I am known for—outdoor sagas with an historical bent, about early mountain climbers, ocean sailors, river rafters, hikers in unfamiliar territory.

My protagonist, a newcomer to the Yukon, is beset by extreme cold as he tries to reach his buddies at a distant camp. There he will find warmth and shelter. He's only a few hours away but the temperature is so cold, minus fifty degrees Fahrenheit, that he has to stop and make a fire along the way. Then the fire goes out. He has a dog with him.

I get to the last paragraph.

"The man held steadily on. He was not much given to thinking, and just then particularly he had nothing to think about save that he would eat lunch at the forks and that at six o'clock he would be in camp with the boys. There was nobody to talk to; and, had there been, speech would have been impossible because of the ice-muzzle on his mouth."

"Okay, I'll stop there. I'll read another 1500 words next week."

Samantha takes over. "Who wants to comment?" she asks.

Bill raises his hand and is called on.

"Jordan, it's interesting, and I see you're building the question of whether the man will make it to his camp, but there are some problems. One is your overuse of semicolons, which I've noted. However, the major problem I find is your excessive use of 'was'. I checked it out on Word. You used 'was' 52 times, and frankly the repetition is tiring to the reader. Allow me to read three sentences in your first paragraph."

Bill picks up his copy and starts reading, emphasizing each 'was'.

"It *was* a steep bank, and he paused for breath at the top, excusing the act to himself by looking at his watch. It *was* nine o'clock. There *was* no sun nor hint of sun, though there *was* not a cloud in the sky."

"Here's a suggestion for rewriting just those sentences," he says, and begins reading his rewrite. 'The bank proved steep, and he paused for breath...Nine o'clock already, he thought. Sun's not out, though the sky is cloudless.' That's just a suggestion, Jordan. I would try to change most of the 'wases' to some other verb form."

"Thanks," I reply. "I'll consider that."

Mike quickly raises his hand and begins speaking. "Interesting, your last comment, Jordan. You said, 'I'll consider *that*'. I counted thirty uses of 'that' in this excerpt. Let me just quote two sentences, beginning on line twenty-nine."

"Fifty degrees below zero stood for a bite of frost *that* hurt and *that* must be guarded against by the use of mittens, ear-flaps, warm moccasins, and thick socks... *That* there should be anything more to it than *that* was a thought *that* never entered his head."

"Excessive use of 'that' is generally a sign of weak writing," adds Mike. "You're a good writer, and I'm frankly surprised you used 'that' so often."

"Perhaps you're right, Mike," I reply. "I'll look into *that*." My comment elicits some laughter. We're really a friendly group, all seeking to improve our writing.

"Anyone else?" asks Samantha.

Alice offers a comment. "I pretty much agree with what's been said so far. Just seems like a lot of overwriting to me. One other area where I think the writing could be sharpened is your repetition of the word 'it.' Just look at that first paragraph again. I won't read the whole thing. All these uses of 'it' are in that one opening paragraph, beginning on line five."

"*It* was a steep bank...."

"*It* was nine o'clock."

"*It* was a clear day."

"Then sentence six of the same paragraph."

"*It* had been days since he had seen the sun."

"Too many 'its'," Alice continues. "Also, you use the first three as a pronoun, and the fourth one as a preposition. All this, I think, draws attention to the grammar and away from your story. At least it does for me."

"How would you change it?" I ask.

"I don't know," she replies, with an air suggesting genuine concern for the story's problems. "It's up to you. Bill offered one suggestion for fixing the 'wases'. I would just pay attention to your use of 'was,' 'that,' and 'it'. You can easily search for these words. Combine phrases so they're hardly needed."

"Any other comments, Alice?" asks our leader.

"Oh, one other. The man has no name. You just call him 'The Man'? Why not give him a name, make it a little more personal. Okay, I'm done. That's all."

Samantha asks if anyone else has a comment. Two members have so far offered no critique, and remain silent. I get the feeling that, by now, they perhaps feel sorry for me and don't want to pile on.

"No other comments? Okay," says Samantha. "I do have a criticism no one's mentioned. The piece starts out giving us the man's point of view, and that is pretty much maintained throughout. The narrator tells us that the gloom of the day 'does not worry the man', that a noise in the forest 'startled him', and that at one point the man noted changes in his cheek from the cold. But then the narrator also gives us, in several places, the *dog's* point of view."

Her emphasis on the word "dog" translates into "Do you know what you're doing?", and elicits a few titters from the group.

Samantha has more to say. "In fact, Jordan, you go back and forth with point of view, between the man and the dog. I personally don't mind the dog having a point of view, some stories are written that way, but a general rule is to keep only one point of view in a short story.

"Where," I ask, "do I have the dog's point of view?"

"Several places. Samantha glances down at her copy. Here, line sixty-two."

"The animal was depressed by the tremendous cold. It knew that it was no time for travelling. Its instinct told it a truer tale than was told to the man by the man's judgment."

"And again, on line sixty-eight."

"But the brute had its instinct. It experienced a vague but menacing apprehension that subdued it and made it slink along at the man's heels...The dog had learned fire, and it wanted fire, or else to burrow under the snow and cuddle its warmth away from the air."

"So, you see, you go back and forth. I am not a stickler for point of view like some people, but do draw the line on interjecting an animal's point of view along with a human's, especially when they are presented by a narrator who is physically removed from the scene. It sounds artificial to me. That's just my opinion."

"Thanks," I reply. "Anything else?"

Brian, heretofore silent, speaks up. "Jordan, you said you have another 5000 words to this story. It's finished?"

"Yes."

"I suggest you go back and rewrite the thing before submitting more to our group. I don't want to be too critical, but do think the points raised here are valid, and seriously weaken your story. You can't hope to get it published in this style of writing."

"Oh, I'm not worried about that, Brian. It's already been published."

"Really, where?"

"I have a confession to make. It's not really my story. The actual title is "To Build a Fire," and it was published in 1908 by Jack London. The only thing I changed is the title. It is still being read in high schools and is widely regarded as a classic man-versus-nature short story." I pause for effect. "A classic."

There are a few guffaws as people stare at their copy. I see Brian doing a fast web search on his smart phone. While he's searching, I take another sip of coffee, and then Mike speaks up.

"You can probably do this with a lot of older literature," says Mike. "Imagine reading *Beowulf* here. This critique group is really for what we ourselves write, not fiction written by others, no matter how famous they may be." He looks to Samantha, as if hoping she will reinforce his disdain for my trickery, but she stays mum.

Brian puts down his smart phone. "Okay, I found 'To Build a Fire'. It popped up in a website 'Twenty Great American Short Stories'. So you fooled us, I admit. But I agree with Mike. The criticisms are still valid for modern writing. Styles change, and what's considered good writing changes over time."

"I suppose so," I reply. "Just thought it would be interesting to see how we respond to what's generally considered great literature, even today. As I said, the story's read in schools across the country."

"So is *Beowulf*," says Mike, fairly dripping with sarcasm. Brian slowly shakes his head, and Alice pointedly does not make eye contact. Still, I have no regrets. I made my point, and offer no more rebuttal.

"Let's move on," Samantha says. "Who's next to read?"

- END -

The Tapper

On their fourth vacation day in Delhi, and second week in India, Brandon Williams and his girlfriend opt for different sightseeing. He chooses Qutb Minar, a World Heritage site outside the city. She wishes to visit no more monuments, and decides to spend the afternoon in the ancient and colorful market Chandni Chowk.

Brandon knows about Qutb Minar from *Fodor's Essential India*: basically an 800-year-old column 100 meters tall, made of red sandstone and marble and surrounded by other medieval structures.

The monument is just five miles from their hotel. Public transportation is not feasible, so he hires a car and driver and prepays $25 U.S. for the round trip. He spends about an hour at the Minar while his driver waits. The monument lives up to its billing and he considers the visit worthwhile.

The return trip begins about an hour before sundown and, as with the ride to the Minar, Brandon sits in the backseat, opposite his driver.

***

The two-lane road is choked with cars, and after three miles of stop-and-go driving all movement ceases, for no apparent reason. Brandon curses the traffic. Worse than Chicago, he comments to his driver, Rangu. Here, you can be stopped cold almost anytime, anywhere, from God knows what: a stubborn cow, an accident, a demonstration, a large pot hole.

Both driver and passenger are in their late twenties, but otherwise share little in common. Conversation had been desultory to this point, but now becomes more animated.

"I've not been to your country. Will go some day," says Rangu.

"You'll like it. Lots of Indian people in my home town. We have great Indian restaurants."

"My English—not so good."

"Good enough," Brandon replies.

From his side window Brandon notes much activity on the berm. People walking while carrying laundry, food, furniture. Some are alone, others in small groups. Also several locals riding bicycles. *Wish I had a bike now. Even walkers are at an advantage.*

Tapping begins on his window: a young Indian woman dressed in colorful rags, holding an infant. *What an annoyance! First, stuck in traffic, and now beggars.* Two things he does not like about India: the poverty and the begging. He thinks ahead, of being with his girlfriend in their four-star hotel, well insulated from the poorest classes.

He remembers a friend telling him about "begging managers" who rent out babies in the morning, to increase the proceeds. At night, his friend said, the babies are returned, to be sent out again the next day. *Probably one of those.*

"Don't respond, Mr. Brandon," says Rangu. "Will just bring more out."

The car is at a standstill. She continues tapping. *Damn! I wish to hell we'd move. I'm obviously well off to her, a foreigner with a driver.* He stares for just a moment. She is *National Geographic* poor: face gaunt, eyes wide open, pleading.

Through the mirror Rangu sees him looking out the window. "Don't look! Brings others." Rangu honks his horn, to no effect.

Brandon obeys and turns his gaze forward. He is feeling more uncomfortable by the minute. His brief look has encouraged the woman. The baby starts crying. He wonders, has she pinched the child?

The woman continues tapping. A strong middle finger, he notes. Tap, tap, tap.

Brandon starts to roll down the window. *Maybe a dollar will make her stop.*

"Don't roll down the window, Mr. Brandon, please." Rangu honks his horn. The baby cries.

Tap, tap, tap, tap, tap, tap.

He looks again at the woman. Her eyes implore. She holds the baby out a few inches with one arm, and with her other hand puts two fingers to her lips. He knows the meaning: *My baby is hungry.*

"Look away, move over behind me," implores Rangu, and he honks again. "Come. Sit behind me, away from that window."

Many tourists, many beggars, in India. And now Brandon remembers advice he's heard over the past week, from both natives like Rangu and fellow tourists. Always some variation of 'don't feed the beggars.' It reminds him of zoo warnings. 'Don't feed the animals.'

Brandon opens the car door.

"Where are you going?" yells Rangu.

Half out the car, Brandon says, calmly, "Leave me here, Rangu. I'll walk back to the hotel."

Brandon closes the door. Just then the cars in front begin to move, albeit slowly, and now the car behind honks. Brandon knows Rangu has been distracted. He moves away from the car as it catches up with the traffic, and then sees Rangu twist around to look out the rear window. Brandon waves him to go on.

Now alone, Brandon faces the woman with child. She does not let go of his eyes. He pulls out some bills, gives her an American dollar and fifty rupees. She steps back and more beggars appear. He begins distributing all the money in his pockets, about twenty-five American dollars, plus another ten in rupees. He fills each outstretched hand with a little bit of paper money, until there is no more. The only thing still of value on his person are a passport and credit card, sealed in an inner pocket.

More beggars come and implore in their native tongue. He hears no English. He pulls out his pockets to show they are empty. "No more," he says, over and over. Gradually they walk away, to seek handouts elsewhere.

The tapping woman approaches him. She no longer holds the baby; it has served its purpose, he assumes, and is perhaps with another beggar. She reaches for his hand – the money hand – and kisses it. Then she bows and walks away.

Brandon smiles, glad to be free of the car, and of his anxiety and discomfort. *I deserve no praise. I did it for me, and I am happy for it.*

It is now twilight and will soon be dark. He figures it's about two miles back to the hotel. He walks the distance, unmolested.

- END -

Crusade

Dr. Lewis Miller always struggled to get his smoking patients to quit. He cajoled, he pontificated, he pointed out facts. When all that failed, he used his funeral home gambit.

"Mable," he would say to his patient, when her smoking habit came up, "What funeral home do you do business with?"

This question would, of course, get Mabel's attention. After her 'why-the-heck-are-you-asking me-that?' response, he would go into his the-cigarettes-are-killing-you-quick spiel. He tried some variation of this question with most of his addicted patients. Sometimes it worked, but most often not. Still, he kept trying.

And if one of his smokers was admitted to the hospital, for whatever reason, he would, in the middle of examining the patient, ask where they stashed the cigarettes.

"My cigarettes?"

"Yes, the ones you brought with you."

Outed, the patient would invariably reveal the hiding place, usually a purse or the bedside drawer.

"May I have them, please?" the doctor would ask,

ever so politely. "You won't be smoking in the hospital." And usually, without a fuss, the patient would turn them over. Like his other methods, though, this gambit seldom worked to break their habit. Still, he felt it a duty to always try something, and he liked inventing new ways.

Which brings us to the case of Amanda Wiggins, a middle-aged woman with chronic lung disease whose chief complaint was always some variation of "I am short-winded." She had gone through several hospitalizations for chronic lung disease, yet continued to smoke *even when in the hospital*, this being an era when "smoking rooms" were available for tobacco-addicted patients.

Neither fear of funeral homes, emergency rooms, artificial breathing machines, lung cancer, nor skin wrinkles—all warnings offered by Dr. Miller—had made any dent in Ms. Wiggins' smoking addiction. She was incorrigible. She continued to smoke in her hospital room, even though that was forbidden, and when reminded of the ban, she got out of bed and walked to the ward's one small area that allowed the stinking habit.

Now you might think there is something wrong with the mind of a patient who continues to abuse the very thing making her sick, and you would be correct. There was a history of depression and a chaotic home life, and she had seen a psychiatrist on occasion, though she was no longer taking prescribed anti-depressant medication. As for Dr. Miller, he practiced pulmonology and did not feel daunted by her psychological problems. He would find a way.

He had come to learn that Ms. Wiggins' anchor in life was the Bible and fundamentalist religion, facts heretofore not mined in his no-smoking crusade. And so, on her second day of yet another hospitalization for chronic lung disease, Dr. Miller made his move. Ms. Wiggins was in bed, reading her Bible. He arranged for her nurse, Emily, to come join him. He needed a witness in case Ms. Wiggins really did quit smoking, someone to testify to his no-smoking creativity. While he stood to the left of the bed, he had Emily stand on the other side, making it easy to observe her reaction as he focused on their patient.

"I want to discuss something with you," he said to Ms. Wiggins.

She put down the book. "Yes?"

"It's about your smoking, Amanda. We can't get you better if you continue to smoke."

There was a short pause, then she said, "I'll quit," in a manner which conveyed just the opposite intention.

"You've got to quit."

"I'll quit. I want to get better."

"You're gonna die!"

"Don't say that, Dr. Miller. If I quit will I get better?"

"How are you going to quit? You've promised me a hundred times, and you always go back to smoking."

"Well, I'll quit now."

"Can I have your cigarettes?" He knew her supply was endless; taking them would be like trying to cut off the flow of cocaine with a single arrest. Still, he figured it would be a step in the right direction.

"Take 'em, Dr. Miller," she said, confidently, pointing to her nightstand. "They're in here."

He opened the drawer and took out two unopened packs of Camel cigarettes.

"Can I have the others?" he asked.

"I don't have any more. That's all I have."

He knew there would be others, easy to obtain.

"Now you've got to swear you'll quit smoking."

"I'll swear," she said, showing no emotion.

He raised his brow slightly to catch Emily's eyes, then returned his gaze to Ms. Wiggins.

"Then swear," he repeated, raising his voice slightly.

"I swear." Still no emotion from his patient. Dr. Miller reached over and picked up her Bible from the bed.

"Swear on this," he commanded.

"Why do I have to swear on the Bible?" Now her voice was rising. "I *said* I wouldn't smoke. Don't you believe me?"

Dr. Miller knew the power of religion, especially her fundamentalist brand. Unless he could get her to swear on the Bible she would never take her promise seriously.

"Ms. Wiggins you've got to swear on the Bible. Otherwise God won't believe you're sincere."

She hesitated and her body began to shake. She looked at Dr. Miller, then at Emily, then at her Bible. She seemed lost in thought. Then, after a few seconds, she looked up again at the doctor.

"Dr. Miller," she said, this time with indignation, her voice trembling a little, "that's the word of the Lord! You want me to swear on the Bible?"

"Swear!" He paused, counted the seconds: one-two-three. "SWEAR!"

"I can't do that!"

"Then you don't intend to quit. You lied to me." He looked again at Emily, wondering if she found his method unprofessional, but she remained an impassive observer.

"But I will quit, Dr. Miller. I promise!"

"Then SWEAR ON THE BIBLE!"

Slowly, with hesitation, she placed her right hand on the holy book. Now he felt the flush of victory for his crusade. He had reached the pinnacle of no-smoking creativity: a unique message tailored to a unique patient.

"Repeat after me," he said. "I, Amanda Wiggins..."

She hesitated and looked again at Emily, who merely nodded her head, affirming Dr. Miller's command. Then Ms. Wiggins looked back at him, and their eyes met. Evangelist and true believer. She repeated his preamble.

"I, Amanda Wiggins..."

"Do swear before God in Heaven..."

"Do swear before God in Heaven..."

"That I will never touch or smoke cigarettes again."

"Oh, Dr. Miller!"

He repeated the command with raised voice, this time a deep baritone. "THAT I WILL NEVER TOUCH OR SMOKE CIGARETTES AGAIN. SWEAR, AMANDA!"

"That I will never touch or smoke cigarettes again," she echoed.

"SO HELP ME GOD!" he bellowed, hoping no one from the hallway would hear him, enter the room and break the spell he was so carefully crafting.

"So help me God," she whispered. With the last word her whole body shook, and she began crying. He checked her pulse and listened to her lungs. No acute problem. She was not having an asthma attack, just a religious experience.

"She's okay," he told Emily. "I think we can go now. She'll be fine, but please check on her in a half hour or so." The two professionals left the room, with Ms. Wiggins sobbing quietly in her bed.

Feeling quite smug about his effort, Dr. Miller went to see other patients. He thought: to get a patient to quit smoking you must learn to communicate on their level, to search out that part of their psyche that will obey the doctor. Why aren't all physicians this creative with their advice?

A half hour later Emily called him to return to the ward. "Check out the smoking room," she said. "You won't believe this." The tone in her voice was like a sharp needle to his inflated balloon. He ran up to the ward.

There, in a chair next to a card table, sat Ms. Wiggins, smoking a cigarette. He noticed only two items on the table, an ashtray and a pack of opened cigarettes. He saw no Bible. Relaxed and calm, she looked up at her physician with not the least hint of anxiety.

"What happened?" he asked, feigning a hurt incredulity. "You PROMISED me you would quit. You promised GOD! You swore on the Bible!"

"I just had to have a cigarette," she said, flashing an innocent smile. "And besides, I had my fingers crossed."

Never again did Dr. Miller try religion to break a patient's habit.

- END -

Robert and His Muse – Writer(s) at Work

For his second novel, Robert could not find a satisfactory ending. Would he again call on his muse for help? He would rather not, and fought the temptation. The muse's advice on his first novel, *The Ventriloquist's Revenge*, was unexpected but helpful, and the book was now a *New York Times* bestseller. Being a professional ventriloquist and a new author brought him some fame, extra income, and speaking appearances.

Everyone asked about his skill at throwing voices, and why he decided to write the novel, and was he working on another. No one enquired about the writing chore itself, if he ever had writer's block, or if, in fact, he even had a muse.

Had they asked, he would have explained that his muse had shown him a way to end the novel, but it came at a cost. If asked further, he would respond: after my muse showed me the way, I felt both relieved and…drained. A strange feeling, really, he would explain, almost a sensation of going mad, schizophrenic, disconnected. But interviewers and audiences never asked, so he never told.

The day came when he could resist no longer. He would call on his muse again, and risk whatever turmoil ensued. To make sure he missed none of her advice, he would record the encounter. If she came through, as she had last time, he would finish the novel. Then, he thought, *perhaps I will kill her*.

To allay his anxiety he took a swig of vodka. Next, he set his smart phone on the bedroom desk, ready to record. He lived alone and no one else was in the house except, of course, his muse.

He went to a large chest beside his bed, opened the lid and pulled out Ginger. She stood about three feet tall, sported a fancy fedora with a large green feather, beneath which sprouted stringy red hair. She had wide eyes and an idiot grin, and altogether the expected charm of a ventriloquist's puppet.

With Ginger on his right knee, Robert sat at the desk so both were visible in his phone screen. He started the video recording, then placed his right hand inside the creature and began speaking.

"How are you today, Ginger?"

"I'm fine Robert, what's up?" she answered, in her usual high-pitched voice.

"Finishing my second novel."

"What's this one called?"

"*The Ventriloquist's Capers.*"

"Sounds exciting," she replied. "Your first one was about a ventriloquist also, as I recall."

"Yes, a guy named Marcus."

"And in this new novel?"

"Same guy. Marcus is a professional ventriloquist, like me. But it's all fiction, you understand."

"Am I in it, Robert?"

"No, afraid not. Marcus has another puppet, named Jimmy. Together, they rob banks, though Jimmy does all the talking, demands the money. Clever, don't you think, since Jimmy's just a dumb puppet?"

"Oh, Robert, you watch your language. I'm also a puppet, you know."

"I hadn't noticed."

"So what happens in the novel?"

"Well, they get caught, eventually."

"That doesn't sound very exciting, Robert."

"Hold on, there's a lot more to it. I go into Marcus's psyche, how it influences his ventriloquism, and leads him to do the robberies. I also reveal Jimmy's attitude about getting involved."

"So you make Jimmy like a real person?"

"Well, in the novel, in Marcus's mind, yes."

"So tell me, already. What happens?"

"Well, as I said, they get caught. They are put in jail, in the same cell. Jimmy begins screaming he can't stay with Marcus, that Marcus framed him, and the guards separate them. That part is written like a humorous interlude, not critical to the plot, but an element of good fiction."

"I don't need a lesson in writing, Robert. I'm not into literature."

"Sorry."

"Go on, how does the thing end?"

"Well, they go to trial, both Marcus and Jimmy."

"Jimmy, too?"

"Yes. Marcus's lawyer argues in a pretrial hearing that Jimmy actually committed the crimes, and Marcus was just along for the ride. An interesting legal theory, don't you think?"

"If you say so."

"So in court, the defense lawyer acts almost as if Marcus doesn't exist, and constantly points to Jimmy as the perpetrator. Now, throughout the trial Jimmy has his own chair, and just sits there like a puppet, which of course he is. He doesn't speak."

"You mean Marcus doesn't speak for him."

"Don't be such a smarty, Ginger."

"Be nice, Robert. I am quite sensitive, you know."

"Anyway, Marcus is put on the stand and the prosecution asks him: 'Don't you speak for the dummy? Wasn't the demand for money coming from your vocal cords?' All the obvious questions. Marcus waffles, says Jimmy speaks for himself. The jury guffaws. The attorney tells Marcus perjury is a crime."

"This is getting interesting, Robert."

"Yes. Then the defense puts Jimmy on the stand! Marcus holds Jimmy just like I'm holding you, in such a way that Jimmy appears to be responding directly to the questions. And Jimmy admits – ready for this? – the robberies were all *his* doing, that Marcus is innocent."

"Hold on, Robert. I thought Jimmy claimed in jail that he was framed."

"That was a jailhouse tactic, so Marcus could be alone with his thoughts."

"You're one smart dude, Robert."

"Don't be snide, Ginger, or I'll put you back in the box."

"I thought you needed my help."

"Okay, I do. Let me finish."

"I'm all ears, Mr. Ventriloquist."

"Well, there are objections from the prosecution, but the judge allows everything to continue."

"Is the judge an idiot? This doesn't sound credible."

"It's fiction, Ginger. Please let me finish."

"Sorry, go on."

"That's the problem. And why I called on you."

"You can't decide on the ending?"

"Exactly. Everything's so good to this point. I'm stuck on how to end it. You're my muse. What do you suggest?"

Ginger did not respond for a good minute, and instead twisted her head to look around the room. Then she peered up at her handler. Robert's eyes were closed and he appeared to be in deep thought.

"Robert, are you there?"

He opened his eyes. "Yes."

"The jury finds Jimmy guilty."

"Oh? And Marcus?" asked Robert.

"Innocent."

"Based on?"

Without pause, Ginger continued. "Jimmy has the brains, will power, smarts. Jimmy chose to do those robberies. Marcus was an innocent bystander, a mere pawn in the affair. The jury finds Jimmy real, and in control. Just like me."

"You're one smart cookie, Ginger."

151

"I don't like cookies. Call me something else. How about muse. One smart muse."

Robert stared at Ginger. The feeling came upon him... again. *Disconnected. I've got to destroy her.* With his left hand he lunged for her throat, began to squeeze.

"Robert, don't do that! Robert, stop! STOP!"

Robert stood, felt faint, moved to his bed and collapsed. He awoke minutes later, drenched in sweat. His phone was still recording. He went to the desk, turned it off, then looked for Ginger. She lay on the floor, crumpled, lifeless.

The Ventriloquist's Capers came out six months later. It was critically acclaimed and soon made the bestseller list. Several five-star reviews commented on its unique and unexpected ending.

- END –

Novel Excerpts

The first three chapters of six novels are presented in Part 3. They begin with three works of historical fiction, the Savannah Trilogy, published 2012, 2014 and 2017. The other novels excerpted are in different genres: contemporary adult fiction (*The Wall* and *Consenting Adults Only*) and middle-grade fiction (*The Boy Who Dreamed Mount Everest*)

Sherman's Mistress in Savannah

Available in paperback and as an ebook:
https://books2read.com/u/38EjG6

After their infamous 'March to the Sea,' General William Tecumseh Sherman and his 62,000-man army occupied Savannah during December 1864 – January 1865. Sherman took as his army headquarters the mansion of Englishman Charles Green on Madison Square. Against this historical backdrop the novel introduces a young war widow, Belle Anderson, who becomes the general's willing mistress. She discovers true sexual freedom and something else – a bordello operator who stalks her at night and threatens to expose the affair. Sherman's Mistress interweaves the fictional story with many historical characters of the period, including Secretary of War Edwin Stanton, Savannah Mayor Richard Arnold, diarist Fanny Yates Cohen, blockade runner Gazaway Lamar, Major Henry Hitchcock, and Union Generals John Geary and Jefferson C. Davis.

Chapter 1

[Tuesday, Dec 20 – Wednesday, Dec 21, 1864]

"What's going on?" asked Henry Brigham. "Why do you need the alderman at City Exchange this hour?"

"Gentlemen, the situation is dire," replied Mayor Arnold. "Hardee has begun his evacuation."

"How can that be Richard? I hear guns in the distance. Surely we are being defended."

"Surely not," Arnold shot back. "Hardee began evacuating one hour ago. The gun fire is to cover their retreat. Go down to Anderson's Wharf on West Broad after you leave here. You'll find a pontoon bridge over to Hutchinson Island, and then another bridge to South Carolina. That's why I called you in now. It's just 9 pm. By 3 am our troops will all be gone from the city and you won't hear any more Confederate shelling. The [ironclad] *Savannah* has been scuttled and Fort Jackson by now should be empty of all soldiers. The only troops remaining in Savannah will be the sick, the infirm, and those who faked illness to stay behind. Probably many of those, I'm afraid."

"How do you know all this?"

"Hardee met with me twice, Monday night and again this morning. He showed me the order. It's from General Beauregard. Hardee is to defend Savannah, but if it's between Savannah and the army, save the army. Our men are needed in South Carolina, where Sherman is sure to go next. He says Sherman has well over 62,000 battle-ready troops. They were resupplied after we lost Ft. McAllister. Hardee has but 10,000."

"What did he tell you to do?" asked George Wylly.

"Pray."

"Pray? You're the doctor, Richard. Surely you have a better remedy."

"Yes, Richard, what do you propose?" asked Christopher Casey, a middle-aged, paunchy alderman. He puffed on his cigar as if this affair didn't concern him as much as the others.

"We must meet with General Geary. His division is closest to the city, and is poised to enter. He's with General Slocum's Corps. Geary will march as soon as he realizes our troops are gone. Sherman may have already given orders to burn the downtown, but we must implore him not to. If we can just get him in peacefully, so he can see what we have, see that he is truly welcome and will not be snipered, I trust they will spare us."

Henry C. Freeman, unmarried and with no close family, spoke up: "Sherman has burned everything so far: Atlanta, Milledgeville, farms, homesteads. He's torn up the railroads. The man is a monster. You have read the papers. We should join Hardee and get the hell out, I say."

"A lot of that's hearsay, we don't know what he plans to do here. We really have nothing strategic of value except the cotton."

"Maybe hearsay," said Casey, but I do hear a lot of people say it. A plantation owner came into the shop just yesterday. His place near Millen was pillaged, then burned to the ground. He saw it all from a redoubt. Nothing he could do. He skedaddled here with this wife and two kids. I don't think he made any of it up. He said it was like that all around Millen; plantations that owned slaves have been stripped bare, the slaves gone and in most cases the houses burned. And we know for a fact Sherman uprooted all the citizens of Atlanta before burning it to the ground. Sherman's been on his goddamn March since middle November. It's now December 20th. That's five weeks of burning, pillaging, stealing, raping."

"It's war, Chris. And we're out of bargaining chips, or fighting chips, or any chips."

"We should get in line with Hardee," blurted out Freeman

"And your wives and children?" Arnold asked of the other aldermen. "What of them? And your property? I'm not talking about your slaves, they are no longer your property, at least not after Sherman gets here. How many of you even own slaves?"

Four of the eight raised a hand.

"Well, if not already, they will be free by tomorrow morning. Unless you don't understand Lincoln's Emancipation Proclamation." He pronounced the document with sarcasm: e-Man-ci-PA-shun Pro-cla-MA-shun.

"But what of your homes, your horses?" continued Arnold. "Give it all up? I say there is a better way. I say as the last of our troops cross over the river, that we rush to meet Geary, catch him before he has a chance to do any damage. I propose to formally surrender the city."

"How can *you* surrender? Last I heard that's a military tactic."

Arnold ignored the comment. "As painful as it may seem gentleman, we have no other choice. I will go alone if I have to, but I sincerely wish us to be unified in this matter, to represent the city government. We may be vilified by the citizens, at least in the beginning, but soon they will come around and be thankful if we can save Savannah."

Freeman did not respond and the others murmured agreement. None of them really wanted to march across a wooden pontoon bridge into the marshes of South Carolina.

"Good, then we are agreed. Let's meet here at one o'clock. All the carriages are gone, taken by the troops. So we will have to go out on our own horses. George [Wylly] and Edward [Wade], you two came by foot tonight. Do you have a fresh horse you can bring?" Yes, they said.

"OK, that will make eight of us altogether. I have a good idea where Geary is camped, out on Augusta Road. We best ride from here to Anderson's Wharf together. As soon as the last troops enter the bridge, we'll head out to meet Geary. I think we'll find Union blue in no time and they can take us to him."

The night was cold, about 45 degrees, and rainy. The city officials rode their horses down Bay Street to West Broad, then to the pontoon landing. Hundreds of troops were milling about, waiting their turn. Straw had been placed on the pontoons to minimize the sound of footsteps. General Hardee was already in South Carolina. The ranking officer approached Mayor Arnold.

"Dr. Arnold, are you planning to cross over?"

"No, we are going to search for General Geary after you leave, to negotiate something. How many are going across?"

"We estimate about ten thousand altogether. We're leaving a whole lot of guns and ammunition behind. General Geary should be happy with that. Wish we could help you, Dr. Arnold, but orders is orders."

"I completely understand, Colonel."

An hour later ties to the first pontoon were cut, letting it drift into the river. At that, Arnold and his party rode south on West Broad, then turned right on Augusta Road. Arnold carried a white flag and a letter of surrender in his saddle bag. In the rain the horsemen spread out some distance and became separated. Arnold and four others turned down a narrow lane, while the remaining three – John O'Byrne, Robert Lachlison and Christopher Casey – stayed on Augusta Road. Just when the separation became apparent the Augusta Road group ran into a roadblock manned by a dozen Union troops.

"Who goes there?"

"We are here to surrender Savannah," said O'Byrne.

The Union Captain approached with a torch. Rifleman on each side stood ready to shoot

"Yeh? Who is we? Dismount or risk being shot."

They all dismounted, not sure what else to do but raise hands in the air. "We are Mayor Richard Arnold and seven of his alderman. Can you take us to General Geary? We want to surrender Savannah."

"I only see three. Three ain't eight. Where are the others?"

"They split off, took another road. The mayor is with them, but they will find us shortly."

Surrounded by bluecoats, the three hapless aldermen were marched 200 yards beyond the roadblock, to a small tent city.

"Wait here." A bluecoat went into one of the tents and awakened the General, who promptly came out in coat and hat. He did not seem pleased.

"I am Geary. Which of you is the mayor?"

"O'Byrne explained the night's events, that the mayor was temporarily separated from them, but that their intent – unanimous – was to surrender the city.

"Well that explains the silence over the past half hour. Not a word nor any response from Hardee's boys. Skipped to South Carolina, heh? So who's defending your city?"

"No one, sir. The only Confederates you'll find are those too ill to leave. That's a fact."

"Well, which direction did your infernal mayor go?"

They gave him an idea, and he dispatched half a dozen soldiers to find Arnold and bring him to camp.

Thirty minutes later Arnold and the others rode in, surrounded by bluecoats on horseback. In his right hand the mayor carried a white flag on a short pole.

Geary yelled out. "Flag's not needed. Got your message. Mayor Arnold, I presume?"

"General, I am Dr. Richard Arnold, mayor of Savannah. Thank you for meeting with us." He dismounted and bowed, as if meeting a European potentate.

"General Hardee has left the city and we are defenseless. We ask of you, protection of the lives and private properly of the citizens and of our women and children. We have no troops, no one to fight you. I think you will enjoy our beautiful city and our hospitality. You will see it is well worth preserving. I have prepared a formal letter of surrender," and with that he handed the letter to Geary.

* * * * *

SIR: The city of Savannah was last night evacuated by the Confederate military and is now entirely defenseless. As chief magistrate of the city I respectfully request your protection of the lives and private property of the citizens and of our women and children. Trusting that this appeal to your generosity and humanity may favorably influence your action, I have the honor to be, your obedient servant. Richard D. Arnold, Mayor
December 21, 1864

* * * * *

"Sir, may I meet with General Sherman?"

"Sherman's not here, and that won't be necessary. But you can lead us into Savannah. If it's as you say, no harm will come to your city."

Arnold and his aldermen led a 1000-strong Union division up West Broad. Heads poked out of 2nd floor windows along the street, believing and not believing. They encountered a black freedman on the street, perhaps slightly inebriated, bowing profusely and yelling "Praise the Lord, Sherman is come!" The soldiers were led down Bay Street. When they left camp the sky was still dark with a wet drizzle. By the time they reached West Broad and Bay the sun was lighting up the morning sky.

It became apparent with daylight that looting had been going on all night. Word of the evacuation spread fast, and shops were being vandalized by lower class whites, but also some blacks, as well as Confederates soldiers who had stayed behind. Some of the looting was motivated by hunger, but there was no way to separate out the desperate from the despicable. Several times Geary dispatched a small contingent to put a stop to the looting. Each time Arnold chimed in with "Thank you

General, we are so glad you're here." In truth, Arnold was glad. He shuddered to think what chaos might ensue without the Federal presence.

Two blocks from Bull Street a shot pierced the air, then a scream. Geary turned his head briefly, then kept riding. He knew the sound -- a Union rifle. Arnold, just a few yards to the side of Geary, was very curious but said nothing and kept riding. A few minutes later a Yankee captain galloped past the marching columns and trotted next to Geary, saluting smartly. They exchanged a few words and the young officer rode off. Geary then spoke, with a hint of sarcasm,

"You have one less looter to worry about, Mr. Mayor."

The troops stopped in front of the Customs House at the corner of Bay and Bull Streets. Geary and Arnold climbed to the base of the spire to reach a spacious four-sided balcony. From there Geary could survey the city in all directions, as his aides raised the American flag and lowered the Confederate one. Alongside the stars and stripes they also raised the flag of Geary's XX Corps. A complete transfer of power had just occurred with no shots fired (save against looters).

The sun was now fully above the horizon. The city was, Geary confessed to Arnold, just as he had heard: a grand and beautiful place, full of small parks or squares, handsome buildings, and a series of capacious warehouses fronting the Savannah River. In them were thousands of bales of cotton -- cotton that would no longer be of service to the Confederacy. They climbed back down to Bay Street and Geary gave orders to encamp on the nearby squares. He then sent orders for the rest of his division to deploy.

"Where the hell is Sherman?" Geary muttered to himself.

Even as events were unfolding, The *Savannah Republican*, one of the city's two daily papers, was on the streets with a most timely editorial.

* * * * *

160

Savannah Republican

December 21, 1864

Citizens of Savannah:

By the fortunes of war we pass today under the authority of the Federal military forces. The evacuation of Savannah by the Confederate army, which took place last night, left the gates to the city open, and General Sherman, with his army will, no doubt, to-day take possession.

The Mayor and Common Counsel leave under a flag of truce this morning, for the headquarters of Gen. Sherman, to offer the surrender of the city, and ask terms of capitulation by which private property and citizens may be respected.

We desire to counsel obedience and all proper respect on the part of our citizens, and to express the belief that their property and persons will be respected by our military ruler. The fear expressed by many that Gen. Sherman will repeat the order of expulsion from their homes which he enforced against the citizens of Atlanta, we think to be without foundation. He assigned his reason in that case as a military necessity, it was a question of food. He could not supply his army and the citizens with food, and he stated that he must have full and sole occupation. But in our case food can be abundantly supplied for both army and civilians.

We would not be understood as even intimating that we are to be fed at the cost of the Federal Government, but that food can be easily obtained in all probability, by all who can afford to pay in the Federal currency.

It behooves all to keep within their homes until Gen. Sherman shall have organized a provost system and such police as will insure safety in persons as well as property.

Let our conduct be such as to win the admiration of a magnanimous foe, and give no ground for complaint or harsh treatment on the part of him who will for an indefinite period hold possession of our city.

In our city there are, as in other communities, a large proportion of poor and needy families, who, in the present situation of affairs, brought about by the privations of war, will be thrown upon the bounty of their more fortunate neighbors. Deal with them kindly, exercise your philanthropy and benevolence, and let the heart of the unfortunate not be deserted by your friendly aid.

✳ ✳ ✳ ✳ ✳

All day troops poured into Savannah, most mighty impressed by their prize: a beautiful port city, and it wasn't to be burned or despoiled. True, the night's looters had done their best to mess things up a bit, but that was fixable. For most of the soldiers Savannah was a welcome respite from marching through piney woods, around flooded rice fields and over swollen streams on pontoon bridges. Here was a city with streets and houses, many parks and beautiful oak trees, and – god bless 'em – women. In late 1864, because of the war, women in Southern cities greatly outnumbered men.

Some soldiers kept diaries, none more assiduously than Lt. Cornelius C. Platter, of the 81st Ohio Infantry Volunteers, who made the entire march from Atlanta. In a hardbound accounting ledger he jotted down thoughts and observations, starting from November. On December 21st, the first day of occupation, Platter wrote:

* * * * *

This morning after breakfast we were informed that the "Rebs" had taken up their departure last night not believing it I went down to the front and seen for myself that the enemy had indeed left. We were immediately ordered to cross. 81st and 66th crossed in a pontoon boat at the same point where Lt [Lieutenant] Pittman and party effected a crossing. We supposed at first that the enemy had only fallen back to a stronger line of works. - so after crossing we advanced cautiously - but soon discovered that they had bid the city of Savannah adieu.

-- We soon struck the Gulf RR and proceeded directly towards the City - down the RR track - Major Henry & I had left our horses on the other side of the "Little Ogeechee - so we took it "afoot" and reached the "suburbs" of S about 3 PM and went into camp southeast of the city among the "dutch gardens" Which are full of all kinds of vegetables. As soon as our horses arrived Maj [Major] H and I rode into the city -- With the exception of Huntsville it is the prettiest city I have seen in the 'Southern Confederacy" - The "Wharfs and docks" are magnificent but on account of the obstructions in the River below [Fort] Jackson our fleet cannot come up. The town was quite full of Soldiers - quite a number of stores were plundered by soldiers assisted by negros and "poor white folks" who seemed delighted at having a chance to pillage - As a general thing the Citizens kept 'in doors". Saw the Rebel [gunship] Savannah and a gun boat laying on the opposite side of the river -- The enemy finished crossing this morning about daylight and are supposed to be making for Charleston. I think Sherman has rather been "out generaled" by Hardee. or since he couldn't have gotten away so easily - Who is to blame for allowing him to escape -- time alone can tell. but it is the general [informs] us that Gen [General] Foster is the "guilty man" -- We found a great many Guns Cotton & c [et cetera] which the enemy had to leave. Cold and windy this evening -- Procured some nice riding bridles today Retired early.

* * * * *

Where *was* Sherman? Having secured Foster's cooperation for the coming siege, General Sherman was having trouble getting back to Savannah. The steamer *Harvest Moon* ran into high winds and waves, and became lodged on a mud bar at low tide. The crew could not free the ship and Sherman had to transfer to Admiral Dahlgren's low-draft barge to complete the trip. Rowed by a dozen sailors, the barge made its way slowly up the Ogeechee River, headed for Kings Point. Along the way it was met by the Union tugboat *Red Legs* with messages for the general, including word of Savannah's surrender.

Finally, late on Wednesday, December 21st, Sherman reached camp at Kings Point, where he spent the night. Hardee had escaped and Sherman had missed the first march of troops into Savannah, for which he had regrets. But he also had much reason to be pleased. Savannah was captured without a battle, and he could now relax while the army was resupplied and its energy replenished. As per his master plan, the southern march was not even half over. The Carolinas were next, then on to Virginia. And then? 'It will be done', he thought. This long civil war, he now saw with clarity, was soon to end in complete Union victory.

Chapter 2

[Thursday, December 22, 1864]

Thursday morning General Sherman and his party rode by horseback into the city. He felt triumphant, but at the same time somewhat chagrined that Hardee had escaped. That was the whole point of his sojourn to Hilton Head, to prevent the escape. It was a wasted effort and he missed marching in with his troops the day before.

His first stop was the Customs House on Bay Street and its rooftop balcony. He had earlier dispatched a messenger to fetch General Geary, who was able to join him in the view. Sherman liked what he saw. To the north, just across Bay street was Factors Walk and the Cotton Exchange, and behind that the Savannah River, divided by Hutchinson's Island. Just across the back channel lay South Carolina. Three miles east lay Fort Jackson with its many guns, never used in battle. They would be a nice addition to his arsenal. To the west lay West Broad Street and the Freedman's Quarters, called Shantytown. And to the south lay the heart of the city, with its 22 magnificent squares fulfilling a plan first envisioned by James Oglethorpe 130 years earlier. Churches, stores, warehouses, magnificent homes, and in the distance Forsythe Park with its fountain and large parade ground. He liked this city! He liked it even more that Savannah had been secured without any loss of life. His next stop: Pulaski House Hotel at the corner of West Bryan and Bull Streets., across from Johnson Square.

Pulaski House was Savannah's eminent hotel, where all dignitaries stayed. Sherman had actually stayed there as a young man. After graduation from West Point in 1840 he spent 5 years in the south, with stints in Charleston and northern Florida. His travels brought him through Savannah several times, and he was familiar with the hotel. He figured it was as good a place as any to set up army headquarters (he could pretty much take any establishment he wanted). The only problem was securing a nearby stable for his horses.

The proprietor was someone he knew from New Orleans, a Vermont native. After cordialities, the Vermonter expressed his concern: Well, of course the General and his large staff could stay, but would the Hotel be paid?

"We'll see," said Sherman, non-committal. When you command 62,000 soldiers and can do literally anything you want, you don't have to be committal. Sherman sent a captain to look for nearby stables, and settled in the lobby to confer with his generals. There was much to discuss, not least how to feed and house the army while in Savannah.

Within 15 minutes two well-dressed men approached the group: Mayor Arnold and Charles Green.

"General Sherman," Arnold bowed, "I am pleased to meet you. I have met General Geary and welcomed him to our city."

Sherman nodded his head. They shook hands. "Yes, I know, I have learned such from General Geary already."

"General, I would like to introduce you to Mr. Charles Green, who has a proposal. Mr. Green is an Englishman." Green shook Sherman's hand profusely.

"Your reputation has preceded you, General." Sherman arched his eyebrow. Was that a slam or a compliment? Green, two inches shorter than Sherman, and amply proportioned at 190 lbs., sported an expensive haircut and full beard. He was well dressed with a coat of fine English cloth, shoes shined and free of grime, something hard to achieve on Savannah's muddy streets. There was a faint smell of cologne, or was it horse manure? He spoke with a British accent but not rapidly, and was easily understood. Sherman, who had just marched 300 miles with his men, living mostly off the land, wondered if this sophisticate had ever spent a night outdoors. A one-word pejorative popped into his head: dandy.

"General," said Green, "I spoke earlier with General Howard, and he agreed that you would most enjoy your stay in my own home. I have a large home on Madison Square, built in the 1850s, and if I may so say, the grandest in the city. You are welcome to use it as your headquarters during your stay. Gratis, as my guest."

"Thank you Mr. Green, but that should not be necessary. I have instructed my adjutant to look for a stable for our horses, and when that is secured we will be lodging here in Pulaski house. Should we not make suitable arrangements, I will let you know." Sherman felt leery of taking over a private home, afraid it might engender ill will. He wanted to win over the people of Savannah, notwithstanding the carnage caused during his month long march through Georgia.

"At your pleasure, general, I can be found at home. My offer is open ended. And I don't think you will find a grander place for your headquarters."

In fact suitable stables were not found and Sherman thought more of the offer. His generals agreed with the idea, as the home was centrally located and reportedly magnificent. Sherman really didn't care about ulterior motive: that Green was a successful cotton merchant and wanted his house protected and his cotton not to be confiscated. Sherman sent an aide to Madison Square, to inform Mr. Green he would be coming. Within the hour the group packed up and left Pulaski House for the 15 minute horse ride down Bull St., past Liberty St. to Madison Square, and then to Macon St., just off the Square.

Green's house was designed by famous architect John S. Norris, who lived in Savannah from 1846 to 1861. Norris also designed the Customs House on Bay St. It style was Gothic Revival, and cost $93,000. Green had spared no expense on furnishings. As with most wealthy Savannahians, his tastes far exceeded what the old South could produce, and most furniture and wall coverings were imported.

Green came to the city in 1833 at age 26, essentially penniless. He made his fortune after arrival, as cotton merchant and ship owner. This was an advantage in constructing the mansion, for he was able to bring over from England heavy building materials (bricks, flagstones, planks) as ballast on her ships.

Green's house was a rectangular structure, two stories tall, with flat roof punctuated by a skylight. The front of the house, with its ornate entrance consisting of three sets of doors, faced the church. The east side of the house, which faced Madison Square, was notable for its three-dimensional 'oriel' windows. On the other side of the house, facing Whittaker St., were stables for half a dozen horses and the servants' quarters. Directly across from the Green home was handsome St. John's Episcopal Church, completed in 1853, also in a gothic style.

Green did not give the Union entourage a chance to knock. The front doors were already open when they arrived. He led the party into his large foyer, whose ceiling easily exceeded 20 feet, then gave a quick tour of the spacious first floor. He next took Sherman upstairs to what would become his private quarters, a large office and bedroom. Between them, connected by hallway, was an unexpected feature: a genuine bathroom, with tub and water closet.

"General, you will be very happy with this convenience, I assure you. I am told only a half dozen homes in the city have one. The tub and toilet are fed by cisterns on the roof. Make yourself at home. I will leave it to you as to whom among your staff will also stay here. I believe the house can comfortably hold half a dozen or so. The stables are out back, and your horses are already being well cared for. As for myself, I will occupy just two rooms over the dining room. I have moved my wife and children to other quarters, and I promise you will not be disturbed."

"Thank you Mr. Green. I should very much appreciate if you would join me for dinner tonight, so we might get better acquainted. If your wife is free of domestic duties, please bring her as well. I will have some of my men with me, but just a small dinner party, nothing fancy."

"I'd be delighted, general." To this point Green had made no mention of his motives, or of his cotton. But, really, what better insurance for his home and tangibles than to have the commanding general as a guest? As to the cotton, as Green would soon learn, that item was not negotiable. But the house itself would remain fully intact, respected and cared for by the General and his staff.

Within an hour of taking up residence Sherman had his first visitor: Mr. Albert Gallatin Browne, of Salem, Massachusetts, United States Treasury agent for the Department of the South. He had been waiting in Hilton Head until the city was seized by U.S. troops.

"What brings you here, Mr. Browne?"

"I am here to claim possession, in the name of the Treasury Department, of all the cotton and rice your men have captured. And may I say, magnificent march, General. Magnificent! The whole country is marveling."

"Well, these items were fairly won, Mr. Browne, and I must say, I am first beholden to the army, so they can be fully provisioned."

"I understand, I understand. But these goods were won by the United States Army, and rightly belong to the treasury. I must assure that whatever is not vital to your army, befalls to the U.S. I'm sorry General, but that's my job. I will off course defer to you in all things military, but must file my report soon."

"I have marched 300 miles in 30 days, risked life and limb of 60,000 of our finest troops, and just arrived in town. I have 10,000 poor Negroes to get fed and housed, and a civilian population that hasn't yet come to grips with their defeat, who may yet turn outwardly hostile. I am in possession of southern cotton and guns and god knows what else, and there is as yet no accurate inventory of all that. And the first greeting I get is 'give me all your goods'? Is that what I am hearing, Mr. Browne?"

"I am sorry, but I am just doing as instructed."

"Well, you are sorry, sir. I am not ready to surrender possession just yet. The quartermaster and commissary will manage these spoils for now. After proper inventories are prepared, whatever we have no special use for, I will turn over to you, but not before."

"Yes, sir" said Browne, deferentially. "What is your estimate?"

"Oh, I estimate that the warehouses store at least twenty-five thousand bales of cotton, and in the forts probably hundred and fifty large guns."

"That's a good amount. I have an idea, as Christmas is upon us in a few days. The Golden Gate is this very afternoon to sail for Fortress Monroe, Virginia. If she has good weather off Cape Hatteras, she will reach the fort by Christmas day. Might I suggest that you send President Lincoln a welcome telegram offering him as Christmas gift this bounty? He likes such peculiarities, you know."

The idea intrigued Sherman, and warmed him to this Mr. Browne.

"Good idea." Sherman sat down and wrote out the following on a sheet of paper:

* * * * *

Savannah Georgia, December 22, 1864
To His Excellency President Lincoln, Washington, D.C.:
I beg to preset you as a Christmas-gift the city of Savannah, with one hundred and fifty heavy guns and

168

plenty of ammunition, also about twenty-five
thousand bales of cotton.
W.T. Sherman, Major-General
* * * * *

"There, that should do it."

Browne read the missive. "Splendid. Mr. Lincoln will enjoy this," and he pocketed the note. "Well, General, it's been a real pleasure meeting you. I'm going to the ship to now, and will see that this is handled with special care."

With that, Browne left the mansion on horseback and reached the Golden Gate but an hour before she sailed.

People were already coming to the mansion, to see the general, to petition for food or redress, or just to gawk. The audience included many blacks who just wanted to see "Massa Sherman" or "Moses Sherman" as some called him. A dozen sentries now surrounded the house, and a hundred soldiers were setting up camp in Madison Square across the street. Similar housing – mainly tents and wooden huts – was being erected in the other squares, and also large camp sites in Forsythe Park and old Colonial Cemetery.

At 4 pm a young woman approached two sentries guarding the main entrance on Macon Street. She was dressed in fine clothes, with a long brown coat, for the air was a chilly 56 degrees. It does not snow in Savannah (almost never) but winters are cool. The weather was worse in middle Georgia. Before reaching Savannah many soldiers suffered long nights due to frigid temperature and lack of adequate bedding.

She stood 5'5", about 140 lbs, appeared to be in her early 20s and had little makeup. Fur from the coat was up around her ears and she wore no hat. Her reddish-brown hair waved with each step. She was pretty, in the way of southern ladies who don't try to affect airs, and attractive even from a distance. Heads turned among several Union men as she strolled by Madison Square. The only women they had seen in months were either ex-slaves or what they considered southern 'white trash'.

Her speech, a lilting southern drawl, was addressed to the left sentry. "I understand General Sherman has this morning taken up residence in Mr. Green's home?"

"Yes, Ma'am."

169

"I have a written message for Mr. Sherman. I have been told to deliver it in person."

"I'm sorry, Ma'am, the general is not accepting Savannah citizens today. He's just arrived. But I am authorized to say he will see civilians tomorrow, starting at 1 pm. However, if you have a written message, I can see that it is delivered to him."

"No, thank you. I have been instructed quite clearly I must deliver it in person. I will return to tomorrow. One pm you say?"

"Yes, Ma'am, but we've had many enquiries, so I don't know how long you will have to wait."

"And to what time will he be taking visitors, sir?"

"Not sure, Ma'am. That's up to the General. He's mighty busy."

"Thank you corporal. It is corporal, isn't it?"

"Yes, Ma'am."

"Thank you."

After she left the other sentry spoke up. "The Savannah ladies are lovely, are they not?"

"Yea," said the sentry. "And Uncle Billy will have us shot if we bother them. He's made that clear."

All afternoon there was a scurrying of army staff to provide sentries, add kitchen help, order supplies and accomplish other tasks to establish Army HQ. One of the perquisites of being major-general was that you didn't have to worry about domestic affairs. Your quartermaster, secretary and personal valet (which Sherman also had) would get the job done.

Charles Green's second wife Lucinda, a 36-year-old native of Virginia, was a smart woman who recognized Sherman's presence was also in her best long term interest -- even though it meant moving out of the house with her 6 children, who ranged in age from 6 months to 12 years. There was probably no better way to keep the precious art and antiques from being looted than to have Sherman as their guest. Green kept two rooms in the house to look after things, but would spend much of his time with Lucinda and children in a large rented home next door to his sister and brother and law, the equally wealthy Andrew Low.

Charles and Lucinda Green arrived to the dining room at precisely 6 pm. Sherman was already there with his military entourage, talking business. With him were: General Geary, responsible for the military oversight of Savannah; Sherman's personal secretary Major Henry Hitchcock; and Captain George W. Nichols, mess manager. As manager, Nichols was to hire new domestic staff, order all food and other supplies and keep the place in good repair. The Yankees stood to greet their hosts. Lucinda's Virginia accent contrasted with Charles' British accent – both foreign to Sherman's ears. Apart from some slaves and angry rebels on the march, Sherman had not had conversation with a Southern woman since his Louisiana days. He found her way of speaking – 'Ah am honored, gen'ral' -- oddly comforting.

"Mrs. Green, so nice to meet you. Me and my staff want to thank you for letting us use your home during this difficult period. We will stay out of your hair."

"General," said Mr. Green, "it is we who will stay out of your way. My wife and our six children will be staying in another home, which I assure you is quite spacious and with many amenities. As I explained earlier, I will be occupying two of the rooms upstairs, just to keep an eye on things, but will of course also be spending time with Lucinda and our children."

Wine was served and the conversation picked up.

"Well, you have a lovely wife, and at your age you say you have young children?"

"Yes, six with Lucinda. My first wife died of consumption in '46. We had four children together, although one lived only a year. They are now, let's see, 26, 21 and 18. So altogether I have 9 children."

"Well that beats me," said Sherman, slapping his thigh. Of course you've got me by 10 years in age, and one extra wife."

Where is your family now, general?

"Now they are in Indiana, but we're all from Ohio. Lancaster, Ohio."

"And how many children?

"Five now. We lost a son last year. Typhoid fever."

"Oh, I'm sorry."

Sherman continued, unwilling to wallow in the past: "So Mr. Green…"

"General, you can call me Charles."

"OK, Charles. Please, tell us about your house. When was it built?"

"We started the plans in 1850, but with all the materials we imported, didn't really get the frame up until '53. We moved in in '56. As you may know, it was designed by John Norris. He also did the Customs House and some other prominent buildings around town. I told him to spare no expense, and he didn't. Cost me a total of ninety-three thousand."

"So I've heard," said Sherman. At his current rate of army pay it would take 12 years to make that amount.

"Besides cotton, you are in other areas also?" asked Geary.

"Yes, shipping, importing and exporting. That sort of thing."

"Goods from England?

"Well, yes, quite a bit before your blockade. But we've still kept busy."

Two black servants brought out trays of meat and potatoes. They started the serving with Mrs. Green and General Sherman, then worked their way to the others.

"Had a little legal problem few years ago I understand?" said Sherman. Here he was referring to Green's arrest in 1861 on charges of smuggling goods from Europe into the Confederacy.

"Yes, yes, all a misunderstanding. They arrested me on my way back from England, when I entered Detroit from Canada. Accused me of all sorts of skullduggery, smuggling arms, that sort of thing. Kept me locked up at Fort Warren in Boston for three bloody months. Being innocent of all charges, I was released. I came back home and haven't left since. War makes people skittish, I should say."

"Yes, well, we Yankees are a pretty determined bunch. There was a time the British were actively aiding the South. It came close to having them recognize the Confederate states as a legitimate country, but Antietam and Gettysburg stopped that bit of nonsense."

"I won't deny my sympathies have been with the south – it is my home for all that – but we can do business under any flag, as long as there are recognized property rights and the rule of law. We English may have lost the colonies but we damn well gave the United States a proper send off. Now our two countries aren't all that much different. Common language, common laws, much trade between us."

"I would say that's true," said Sherman. "As soon as we get rid of this damn curse of slavery. How many do you have, Charles?"

"Just two, but we never thought of them as slaves. I grew up in England without slavery of course, and over here was shocked that you had to buy your help. I always think of them as just house servants, not slaves. Of course they're free now, but we always treated them well. You can ask them."

"Charles, how did you end up in Savannah in the first place?" asked Nichols.

"I did some business with Mr. Andrew Low in England. Then he met my sister, she came over to marry him and I followed to join his business."

"I believe he's another cotton merchant like yourself?" asked Sherman.

"Yes, we worked together, shortly after I arrived in '33. I was taken with the warm climate and bustling city, and stayed. We like it here. Helps to have some money, though. It would not be pleasant if you were poor."

"That's probably true anywhere," said Sherman. "Mrs. Green, you are from Virginia, I take it?"

"Yes, Prince William County. I met Charles on a trip to Savannah. I do think the weather's much better in Virginia, and we go back once a year. We have a farm in Greenwich, though I understand some Yankees are staying there at this time."

"Well, that may be," said Sherman, "but I'm sure they are treating your property with respect, and it will be returned to you in good shape."

"Well, I hope so, general."

"Virginia's a mighty fine place," continued Sherman. "Too bad Lee sided with the secession. I know his loyalty was with Virginia, first and foremost. He would probably have General Grant's job now had he stayed with the Union."

"Did you ever meet General Lee?" asked Mr. Green.

"No, Ma'am. But I hope to soon, when he surrenders."

There was more small talk, a toast to the Greens, and soon dinner was over. As the men rose to leave, Green asked, "General, may I have a word with you in private?"

"Certainly," and the two men walked over to the library.

With the door shut, Green spoke. "As I said, our home is yours during this occupation. I would like to ask, if I may, what you plan to do with all the cotton, some of which I personally own. I don't consider it war materiel, and do believe it should revert to its rightful owners."

Sherman was not put off by this bold solicitation. He didn't expect to sleep in Green's house without some attempt at quid pro quo, and welcomed the chance to get past the question of cotton ownership.

"I do understand your situation, Charles. General Geary has also received entreaty from other merchants. But in situations like this it is, fortunately, out of my control. Technically the cotton belongs to the United States, simply because it *can* be construed as war materiel, as you put it. It could be used, for example, to make uniforms, or be traded for guns and bullets. I believe you are familiar with that sort of business." Sherman gave a wry smile, for he knew Green had been involved in smuggling, and Green knew he knew. Green, for his part, kept a stoical countenance, not admitting or denying anything.

"In matters like this," continued Sherman, "the army has to defer to the civilian authorities. I have just today informed President Lincoln of our spoils, which include all the cotton and many large guns. So I appreciate your question, but don't have a satisfactory answer for you. I will say that private property with no possible military use will be respected."

"Thank you, general. And I appreciate your consideration. If any questions arise relating to the cotton's rightful owners, apart from the United States of course, I trust you will call upon me."

"Certainly, certainly."

Chapter 3

[Friday, December 23, 1864]

Sherman spent Friday morning traveling among his troops, now deployed throughout Savannah and environs. Slocum's left wing was encamped in the city itself while Howard's right wing spread throughout Chatham County and into adjacent Bryan County and Fort McAllister. Each of the city's squares covered about 4 acres and could hold up to 100 soldiers, in makeshift barracks and tents. These camps – with their latrines and cooking fires -- were little different than what the men experience on the long march, except for the surroundings: homes and shops instead of piney woods. The army was resupplied from navy ships via both the Savannah and Ogeechee Rivers, though the former still had many barricades that had to be removed (some placed two years earlier by Union forces to prevent blockade running).

Savannah was spared destruction but the citizen's needs were great. The blockade had taken a heavy toll and the poor suffered from inadequate nutrition and housing. In addition to 62,000 troops, Sherman also had to worry about feeding thousands of refugees – Negroes who had accompanied his army into Savannah.

At 11 am he met with Mayor Arnold in his Bay Street office. When the meeting was arranged Arnold had asked if his alderman should be present. Sherman said no, he didn't want to deal with a committee. Sherman brought along three officers, two of whom were journalists in civilian life.

"There are also some local policies which I expect you to carry out, Dr. Arnold."

"General Sherman, please call me Richard."

"My plan is for you and your council to continue running the city as you've been doing. General Geary will be in charge of military order, and assure there is no looting or fighting. You may not know, Richard, but he used to be Mayor of San Francisco, so he knows a thing or two about managing cities."

"No, I didn't know that. I'm surprised he didn't tell me when we marched into town together."

"That's John for you, rather modest in his accomplishments. But don't underestimate him. He does not brook incivility. He will leave it up to your office to manage the fire, police and other routine functions. In items of significant dispute, expect Geary to have the final say. Captain Rodgers here will be assigned to the City Exchange, to assist in any way possible as liaison to General Geary. He will attend all council meetings but only as an observer, and to answer questions that may arise regarding the military. "

"That's good, General. Cooperation is most important."

"On the issue of food, I am releasing all rice stores to help feed the poor. I want your office to ascertain as soon as possible the names of all worthy families that need assistance, and set up a distribution system, so they may receive whatever food is available. As soon as we can clear the Savannah River of most barricades shipping will resume, and more food can be brought in."

"Excellent. We'll get right on it."

"I should also tell you we are instituting a 9 pm curfew. That should not cause discomfort to proper citizens. People on official business, of course, are exempt. As to people who cannot abide by our laws, or feel disposed to continue their fight, we will make arrangements to have them transported to Charleston. We don't want anyone remaining in Savannah who cannot conduct themselves as good citizens."

"Yes, I've already been contacted by some officer's wives who wish to get out of town. They will be pleased. When do you expect a ship will be ready?"

"Certainly within the week. We will place notice in the newspapers, and have requestors sign up with your office."

"Unfortunately, the newspapers have ceased publication. The *Savannah Morning News* stopped on the 20th, the *Savannah Republican* on the 21st."

"I know. That's why I brought along these two fine journalists." And with that Sherman formally introduced Samuel W. Mason and John Hayes.

"Mr. Samuel Mason was editor of an army newspaper in Port Royal. He will take over the *Morning News*, and change its name to the *Savannah Daily Herald*. No more firebrand editorializing."

"It's just as well," said Arnold. "The *Morning News* editors fled last week."

"Glad to meet you," said the taciturn Mason, who had not yet spoken.

"And Mr. John Hayes, he was a war reporter for the New York Tribune. He will oversee the *Savannah Republican*." Hayes nodded to the mayor and they shook hands. Sherman continued: "It will take them a few days to start up the papers again. All previous employees will be retained if they wish, but they may no longer publish lies and slander. What they print must be fair minded and not against the United States government. I will not tolerate any slander or anti-Union propaganda, even if it's republished from another source."

Arnold wondered if Sherman was referring to some of his own speeches, which were printed in the rabble-rousing *Republican*. He chose not to enquire, and just nodded his head in agreement. Then he piped up with a question.

"But there will still be freedom of the press? If we are now to re-join the United States, I do believe it is guaranteed by the U.S. Constitution."

At that, Sherman showed his first sign of testiness. "May I remind you, Richard, we are still at war, even if Savannah is not. My orders are strictly a matter of military necessity. I am all for freedom of the press, as soon as the Union is whole again. When the war is over, you will find I have as much power over your newspapers as the man who sweeps the floor."

"Yes, yes, of course. I understand, General. You have my complete cooperation. I most appreciate your understanding and will do my best to make sure the city runs smoothly."

"Excellent."

Back at the Green mansion Sherman had a brief lunch and prepared to greet visitors. His goal was an hour or two a day with ordinary citizens. A group of 20 or so had already assembled in the downstairs foyer, including yesterday's Macon St. visitor. Sherman would give each a few minutes. People should see for themselves that he is not a monster, but an amiable soldier who wants nothing more than peace and Union. To get from the foyer to his office visitors climbed a grand spiral staircase, perhaps the most prominent single feature of the mansion. Sherman arranged for an aide to record names and a sentry inside the doorway should there be any disorder. An attempted assault was not implausible.

The first visitor escorted up the stairs was a black man, Isaac Butterfield, about 50, of West Broad St. Hat in hand, he walked into the room, head bowed. Sherman approached to shake his hand. Isaac looked up to Sherman's full red beard and craggy face.

"Is you Sherman?"

"That's me."

"I sure am mos' happy to meet you. You *are* Mistah Sherman. God help us all. You are a great man. Been prayin' for you all for a long time, Sir, prayin' day and night for you, and now, bless god, you is come. We is free. We is free!"

"That's true, my man. You are no longer a slave."

"That's all I wants to say. God bless you Mr. Sherman." And with that he was escorted out.

Visitors came just to introduce themselves, to welcome him to the city, or to ask for sustenance for hungry citizens, of which there were many. Sherman wanted to hear from these people and welcomed all such questions, which he answered with sincerity.

"We're working on that."

"Give us a few days."

"I do understand. I'll do my best."

A middle-aged, well-dressed man was ushered in. "General, I am Mr. Noble A. Hardee. I think you know my brother."

"General John Hardee, I presume."

"Yes, General. I am a civilian, a businessman, and though a supporter of the Cause, I have never taken up arms. He asked me to give you this note. He's sorry he couldn't be here to deliver it in person. He had to leave town rather unexpectedly." A smile crossed Mr. Hardee's lips, met with an equal smile from General Sherman. Hardee's little sarcasm was not offensive. The note asked for protection for Noble Hardee, and was signed by General John Hardee.

Downstairs, the young woman waited patiently. She noted among the group only two other women, both in their 40s. The rest of the visitors were men, black and white, young and old. The two older women sat together, and when a seat opened next to one of them they motioned the younger woman over, so as to make conversation easier. They were curious about her.

"I'm sorry, I don't think I know you. You are...?"

"Belle Anderson. I live in the city and have come to greet the general." She was purposely vague, as her business was none of theirs.

"Well," said one of the women, "my husband is Confederate General G.W. Smith. He just left two days ago with General Hardee's forces. You know they crossed the Savannah River on that makeshift bridge. G.W. -- that's my husband, what everyone calls him -- knows General Sherman from West Point. I have a letter from G.W. for the general, to make sure I have his protection. These generals are honorable men and they respect each other, they do. G.W. would do the same for Sherman's family, were the tables turned."

"And my husband is General A. P. Stewart." said the other woman. "He's with General Hood's army up in Tennessee. Or was. I'm not sure where he is, now that Atlanta's been taken. I don't have a letter, for obvious reasons, but I deserve the same protection as Mrs. Smith."

"Neither one of you sound like you're from Savannah."

"Oh, no," said Mrs. Smith. I'm from New London, Connecticut."

"And I'm from Cincinnati," said Mrs. Stewart. "We came here because our husbands are fighting for the Confederacy. It's such a beautiful city, we hope General Sherman continues to show his generosity."

"Is your husband in the army Mrs. Anderson?" asked Mrs. Stewart. It was a probing question, given that Belle wore no ring.

"My husband died fighting at Second Manassas."

"Oh, I'm sorry," she replied, sounding more embarrassed than sorry.

"Thank you."

"Mrs. Anderson, I don't mean to be too personal, but how can you bear to meet Mr. Sherman?"

"That *is* somewhat of a personal question, Mrs. Smith, but the truth is, I don't hold it against him. We started the war, and the general is just doing his job. And the general was not at Second Manassas."

"I suppose you're right. I'm sure my husband has made many Yankee women into widows. War is so cruel," said Mrs. Smith, who only wished it could be crueler for the Yankees.

Mercifully, Mrs. Smith's turn to see Sherman came and she ascended the staircase. Mrs. Stewart continued her tête-à-tête with Belle.

"Belle, I remember reading about your father last year. He died a hero, at Chancellorsville, as I recall."

"Yes, that's correct."

" My sincere condolences. Your father *and* your husband."

"Yes, and I have a brother, Abner Wickham, with Lee in Virginia at this very moment. Third Georgia Regiment."

"My, oh my. This is hellish. I wish the damn war was over. Thank goodness the city has been spared. Maybe Sherman isn't the monster we've heard about from the papers after all."

Belle didn't respond, and the conversation ended there. A few minutes later Mrs. Stewart was called up. She stayed in Sherman's office no more than 5 minutes. Finally, after waiting over hour and a half, it was Belle's turn. There were only a few others left in the foyer as she ascended the staircase. Her first impression on entering his office was that Sherman looked tired, and that he was taller than she expected, about 6 feet. He had deep red hair and a short rusty beard. His face was marked with what she called worry lines but other people might call wrinkles. She inferred his thinking at that moment: 'Oh, no, not another wife asking for protection'.

"Your name, Ma'am?" asked the aide.

"Mrs. Belle Anderson."

"Address?"

"106 Jones St., Savannah."

"And your business with the general?"

Speaking to the aide, she began: "My mother, who has recently…"

"I'm sorry, Ma'am, you may address the General directly."

Belled turned toward Sherman, who was still standing, and she started over. "My mother, who has recently deceased, begged me – asked me – to bring you this letter, General. It is sealed and I have not read it. As horrible as this war has been, and as much as you have made it so, I must honor my mother's dying wish." This was clearly a rehearsed line, and said with aplomb. The aide stiffened a bit but Sherman just smiled. She went on.

"My mother had a premonition you would show up here."

"I'm sorry about her passing. Premonition? When did she die, and from what cause?"

"She died a few weeks after the fall of Atlanta, in late September, from cancer. She was 46. She said: "Belle, Sherman has taken Atlanta. He will come here next, I feel it. If he does come, you will please deliver to him this note. In person, I beg you. Do not trust it to any of his lieutenants. And please don't ask me what is in it." "

"Again, accept my condolences, Mrs. Anderson. Please understand that I want this war to end as much as you do. Should I read it now?"

"If you wish." Belle hadn't thought of that question. Would he read it now or later? It was really up to him. He could pocket the thing and send her away. She was of course curious and did not move, but quickly added, "Yes, please."

Sherman did remember a woman named Anderson from long ago, but in the flush of meeting Belle the details didn't register immediately, or he might have pocketed the note for a later time. Instead, out of simple curiosity and to get this visit over, he opened the sealed envelope and removed a single slip of paper. As he read Belle could see her mother's handwriting but not make out any words. His smirk turned to a frown. He read the letter again, cleared his throat slightly and looked at the young woman. Then to the aide and sentry:

"I wish to have a private discussion with Mrs. Anderson. Could you please leave us alone for a few minutes? You can wait in the hallway," and he motioned them to the door.

"But sir," protested the aide, concerned to leave their Uncle Billy alone with this unknown woman in a Confederate's house.

"It's OK. It'll be OK. That's an order." They did as told, closing the door behind them. Sherman walked to the window overlooking Macon St. and motioned Belle to follow.

He held the letter in his hand and looked hard at Belle, then turned away to face the window for a full half minute. Belle thought this was certainly one of the more awkward moments of her young life. She saw him bite his lip just before he turned around. The letter jarred every bit of his memory, down to the last minute detail of their encounter so long ago.

"So, you have not read this, really?"

"No, you saw it was sealed. You knew her?"

"Yes."

"May I ask in what capacity"?

"Good friend. Dear friend. I was in Savannah years ago, actually 20 years ago, and we met at the Pulaski House. She was working as a receptionist."

"And?"

"I shan't discuss it further."

"May I infer, dear sir?"

"You may infer all you wish. I am a happily married man, and I do not wish to bring up a bygone era that can do no one any good. This was 20 years ago. You were how old then?"

"Four. My father's cousin owed the hotel when I was a child, I do remember that. And my father…was he away at sea?"

"I believe so, yes."

"So it was more than a passing 'How do you do, Lieutenant Sherman'? I suppose it was Lieutenant Sherman then."

"Yes."

"Good friends?"

"Yes." All Sherman had to do was leave it at that. He had no obligation to show her the letter or discuss its contents, but something propelled him forward – to share this private history and see where it might lead.

"You want to read it?"

"Yes."

He handed over the slip of paper. She read it quickly, half afraid he might snatch it back.

September 15, 1864
Dear William
You have made it back to Savannah. I somehow knew you would. As I write this, I know I won't be around to 'welcome' you. I hope the citizens of our city have not suffered too greatly. You are a Union soldier through and through, and I respect that. My husband and son-in-law died fighting for the Confederacy, and now I am dying of natural cause – a cancer, my doctors tell me. My only comfort – now and in the life hereafter – is Belle, a child whom you never met when you were here, and her son. Belle is a beautiful young woman now, alas a war widow. I would ask only one favor from the grave. Please, to the fullest extent within your power, please make

*sure no harm comes to them. I do fear for their future when –
as now seems inevitable – the South will fall and Savannah will
be at the will and mercy of your army. With affection from the
beyond,*
Maryjane ("Marcie") Wickham

Belle fought back tears. "Had I known the contents, sir, I
would not have honored my mother's wish. We do not need
your protection, at least I sincerely hope not."

"She doesn't mention the boy's father. Where is he?"

"Edward was killed at Second Manassas. A bullet through
the heart, I am told. He died a hero, sir."

"And your father?"

"Chancellorsville. He also died the hero's death." Then,
almost inaudibly, "A hero is a man who is afraid to run away."

"What?"

"Nothing. Just that the word is sometimes overused, I
think, and does not really soothe the widow or the child."

"I see." Sherman had witnessed thousands of battlefield
deaths and was hardened to this sort of personal history.
Husbands, sons, brothers -- a multitude killed since the summer
of 1861. On a personal level it was always tragic. As a
commanding general it was the cost of doing business.

"So there's just you and your son?"

"We live with my aunt, my father's older sister, who I'm
afraid has a touch of senility. She's forgetful, and rarely leaves
the house unless someone goes along."

"Slaves?"

"We had two but my father freed them when he entered the
army. He too had a premonition that this day might come. He
didn't want our servants to feel hostility toward us, to abandon
us if we lost the war, which is what most slaves surely will do
now that they are liberated. So in 1861 they became freed
Negroes, and we pay them and they understand they are free to
leave if they wish. And that was long before Mr. Lincoln's
Proclamation. Savannah had almost 1000 free blacks before
you arrived."

"So I've learned. Now you have thousands more."

"Ours stayed with us. You won't find two more devoted
and loyal people anywhere in this city. Mabel, also a widow,
I've known her since childhood and she lives with us and helps

raise my son. She's with him now. And Hosiah Jackson has been with us for years. He helps maintain the house, the horse and carriage. He goes home to his own family at night."

"And your means of support, if I may ask?"

"An inheritance I have is sufficient to pay them and support us. And I do some private teaching in my home, that helps."

"In your own home?"

"Just three children. I used to teach in the Mayberry School here in town, but now I just do it privately. We are in recess for the holidays. Our home is quite nice, so I have no personal needs. Unlike a lot of people in Savannah right now."

"So I have learned in my short stay here. Half the people I met today begged me to get more food for the city. It's a problem. And you know what the other half asked?"

"If I may surmise from the two women before me, protection for their persons and property. But *I* didn't ask General, my mother did."

"Would you believe," and here Sherman gave out a loud chuckle, "General Hardee even had the temerity to ask me to protect his brother! I'm supposed to be a monster, a devourer of flesh, a burner of homes, and yet three Confederate generals have asked me to protect their families! Shows you the hypocrisy of all those newspaper articles about me. The generals surely know I am an honorable soldier, or they wouldn't trust me with such requests."

"I should think there is a lot of puffoonery on both sides, General. What you read about southerners in northern papers is just as outlandish, I'm sure. You'll find more tolerance and decency here than you would ever expect from northern propaganda."

"Well, yes, you have a point Mrs. Anderson. I've said that myself. You do have a point."

"And your family sir?"

"I have not seen my wife Ellen in 9 months. A son died last year, at age 9. I have 5 children, including a son just 6 months old. I've never seen him. They are all in Indiana now. Separation is painful. Nothing good about this war. I want it to be over and will do everything I can to make that happen. War affects everyone. We did not start this war, Mrs. Anderson, but we will finish it."

"I don't doubt that, General. Well, I better be going."

"Won't you come again? The sentries don't bite."

"Thank you, but I don't think we really have anything more to discuss, General. But you have been most kind."

Belle did not want to go but her head told her she must. They felt a mutual, physical attraction, a longing really, but it was so repressed that a casual observer would miss it. Belle wondered: Is Mama reaching out through me? And for the first time in months Sherman felt a strong desire to hold and caress a woman.

"Our troops are putting on a grand parade at noon tomorrow, on Bay Street. We'll have bands, color guards, it'll be a spectacle. The Mayor and aldermen will be there. I think your boy may like it. You should come. The soldiers are to pass our stands at noon, corner of Bull and Bay. Then they have me scheduled to greet visitors after the parade. I should like to meet your son."

"Thank you, General. I'll look into it. Good day."

"Mr. Campbell," he yelled. "You and the Corporal may enter now. Mrs. Anderson is leaving. Please escort her out."

Then in low voice to Belle: "Thank you for coming. I really mean that."

They shook hands and Belle left the room.

✻ ✻ ✻

Available in paperback and as an ebook:
https://books2read.com/u/38EjG6

Out of Time: An Alternative Outcome to the Civil War

Available in paperback and as ebook:
https://books2read.com/u/47E7wA

It is November 1864 and General Sherman's army is marching through Georgia. Sherman has recently burned much of Atlanta and meets very little opposition as his 60,000-man army aims for Savannah. General Hood's Confederate army will soon be defeated in Tennessee by General Thomas's Union forces. General Grant is squeezing the vise he has placed around Petersburg, and the Confederate capital Richmond is threatened. General Lee's troops are demoralized, many shoeless, and some are deserting to return home so they can help feed and protect their family. The South has all but lost the Civil War and leaders on both sides sense the end is near. It is just a matter of time, yet the Confederates do not give up or in. They are hoping for a miracle.

Across the ocean comes a foreign fleet of submarines, promising to save the South from inevitable defeat. Is that possible? What could be their motive? And why -- oh why -- do they come at the last hour?

This 'alternative history' of how the Civil War ends presents both real and imagined events of that momentous conflict. Alternate Civil War history is now a common genre, with many essays and novels that posit a different ending. A subgroup of this genre invokes time travel to effect a different ending to the war. In Out of Time you will find my own unique alternate-outcome scenario.

Chapter 1

Monday, December 12, 1864 -- Union army camp near Savannah, Georgia

At four in the afternoon tall and uniform-dressed Major Walter Garrison strode briskly toward General William Tecumseh Sherman's tent. A much shorter black man clothed in rags and walking with a slight limp followed a few steps behind. As they approached the tent Sherman's adjutant, sitting just outside the flap, stood quickly and saluted.

"Sir?"

"Major Garrison. I am here to see General Sherman."

"He's expecting you, sir?"

"Yes, he received my message this morning."

"The Negro too, sir?"

"He'll wait outside. We'll call for him shortly."

The adjutant turned to enter the tent but was met by Sherman coming out. "Major Garrison, come in. I did get your message. Come inside." In contrast to Garrison the general appeared almost slovenly, with shirt tail hanging over unpressed pants, red hair and beard unkempt. They had both come 300 miles from Atlanta in less than a month, mainly (since they were officers) on horseback. Sherman, for his part, had no one to impress. "What is so damn urgent, Major?"

"The Negro with me. My men caught him last night. Or I should say he caught us. He's a runaway from Fort McAllister. Came up to our lines about two miles down river from here. Quite flea bitten and half starving, but coherent for all that. We gave him some rations and clothes and did a general debriefing."

"Well, Major, we already know from deserters the fort's complement of men and guns. All their big cannon are pointed to the river. We're attacking from the land side. It's never been attacked that way before, so I don't care what's pointing at the river. I don't expect much in the way of resistance. They can't have more than 200 troops."

"Tomorrow is it, sir?"

"Yes. I've chosen General Hazen's division for the task. He'll throw up three of his 4,000 men against their small number and we'll surround them from three sides. Shouldn't take long. Is that what this is about?"

"Yes. I think you should listen to what Moses has to say. That's his name."

"Fine name. Summarize it before we call him in."

"They have fresh troops and some new kinds of weapons. If what he says is accurate, they may be from a foreign nation. "

"Bring him in."

Moses entered the tent. He looked older than his forty-five years, and carried himself with head tilted slightly forward. His already-gray hair was balding in front, and there were several teeth missing. At the sight of Sherman the Negro's eyes opened wide. Whether affected or not, his manner showed deference and pleasure. He had heard plenty about William Tecumseh Sherman and like most slaves about Savannah viewed the general as savior to his people.

"Moses, this here is General Sherman. He's the boss of all the troops about Savannah. Don't be afraid. Just tell him what you know about Fort McAllister. What you told us last night."

Sherman made a point of shaking Moses' hand, to put him at ease. "Here, Moses, sit down. You're in safe territory now. No one will harm you. How'd you run away?"

"At night. They don't lock us up. They figured we got no place to go, the swamps will kill us no how. But I knows this area and mos' important I knows da Yanks is about and I know Mr. Linkum done freed us some time ago, so I just got to find me da Yankees. And damn if I didn't find the mightiest. Sho is a pleasure, Mr. Sherman."

Sherman was amused. "Well, you're right on all accounts so far. So what's going on at the fort? They moved in some fresh troops? That's not surprising."

"And some new-fangled guns, too. Ain't never seen them befo."

"Tell us what you saw."

"Well, the new troops they came inside a long iron boat also new to Moses. Real low in da water, no sails, just one smokestack. And a second boat right beside it was came full of wood boxes that me and da other slaves unloaded, but we had help from da troops also. Took all day to bring out da boxes and into da fort. The boss man in charge from dat boat had yellow hair and a funny way o' talking, what they tell me is an axent, they say, and not from 'round these parts. My buddies say he over from 'urope, but I don't know. Don't really know where this 'urope be no how. Anyway, they came about a week ago. After we get all da boxes into da fort, they don't let us touch the weapons inside. Only da troops."

"But you've seen the weapons that were in the boxes?"

"Oh, yeh, I seen 'em alright. They been playin' with 'em all week."

"Can you describe them for me?"

"Yessir. One of them is long and gots a barrel with holes in it. Looks like a rifle but fires real rapid like, many bullets with just one pull o' da trigger. Da man carrying' da gun, he always has another soldier behind, carrying more bullets in dese round cans. Soon as one can empty, the shooter gets another can. Funny damn gun, dat way."

"Sounds like a fancy repeater, Walter. Fancier than our Spencers, which can fire seven bullets from a tube magazine. But not with one pull of the trigger. Each shell has to be chambered and the rifle cocked before it'll fire."

"Right, sir," said Garrison. "We have a number of those among our troops, though most of the men still carry their muzzle loaders."

"Moses, you're sure it fired many bullets with only one pull of the trigger?" asked Sherman.

"Oh, yessir. The mens hollerin' about that feature."

"I understand. Go on."

"Another type is bigger and heavier, and sits on two legs. It takes four mens to operate, one to pull the trigger, one to hold a long belt with all da bullets what goes into the gun, another to put water in da barrel when it gets too hot, and yet another to go get stuff what needs gettin'. Sometimes dey change places, but always four men w' dis gun. And it shoots so many bullets, ol' Moses can't count em. Coss I can't count no how but it sho shoots more bullets in a split second den I got fingers and toes."

"A repeater cannon," Sherman offered. "Why did they fire them? Were they testing them or was there some kind of battle?" Sherman wondered if one of the Union ships had approached the fort.

"Ain't no battle, just whole lot o' testing and whooping and hollerin. Never seen such happy soldiers. Da mens from da boat teachin' the mens already at the fort how to use 'em. Sure waste a lot of bullets."

"You said there were three types. What is the other one?"

"The other type, it be like a small cannon, and also four mens with dis one. It shoots a shell that don't make a lot of noise, just goes 'whiff' and then explodes in the distance with lots of green and yellow smoke. Ain't never seen that befo, neither, but I only knows McAllister."

"How many of each type of weapon would you say they have?"

"I don't rightly know. We carried dem boxes all day, mighty heavy, but dey didn't let us touch what was inside. Most of da men has one of them skinny rifles I described befo. And da kind with the two legs, I only seen this many (he held up both hands). The ones w' da shells that make the yellow smoke, maybe the same as all my fingers, no more."

"So they have some new guns. We can get past that. We have repeaters also, though not as fancy. How many new soldiers came from that boat, Moses?"

"Well, I heard one o' da officers say the fort had three hundred men after dey all came in."

"So it's less than a hundred new men, that's for sure. How the hell did they get past the blockade?"

"Suh?" answered Moses, not fully understanding the question.

"Could have been at night, Sir," offered Major Garrison. "He describes them as long, low profile iron boats."

"Possibly," agreed Sherman.

"The new soldiers, they have an accent too?"

"A couple of dem, yea, including da man what watched us unload da boxes. But the others just regular southern boys."

"Is Major George Anderson still in charge?"

"Yessir. He's there, but now he always have that yellow-hair foreign guy by his side. And dey been practicing mighty hard with their new guns, and teaching de troops dat was already there."

"Well, that's mighty helpful, Moses. Anything else you noticed different?"

"One mo' thing."

"What's that?"

"Whenever they fire dem small cannons what make the green smoke, first they keep looking at the flag, to see which way da wind is blowing. Then everyone's got to put on a heavy mask. Even dis here nigger had to put one over his face. Most uncomfortable. Dey say if you don't, you could die from da smoke."

"Describe the mask," said Sherman matter-of-factly.

"It fits over the front of the face and has these two big eyes covered in glass. Hangin' from the front is somethin' round and made of metal. I sure ain't ever seen anything like it befo. We looks like de devil with it on. And glad when we can take it off."

"How many times did you have to put it on?"

"Three times, as I recall. Whenever they practiced with dem cannons I jus told you bout."

"But not with the repeating guns?"

"No, never wi' those guns."

"So the masks were only for shooting the small cannons?"

"Yessir. Only after all da mens had da masks on. The foreigner, he kept yelling "ready gas masks" until everyone had it over his face. Some had trouble and needed help puttin' it on."

"How long did you wear it for?"

"Oh, a long time. Each time the sun went from here to here on da ground." He held his hands apart about 2 feet to show the movement of the sun's shadow.

"About an hour," Sherman muttered to Garrison, who acknowledged the fact.

"What'd you smell when you took the mask off?"

"Like a funny smell, don't rightly know how to describe it. Not like gun smoke, dat for sure. Made my eyes run a little, but it went away. Some o' the men coughed, and one man emptied his stomach. But da smoke from da cannon was mostly gone by then"

"Did the smoke drift toward the fort?

"Maybe a little bit, nothin' you could see. But you could see smoke out where the shells landed. Big yellow and green clouds of smoke. Far off."

"How far would you say, Moses?"

"Don't rightly know. I'd say 'bout as far as from here to da river bank." Moses pointed to show he meant the river near Sherman's camp.

"Um, that's about three hundred yards, I'd guess," said Sherman. "From the time these new men arrived until you escaped, how many days passed?"

"About four or five, I reckon."

"OK, Moses, you've been very helpful. You can go now, but you will stay with my camp."

"Don't mind my askin', Mr. Sherman, but is we gonna be free soon? My people been waitin' a long time."

"Yes, Moses, real soon. I promise." Sherman ordered his aide to get Moses some new clothes and a labor position with other blacks in the camp.

Moses bowed, said "Real nice to meet you, gen'rl" and left with the adjutant.

"Well, Major Garrison, "What do you make of it?"

"Sounds like they're better defended than we thought from the white deserters. I am certainly not familiar with the type of rifle Moses described."

"He didn't describe any army issue rifle. Sounds more like a fancy repeater gun. As for the larger repeaters – the ones that sit on two legs – they sound like an improved version of the Gatling guns Grant is supposed to have up in Virginia. But I hear the Gatlings are very bulky and prone to overheating, and take half a regiment to operate. Not ready for widespread use, that's for sure. And what about those masks? Our cannons make a lot of smoke but the men don't get sick from smoke drifting back to their position. Do you think Moses was set free to scare us away, his story made up?"

"The thought did cross my mind, General. But his remarks are consistent from yesterday, and in any case, why would they choose a slave? Hell, he'd want us to attack the fort, not scare us away. Moses is clearly uneducated. They could not rely on him to get the story straight if it was made up. They're not that stupid."

"I agree. They're out-manned, but not stupid. Or this war would have been over a lot soon," remarked Sherman.

"And the masks," sir. "Why would they ever invent an idea of using masks in battle? No, the masks must be real. And if real, they must have a real purpose. His story is too far-fetched to think it's invented just to scare us. They wouldn't make up stuff like this and then trust it to a slave. I do think he's a runaway and nothing is invented."

"Yes, seems clear. As you explain it, there is no reason to doubt what he says."

"Are we still going to attack?"

"Hell yes, tomorrow afternoon. We'll prevail on numbers and skill. Every new weapon is always trouble the first time around. They are too few, they jam or overheat, or the troops need more training to use them effectively. He described about ten of the Gatling type. I trust our snipers can take them out from a great distance. How many men have Spencers, if you know?

"Probably about a tenth of the men, I estimate. Not that many. Are you going to inform General Hazen of this new development?"

"Yes, I'm meeting with him this evening to go over final plans. If I know Bill Hazen, he'll look upon this development as just another obstacle to overcome. We may be up against more firepower than we first thought, but I don't see how our men can fail."

The major left and Sherman sat alone at his small wooden table. He studied and re-studied a map of the fort and surrounding area. Fort McAllister was built on the southern bank of the Ogeechee River, twelve miles south of Savannah, to prevent Union ships from reaching the city via Ossabaw Sound. In the past two years it had been attacked seven times by federal navy ships and repulsed each attack. McAllister was just about invulnerable from river bombardment because its sand-constructed walls absorbed any cannon balls without much damage, and could be quickly repaired in a day. In contrast, the once-thought-impregnable Fort Pulaski, with brick walls seven feet thick, fell to the Union's rifled cannon on just the second day of bombardment, April 11, 1862. Pulaski was still in Union hands.

Savannah itself remained unscathed by Union ships because they could not travel safely up the Savannah River. Once past Fort Pulaski U.S. Navy ships had to contend with close-in Fort Jackson (three miles from the city), plus batteries along the banks and massive cribs that literally blocked any movement past Elba Island. All of these ruled out the Savannah River for resupplying Sherman's troops. That task could only be accomplished on the Ogeechee River.

Sherman had to have Fort McAllister. And why not? Nothing had stopped him so far in his splendid march from Atlanta. Reaching Savannah's outskirts had been like a country walk for his army, with few casualties and no real impediments. Soldiers called him "Uncle Billy," an endearing title that suggested his army was like one big happy family.

Yet…for the first time since leaving Atlanta, doubt crept in. Was there something new here he didn't understand? Was he being cavalier about the repeaters Moses described? And what about the strange masks? Did they have a true military purpose? Sherman didn't honestly know, but this fleeting doubt only renewed determination to take the fort and get his army resupplied. Savannah was but the halfway point of a long southern campaign that began in Tennessee. He folded up the map with a single thought: *From here I will march to Virginia, join up with Grant and help end this war once and for all.*

***

That same evening, 12 miles away in Savannah, a comely eighteen-year-old girl lay in bed, not quite ready for sleep. Julia Goodfellow, daughter of prosperous parents (her father was now off fighting for the South), had only this year finished high school and taken position as a school teacher. A kerosene lamp on the bedside table allowed her to re-read a letter received that day, from a twenty-year-old soldier. Though not yet engaged, she and the letter writer agreed to marry as soon as the war was over. Assuming, of course, as he not infrequently reminded her, that he survived.

December 9, 1864
Dearest Julia,
I hope this letter finds its way to you. Never know what with the mail these days and the blockade, though I am only a few miles away, in Fort McAllister. The colonel said we could write and they would find a way to get the mail to Savannah, but when, he couldn't say. We arrived here recently and I cannot divulge anything else, as I am sure you understand, but am well and we are itchin for a fight, but don't know if and when, etc. The afternoon we spent together Saturday last is forever etched in my heart and soul. I loved you before and even more since

then, if such a thing is possible. I pray to god this war will soon be over and we can join and live our lives together as husband and wife, as we are surely meant to be. You are the most wonderful, remarkable woman – (not girl!) – in the world. With all my love,
Jimmy,

Julia held the letter to her bosom and sighed. Her yearning was deep and she fantasized another afternoon alone with Jimmy. She put the letter inside the pages of a book whose cover was only a plain brown wrapper, no title or identifying words. Inside, the first printed page stated in small print:

The Art of Making Love.
For the Modern Woman.
Prince Philipe Gusteau, Paris, 1862.
Translated from the French.

The author was a pseudonym and *The Art* was no translation at all, having been written and published in New York, then disseminated under the counter to enlightened females north and south. This was Julia's second reading. From the Introduction:

In my affairs with Parisian women I have learned much about the fairer sex. That this information is repressed and hidden by our society is unfortunate, but these pages are meant to unfold the truths of all womanhood. And make no mistake. Women are the same in London and New York and Moscow, as in Paris. Native cultures only alter the outward appearances, the dress perhaps, or the manners shown in polite society. Cultures do not -- cannot -- alter the inner soul of the intelligent woman, what they want and desire, how they behave in the uninhibited confines of the marriage chamber.

...women want to be held and caressed, which they sometimes mistaken for "love" or "affection." No! It is the physical need to be held and caressed by a man that they want. Yes, it is true that the man must care for his woman in the personal sense, to be kind and gentle and considerate. But all the "love" and "affection" expressed in ways other than physical will not satisfy -- nor should it -- the modern woman.

The key is for the modern woman to understand that she has as much a right to physical satisfaction as her male companion, that she has the same physical needs as he does, and to work toward that mutual satisfaction. These pages will tell you how to accomplish that goal. For readers of my work outside Paris, I trust the translation will not stint on the details...

Chapter 2

July 1, 1918 – Kaiser Wilhelm II's Imperial Office, Berlin, Germany

Kaiser Wilhelm II sat in his ornate, high-backed chair as three men entered through a side door. One man was dressed in crisp military uniform, with medals over his left chest. The other two wore suits and ties suitable for a formal occasion. Each walked in slowly, with head up, looking toward the Kaiser. As they gained his eye they nodded, and he returned the nod.

The office for this meeting was more like a small ballroom, 3000 square feet, with faux columns and gold edged moldings. Wilhelm would have preferred meeting in his castle in Pszczyna, but it was too far south. Decisions had to be made in Berlin, the Prussian capital and much closer to the North Sea Fleet.

The office dated to his grandfather, Kaiser Wilhelm I. On its walls hung photos of both Kaisers, along with assorted European royalty related to them in some fashion. Absent from the picture gallery were two notables: his grandmother, England's revered Queen Victoria, whose country he was trying to crush by any means possible; and distant cousin Albert, King of Belgium, whose country he had overrun in August, 1914.

As the men entered Wilhelm did not stand nor speak. They took seats at an immense table opposite the Kaiser and remained silent. Admiral Eduard von Capelle, Secretary of the Reichsmarineamt, was 63. He had replaced Admiral Alfred von Tirpitz 2 years earlier, and was soon himself to be replaced. For now, though, he had the Kaiser's confidence. Capelle wore the navy uniform and was the only one of the three under Wilhelm's military command.

Sixty-one-year old Kurt Krebs, a civilian and head of military research, was the scientific genius behind what was now a desperate proposal to win the war. He wore a stiff suit with a thin German tie and was the only one of the three to have uncombed hair, which befit the image of scientist.

Johann Friedrich Goethe, professor of history at the University of Berlin, was there because his knowledge of 19th century American history was crucial to the plan's execution. His suit was similar to the scientist's, possibly from the same rack, but the two would not be confused; Goethe wore his hair combed back into a pony tail, an affectation of some university intelligentsia.

Wilhelm doodled with a pen in his right hand. His shortened left arm, a birth defect, stayed hidden under the table. Now fifty-nine, he had reigned since his father's death in 1888. In the decades since there had been great advances in photography, a great boon to his narcissism. Wilhelm was the most photographed man in Europe. Most images showed him wearing the Pickelhaube, what many non-Germans referred to as "that funny spiked helmet" -- a useless appendage of the German military uniform. *All* photos showed him with his distinctive mustache; a long, flattened W. People joked that the pointy ends matched his pointy helmet.

Now dressed in full military uniform (absent the spiked helmet), Wilhelm appeared as in a reverie. He looked *through* the eyes of Capelle, then Krebs and Goethe. They stared back uncomfortably, protocol requiring that he initiate conversation. If you could read their minds you would find, beneath outward deference, a measured contempt for their Kaiser. Capelle, for his part, had urged the policy of unrestricted submarine warfare, which more than anything else brought the United States *into* the war. But to him it was really blunders on the battlefield, both tactical and strategic, that led to this unhappy summer. And Wilhelm II -- supreme military commander -- was responsible. The two civilians certainly thought so, as did most of the German high command. Rumors were rife about his possible abdication for losing the war.

Goethe, the historian, laid the beginning of Germany's descent to 1890, when Wilhelm fired Chancellor Otto Von Bismarck. Though Bismarck was 75 at the time, and would have died before the Great War, his firing -- and subsequent events -- showed Wilhelm to be a military and political *incompetent.* Goethe counted mistakes he blamed on the Kaiser: unrestricted submarine warfare (including sinking of the *Lusitania*); unwinnable and unnecessary battles (Jutland, Verdun); invading Russia before the fall of France (that wasn't the Schlieffen plan!); and perhaps worst of all, assumptions about the enemy based on wishful thinking. "Oh, the

Americans can't even mobilize before 1919," Wilhelm famously said. Yet now the Yanks were in France, a million strong and eager to fight.

Not all was his fault. Much of the blame lay at the feet of Generals Erich Ludendorff and Paul von Hindenburg, the former a fanatic who seemed to be systematically destroying Germany with futile land offensives. A March 1918 offensive had been temporarily successful and for that Wilhelm awarded each the Merit of Honor. This medal only deluded them further and led to more deaths in April, May and June. A *million* young German men killed or wounded since 1914, the country starving and all but bankrupt, and no end in sight – except with capitulation. Bismarck had ruled with common sense and political savvy, backed by military strength. Wilhelm ruled by gut feelings and military assessments not consistent with reality. Under a different leader -- a *Bismarckian* Kaiser -- Germany would not now be in such dire circumstances. Dire they were, but the bumbling Wilhelm was still supreme commander and the men before him could not proceed without his approval.

Wilhelm finally broke his reverie. "Thank you for coming. Let's not flatter ourselves, gentlemen. We are losing the war. It is the Jews on our left and now the Americans on our right. What started so gloriously is ending in farce. FARCE! We had the French and British licked, kaput! Somme. Verdun. Gallipoli. Jutland." In fact the Jews had nothing to do with the outcome, and Somme and Verdun were stalemates, not German victories. Gallipoli was a battle fought between England and the Turks, and the Turks (a German ally) won. And although England lost more ships and men than Germany at Jutland, the German fleet retreated to its base and did not sail again.

So misinformed! thought Goethe. But it was clear to him – and the other two -- that Wilhelm was fixed in these beliefs and no one wished to offer any corrections.

"Even Russia gave in, and we have now concentrated all our troops at the Western Front. But then the Americans showed up, with their Jewish money and guns. We cannot beat them *and* the French *and* the British. WHAT DO YOU HAVE TO SAY?" he screamed. This was his way and they did not take it personally.

"We must think a new way, try a new tactic, Herr Kaiser," spoke Krebs. This "new way" had been hashed out in a series of secret meetings and memos over the previous two months. First the idea was fantasy, then it became a mere possibility, then a concrete plan. With each military setback at the front Wilhelm became more and more receptive until now; now he wanted assurance it *could* work. Now he was desperate; any plan was acceptable, even one totally beyond his comprehension.

"Yes, yes, that's why you are here. To make a final decision. I want to decide today if we are to implement the plan. Reverse Time, you call it. You have all studied the secret documents. Let's have it out. You first, Krebs," he commanded.

"There is an excellent chance the time shift will work sir. Excellent. We have sent men and sizable objects back in time, and received indirect confirmation of their arrival, though the time they arrived was not always what we intended. We can send submarines as well, I am certain. What we don't know is just when they will enter the past. We can't be precise and once the transfer is done it cannot be undone. And we may never be certain that the desired changes will take place."

"Ah yes," said the Kaiser, "so I've heard many times since first learning of your marvelous time machine." For all his faults – including helping to instigate the Great War (notwithstanding the Sarajevo assassination, really just a local dispute between Austria-Hungary and Serbia) and an egomaniacal lust for empire – Wilhelm could think logically when necessary. "If we are successful, why won't we know that right away? Why won't the Americans evaporate from the Western Front so that we can fight England and France alone and FINALLY CONQUER? That seems an obvious conclusion if YOUR machine works." Then, turning his glance toward Goethe, "if YOUR history is correct."

"I wish it were so," said Krebs. "But we are trying to *alter* history. If we are successful, and America does not enter this war against us, perhaps something else happens, something that is unforeseen and unforeseeable."

"Like what?" the Kaiser snapped.

"One could hypothesize an infinite variety of events, your Excellency. Perhaps the Confederates don't become a major power, and lose a later war to the northern states. Perhaps

England, sensing a threat from a divided North America in the late nineteenth century, builds a bigger and stronger army and navy, and easily defeats our troops well before America declares war in 1917. Perhaps Russia, spurred by mid-nineteenth century events in North America, has its revolution well before 1917, and defeats us on the eastern front. These are just some obvious possibilities. There are many more we can't even think of. As much as I believe in our project, and want it to succeed, Herr Kaiser, I must acknowledge that one can't alter history and predict how it will play out 50 years later."

"Sir, if I may speak," said Goethe. At 56 Goethe was the youngest and most widely respected of the three experts, in part because he was recruited late to the project and had not been part of the war effort. Goethe also won respect for his ancestry; he was a direct descendent of literary giant Johann Wolfgang von Goethe. Johann Friedrich Goethe's specialty of 19th century American history was an arcane subject for a *German* professor, but offered some advantages. For one, it guaranteed very little academic competition. And now this; he never dreamed his specialty would one day put him before the Kaiser to help save Germany.

"Krebs is correct on all points. However, my study of the American Civil War does suggest that an independent Southern Confederacy will only grow stronger with time, and eventually *will* throw off the yoke of slavery and build a strong military. If there is still to be a great war – and given the belligerence of the nations we are fighting, there surely will be even if America is divided – I do think the American Confederacy will become our ally. And as result, stay out of our conflict. Other than that, I have to agree, we don't know how it will ultimately play out."

"I want them ON OUR SIDE, not just "out of our conflict." Will they invade the United States to abort the American Expeditionary Force? Even better, will the Confederacy send troops over here, to help us win this GODDAMN WAR!"

"Possibly, Herr Kaiser, but if they just work to prevent the United States from getting involved, won't that be enough to secure our victory? What is the assessment of Ludendorff at the front?"

"General Ludendorff IS AN IDIOT! Everything is good, one more assault, one more division, one more this, one more that. Yes, Ludendorff is confident we could prevail without the

Americans, but he's been confident of other battles that cost us dearly and lost us ground. Hindenburg is more sensible. Without the American intervention, he believes the war might already be over. America's entry last year, even before their first boat sailed to Europe, re-energized the French and British. Just the anticipation of America's help gave them new life, a new will to fight on. So yes, my own assessment is that we would win this war if America had remained neutral. Why else would I go along with your crazy scheme? Capelle, is the navy prepared?"

"I have the volunteers and the submarines are ready, Herr Kaiser. It was not difficult. Three hundred of our best men, including naval architects, gunnery experts and of course submariners. Two dozen or so actually speak very good English."

"They know they won't return?"

"They have been told so."

"You assure me they are volunteers?"

"To a man." Capelle paused for a moment to consider: How strange. Wilhelm has never shown any concern for the hundreds of thousands young Germans killed at the front, or in iron casket submarines, and now he expresses concern about volunteers who agree on a no-return mission. Perhaps to him time travel is worse than being riddled with bullets.

"We have explained it is a submarine convoy," Capelle continued, "to North America to secure aid that will allow us to win the war, that the boats will not be returning, that the men will find a primitive country across the ocean. Some know of New York and its wealth, but the American South is a blank and they accept that it is bereft of modern conveniences. We do not think the men would believe us if we talked of time travel. We have said, 'men, do not volunteer if you are married or have a family you cannot leave. The risk of dying on this mission is very low, and the risk of succeeding to save Germany is very high. Just do not expect to return to Germany. You will be emigrating to America, to start a new life there'. That is a paraphrase of what we told them. And when I listed the sub commanders, that helped decide the issue. The volunteer captains are well respected, and excited for this project. To a man they would sacrifice all for a greater Germany. They and a small circle of officers know the true plan, but for the others

202

our message was honest but vague. Three hundred volunteers. We turned many away, and took only the most qualified. They are looking for adventure and a new life in America."

"Good, good. Goethe, tell me more about this stupid American Civil War. Why did it last so long?"

"Excellent question, Herr Kaiser. The Yankee – that is, the Northern – generals were mostly incompetent. One of them, a General George McClellan, was fired twice by President Lincoln for incompetence. The Southern Army was much better led, but it was considerably smaller. Consider our war with Belgium in August 1914. Without our brilliant generals, it might have dragged on for much longer than a few weeks, given the resistance put up by the Belgians. But the outcome was inevitable given our superior numbers and greater armaments and industry, and we quickly dispatched the resisters. That should have been the case with the Northern states in 1861. The North had twice the manpower to draw from, and several times the industrial might compared to the Southern rebels. That war should have been over in months, not years. Only when Yankee generals named Grant and Sherman took charge in 1864 did the North ultimately prevail. But up until then, there was always hope for the South – because the Northern leaders were so inept."

"So when would you have us intervene?"

"Another excellent question, Herr Kaiser. We should not intervene too early, because a quick Confederate victory could lead to an early return of Northern hostility. I think the middle of the war is best, when the North is weary of fighting, and ready to settle, to capitulate. I believe the ideal time is what the Americans call the battle of Gettysburg, Pennsylvania, in July 1863. It is considered the pivotal battle of the war, and the Southern Army was repulsed. General Lee and his men had to retreat back to Virginia, and it was all downhill for the South from then on. If the Southern Army under Lee had won that battle, the outcome would likely have been Northern capitulation sooner or later."

"If I may interrupt," said Krebs. "We will be lucky to achieve a point within a year or two of our desired arrival. The machinery is not precise, as I have said. It would be best to aim for 1861 or 1862, to give us some leeway. That way, if Goethe is right, then our men could wait until the right time to intervene."

"No, No, that's not good," said Capelle. "My men are soldiers, marines. They cannot sit for a year or two on our boats doing nothing. That could lead to lethargy, weakness, even mutiny. They must engage upon arrival, or shortly thereafter. No earlier than spring of 1863. Also, our subs will degrade over time, without modern shipyards to restore and repair them. I estimate the useful life of each sub, without ability to make major repairs, a year at most. We will go out on diesel fuel, but the supply won't last more than 6 months. The subs can be retrofitted to run on coal, and we are carrying equipment for that purpose. Coal should be plentiful in North America, but even then the machinery will degrade over time. And for obvious reasons, we won't have access to Northern foundries to quickly build new boilers. No, our ships must engage on arrival to North America, or soon afterwards. I thought I made that clear in my previous memos."

The Kaiser smiled at his experts. "So we have a machine that may send men and subs back in time, but not the precise time we desire. The men and subs must engage the enemy shortly after arrival, or see their effectiveness degraded. Our time travel party may influence the result of a distant foreign war, but the change in the outcome may or may not be favorable for our own 20th century conflict. And I am supposed to be encouraged?"

"As I have proposed before, sir," said Krebs, "it would be far easier to send a small group of men back in time to assassinate U.S. President Abraham Lincoln, who is uniquely responsible for the American Civil War. Or rather, to kill him before he becomes president. That way we could aim for any time in the 1850s."

Krebs also considered suggesting the Kaiser himself go back in time, so he could make different decisions and prevent war in the first place. But Krebs' idea died aborning. The Kaiser didn't really think the war was a mistake, and going back, say, to 1914, might change a battle strategy or two, but not the fatal decision to declare war on France and Russia. Worse, such a proposal might be taken by Wilhelm as an invitation to commit suicide (suppose the time travel failed?), lead to Krebs' immediate dismissal and destroy all hope for the

Civil War mission. As much as he wanted to, Krebs would not suggest the Kaiser go back in time.

"I have already addressed that scenario in one of my memos," objected Goethe. "Lincoln was the catalyst, like Serbia's Gavrilo Princip, but the seeds of America's civil war were present for decades before Lincoln became president, and would have sprouted without him. So I respectfully disagree with Herr Krebs. Assassinating a single leader would not change the deep-seated animosity between North and South. It must be an outright Southern victory to be effective, to prove to the Northern aggressors not to interfere with the Confederacy. And also to prove to the Confederacy that they must change from an agrarian economy to an industrial one, in order to maintain a strong army and navy. At least that is my considered opinion."

"And you still plan to go on this suicide mission?" The Kaiser chuckled.

"Yes, Herr Kaiser," Goethe replied, with the enthusiasm of an explorer to whom risks are secondary to discovery. "I am a widower, and my son died at the front." The Kaiser nodded his head, as if in appreciation of the sacrifice. "This will be the opportunity of a lifetime. Admiral Capelle will appoint me an officer in the navy, answerable only to the boat captains. They will need me to direct the itinerary, which will depend on exactly when we arrive to North America. The war changed daily, and landing at the wrong port at the wrong time could jeopardize our mission. I will never feel so needed as on this mission. I am honored to go."

"This is good. Your desires and Germany's needs mesh beautifully. Good." The Kaiser pointed to Krebs and Capelle: "And you two are staying?"

"Yes," said Capelle. "We still have a war to run, a navy to manage."

"And as much as I would love to be part of the experiment," answered Krebs, "I must supervise the time transfer. And continue my work to make it more precise."

"Tell me Capelle: If your men are at sea, how will they know what year, what month it is? I know radio communication is of recent origin."

"Yes, the ships will be able to communicate with each other, but there will be no radio on any land mass. This of course has the advantage that no one will ever be able to intercept our signals. After the subs go through our time portal they will sail past one of Germany's North Sea islands. About five miles offshore the *Deutschland* will send out a small life boat with two officers and a group of rowers, so it will not look like a vessel from the 20th century. Once they land the men will buy a few supplies, and through conversation ascertain the day, month and year. We have some old German marks for this purpose. And, since our subs will be well offshore, they should not arouse suspicion if we choose our sea lanes carefully. We of course have detailed charts of the area from the mid- 19th century."

"Which island, if you know?"

"Probably Borkum. That looks most promising."

"Good. And just how many subs are we sending back in time?" asked the Kaiser.

"We can safely put eight vessels through," said Krebs. "Two are fighting subs, torpedo-equipped U-151s, and six are of the *Deutschland* class, U-boats converted to carry cargo. When empty of cargo they can be quickly converted back to fighter subs, so we'll always have the capacity to fire torpedoes. But it's most important to transport enough guns and ammunition to get the job done. It will take about half an hour for each sub to pass through the time portal, and they all must do so in a narrow window so they can re-enter on the same day. Eight is a safe number, with some leeway."

"I should add," chimed in Capelle, "that each cargo boat can each carry up to 800 tons of guns, fuel and torpedoes, plus a crew of thirty. That's almost 5000 tons of weapons. Three hundred tons of underwater missiles and the rest guns, artillery, shells and bullets. A fair amount for any army."

"Good, excellent planning. And the subs should have no trouble getting past the British blockade," added Wilhelm. Capelle was about to reply but Wilhelm quickly corrected himself. "Of, but of course. I forgot. They will be in the North Sea in the mid nineteenth century. No English blockade. One forgets these little trivialities. You have the list?"

"Yes, Herr Kaiser." Capelle reached into a folder on his lap and removed a single sheet of paper. He leaned way over the immense desk so Wilhelm could reach it with his good arm. The Kaiser scanned the typed page.

Project Reverse Time – Candidates

Class	Type	Name	Captain
U-151	Fighter	*Heidelberg*	Lurs Hurschel
U-152	Fighter	*Dusseldorf*	Karl Steuben
U-153	Cargo	*Bismarck*	Erich Eckelmann
U-154	Cargo	*Hindenburg*	Otto Whimer
U-155	Cargo	*Deutschland*	Gerhard Schnitzler
U-156	Cargo	*Munich*	Paul Konig
U-157	Cargo	*Wilhelm*	Karl Meusel
U-158	Cargo	*Danzig*	Ferdinand Studt

Capelle gave Wilhelm a minute to peruse the sheet, then spoke: "Yes, two subs are torpedo ready, with capacity of eighteen torpedoes each. The other six have been converted into cargo subs, though when emptied they can be quickly converted back to fighter subs. Each boat is equipped with two fifteen centimeter deck guns, which alone can heavily damage a nineteenth century wooden boat. As you know, the *Deutschland* has already made the trip to North America twice, and she will be the lead ship. Gerhard Schnitzler will be the captain of the *Deutschland* and commander of the overall mission. Lurs Hurschel will guide the *Heidelberg* and serve as the second in command. They have of course volunteered."

"Yes, I see. Schnitzler and Hurschel, good men," said Wilhelm. "I will be sorry to lose them from our era."

"They will save Germany, in the end. They feel so and are compelled to go. And we have enough redundancy that even if we lose two or three subs to weather or an unexpected error in the time warp, there will still be plenty of firepower for the Southern armies. With our advanced armaments, even if only one of the fighting subs and two cargo subs make it to North America, they will be a force untouchable by any mid-19th century navy."

"Do not be so smug," retorted the Kaiser. "I remember well all the promises our generals gave about Belgium and France. We cannot predict these things. I understand they had armored ships and submarines in the 1860s."

"Yes, but primitive by twentieth century standards. Of course you are right, Herr Kaiser, we should not be complacent about this endeavor. Which is why we have built in redundancy, and taken only the best of our men to meet this challenge."

"But why no battleship? I would think that could do the job all by itself." Capelle turned toward Krebs, acknowledging that the scientist should answer.

"We strongly considered sending one or even two battleships," said Krebs. "They could certainly do much damage to the cities of Washington and New York. But the mass of a battleship is six times that of a submarine, and would require a much larger portal then we have set for the submarines. And the larger the portal, the more risk there is of time warp failure. Also, according to Professor Goethe's analysis, a battleship may not be the best weapon for our purpose."

"Yes," agreed Goethe, "a battleship bombardment of Washington or New York would kill a lot of civilians, and perhaps energize the Northern population to fight harder. Also, even if Lincoln was killed or he surrendered, it would not mean a defeat of the Northern armies. They could rebuild over a few years and launch another war. During that time the North could also learn to duplicate the very weapons we plan to provide the Confederates. And as the Admiral has pointed out, without modern shipyards and access to foundries, any ship we send will degrade and become useless in a year or two. So a battleship might be very effective in the short term, but to secure a lasting victory, the South must defeat the Northern armies. Instead of General Lee surrendering to General Grant in Virginia, it must be the other way around. Ultimately, despite what we expect of our submarines, this war has to be fought and won on the ground, with guns we can bring to the South. We have thought this through very carefully."

"Then you truly are ready."

"Yes," replied all three, in near unison. "With your permission," said Krebs, "our transit will begin three days hence, July 4, 1918."

"Then it shall be. You have my authority. See to it."

Only Goethe appreciated the irony of the launch date: American Independence Day. Without another word the three men stood, bowed before the Kaiser and left the room.

Chapter 3

Mid-afternoon, November 25, 1864, in the Atlantic Ocean

One hundred miles off Georgia's coast the submarine convoy cut all engines. The sea was glassy calm, an ideal time to stop and consider the next move. Eight subs spread out in a 5-mile wide semicircle, with *Deutschland* in the middle. Telegraphy among the ships worked perfectly. The air was *radio pure* – no interfering signals from anywhere on the ocean. A dinghy from the *Heidelberg* ferried Captain Lurs Hurschel to the *Deutschland*, to meet with Captain Schnitzler and Goethe. Together, the three men would decide the course of action and, presumably, the fate of Germany in the 20th century. Captains of the other subs would be notified by telegraph and they would follow orders to the letter.

Schnitzler sat with Goethe in his Captain's quarters, waiting arrival of Hurschel. "So far, uneventful, Herr Goethe. How are you holding out?"

"I am fine, occasional sea sickness, nothing major. The moments we've been under water were smoother, but I understand the need to travel like a regular ship."

"Yes, under water is for only when we must hide, or avoid bad weather. Otherwise it is much more efficient to ride the surface. It gives us faster speed, for one thing. And oxygen from the air, so the diesels can charge their batteries. Until we reach North America, I doubt we'll encounter anything to make us submerge. Bad weather perhaps, but we've been lucky so far."

"Yes, I can't complain."

"Tell my, Herr Goethe, how did you come to your expertise in history of America?"

"America has always fascinated me. An uncle immigrated to New York in 1888, and sent us pictures and descriptions. I began reading and learned of their Civil War. It killed hundreds of thousands, but forged a great nation. In my dissertation I had the opportunity to write on any subject, so I chose the American Civil War and its aftermath, what they called Reconstruction. My professors accepted the thesis. The rest, as they say, is history. Pun intended."

Schnitzler did not show any appreciation of the pun. "Reconstruction? You mean putting the country back together again?"

"Partially. The United States remained very divided for decades, but at least they weren't killing each other. Yet, it was a painful period for the underclass, particularly the freed slaves. Even to this day – I mean the era we just left – the Negroes and many immigrants are treated as second class citizens. "

"I suppose," said Schnitzler, "but we are in 1864 now. Tell me about America, the everyday life there, what we can expect after their war is over."

"I have never been there. I know battles, generals, political history, geography and such. But, of everyday American life I am quite an ignoramus. I can infer some things, but that's about all."

"Well, infer for me. What will it be like to live there? What will we miss?"

"Life I'm sure will be primitive compared to modern German standards. Let's see, Captain. No toilets, no indoor sinks, no electricity, no automobiles or trucks, no telephone. It's true many Germans in our own era don't have access to these marvels, but you and I are used to them, so they will no doubt be missed."

"Yes, yes, of course. But in my home we did not have electricity until I was 18. I have never had an automobile or flown in an aeroplane. I will miss the toilets and the sinks, but have spent many days without them, in training camps. What I want to know more about is the people. I understand their war was over slavery, which the South was determined to keep, but otherwise are the North and South cultures so different?"

"I would imagine so, only because the North is more industrialized with bigger cities and larger population, and doesn't depend on slave labor. But the common laborer in a Northern factory is apt to be just as poor and downtrodden as the slave on a Southern plantation. Also, you will find more of our fellow countrymen in the North compared to the South."

"But there are some Germans in the South?"

"Yes, though remember, there is no Germany as such in 1864. We are still Prussia. Unification came in 1871. So there are German-speakers, from various states, mainly Prussia of course."

"What about the women?"

"Ah, now you are really out of my field. Could you be more specific, Herr Captain?"

"I'm not sure. Let's start with availability."

"Ah, so. Well, if you want to meet a woman, the best places would be the big cities, New York, Philadelphia, Boston. Of course, after our little excursion on behalf of the Confederates, we may perhaps not be welcomed in those northern cities."

"So, in the South?"

"There are no large southern cities. Savannah, Charleston and Richmond are urban areas that should be most favorable for meeting unattached woman. But again, Captain, this is not my area. You are not married, I take it?"

"No, I am not. I am not without experience with the opposite sex, but the thought has occurred to me to find a woman and settle down, when our service to Germany is completed. You were married, I understand?"

"Yes, my wife died of typhus. My son was killed at the front. For me it is truly a new beginning."

"Then we are similar, though I have not suffered your personal tragedies."

"How old are you Captain, if I may ask?"

"Thirty-eight. And you, Herr Goethe?"

"Fifty-six. A generation older. Not wiser, Herr Captain, just older."

"I am a submariner, you an historian. Germany needs both."

"Yes, I suppose."

Their conversation was becoming banal and both men welcomed a knock on the door. "Who is it?"

"First Mate Rosenberg, sir. Captain Hurschel has arrived, sir."

Schnitzler quickly opened the door and warmly greeted the *Heidelberg*'s captain. "Lurs, come in, come in, come in. We are expecting you." The three men barely fit into the tight quarters, which included a small table and chair. On the table lay a nautical chart of the coast between Charleston and Georgia's sea islands.

"How does it go on the *Heidelberg*? asked Schnitzler. "All your men have been informed, I trust?"

"Yes, of course. No more secrets. And the men are in good spirits. They don't all believe it is 1864, of course, and make many jokes about time travel. 'You going to screw your grandmother, then you'll be your own grandfather!' Or, 'Now you can kill the bastard that diddled your mother before you were even born.' That type of crudity. All in good fun, of course. So far the trip is a novelty. They know their situation is much better than regular submariners during the war, or their brethren fighting in the trenches. This good humor could disintegrate, of course, when they finally accept that Germany for them is no more, that their life will now be in North America."

"Ah," replied Schnitzler, "same on the *Deutschland*. We have picked good men. They will do fine. It is our job to lead and guide them. You told them about the bonus?"

"Yes, yes, of course. Each man gets a bonus in gold once the war is over -- that being the American Civil War of course. I don't think we run much risk of desertions before that point."

"Yes," Schnitzler. "No point in sending us back to a primitive era only to jeopardize the mission for lack of proper incentive. A sailor could leave us any time we're on land and be gone forever. There is no way he could be found for proper punishment, as back home."

"Gentleman, Captains," interjected Goethe, "we have a monumental task. I am but an historian, albeit with some knowledge of the current -- that is, 1864 -- geopolitical situation. But exactly how we execute this plan is a military decision, and decision time is at hand. Will you permit me to outline what I know about our position?"

"Please do," Schnitzler advised. "We are ready to act."

"At our current speed we will arrive at the Georgia coast in less than a day. Look at this chart. The coast, from roughly here to here, contains over a dozen, perhaps two dozen Union war ships." Goethe's pencil drew a line from Port Royal South Carolina to the sea islands of Georgia. They are there for two purposes. One, to blockade the southern ports so the Confederacy can't be resupplied from Europe or Bermuda. And two, to resupply the army of General Sherman when it reaches Savannah. His army will reach the outskirts in about two weeks, and enter the city without any resistance on the twenty-first of December. But first he has to take over this fort," and here Goethe pointed to a small dot on the Ogeechee

River south of Savannah. "Fort McAllister, which his army will overcome in a 15-minute siege on December 13, 1864."

"Fifteen minutes? Is that a world record for seizing a fort?" joked Hurschel.

"Perhaps, but the fort does not have many men. The ratio will be something like ten Union soldiers to one Confederate. Remember, this war is almost over and the South will surrender in a little over 4 months. I have directed us to Savannah because I think General Sherman has to be defeated there, before our boats head to Virginia. His march through Georgia has demoralized the South and is causing desertion of soldiers fighting with General Lee in Virginia. Once Sherman's defeated we will still have plenty of time to help Lee defeat Grant. That is my plan and you have agreed."

"Yes, said Schnitzler, "and you have made us understand that it is the Union army that must be defeated. So what do you propose we do with Union ships we encounter *here*?" Schnitzler pointed his pencil at the mouth of the Savannah River.

"Here's what I think," chimed in Hurschel. "Let's keep in mind our goal is to defeat a Union army, one that must be resupplied before heading north. While our subs could probably destroy all these boats – how many did you say?"

"Perhaps up to two dozen,"

"Well, then, twenty-four ships, that's twenty-four torpedoes, all in a day's work. We could do it with just two fighting subs, and probably not sustain any damage. But…it takes out the element of surprise if we do this right away. No matter how primitive nineteenth century communications, General Sherman will find out and divert his army northward before the Confederates can degrade it. Then he will join Grant and possibly defeat Lee even sooner than your April date. So if our goal is to defeat Sherman in Savannah, then we have to make him think his ships are waiting for him, and he continues with the attack on this fort. You agree?"

"Yes, I agree completely," said Goethe. "That is why we have to sneak in without engaging the Union ships until we can meet with the Confederates and give them our weapons. But again, there are many ships patrolling this area, so how do we do that?"

"I think I have a plan," said Schnitzler. "You have told us about this fort that guards the Savannah River, Pulaski, they call it. A Polish name, yes?"

"Yes, he was a Polish warrior in the American Revolutionary War. Lost his life fighting for the Americans in Savannah. He's a hero there."

"Here is the fort on Cockspur Island," said Schnitzler, pointing to a small island at the mouth of the Savannah River. "The fort has nineteenth century guns and could not do us much damage but," and here he paused for effect, "they could perhaps do *some* damage. AND, if we get past them, they could block our exit by sinking ships or piling ballast near the river's mouth. It is a shallow river, I know from the charts. With the high tide, the maximum depth is only twenty-five feet depth. We cannot go in under water."

"Captain Schnitzler, that is why you are a sea captain and I am but a lowly historian."

"We are both essential to the war effort, Herr Goethe."

"So what do you propose?"

"Again, we could destroy the blockading ships right away and cut off Sherman's supplies, but he is no doubt resourceful and would find his way up north, his army intact. That plan would not likely help the Confederate cause. So I propose that only two ships, *Deutschland* and *Heidelberg*, enter the river. At night, at high speed and under cover of darkness to get by Fort Pulaski. The rest of the fleet should stay out of view of the Union ships, until we have had a chance to meet with the Confederates, supply their local army and defeat Sherman. Or at least keep him from being resupplied."

"But wait," said Hurschel, pointing to an area of the Savannah River upstream from Pulaski, three miles from the city center. "There is a Confederate Fort Jackson here. How will they know we are not the enemy? And how far could we get upriver anyway, if it is blocked with either Confederate warships or perhaps even mined?"

"Likely both," said Schnitzler.

"There is even more," said Goethe, before Schnitzler could continue. "The Confederate ironclad *Georgia* is moored here," and he pointed to a spot north of Elba Island, opposite Fort Jackson. "It is under-powered, and can only be moved by tugs, so it is really just a floating battery. But anything approaching the *Georgia* could be attacked. Also, because it hides behind a crib, torpedoes can't touch it. A floating battery behind a wall. Potentially dangerous."

"So," said Schnitzler, "there is clearly some risk in trying to reach out to the Confederates, no doubt about it, once we're past Fort Pulaski. That is why, three or four miles upriver from the fort, out of their cannon range, we will fly the Confederate flag!"

"They have their own flag?" asked Hurschel.

"Of course!" exclaimed Goethe, in childlike enthusiasm. "And we have half a dozen of them!"

"We do?"

"Yes. We made them!" and here Goethe slapped his knee in glee. "It was my idea."

"Brilliant!" exclaimed Hurschel. "I never would have thought of it. Where are they?"

Schnitzler turned around and opened a small cupboard above the table. With two hands he removed a heavy fabric that, to Hurschel, looked like a large folded table cloth. Schnitzler and Goethe unfolded the cloth in the cramped quarters, its 2 x 3 meter size filling the room. They held before Hurschel a bright red flag set with a wide, deep blue X touching all corners and containing 13 white stars.

Saturday, November 26, 1864, near the Georgia coast

Captain Lockhart, we see steam in the distance," warned *Norwich's* first mate. "Looks like two low profile ships, on course for the Savannah River."

"From what direction?"

"Not from Port Royal, sir, that seems certain. Coordinates show they have come from the direction of Europe, sir."

"Blockade runners, no doubt. You say it's two of them?"

"Appears so, by telescope. Two points of steam."

"That's strange." Lockhart grabbed the telescope while his seaman pointed to the area of concern. The Captain looked for a good three minutes. "They are low profile, alright. And they look like ironclads. Nothing I've seen before. Where is our blockading fleet?"

"We are twenty miles out, sir. We could signal them with flares, or let these ships pass and have the fleet deal with them."

"No, they must be stopped sooner rather than later. They could sneak in, if the fleet is not warned. Send out flares in the distress pattern. The closest ships should see them and head in our direction. Until then we'll have to deal with the situation ourselves. Let me look again. They could have come from the North Carolina coast, swinging in a wide arc to approach from this angle and make a dead run for the river. But to my knowledge the Confederates have no ships of this type. Could be foreign. I don't see any flags." A minute later three flares shot up westward, signaling 'all available ships come at once'. This was standard for a Union ship in distress or in need of immediate assistance.

President Lincoln imposed the Southern blockade in April 1861. By 1864 the Atlantic effort was divided between the North and South Atlantic Blockading Squadrons. In the first year of the war it was relatively easy for runners to sneak through, but with the fall of Fort Pulaski to Union forces in April 1862, and with an ever expanding Union fleet, the blockade became highly effective. By 1864, under command of Admiral John Dahlgren, the SABS had effectively stopped almost all shipping into Savannah, Charleston and other southeastern ports. A successful runner was now rare. Ships that made it through were small and fast, and certainly devoid of heavy weapons that might slow them down.

"How fast are they moving, Captain?"

"Running at least twelve knots. I estimate the first ship will pass us about a mile to starboard from where we are now. I think we can attack without risk of being counterattacked. Whether our cannon will do any good, it's hard to say. If the hull is iron, probably not. But if we can inflict some damage that should deter them. We'll go broadside and try to signal them from fifteen hundred yards off. If they are hostile we'll fire."

Lockhart then gave orders to move his ship perpendicular to the path of the first boat. In fifteen minutes *Norwich* was only a mile away, traveling at eight knots while the unknown ship was moving at a brisk twelve knots. At this rate the low profile vessel would pass him at a distance of about five hundred yards. He gave the message to his signalman, who held flags ready.

"Signal 'Stop and identify. River is closed'. Repeat three times." Flags waved in the air. "Message conveyed three times, sir."

"Good." Lockhart looked through his telescope. No response but then there was no one on deck who might have seen the signals either. He did not see a country flag flying, which confirmed that the two ships were blockade runners. He felt certain there was no inventory in either the Union or Confederate navy like these ships. Being slender and of low profile, they seemed built for blockade running. His own ship was a high profile screw steamer, 132 feet long, beam 24 feet, and made of solid timber. She carried two 30-pounder Parrott cannon and 4 eight-inch (200 mm) guns. He should be able to blow this low profile boat out of the water. Blockade runners were designed to be fast and evasive, not to engage in direct battle. Captain Lockhart surmised the two boats planned to succeed by sheer speed. He could not help but contemplate accolades that might accrue for capturing one of them. He had no intention of standing by to let them pass.

"Prepare to fire. Direct cannon to the center of the boat. If she has an iron hull our balls may not do much damage until we get closer. If they get past us I'll have to leave it to the fleet and Pulaski's guns to stop them."

"Cannon ready, sir."

"Fire!"

The two cannon blasted balls toward the boat as it sailed past, about a thousand yards distant. One ball hit the hull and bounced into the water; the other missed. The cannon were reloaded and two more balls sent skyward; they too missed. Suddenly the mystery intruder turned south and headed directly for the *Norwich*.

"She's headed our way! Prepare to fire when she gets to within 500 yards!"

At 700 yards the boat presented a slender target. It appeared no more than ten yards in width, with a very low water line. Then to Lockhart's amazement there was *no* water line. The ship had disappeared!

"What the hell?" was all Lockhart could muster. For a full minute he stood gazing at an empty sea where, a moment before, his target had floated. He could still see the other mystery boat about two miles distant. But where was the first

217

one? Then, *BAM!* The *Norwich*'s deck shook, as if the ship hit something submerged. Men stumbled, lost their footing. Before anyone could ask 'What was that?' there was an explosion. Within seconds *Norwich*'s stern fell away and the ship began sinking. Instinctively, without time to investigate or curse God, Lockhart yelled: "Man lifeboats! Abandon ship! All men to life boats!"

The sinking was over in minutes. Of the sixty-four men on board only fourteen made it into two of the lifeboats, and eight more were pulled from the water. Captain Lockhart was one of the lucky ones. To avoid resurfacing debris the survivors quickly rowed away from the area. As they rowed, just ahead appeared a swell in the ocean. The disappeared boat rose to the surface and loomed over their tiny craft. What seemed thin and slender when viewed from the deck of the *Norwich* now appeared long and ominous. A sailor came on the sub's deck with a megaphone and yelled out in heavily accented English: "Row toward us. We will then pull you up."

Captain Lockhart really had no choice but to comply. He was at sea in a lifeboat, with no weapons and few provisions. Whoever was commanding that strange boat was either a good Samaritan or taking him and his men prisoners. He would soon find out.

Norwich's sailors were hoisted aboard the sub, each given a blanket and led away below deck. They were followed by three sailors with guns raised, effectively answering Lockhart's question. They were prisoners. What the hell was going on? Below deck Lockhart was introduced to the ship's captain. "I am Captain Lurs Hurschel. Welcome to the *Heidelberg*." Addressing the senior most prisoner: "You are?"

"Captain James Lockhart, United States Navy."

"Sorry we had to destroy your ship Captain, but it was you who fired on us. My sailors are looking for more survivors."

"Thank you captain Hurschel. May I ask where you are from and what are your intentions?"

"Our boats are from Europe, the country of Prussia. We are headed into the port of Savannah."

"So I assumed. My country has blockaded the port. I think you will meet with heavy fire at the mouth of the river, from more Union ships and Fort Pulaski. Furthermore, the channel is shallow, so I don't think you can submerge. I don't think you will get very far underwater." Lockhart would not have divulged this information except for the fact he truly believed an attempt to run the river would sink the sub, killing himself and the other *Norwich* survivors.

Hurschel did not respond and Lockhart went on. "How did you blow us out of the water?"

"Underwater missile. Something we have perfected."

"I am impressed. We could use a few of those." The sarcasm did not register with Hurschel.

"I am afraid you and your men are to be our prisoners for the duration. We cannot release you at this time. We will treat you most cordially, however."

Soon other Union ships arrived to the area. They encountered only floating debris: clearly a shipwreck of some type. A sailor from the Union ship *Aladdin* spied a large piece of floating wood, about 15 feet long and 2 to 3 feet wide. It seemed to be part of a ship's hull or deck. Two sailors hoisted it aboard with grappling hooks. There was lettering on one end, beginning just where the board had broken from the ship. It read: WICH—

✳ ✳ ✳

Available in paperback and as ebook:
https://books2read.com/u/47E7wA

Liberty Street: A Novel of Late Civil War Savannah

Available in paperback and as ebook:
https://books2read.com/u/bzvY2G

Abigale Tate, 24, has lost her father and husband in the Civil War, and now General Sherman is about to invade Savannah. She feels despondent and cynical. She attends a black church and is enthralled by the reverend, a free colored man. They have a furtive affair, which ends when she meets a Yankee major. Along the way she is beset by a teenage sister who has no boundaries in seeking love, a stalking German immigrant, and an outlaw brother who is hunted by the very man she hopes to marry.

Chapter 1

— Savannah, Georgia – Tuesday, September 20,1864

Around ten in the morning an envelope arrived to the townhouse at 27 Liberty Street, addressed to Mrs. Abigale Tate. Abigale, age twenty-four, was teaching at the Dayton Finishing School, so her negro servant Polly put it on a table in the front parlor.

Abigale's mother, Mrs. Henrietta Gordon, saw the envelope and felt sure of its message. She had received a similar message the year before, announcing her husband's death at Gettysburg. She retired to her bedroom and prayed.

Another daughter, Jane, age seventeen, was in her room reading a book about men and women and love.

Abigale came home for lunch.

"Mail be for you, Miss Abigale," said Polly, pointing to the table.

"Oh?" Abigale opened the envelope to find a one-page letter.

> **Dear Mrs. Tate:**
> *I regret to inform you…Capt. Franklin Tate was mortally wounded on Sept. the first, in Jonesborough, Ga. He fought bravely and succumbed from a bullet to his chest. I do believe he passed without pain. We recovered the body and gave him a full military burial…*

Abigale stared at the letter, then fell to the floor. Polly yelled upstairs: "Miss Henrietta, come quick! Miss Abigale sick!"

Mrs. Gordon ran down the stairs. "Oh, my God, she's fainted!"

Jane appeared. "Mother, what happened? What's going on?"

"The letter. The letter. Help me get her to the couch."

The three women picked up Abigale and laid her on the couch. Jane and Polly rubbed her arms while Abigale's mother read the letter. "I knew it," she said in a low voice.

Abigale awoke, looked at her mother.

"Oh, Abigale, I'm so sorry," said Mrs. Gordon. "I just read the letter. Are you all right?"

Abigale could only scream. "Let ... me ... die! LET ME DIE!"

— *Friday, December 9*

"Stop playing that funeral music!" yelled Jane.

"It's Chopin. Piano Sonata No. 2," retorted Abigale as she lightened her touch on the piano keys.

"I don't care who wrote it. It's driving me crazy."

"Girls, girls," admonished Mrs. Gordon, "must you always argue? Oh, if father were here, he would know what to do."

Abigale stopped playing, turned around on the bench to face her mother. "But father's not here. He's dead. Just like my husband. And just like we'll be soon, when General Sherman arrives."

"Don't say that," said Mrs. Gordon. "Abigale, you've changed so. I don't know what to do with you. You used to be a happy girl." "I'm not a girl anymore. I'm a grown woman. Without a husband. Without a father. And with a brother God knows where, fighting in this damn war."

"Do you think Johnny will be all right?" asked Mrs. Gordon, as if Abigale somehow had the information at hand.

"We don't even know if he's alive," Abigale replied. "When was our last letter from him? Six months ago?"

"Mother, I'm going upstairs," said Jane. "I can't take this family much longer. My sister is a bag of melancholy, and you are in perpetual mourning. I feel as though I am growing up in a funeral home." With that, Jane climbed the townhouse stairs to her second floor bedroom.

"Polly," said Mrs. Gordon. "Go to the kitchen and fetch me some tea. Abigale, would you like some?"

"No thank you."

Polly left the room to do as asked.

"Abigale, I'm worried about Jane. She's only seventeen but puts on airs like a worldly woman. Do you know what I found in her room the other day?"

"I can only imagine."

"A book, with just a brown paper cover. I looked inside. It's called *The Art of Making Love — For The Modern Woman*. By some Frenchman, but it is our language. Where did she get such a thing?"

"Why didn't you ask her?"

"And have her snap at me? Oh, if only your father was here. Would you ask her, when you get a chance? I am afraid it is an evil influence." "

Did you read any of it?"

"Yes. To my dismay. It seems to convey a European viewpoint."

"Tell me. Nothing will surprise me."

"Well, he – this Frenchman – wrote that love between a man and a woman is all about physical attraction, that the woman wants the physical touch as much as the man, and that she won't be satisfied otherwise. And that was just the first page."

"Did you read more?"

"No, that was enough. I think the book is a manual for women seeking intimacy. Even, perhaps, before marriage. Only the French could write such a thing."

"Mother, you want some advice?"

"Yes, please."

"Leave Jane to herself. She is feeling the full blush of womanhood and is affected by our family misfortunes. As am I. One difference is that I have had what she now wants, and am more mature for it."

"What are you speaking of, I—"

"Tea is ready," said Polly, entering the room with a cup on a plate. She handed the cup to Mrs. Gordon.

"Thank you, Polly," said Mrs. Gordon. "Abigale, we can talk later, I am going upstairs to lie down. If you wish to resume playing Chopin, that is all right with me."

"Thank you, mother."

As soon as Mrs. Gordon left, Abigale lowered her head and sighed. Polly walked up to her, placed a hand on Abigale's shoulder and said, "Is you hurtin', Miss Abigale?"

Abigale looked up at her servant. "In ways I cannot express, Polly." She repeated her answer, but in a low voice and slowly, as if speaking only to herself. "In ways I cannot express."

"Sho' is a bad time."

"Polly, what are you going to do when General Sherman comes?"

"Ma'am?"

"He's coming soon. He's marching from Atlanta, and when he gets here he's going to free all the slaves. President Lincoln gave a proclamation to free all of you. General Sherman is coming to enforce it. If he doesn't rob and kill us all first."

"Ma'am, don't you talk like that. You and Mrs. Gordon have treated me right well. And besides, I gots no place to go."

"True enough, and I'll tell you a secret," said Abigale. "I have no place to go either. We are cut off, isolated here, surrounded by Yankees."

"How you knows dis?"

"Oh, everyone knows. Sherman is just outside the city. Do you know what he did to Atlanta?"

"Don't rightly know, ma'am."

"Burned it. Burned it to the ground. He may do that to Savannah."

"Don't know 'bout that, Miss Abigale. But I see what I sees in da Gordon house, and I know what might help you," said Polly.

"Oh, what?"

"You need to come to church with me this Sunday, hear our Reverend Simms. His sermon will make you feel better. He's got powerful speaking, he does."

"A colored church? A black church? Is that where you go every Sunday, on your day off?"

"Yes, ma'am. Ain't no secret."

"No, I suppose I knew that, just never thought much about it. This reverend, he's colored?"

"Yes, ma'am. Rufus Simms, a free colored man. He's got a nice-sized congregation. Third Ogeechee Colored Baptist. You heard of him?"

"No, I don't think so."

"You go with me, Miss Abigale. He'll make you feel better."

"I bet he's happy Sherman is coming."

"Don't know 'bout that. Maybe he'll mention it in his sermon."

Abigale was not partial to religion. Though raised Methodist, the war had left her disillusioned and disinterested in Sunday sermons. She had last been to church in August, when her mother dragged her.

"Do other white people go?"

"Usually a few shows up. You'll sit in the back. You won't be noticed or bothered with."

A colored preacher, thought Abigale. The idea intrigued her. *Why not go? I am willing to try anything to ease my despair.*

Chapter 2

— Sunday, December 11

Polly and Abigale walked the eight blocks to the Third Ogeechee Colored Baptist Church, in the section of Savannah known as Frogtown. The cool morning air and bright sunshine made the walk pleasant enough, except for trash strewn about the streets by local servants. Thankfully, there were no rotting animals. The negro work detail responsible for clearing the trash would show up Monday morning.

Abigale pondered what had become of her city. The war news was all bad. Atlanta had fallen in September, about the time Franklin was killed. In mid-November General Sherman began his huge army's march in a southeast direction. Reports of the march, which included pillaging, arson and wanton destruction of property, grew more frightening day by day. Now he and his army were just outside the city. Any day he will take us over, thought Abigale. Then what?

She also thought of Polly, sure to be freed when Savannah surrenders. Abigale had an affection for the woman, now thirty and with the Gordon household fifteen years, and hoped legal freedom did not diminish her loyalty or induce her to leave. Polly did most of the house chores, including cooking. Unlike many of Savannah's slaves she did not lack for nourishment. Big-boned and several inches shorter than Abigale, she was on the heavy side, with a full, round face.

Polly had married a decade earlier and initially she and her husband lived in the Gordon's basement. She had had no children and after about two years they separated, and though never legally divorced they were fully estranged. He was owned by a prominent Savannah family, the Caseys. Abigale did not know if Polly had another man, but doubted it.

Despite her foreboding Abigale enjoyed the walk, a chance to get outside and exercise. She wore an old deeply-pleated skirt and blouse, with a head bonnet. No new clothes had entered the household since shortly after the war began, and the women repurposed and resewed what they had. Polly wore an old unformed smock with skirt, and a kerchief for head cover. Both women had on jackets, Abigale's made of silk and trimmed with braid, her servant's of cheap pre-war cotton.

Initially, Polly stayed a few steps behind her mistress, as per custom, but Abigale insisted she walk beside her. "I want to ask about your church."

"Yes, ma'am."

"You go to the same church every Sunday?"

"Yes'm. Although Reverend Simms is not always doin' the preachin'. Sometimes others fill in for him."

"What's his regular job?" She knew that colored ministers, of which there were several in Savannah, had regular jobs to sustain themselves.

"He be a carpenter, I believe. He's a free man, though, do what he want."

"Yes, I understand." Well she did. Out of a Savannah population of 22,000, an estimated 7700 were legally slaves, with free blacks counting for another 700. "Free" meant they were not owned by anyone, though each free black person had to have a white "guardian," to represent them in legal matters. Still, they could move about, earn their own living and, if they had the means, even own slaves themselves.

"Does he own any slaves?" Abigale asked.

"Not as I knows, ma'am. He be a man of God."

Abigale pondered the statement. "Owning slaves is not God's way?"

"I don't rightly know, ma'am."

Abigale did not take offense, and let it go. If her servant had abolitionist ideas, they did not show in the household. Besides, everything would change in short order, when General Sherman arrived. Polly would be liberated in name, but Abigale and her mother and sister would still need her services and Polly would still need a job. So perhaps nothing would change for her family. Unless, she thought, Savannah is burned to the ground by that odious Yankee.

A few horse-drawn carriages passed by. The two women were careful to avoid any clouds of dust kicked up by the conveyances. Abigale's family did not own a carriage or she would have taken it to the church, but she didn't mind the walk; it felt good to get outside. She was thankful she had said yes to the invitation. It gave her an excuse to dress up a bit, to feel more like she did before death and destruction entered her life. For the first time in weeks she had an agenda, albeit unusual for a woman of her background. She imagined what others might think of her going to church with Polly, and then realized she didn't care.

After about twenty minutes they crossed West Broad Street and reached the church. Abigale had seen the building before but never paid much attention. It was of the second category of Savannah structures, built of wood rather than masonry or brick. Abigale noted it to be in some disrepair, with its white paint peeling, several window shutters missing, and some wood planks needing replacement.

The two women climbed a few steps and entered the building. A single wood-burning stove adorned the stage, but the air remained cool inside, the stove simply unable to warm the whole interior. In wintertime, parishioners kept their coats on, making the services tolerable.

Abigale noted a similar seating arrangement as in white churches, with two long rows of wooden benches, starting near the entrance door and ending just before a raised stage. The benches could seat 300 people comfortably, and were now half full with negro parishioners. As more people entered behind them, Polly steered Abigale to the rearmost bench on the left, closest to the front doors. The bench was empty and Abigale sat on the end near the aisle. She felt a little awkward as the only white person present, man or woman, but her arrival didn't seem to cause any notice.

"Other whites be coming, Miss Abigale," said Polly, apparently sensing her mistress's discomfort. "We always have a few." The same could not be said of Abigale's First Methodist church, where no blacks were permitted to sit with the congregation.

"I goes up front, Miss Abigale. You'll see and hear fine from here. I'll come for you after Reverend Simms done with his sermon. That's when da service be over."

"If I choose so, Polly, I may go out earlier, so if I'm not here I'll see you back at the house."

"Yes, ma'am," Polly replied, and left Abigale to take her seat up front.

Abigale sat down and surveyed the room. The women mostly wore shawls, the men old jackets, some of them army issue. She wondered if they came from their dead masters.

After a few minutes a portly white gentleman entered the church and excused himself as he squeezed past Abigale to sit on the bench, leaving a space of two feet between them.

"How do you do?" he said, in a guttural German accent, and held out his hand. "I am Gustav Heinz."

She shook his hand. "Pleased to meet you, Mr. Heinz. I'm Abigale Tate. Mrs. Abigale Tate."

"Is this your first time, Mrs. Tate?"

"Here? At Ogeechee Colored Baptist?"

"Yah, yah."

"Yes, I came at the urging of my negro servant. She lured me here, I'm afraid. Said I should come listen to her Reverend Simms."

"Where do you live? On a plantation or in the city?" A fair question, since the city was surrounded by many rice plantations, run by women while their men were off fighting.

"Oh, close by, on Liberty Street," she said.

"I see. I see." He looked her up and down, nodding his head. This made her feel slightly uncomfortable. She turned away and tried to focus on the stage.

She was about to ask why he was staring at her, when he spoke. "You've suffered a loss." It was not a question.

Abigale jerked her head toward him. "What do you mean?"

Now she looked more closely at this figure and noted that perhaps he was not a gentleman at all. She noted unpressed pants and a frayed coat, and he had at least a two day's growth of facial stubble. She guessed his age in the late 40s, close to her father's age if her father had lived. By reputation most German-speaking immigrants, of which there were many in Savannah, were hard working and prosperous, and perhaps Mr. Heinz was too, but something about him suggested a lower middle class background. She smelled a faint body odor, but could not discern if it was sweat or cologne.

"Excuse me," he said. "I don't mean to pry. But I notice these things."

"Oh? What things?"

"For a beautiful woman, which you are, one whose life should be joyful, you do not show a smile. You introduce yourself as Mrs. Tate but wear no ring. And you came with no other family, at the entreaty of your negro servant. And alas, this is war time in America. Am I wrong?"

Though crude, his comment was somewhat reassuring. Even a ten-pound weight loss in recent weeks and a repressed smile did not dim Abigale's beauty. At almost five and a half feet tall, she was well-proportioned with a full bosom which, unlike other curves of the female anatomy, was not hidden by dresses worn in public. Unblemished skin, golden-brown hair and sparkling blue eyes added to her appeal. Gloom in countenance certainly did not diminish her attractiveness to men.

"You are very observant, Mr. Heinz. I am in fact a widow." Why, she wondered, is she even responding to him? Out of courtesy? Curiosity? Loneliness in a sea of black faces? Perhaps all these reasons. "My husband was killed just this year, near Atlanta. And what brings you here to this church, and to Savannah in war time?"

"Ah, before the war, long before the war," replied Gustav. "I came from Frankfurt, in Hesse."

"Hesse?"

"Ah, part of a loose German-speaking Confederation. One day we will all be united. Like your country, it seems." He gave out a short and sardonic laugh, as if responding to a private joke.

Abigale did not share his amusement, but remained polite. It was well known among educated Southern whites that Europe had long ago given up slavery, and that the South's adherence to the institution partly explained why no European country came to its aid. Had France or Britain entered for the South, the war would likely be over by now, and General Sherman would not be at Savannah's doorstep.

"I have been here since fifty-six," said Gustav. "Now proprietor of Savannah Gardens, boarding house on Broughton. You've heard? Fine establishment."

She had heard. Savannah Gardens was a boarding house in name only, a brothel for soldiers being its main function. There was even rumor that he employed one or two young black girls, a premium for white soldiers seeking forbidden fruit. *So Gustav is the proprietor!*

"Yes, I know where it is," she said, showing no surprise. She was careful not to say "what it is."

230

"Yah," he replied. "This war is terrible. Bad for business. Bad for the economy. Reverend Simms is a free black man. He speaks the truth and when I have time I come to listen."

At that point a tall skinny male negro came on the stage and bellowed out "Children of God, let us stand and pray."

"Is that him?" asked Abigale.

"No," said Gustav. "He is the choirmaster. First we have the singing. *Then* comes the Reverend."

Abigale and Gustav stood with the others. Just then an elderly white couple came in and entered their bench. As they squeezed past first Abigale and then Gustav, the Hessian moved closer to her, to give the couple more sitting room, a totally unnecessary maneuver considering the bench was long enough to accommodate eight people. After the opening prayer, with everyone seated, she found him a foot closer than before.

Abigale pondered the irony of being made to feel uncomfortable by a white man in a black church. Should she just leave? For a minute she vacillated over what to do: stay or walk out.

A group of men and women came on stage, hymnals in hand, and the singing began.

No. I'll stay. I'm too damn curious about this Reverend Simms.

Chapter 3

Across the rows of people Abigale saw Reverend Simms stride to the pulpit, attired in a flowing black robe fringed with a white collar that dipped down below his neckline. From the back of the hall he appeared light-skinned, though clearly negro from his dark, thickly-curled hair and general facial features. He was short and stocky, with broad shoulders, and clean shaven except for a small chin beard. Before speaking he stared left and right, then straight ahead. The first words he spoke surprised Abigale. They were not standard English.

"Our Fadduh awt'n Hebb'n, all-duh-weh be dy holy 'n uh rightschus name. Dy kingdom com.' Oh lawd leh yo' holy 'n rightschus woud be done, on dis ert' as-'e tis dun een yo' grayt Hebb'n. 'N ghee we oh Lawd dis day our day-ly bread. "N f'gib we oh Lawd our trus-passes, as we also f'gib doohs who com' sin 'n truspass uhghens us. 'N need-us-snot oh konkuhrin' King een tuh no moh ting like uh sin 'n eeb'l. Fuh dyne oh dyne is duh kingdom, 'n duh kingdom prommus fuh be we ebbuh las'n glory. Amen."

There followed a chorus of "Amens" from the audience, along with stamping of feet.

Gustav leaned over to Abigale. "Gullah," he said. She nodded in agreement. By the time Simms had reached "N f'gib oh Lawd" she surmised it was the low country dialect of slaves imported from Africa. If this was to be Reverend Simms' choice of language, she saw little point in staying. *Another reason to walk out of here.*

"That's just to warm up the audience," Gustav chuckled. "Most of them know Gullah somewhat, especially those who spent time on the Sea Islands. He likes to start out that way."

"Loses me," said Abigale. "Will he speak in English?"

Before Gustav could respond Simms continued, his voice from the pulpit clear throughout the room. "My friends, what a glorious moment we are in. It's been a long hard road, it has. We have lost many brethren in the rice fields, to the plague and to the fevers and, yes, to the taskmaster. And our white folk have lost many of their own, to war and disease and more war. These have been difficult times. Is that right?"

"Difficult times!" the flock yelled in unison.

"Who among us has not suffered some loss, some pain, some hurt?"

"No one among us," they all responded, again in unison. This was not the first time Simms had asked these questions.

"But we see a light now. Yes, we do." He pointed to a man in the first row. "Do you see the light?"

"I do," said the first-row parishioner.

Pointing to a woman in the second row, Simms called out: "And do you see the light?"

"Almighty lawd, yes!"

Simms walked about twenty feet stage left and called on another woman, a middle-aged negro in the first row. "Do YOU see the light?"

"Hallelujah!" she yelled, and began gesticulating and making strange sounds with her tongue. At this the audience chanted "Amen! Amen! Amen!" The tongue-speaking woman had to be restrained by her neighbors, until she finally quieted down.

Simms strode back to the podium and turned to face the assembly. "WE ALL SEE THE LIGHT" he exclaimed. "The Lord is a comin' to deliver us, He is."

Abigale felt uneasy. She did not want to hear any more and stood to leave. Gustav reached for her forearm with one hand and raised his other hand to indicate 'wait a minute'. She was about to pull away and bolt for the door when Simms spoke again.

"And white folks see the light, including war widows and war mothers and war sisters. We have all suffered together, and now we can all see the light. White folk, dark folk. Don't matter. We are all children of God. Is that not so?"

"That is so! That is so!"

Simms smiled and lifted his eyes beyond the sea of black faces to the very rear of the hall. The reverend's gaze and the Hessian's gentle hand persuaded Abigale to sit back down. Gustav let go of her arm.

Abigale was thankful no heads turned in her direction. She would find another moment to make her escape. *Why did he mention 'war widows'?*

The sermon continued. "God has a purpose, he does. We must believe in God to make sense of the last four years. Why would God allow white folks to kill each other in such high

233

numbers? So many deaths. The women folk left behind—those who've lost a father, a brother, a son or a husband, they may feel deep down that God is evil. But is God evil?"

"No!" roared the audience.

"Why would God allow black folks to suffer so, under the yolk of repression? Why would God allow our brethren to be shackled and whipped and torn asunder from their families? Must be an evil God. Is God evil?"

"No!" came the reply, from 300 souls.

Simms raised his voice to seek a louder response. "I say, IS GOD EVIL?"

"NO!"

"No, WHAT?" screamed Simms.

"God is not evil!"

"That's right! God is not evil. He has a purpose. This war has a purpose, as horrible as it is. It will free us. Our savior is coming!"

Abigale wondered how Simms could get away with such blasphemy. *My father and husband didn't fight to free the slaves! If Father was alive and heard this—he wouldn't stand for it, that's for sure. I bet this isn't the first time Simms has spoken such inflammatory rhetoric. Why didn't the authorities stop him? Where are the men in this city? Mayor Arnold and his aldermen? General Hardee and his army? How come only a few white people are hearing this? Can free blacks speak in public this way? In Savannah?*

She glanced over toward the elderly white couple. They seemed unfazed by the speech. Perhaps this is what they came to hear. She did not recognize them and wondered if they were visiting from up north. Then she realized no one was visiting from up north, at least not within the past two years or so.

"You say God is not evil, my friends," Simms continued, "and once again you speak the truth. There is a purpose in all this, God's purpose. We are all creatures of God, and I say this. Count your blessings. For whether you are enslaved by the white man's shackles or you are a prisoner of your own inner demons, there is light coming. There is light coming! DO NOT DESPAIR!"

What does he mean, prisoner of your own inner demons? Do blacks have inner demons? Is he speaking to me? How would he know? Polly! She must have said something to him!

Simms pivoted to New Testament scripture. "Jesus said, in Matthew, 'Ye are the light of the world. A city that is set on a hill cannot be hid. Neither do men light a candle and put it under a bushel, but on a candlestick; and it giveth light unto all that are in the house.' Our light is coming. It is coming."

Simms continued with more biblical quotes, each one powerful yet opaque, allowing him to fit it to the times. He never once mentioned Sherman by name, but didn't have to. Even the least literate among his flock knew, from countless conversations among their brothers and sisters and other kinfolk, that General Sherman was "the light," or was "bringing the light," and that when he arrived there would be a new order.

Simms' sermonizing went on another half hour, as Abigale wrestled with it all. He was infuriating and soothing, treasonous toward her culture and understanding of it as well. He spoke in generalities, yet his words seemed to touch her inner soul. Whenever she decided to leave, the next moment she decided to stay.

The parishioners intrigued her as well, especially when compared with her own Methodist congregation. Apart from race, she noted a striking contrast. Savannah's white Methodists sat in their pews dutifully, stoically, reciting scripture when called on, but without excitement or verve.

Here, when Simms swayed back and forth, so did all the negroes. When he threw up his hands to the Lord, they did as well. When he bellowed out a question, they yelled back the answer. And several times throughout the service, a man or woman would stand, call out "Hallelujah! Praise the Lord" and sit back down after the audience approved with a loud "Amen." Such a thing was unthinkable at her church.

Yes, she thought, verve was the right word. Compared to Simms' flock, the white congregation was sedate: no involvement, no *verve*. Her people attended Sunday service as obligation, lest they rot in Hell after death. Simms' people came to be entertained and uplifted; they attended for the here and now, not for any promise of a better afterlife. Her white church was duty. This black one was joy.

So despite initial misgivings, and the obnoxious Hessian beside her, Abigale decided to stay. As soon as the service was over she would question Polly about what she had told the reverend.

After the last "Amen" the audience rose to exit. Polly rushed to the back bench and before Abigale could speak, pulled on her mistress's arm and said, "Come, Miss Abigale, he wants to meet you."

"Who?"

"Reverend Simms."

"Why? What did you tell him?"

"That you be the nicest mistress in Savannah. He a free colored. He likes to meet nice white folks."

Abigale hesitated and Gustav chimed in. "Ah, you should go, Mrs. Tate. When General Sherman comes, will be helpful perhaps to have connections with the colored elite." He flicked his hand toward her, indicating she should go with her servant.

She did not reply. Instead, she looked down the aisle at the stage, then the opposite way, toward the church doors. Should she now run home? If she left, would Gustav follow her? Going with Polly to the pulpit would be a way of getting rid of him, at least, so she acquiesced. There was another reason; she *was* curious to meet the reverend.

Polly and Abigale fought their way down the aisle, past the exiting crowd, and climbed a few stairs to the stage. Simms was at the pulpit, conversing with several followers. Abigale noted that Simms was only an inch or so taller than herself. She estimated his age around thirty-five to forty.

Polly made a quick introduction. "This be Miss Abigale, Reverend."

He held out his hand and Abigale shook it.

"Nice to meet you," she said. *What am I doing?*

"The pleasure is all mine," he replied. "I hear nice things about you. Sadly, I have also learned of your losses. Please accept my deepest condolences."

"Polly told you?"

"Yes. It is indeed unfortunate."

Abigale gave her servant a disapproving look but said nothing. Simms exchanged a few pleasantries with the remaining parishioners on stage and they dispersed.

He sounds intelligent, she thought. Cultivated, even.

"Thank you for coming to my church," Simms said. "We welcome white folks who have an open mind. I see you sat with the Nelsons and Mr. Heinz."

"They are new to me," she said. "I did meet Mr. Heinz. He told me he comes to hear you often, that you speak the truth." How well did the reverend know Gustav? Was he a patron of Savannah Gardens? Why would she think that? She didn't even know if he was married. Abigale looked back at the bench she had just left and saw Gustav sitting there, now alone, as if waiting for something. Or someone.

"Well, thank you," said Simms, "but I'm afraid the truth depends on whose viewpoint, wouldn't you agree?"

Truth and *viewpoint.* Abigale thought the words sounded strange coming from a colored man, free or not. She chose not to answer his question.

"How did you learn to become a reverend?" she asked.

"Ah, that is an interesting story. Perhaps you and Polly would like to come to my office for a few minutes? We can speak privately there. It's right behind the stage."

"Be fine with me," said Polly.

"Yes, for a few minutes," said Abigale. By then Gustav would be gone, she figured. And besides, there was something about this reverend that stoked her curiosity. *He doesn't seem like any negro I've ever met. If I closed my eyes he would sound like a white man. An* educated *white man.*

✳ ✳ ✳

Available in paperback and as ebook:
https://books2read.com/u/bzvY2G

The Wall: Chronicle of a Scuba Trial

The Wall is available in as an ebook:
https://books2read.com/u/bPRYGr

A young woman is lost on a scuba dive in Grand Cayman. Did she suffer nitrogen narcosis? Or did she commit suicide? Experts argue both scenarios in a civil trial that takes place 14 months later. Her parents are the plaintiffs. The defendants are a large corporation and its dive master on that fateful day. There are several experts called to testify, including the author. The two lawyers object to each other's arguments, cite precedent, drill their experts. Yet one thing is missing: her body. It will never be recovered. The Wall is fiction but it reads like a real case. Put yourself in the jury box, listen to the experts and lawyers battle it out, then make your decision along with the jury. How will you decide? For the plaintiffs or the defense?

Chapter 1

The Dive

The Caribbean water is shimmering and blue, transparent on this sunny day. The dive boat ties up at a preset mooring so no anchor will disturb the delicate coral beneath. One by one, nine scuba divers jump off the boat. Each diver has requisite air tank and regulator, face mask and fins, and most are clad in a brightly-colored, thin wet suit to protect from accidental abrasions.

A young woman, Charlene, is the leader or dive master and she will guide the dive. The other eight are diving for pleasure and buddied up for safety, like kids at a summer camp swim. The eight tread water on the surface next to the boat until the dive master asks for the OK sign. Each diver forms an "O" with thumb and forefinger signaling "I'm OK."

"Let's go!" she says, and the dive commences.

***

The opaque surface gives way to another world below, one alive with fish and invertebrates of odd shapes and beautiful colors. It is a world that Jacques Cousteau brought to millions of television viewers in the 1950s and 1960s. In that era modern scuba gear – invented by Cousteau and Emile Gagnan in France during World War II – made underwater exploration possible for just about anyone with the desire. It took several decades of product development and marketing for scuba – self-contained underwater breathing apparatus – to become a major recreational industry. As an industry, scuba shares features with downhill skiing: high-tech equipment; glossy magazines with colorful covers; air travel usually needed to reach the best sites; emphasis on safety; official acknowledgment that injuries can occur if one is not trained and careful.

Each year millions of divers travel to warm waters all over the globe. Especially popular in the Western Hemisphere, with a plethora of healthy coral reefs, are the Bahamas, several Caribbean islands, and the Yucatan coast of Mexico and Central America.

For people whose image of the sea comes only from the beach or the deck of a boat, the first underwater view of a coral reef is a mind-expanding *New World*. Three sites are famous for offering a far-surpassing experience when viewed in person, compared to just a TV or digital image: Arizona's Grand Canyon; earth from outer space; and the underwater view of a healthy coral reef.

***

It doesn't take the divers long to reach a sandy bottom about forty-five feet below the boat. The sand is punctuated by ridges of high coral heads. Hundreds of yellow grunts and jack fish dart about, oblivious to their new mammalian neighbors.

The divers hover a few feet over the sand while the dive master counts heads and signs to each for their OK signal, then with more sign language she indicates 'follow me'. She is easy to follow as underwater visibility is almost 100 feet in any direction (the typical inland lake has visibility of only two to four feet). These are near-perfect dive conditions. The water is warm, visibility is excellent, sea life is abundant. Less than five minutes into the dive the group reaches the edge of an underwater cliff. Beyond the cliff edge is an empty blueness. Over the cliff and almost straight down is the wall, a 3000-foot descent to a new bottom.

The first few hundred feet of the wall is a natural collage of hard and soft coral, in which live some of the more interesting sea creatures: anemones, shrimps, crabs, eels, octopi, and a variety of tropical fish. Sometimes along the wall you will see pelagic species, such as sharks, barracudas, stingrays and giant turtles. These larger, free-swimming creatures don't stay long before retreating to the open sea. Since scuba divers also cannot stay long before returning to the surface (perhaps twenty minutes or so at moderate depths), most attention is devoted to the wall itself.

The divers float over the cliff's edge, eyes on the wall as they descend: fifty-sixty-seventy feet. Ten minutes into the dive they reach the agreed-upon maximum depth of 100 feet. The coral collage shows no sign of ending, but for safety they will go no deeper. Instead, the dive plan is to start a slow ascent, to let the accumulated nitrogen bubble out of tissues slowly. To go deeper would shorten the safe dive time considerably and risk the bends, a brutal pain that comes from nitrogen escaping too quickly and forming large gas bubbles that interfere with circulation. Another potential problem of going deeper is simply running out of air and drowning.

The beauty of scuba is that you are free of any connection to the surface, and can go where you will. The downside is that you carry your air supply with you, and there is no more to be had if that runs out (except possibly sharing an air hose with your buddy, always a risky proposition). So divers pace themselves and rarely run out of air. Strict guidelines mandate how deep to go, how long to stay and how quickly to ascend. As a result, thousands of dives have been made here, on this wall, with no fatality and only a few mishaps. Problems have occurred mainly when divers foolishly went too deep or stayed too long.

Periodically the dive master turns around to count heads. Otherwise, she is busy searching for life that her less-experienced charges might not see (she has been on this wall many times). Her job is to guide the dive and try to make it memorable, even exciting. Who knows what they might find? At a depth of eighty-two feet she spots a giant crab hiding in a coral crevice. She alerts the other divers, who stop to gawk at the crustacean, or what they can see of it. The crab is at least three feet across, but only the eyes and huge front claws are visible. The claws sweep back and forth, warning intruders to stay away. The crab cannot know these divers mean no harm, and sensibly refuses to come out of its recess. The divers move on.

***

Every square yard of the wall is alive. Brightly colored forms that look like plants or rocks or weeds are really coral, members of the animal kingdom and built up of millions of tiny polyps. Three foot-long orange basket corals, each with an opening two feet in diameter, jut out horizontally from the cliff. In between sway deep-purple gorgonians, corals that look like giant leafs with an intricate, lattice design. And in between them are the pencil thin, ultra-long 'whip' corals that seem to start nowhere in particular and go on forever.

Hugging the wall are rock-hard brain corals, so named because their serpiginous ridges – each an endless colony of tiny corals – are remindful of the human brain. Dotting the coral surface in random fashion are intriguing Christmas tree worms, about two-inches high and an inch wide. They don't look like any kind of worm at all but instead suggest miniature pine trees growing out of a hollow and stationary stalk. A diver pokes his finger toward one of them; with shutter speed the threatened worm retracts into its stalk. (If you wait long enough, and at a distance, you can see it slowly emerge again.)

Colors are muted at depth, due to absorption of the sun's rays by the water. Reds and yellows are the first to go, and beyond sixty feet or so everything tends to have a bluish-brownish tinge – until you shine your underwater light. Then the real colors are restored, and you see ocean life the way it looks just below the surface.

Along the wall are sea anemones, one of the more colorful sea creatures. A sedentary flower-like invertebrate, it sports dozens of bright-white, pink-tipped slender arms that sway gently back and forth, searching for nutrients. Somehow, the anemone manages to cull from the ocean all the food required, and bring it to a centrally-located (but hard to see) mouth. Even more interesting is what can usually be found, almost hidden, among the anemone's arms: a bright red, diaphanous shrimp. The shrimp rests clinging to one arm, waiting. Perhaps to escape its enemies, or to share whatever dinner comes along. Surely this is a symbiotic relationship, but how does the anemone benefit?

You could stay in one place for many minutes and not be bored, there is so much to engage the senses. And the perspective changes depending on your distance and field of view. At a distance of, say, three feet from the wall you see large corals, hard and soft, and whatever fish swim by. At a distance of six inches you see worms, shrimps and other invertebrates, plus the tiny creatures that live in the myriad nooks and crannies found on any coral reef. And with a magnifying lens you would find still more to marvel at, such as the complex anatomy of the individual coral polyp.

In its abundance and variety of life the coral reef is not unlike a tropical rain forest. But imagine a rain forest where you can defy gravity, where you can place yourself at any level at will, from the ground to the tree tops. You do this effortlessly, and as a bonus you don't have to worry about stepping on squiggly things or getting bitten by nasty creatures you can't see. True, your time is limited in this underwater forest, but that seems a small price to pay for the experience. And you can always return for another visit.

***

At seventy feet depth the group comes upon a diver's delight. The dive master has found a large green moray eel, its bulbous head poking out from a crevice in the coral. She gives the snapping hand signal that means "moray" and everyone crowds around the opening. The eel's head is fully occupied by its mouth, a cavernous space that constantly opens and closes, which is nothing more than normal breathing (by forcing water over its gills). When open, you see sharp teeth by which the eel bites its prey. A fascination, this weird sea creature; it could grace the cover of any science fiction magazine as a visual teaser for stories about "strange life on other worlds."

The moray's vision is poor to the point of near blindness and it will bite anything that comes close. Hands are kept away. The moray refuses to reveal more of its sinuous body, which judging by head size is at least five feet long. A minute or two passes and it is time to move on, to ascend some more.

The dive master glances back to count heads. One, two, three…seven. ONLY SEVEN! She scans the horizon frantically. No eighth diver. She started with eight.

Her head counting alerts others. The missing diver's buddy then notices that his partner – a young woman – is no longer among the group. Everyone else looks around and counts: one-two-three-four—seven, plus the dive master. No mistake. Instinctively, everyone looks up; they can see to the surface: all clear. Then they look down and see, perhaps seventy-five feet *below*, a silver scuba tank on the back of a diver, moving away from them. Still descending!

The dive master signals the others to continue their slow ascent and get back to the boat. The buddy of the wayward diver instead begins to descend, intending to rescue his sinking partner. The dive master pulls on his arm and shakes her head. Unmistakably, with eyes and hands, she gestures No! No! He is to ascend and return to the boat with the others. He is not trained to go deeper, or to attempt any sort of rescue.

The seven divers obey and continue their ascent, while the dive master descends toward the sinking scuba tank. At 130 feet she realizes catching up is hopeless. The lost diver is now at a depth of at least 200 feet and continuing to fall. To follow the diver is to risk joining her in death. Beyond 200 feet the dive master would run out of air before returning to the surface and her quest (alive? dead already?) is still descending.

Seven minutes later the other divers surface, 100 yards from their boat. They were not supposed to surface just yet, or this far away. The boat captain and an on-board spotter see them waving arms frantically, the sign of diver distress. But their distress is for the one lost; they themselves are in no physical danger. The surface is calm and they are now breathing earth's bountiful atmosphere.

The captain releases the mooring line and brings the boat around. One by one the divers climb aboard. The spotter helps them remove their heavy tanks.

"What happened?"

"We lost a diver!"

"What happened?"

"We don't know!"

"Where's Charlene?"

"She dove deeper to try to get her! We left her at seventy feet."

"What happened?"

"We don't know. It all happened so fast. We were at the wall, looking at a Moray. When we turned around she was gone."

"Who is she?"

Only the lost diver's buddy knows her name. "She's Jennie Knowlton. My girlfriend." He begins to cry and vomit mucus at the same time.

The captain is in a whirlwind. A scuba instructor himself, he must now act quickly as both captain and diver, and on limited information from his stunned passengers. First, secure their safety. That done, he brings the boat back to the mooring while making a distress call to the dive shop.

"This is *Coral Cruiser* at the North Wall," he says. "We have two down divers at the North Wall, buoy 254-K. Repeat, buoy 254-K, North Wall. I need boat assistance and rescue divers immediately. Both divers may be at great depth. I am going down now and Johnnie Ebanks, my spotter, will stay on the boat." There is more give and take on the radio, and it is clear that help will be coming quickly.

Ebanks secures the mooring while the Captain dons scuba gear with the speed of a professional. A minute later he is in the water, heading toward the wall. As he reaches the wall's edge he sees his dive master coming up, alone. They rendezvous on the sandy bottom. She takes out her dive slate and writes: "Disapp. @ 200 ft & still sinking." The message is sufficient and final.

Charlene must remain under water for several more minutes to decompress. The captain returns to his boat.

Ten minutes later Charlene surfaces and climbs aboard. The pressure marks from her face mask frame sad eyes, not filled with tears but with a mixture of terror and anger. There is no worse tragedy for a professional in the scuba business than losing a diver. Her first words are to the victim's buddy, Jonathan Archer.

"What happened?" Her tone is accusatory.

"I don't know," he cries. He, too, is scared. It is not like some friend is lost in the woods, or in a cave, or on a boat at sea; in those situations, there is always hope. People lost for days or weeks in those circumstances can survive. But underwater you have only minutes because *you run out of air*. Now his girlfriend is lost at the bottom of the ocean, from which there can be no return.

Archer offers no explanation. He is intimidated by the diver master's glare, by the silence of everyone about him, indeed by the silence of the sea itself. There is nothing to intrude on his answer. He mumbles something about looking at the moray eel, of not knowing his girlfriend was sinking, of everything happening so fast. The dive master realizes further questioning will lead nowhere, at least not now. She confers with the boat captain and spotter at the front of the boat. Then she takes to the radio and speaks with the shop manager. The shop is located at the dock, from where the rescue boat *Turtle Cove* has just left, about three miles away. Dive master and captain are told to stay put, help is coming.

The dive master is too upset to query the other divers, who are getting out of wet suits and putting their gear away. The captain speaks to them. We have lost a diver, he says. We have another boat coming to look for her. I am sorry but I cannot take you back just yet. We will need to stay here awhile. He does not say so outright, but everyone knows she is dead or soon will be, and there is no hope.

The divers have many questions but also don't want to make things worse by interrogating Archer. They want to know if his girlfriend was sick, if she had any history of seizures or asthma, medical problems that have felled other divers under water. They want to ask if he knew she was falling away; after all, buddies are supposed to keep track of each other under water. They want to ask him, quite simply, what happened? But they ask nothing. There is silence, except for the sound of gentle wavelets slapping against the boat's hull. For all aboard *Coral Cruiser*, on this gloriously sunny day, a beautiful dive has turned into a nightmare.

A few minutes later the *Turtle Cove* arrives and pulls up beside *Coral Cruiser*, close enough for Charlene to climb aboard. She confers with two male rescue divers on the second boat, each of whom has dual air tanks strapped on. They are planning a quick search. She knows it will be fruitless but is thankful for their assistance. Having just left the water at great depth, she cannot go back down the wall, but she can go to a shallower area and point out where the sinking took place.

The three divers jump in. Charlene stays at cliff's edge (forty-five feet depth) while the other two go deeper. They reach a depth of about 150 feet and can see another 100 feet further down; no scuba tank, no human form is visible below them. They cannot go deeper without risking the bends. Having reached this depth they must now ascend, but because they went so deep they have to hover twenty feet below the surface for several minutes; this will allow excess nitrogen to bubble off safely. Meanwhile, Charlene returns to her boat, which waits until the rescue divers surface and get back on board their boat. Together, *Coral Cruiser* and *Turtle Cove* return to the dock. The search is over.

Chapter 2

Day One of Civil Trial in Cleveland, 14 Months Later

The first order of business on this Monday morning - before the trial begins, before potential jurors are questioned – are three defense motions for dismissal. Knowlton. vs. Ocean Realm International, et. al., is a civil case, for monetary compensation only. The plaintiffs are Mr. and Mrs. Knowlton. The complaint is wrongful death of their twenty-year-old daughter due to "reckless negligence." Since there is no criminal charge there is no official interest by the state. The parents seek a monetary award, plus the kind of release that can only come with a guilty verdict against someone – even if a faceless corporation – who might be responsible.

To get to Judge Mabel Whittaker's Cleveland courtroom the case has taken the usual circuitous route such cases often travel, only perhaps a bit more so, since Jennie died in the waters off Grand Cayman Island, an independent country of British ancestry 500 miles south of Miami. Considering the large volume of discovery since Jennie Knowlton's death – investigations, interviews, pre-trial hearings, depositions, even an on-site visit to the underwater wall where she disappeared – it seems unlikely any of the dismissal motions will prevail. By the day of trial it is palpably apparent to those involved that inertia favors getting on with the case already.

In truth, defense does not expect any dismissal motion to prevail just now, but the motions will be entered nonetheless, as a basis for later appeal (if necessary). The defense's tone is the assumptive 'your- honor-you-must-dismiss-this-case-it-is-without-merit' style peculiar to lawyers. (It doesn't hurt trying. The defense always hopes a cogent point will catch a sympathetic judge's fancy and result in a quick "motion granted, case dismissed.")

The three defense arguments are not without merit, and in various incantations have been invoked in cases of similar stripe. Speaking for the defense team is lead council Lane Kirkland, a thin man with the body of a long-distance runner, in his late 40s and showing his age mainly by some frontal balding. He stands before the judge to offer his motions.

"Your honor, we request dismissal of this case on the grounds that there is no body. Plaintiff has produced no physical evidence that one Jennie Knowlton is in fact dead, other than hearsay from people working in a foreign country. Young people disappear all the time, only to appear months or years later. It is entirely possible that Miss Knowlton did not die in Grand Cayman, that what happened is some sort of prank, and that she is alive. Whatever happened to her, your honor, there can be no charge of negligence against our client without proof of demise, and to have that proof we need the body. We demand dismissal on this ground, and cite the appellate decision in Johnson vs. Dolphin Yacht Charters, Appeal from the United States Court for the Western District of Pennsylvania (Civil No. 94-4321), to wit:

... Since no body was produced, and while the possibility exists that the alleged deceased was eaten by sharks, the lack of any physical evidence for subject's demise argues strongly against granting plaintiff's claim of death by negligence. We therefore uphold the lower court decision...

Whereupon Mr. Kirkland hands the judge a neat sheaf of papers, which encompass the cited decision.

Plaintiff's lead attorney Chester Pearson, senior partner in the small Cleveland personal injury firm Pearson, McDermott and McFall, stands to speak. He is tall, fiftyish, well-coifed. Like his counterpart, he is dressed in suit and tie.

"Your honor, this is a bogus defense request and an insult to the Knowlton family. Their daughter Jennie has been certified deceased by the appropriate authorities of the Cayman Islands and we have the death certificate, which will be entered into evidence. She died on July 15, 2014. Moreover, your honor, evidence for this death can in no way be called "hearsay," We have eyewitnesses to the exact circumstances that led to her death, and these eyewitnesses include both employees of the company and U.S. citizens vacationing on the island. The circumstances are such that her body can never be produced, at least not within the constraints of technology and resources available to the Cayman government.

"Furthermore, your honor, the case of Johnson vs. Dolphin World was entirely different from the one before the court today. In that case a man fell overboard on a yacht in the Caribbean Sea, and there were no eyewitnesses. The man's insurer refused to pay the death claim because no death certificate was issued. His wife sued the yacht company and lost because she could not prove he was dead, and there was at least some circumstantial evidence he was not. In fact, your honor, it was reported in the newspapers shortly after the appellate decision that he was alive, and that the death had been faked.

"In our case, your honor," Pearson continued, "there is no life insurance claim *and* we have eyewitnesses to the tragic event. We know where Jennie's body is, but it is unfortunately not recoverable. To dismiss our claim on the grounds cited by defense would be a gross injustice, your honor, and deny due process to the aggrieved parents." Whereupon Mr. Pearson also hands the judge some papers, including the cited death certificate.

Judge Whittaker is in her mid-forties, short, brunette. Her trademark is out-of-fashion thick-framed glasses. Her reputation is good: competent *and* efficient, paired attributes not found in all of her colleagues. She has before her two experienced lawyers in the field of wrongful-death civil litigation, which for her is a pleasure. Like all judges, she has suffered incompetent or ill-prepared attorneys, and knows this will not be one of those occasions.

Judge Whittaker disdains the poker-face countenance adopted by some of her male colleagues. Instead, she listens with emotion, raising her eyebrows when something sounds startling, out of order, or ridiculously exaggerated. Her eyebrows raise more with defense than with plaintiff arguments. Hardly does Pearson say "aggrieved parents" then judge Whittaker responds.

"There seems to be sufficient evidence that Miss Knowlton did in fact die on the date and in the manner indicated. If any evidence to the contrary surfaces during the trial, the court will take it into consideration. Therefore, defense motion is denied."

Kirkland is unfazed and prepares for another motion. For effect, he pauses about fifteen seconds, straightens his tie and shuffles some papers at the table, then approaches the bench. "Your honor, we have a second motion for dismissal. This alleged disappearance took place in a foreign country, Cayman Islands, and must be tried there under British authority, not in the U.S." (Not that defense counsel really wants to try the case in Grand Cayman, but granting this motion would make it far more difficult for plaintiffs to mount their case; they would have to hire new lawyers and pay them by the hour, regardless of the verdict. British law does not have a U.S.-style contingency fee system.)

"Your honor," Pearson interjects, "Miss Knowlton died while she was a guest of Ocean Realm International, a United States-chartered company indeed while scuba diving with the very dive shop they operate upon their premises." Pearson then hands the judge a pile of credit card receipts Jennie and her boyfriend generated over the three vacation days before her demise, including ones for the hotel and the scuba diving trips.

Kirkland retorts: "Your honor, we don't dispute that Jennie and her boyfriend were guests at the resort, or that they dove with an operation run by the company. Those facts, however, are beside the point, which is that this court has no jurisdiction over the alleged incident. Notwithstanding the alleged disappearance, British and U.S. admiralty law – established over two centuries – has clearly upheld the sovereignty of each nation to try the cases that originate in either waters, irrespective of the citizenship of the people involved. To demonstrate this point I will cite the appellate case of Cockroy vs. Regency Cruise Lines, which also involves a diving incident in Grand Cayman Island. The decision was handed down by the Southern District of New York, in 1995. Since the case went no further, the decision stands. If I may, your honor, I would like to read the most cogent paragraphs into the court record."

He hands her the decision, which she scans.

"How much do you plan to read?"

"Just the part I've outlined in yellow. Two minutes, tops."

"Proceed."

Kirkland begins reading. Judge Whittaker follows him along in her copy.

The lower court determined that Cockroy was entitled to damages of $300,000 for neurologic impairment following

a scuba diving accident, which occurred while he was on a day excursion from a Regency-operated cruise ship. Regency arranged for the scuba diving, and Cockroy had charged the activity to his cruise ship bill. Notwithstanding that Cockroy is a U.S. citizen and Regency Cruise Lines is a U.S.-based corporation, the dive shop is a registered Cayman Islands business, one that contracts with dozens of cruise ships. To absolve the dive shop of any negligence and to burden the cruise line with all liability - when it functioned merely as a middle man in this activity - is to ignore the culpable business...It has been claimed that the plaintiff would be unfairly inconvenienced by trial in Grand Cayman, but appropriateness and inconvenience are two unrelated matters. Discounting any claim of inconvenience, it is not clear why a forum in Grand Cayman would be inappropriate. No credible evidence has been presented that Grand Cayman would not entertain such a suit against the local dive shop or that there are other barriers to hearing the suit in that jurisdiction. Since plaintiff bears the burden of proof on this issue, we find in favor of the appeal...we agree with the defense argument that the proper venue for this trial is in George Town, Grand Cayman Island, not in Denver [Cockroy's home town]. We therefore reverse the lower court decision and remand the case to its proper venue.

Kirkland looks up, a signal he is finished reading. "Now your honor, before Mr. Pearson objects, let me add that we don't want to deny the Knowlton family their day in court. But the hotel that Jennie and her boyfriend stayed in is in fact a registered Cayman Island business, one that pays taxes to the Cayman government. Irrespective of its association with the parent organization here in the U.S., this 1995 appellate decision clearly states that the proper venue for this claim is back in the Caymans, not in the U.S."

"Your honor!" Pearson rises, prepared for rebuttal.

"Just a minute," the judge says. "Mr. Kirkland, are you finished with this part of your motion?"

"Yes, your honor."

"OK, Mr. Pearson, you may continue."

"Your honor, Mr. Kirkland is mixing apples with cumquats. The 1995 decision he quotes dealt with a diving outfit in no way controlled by Regency Cruise Lines. There was an arm's length business arrangement whereby Regency collected the money and kept a percentage as a booking fee. In the Knowlton case both the hotel and the dive shop were and are owned by the same corporation. The fact that Ocean Realm's operation on Grand Cayman pays taxes to the Cayman government is immaterial. It does not affect ownership and it does not affect culpability, your honor."

"I beg to differ" replies Kirkland, who is now on his feet as well. "Ownership is *not* the reason the appellate court overturned the lower decision in Cockroy. The reason is *location*. The accident took place in Grand Cayman, and the court recognized this fact. That's why the trial was remanded to the Cayman Islands, not because of ownership, your honor."

Judge Whittaker is mindful that the record is being set up for possible appeal, and wants to review the Cockroy case in more detail before making a decision. "The court will take a ten-minute recess," she says, "while I have time to go over this decision." She retires to her chambers.

Fifteen minutes later she returns. It seems that the year-long period of discovery, the legal legwork that has occurred to this point, the anticipation of all participants – and perhaps judge Whittaker's own curiosity – have created a momentum to push this case forward.

"I must disagree with defense in this instance," she begins. "The appellate decision makes specific mention of the fact that Regency Cruise Lines and Jeff's Dive Shoppes [the outfit Cockroy dove with] were separate companies, with different insurers and different governing boards. In the case before this court today, the parent company and the Cayman subsidiary have the same insurer and the same governing board. It is the opinion of this court that U.S. jurisdiction is proper and established. Motion denied."

Only about an hour has passed so far. The audience – Jennie's parents and relatives, an executive from Ocean Realm, a newspaper reporter who will write about the case, plus bailiff and court stenographer – are perhaps a little bored and want the main event to begin already. But there is one more motion to present, to at least get established on the record.

"Your honor," Kirkland begins. "If in fact Jennie is deceased, the evidence is overwhelming that she died an accidental death, and that there are no culpable parties. There can be no wrongful death claim in an accidental situation involving scuba diving, your honor. Scuba is an inherently risky sport, more so than laying on the beach or snorkeling. Furthermore, she signed a waiver for all accidents, acknowledging the risks involved, and I have a copy of it here." He places the waiver before the judge. "I will quote, from the bottom paragraph:"

I agree to hold harmless Ocean Realm International and all its subsidiaries for any accident that may befall me. I understand that scuba diving is inherently risky, and that I may be subject to the bends, to running out of air, or to drowning. This release shall inure to my relatives, to my heirs, and to any relation that may make claim on my behalf for said accident. [Signed, Jennie Knowlton, 7/13/2014].

Looking up at the Judge, Kirkland finishes: "We therefore request that this case be dismissed on grounds that there is not a shred of evidence for negligence, that Jennie willfully undertook a risky sport, and in fact signed a waiver acknowledging the risks involved."

Jennie's mother sobs from the back of the room. She is consoled by Mr. Knowlton. Both are in their late 40s, and for the trial are dressed in grey and black. You could not know anything about this trial but would be able to pick them out as a couple who have suffered some kind of horrible loss.

"Order, please," from Judge Whittaker. She is gentle, recognizing the emotive power of Kirkland's statements. The crying is muted and Kirkland continues.

"Your honor, we also submit before the court the coroner's assessment from George Town, Grand Cayman. I will quote briefly from this document:"

George Town, Grand Cayman, July 18, 2014. It is therefore the finding of this hearing officer that on July 16, 2014, Jennie Knowlton, 20, residing at — St., Shaker Heights, Ohio, USA, did drown while scuba diving under the auspices of Ocean Realm International Corp., subsidiary Ocean Realm Scuba on 7-Mile Beach, Grand Cayman, BWI. Interviews with Charlene Marvich [dive master], Timothy Jenkins [rescue diver], William Bly [rescue diver],

Tilade Greene [boat captain], Johnnie Ebanks [boat spotter], Jonathan Archer [boyfriend of Jennie], Mae Jayne Smith, Darwin Williams and Debbie Schwartz [vacationing divers on Jennie's boat] indicate and corroborate the circumstances of her death. We rule her death was accidental.

Pearson rises abruptly. "Your honor, this is disgraceful, and I apologize for Mr. Kirkland's gracelessness before the Knowlton family. The girl is deceased, and to imply that her signature on a pro forma waiver absolves the company of negligence is an insult. Obviously her death was an accident. We are not here to press criminal charges, and he is well aware of that fact. We are here to prove negligence, your honor. Mr. Kirkland is here to defend that charge. That's what the case is about. To dismiss because it was an accident is to deny due process."

"Then what is the meaning of a waiver such as the girl signed?" asks Judge Whittaker. For the first time there is a trace of doubt in her voice, as if perhaps Kirkland has a point after all.

"Your honor, that question has been thoroughly explored in numerous cases involving scuba divers, and there are at least two appellate decisions. The basic reason for the waiver is to remove true nuisance suits from litigation; a diver scratches herself, or gets bitten by a shark, or develops the bends – in other words, conditions that may be construed as an inherent part of diving. There is no basis for a lawsuit in those cases. An injured diver knew the risks, took the risks, and there is no negligence. However, in the 1991 case of Kutinsky, et. al. vs. Largo Sea Charters, which took place in Monroe County, Florida, the state appeals court made clear that the waivers didn't apply. In that case a dive boat sunk because of improper maintenance, and two divers were badly injured. They sued and defense claimed that the divers' waiver signatures invalidated the suits. The claimants won in court, and on several appeals the decision was upheld. If I may, I will quote from the Florida State Supreme Court, February 24, 1995."

"Is it brief?"

"Very, your honor, less than a minute."

Pearson places the appellate decision on the Judge's growing pile of papers. She nods approval and he begins reading.

Waivers serve a useful purpose, but in the final analysis each claim must be judged on its merits. The signed waiver for scuba or other sports –including team sports such as baseball and football — is not intended to deny due process. Thus, the purpose of participant waivers is not to absolve businesses and local proprietors of true negligence, but only of accidents for which reasonable preparation could not avoid. In this case, as has been repeatedly pointed out, the boat's maintenance was deficient by both U.S. Coast Guard and Florida state standards, and divers suffered when the boat floundered. The divers in question did not intend their signature to waive such negligence, and the court does not construe such. We affirm the lower court decision.

"Furthermore," Pearson continues, now addressing the judge, "if I may continue for a minute, less than an hour ago my esteemed colleague was arguing that the girl was *not* dead, that there was some prank involved. Now he's implying – no, in fact he's stating – that she suffered an accidental *death*. Yes, I believe he did use the "d" word, your honor. Clearly, the only prank in this case is the contradictory argument presented by Mr. Kirkland himself. In any case, your honor, we are fully prepared to make the argument that Jennie would be alive and well today but for the negligence of Ocean Realm personnel. Her signature on a piece of paper cannot be used to absolve Ocean Realm of negligence."

The judge did not hesitate. "I agree, Mr. Pearson. Motion denied."

Kirkland is not dismayed. Each argument is made independently of the others, and can be appealed on its own merits.

"Your honor," Kirkland says, "Mr. Pearson's protestations notwithstanding, let it be stated for the record that an establishment of accidental death with prior signature on a waiver countermands any award for damages or compensation."

"Thank you, Mr. Kirkland. Do you have any other arguments before this court, before we proceed with jury selection?"

"No, your honor."

"We'll take a ten-minute break."

Chapter 3

Day One (continued)

Forget Court TV. Most trials are tedious, often boring. Very few trial decisions lead to any legal precedent, and most are just humdrum affairs of interest only to the lawyers and litigants. Even the criminal trials that excite the public, such as the OJ Simpson case, the Oklahoma City bombing, the Boston Marathon Massacre – are often like turtles at a road crossing; it'll get there, but when?

And civil trials are worse. Their outcome is apt to be nothing more than the exchange or non-exchange of money. Some judges bridle at the use of their courtroom for the attempted transfer of wealth, particularly when the case won't make the newspapers or affect the future of the civilized world; they see their important role in criminal cases. It is routine for judges during a civil case to intersperse non-juried felony decisions, such as drug dealer-sentencing, parole violation or a burglary plea bargain.

Judge Whittaker has several on-going felony cases that require decisions and she will insinuate them into Knowlton vs. Ocean Realm whenever possible. Anyone in the courtroom may watch these proceedings, which usually take place right before or after a break.

With the break over, a parole violator is escorted in by a deputy. The felon is in chains and wearing the orange jump suit of a county prisoner. With his court-appointed lawyer beside him, Judge Whittaker admonishes him for violating parole (he was arrested for possession of an unlicensed weapon). His lawyer mentions "extenuating circumstances that have been presented before this court." There is some given and take, and the prisoner is sentenced to one year in jail. The deputy escorts him away.

Again without announcement, another felon is brought in, similarly shackled and clothed. He is a convicted drug dealer, who comes before the judge with his private attorney. He has pleaded guilty and his lawyer asks for mercy from the court. The judge reminds the attorney that his client has a previous drug-related conviction (for possession) and sentences him to two years in prison. Two people in the gallery, who entered just before the sentencing, wince but say nothing. The prisoner is led away.

Judge Whittaker apologizes to Pearson and Kirkland for the delay, and asks her bailiff to call in the jury pool. Twenty people are marched in, all randomly selected from voting records. They are seated in the jury box, ready for questioning by the two attorneys.

* * *

Lawyers for each side have three dismissals of potential jurors, and each side uses all three. Defense dismisses one potential juror because, on questioning, he admits to having once sued a neighbor. The neighbor ran over the would-be juror's dog, which was unleashed and laying on the neighbor's driveway. In other words, hyper-litigious. Defense also dismisses a woman who lost an 18-year-old daughter to a rare disease. Best not to chance seating an overly sympathetic juror.

Plaintiff's counsel dismisses a female nurse who seems perhaps a bit too opinionated about medically-related issues. Just a hunch, of course, but she's gone. He also dismisses a man who is vice-president of a small manufacturing company. The man is clearly is not happy about being selected for jury duty, and comes across as anti- anything that interferes with business and making money.

And so it goes. Selecting jurors is often intuitive, and the lawyers intuit as best they can. When jury selection is over a panel of ten people is seated, eight jurors and two alternates. They are evenly divided at five men and five women, with ages ranging from twenty-seven to sixty-eight. Only two have ever engaged in scuba diving, and only one has been under water within the past three years.

* * *

In trials plaintiffs must make their case first, and then defense can cross examine plaintiff's witnesses. Then defense calls its experts, who can be cross-examined by plaintiff's attorney. It's a formula for which there are many variations.

Judge Whittaker's courtroom is located in the Old Cuyahoga County Courthouse, an early 20th century (1905-1912) Beaux-Arts design across the street from the raw, vertical "Justice Center Complex" built to replace it. The old courthouse features an ornate, columned facade that pleases the eye, unlike its ugly modern neighbor which shows only a monotony of windows separated by bland concrete.

The differences are more striking inside the two buildings. The old structure's grand lobby, with its gently sloping central staircase, contrasts with the Justice Center's sterile sharp-angled interior. Ceilings in the old building's courtrooms are twenty feet high, and where ceiling meets wall are carved moldings of deep chestnut. The grandeur is somewhat faded after a century of wear, but ask any lawyer or judge – they usually prefer the Old Courthouse to the lifeless rooms across the street.

Judge Whittaker's bench – a raised dais – is at the back of the courtroom from the main entrance. To its immediate left is the witness chair, and to its left and in front is the jury box. The box holds twenty seats, but only ten are occupied for this trial. Opposite the jury, on the judge's right hand side, sits the court reporter with her stenography machine, anachronistic in the 21st century but still widely used. Toward the front of the room are two long tables, side by side. At one of the tables sit defense attorneys (Kirkland and an associate) and at the other table, Plaintiff's attorneys (Pearson and an associate). The Knowltons were invited to sit at Pearson's table, but they declined, preferring to watch proceedings from the back of the courtroom, in the visitor gallery. Also in the gallery are Jennie's older sister; a *Cleveland Plain Dealer* reporter; a representative of Ocean Realm International; and two or three strangers, people who are in some way connected with the litigants.

Also in the room are two big easels containing removable posters. On one of the easels is a large head-and-shoulder studio picture of Jennie Knowlton, in color and unframed. It will remain throughout the trial, a constant reminder of the deceased. On the other easel are a stack of poster-sized drawings. The front poster is a professional line drawing of a female scuba diver dressed with all her equipment.

The first plaintiff's expert is Giles Morgan, a dive instructor with Scuba Unlimited of Miami, Florida. Of medium build, with a slight paunch, he wears a deep purple shirt and light grey sport coat with yellow tie and checkered cotton pants, a jarring selection. But he is dressed neatly, and the style is interesting.

Morgan takes his seat, swears an oath to tell the truth, and Pearson begins his interrogation.

"Please state your full name and where you live, and your age."

"Giles Girard Morgan, Miami, Florida. I am thirty-eight."

"And your occupation, Mr. Morgan?"

"I'm a master scuba instructor."

"Will you please tell the jury what that means, master scuba instructor?"

"Yes. I am qualified to teach scuba diving at the entry level, which is for people who have never dived before. And I am also qualified to teach advanced diving courses, to people who want to become professionals in the field."

"Does that mean you teach the teachers?"

"Yes, you could put it that way. I teach the people who will certainly become the teachers."

"So if I have never been scuba diving before, and want to learn, I could come to you for lessons?"

"Yes. Well, actually you would come to our scuba shop, and I or one of a dozen other people could give you the standard scuba entry course. We call it the basic certification course."

"I see. And if I already know how to dive, but I want to become a scuba teacher, a professional in the field, you could teach me?"

"Yes, but again, there is a standard instructor course, and I am one of several who would be involved."

"But there is a difference between, let's say, an ordinary scuba instructor, and one who teaches the teachers?"

"Yes, there are perhaps 20,000 regular scuba instructors in the country, but only about 350 master scuba instructors."

"Mr. Morgan, how long have you been a scuba diving instructor?"

"Fifteen years."

"And how many dives have you yourself made?"

"I estimate about 4,000."

"Is that a lot?"

"Yes, I would say so. A few people I know have done more."

"Well tell me, for the typical recreational diver, someone who just goes on vacation to dive, how many dives do they do?"

"You mean per year?"

"Yes, just to give us an idea."

"I would say the typical recreational scuba diver does maybe ten to twenty dives a year, that is, when they are active divers. Many divers after becoming certified drop out and don't do any diving at all."

"OK, so 4,000 is really a lot of dives. Mr. Morgan, most of our jury has never been scuba diving at all. Could you please explain, briefly, what it means to scuba dive? I believe you have brought a video and some teaching aids for that purpose?"

"Yes, that's correct. Should I show the video first?"

"Yes, that's a good idea. Just please tell the jury what this video is about."

"It's a simple video posted on YouTube, just to show what the scuba diver looks like in terms of equipment, being under water and so forth. It's really just to show the basic activity, for someone who has never dove before."

"And you are the diver in this video?"

"Yes. There's no sound, so I'll narrate. It's just a couple of minutes."

Morgan's laptop is already connected to the court's fifty-inch TV. He presses a few buttons and the video begins, showing Morgan on a dive boat somewhere warm. He speaks to the jury.

"Here I am with all the equipment in place. You can see there's a lot of equipment. A mask and snorkel, some fins, a wet suit..." He points to each item as it is mentioned.

"Now I turn around and you can see the air tank. You can't dive without an air tank. It's heavy on land, but weightless under water. OK...now I'm going to do a back flip into the water. You can't see the video guy, but he's right there with me, and will follow me under water.

"OK, now I'm under water. I will descend to the bottom, which is about thirty feet. At that depth there's still plenty of sunlight. You feel weightless under water. OK, I have reached near the bottom but won't touch it. Notice I am floating. That's one of the pleasures of scuba diving. I can easily hover over the surface, glide around the coral you see there, and take in the underwater beauty. I am careful not to touch any coral, as it's all alive. So here I am with arms folded, not moving my legs, and lying motionless just a few feet off the bottom. This means

I am neutrally buoyant. Now I'm going to take a deep breath, which inflates my lungs with air and allows me to rise a few feet. There. Now I'm going to exhale and fall back down. So when I am neutrally buoyant, I can control my ascent and descent just with breathing."

The video hits the spot with the jurors, who seem to appreciate the underwater scenery, a break from the sterile courtroom environment.

"I could stay down a long time, almost an hour at this depth, but will now drift back up to the boat. OK, here I am back on the boat's ladder. Out of water the tank feels very heavy and I will take it off as soon as I get back on deck. So that's a very brief, shallow scuba dive. Typically, divers go down for half hour to an hour, and usually deeper than I went. But this is just to show you what it is."

"Thank you," says Pearson. "That was short and helpful. Now if you would, please go the posters. And please bring the easel closer to the jury, so it's easier to see. Is that OK, your honor?"

The judge nods yes, and Mr. Morgan walks to the easel, moves it closer to jury box, angled so the judge can see as well. Morgan's style and rhythm show he is a good teacher, someone comfortable with his subject. He takes out a pocket pointer.

"This drawing of a scuba diver looks like she's carrying a lot of equipment, but it's all essential, and when you get used to using it, it's not really a problem. First, to go under water and be able to breathe, you need to carry your own tank of air, as I just showed on the video." He points to the tank on the diver's back.

It's heavy on land but is weightless under the water. Then you need a way to get the air to your lungs, so we have a hose connected to a mouthpiece," and he points to this apparatus.

"There is some more equipment you need," he continues. "To swim under water you need fins on your feet. To help regulate buoyancy under water you wear an inflatable vest, one that can be inflated or deflated with two simple buttons that the diver controls. One lets air in and the other lets air out. We call this vest a buoyancy compensator or BC for short.

"To keep warm in the water you may need a wet suit that covers most of the body. Finally, to be able to see underwater you need a face mask that covers your eyes and nose as you see here. With this equipment, anyone with healthy heart or lungs can go under water and breathe comfortably for a half hour to an hour, depending on how deep you go."

"Mr. Morgan, what keeps the diver from sinking once she gets into the water?" Pearson has never scuba dived and this question sounds logical to him. But mainly he wants to tell the jury how a diver controls depth under water, and this question is Morgan's lead-in.

In our legal system jury members cannot ask questions. While this could conceivably be cumbersome if uncontrolled, written jury questions funneled through the judge would help facilitate understanding of unfamiliar topics. Instead, jurors have to rely on the lawyer's questions to make sure the expert's explanation is adequate. Jurors are often frustrated because a simple but important question goes unanswered, despite the expert's best intentions.

"Actually you want to sink. In fact, I neglected to mention the lead weights that every diver wears on a belt. You see two weights in this drawing, attached to her belt. For balance there should be two on the other side as well. They could be one to four pounds each, though most divers in warm water would probably use no more than twelve pounds total. The weights allow her to sink below the surface. So these lead weights typically add up to anywhere from four to twelve pounds, and are worn as shown in a belt around the waist. Without these weights, you would actually be stuck on the surface; it would be almost impossible to go down and stay down wearing all this equipment."

"Why is that?"

"The reason is because the wet suit and BC vest make you float; they have a lot of buoyancy. So by using lead weights, when you first jump in the water, if there is no air in your vest, you can easily control your buoyancy, and if you want to dive all you have to do is empty your lungs and you'll sink. That's called being neutrally buoyant. Then, if you sink too much, or go deeper than you want to go, you can simply kick yourself up or, in some circumstances, put some air in your vest – that will make you rise up a little. All this is actually something we teach divers, and they learn how to control their buoyancy over time."

"Just so the jury understands, buoyancy means what?"

"It just means whether you tend to rise or fall in the water. Some people naturally sink when they try to float in a pool, so they are negatively buoyant. Other people naturally float in a pool, so they are positively buoyant. The same thing holds under water. And under water, if you stay at a certain depth without going up or down, we say you are neutrally buoyant."

"So during a dive, you are neutrally buoyant?"

"Well, that's the ideal, but it's hard to achieve. You sort of want to be close to neutrally buoyant, but that takes some experience. Most novice divers tend to have problems with buoyancy, and they are negatively buoyant at the start of the dive and then when they use up their tank air, positively buoyant at the end."

"I see," says Pearson. "Well, would being negatively buoyant make a diver sink further than she is supposed to go?"

"Yes, but again, that's easy to control. When you see yourself falling, all you have to do is kick yourself up, or in some cases add a little air to your BC vest, and you will stop falling."

"Well, then, what could make a diver fall much lower than she is supposed to?"

"Lots of things could. First of all, if you don't check your depth gauge, you can go deeper than you intended and not even know it. It's difficult to know how deep you really are at any one time because there is no visual frame of reference; you can't tell by looking up at the surface or at anything around you. There are no street signs, as it were. For this reason all divers carry a depth gauge to tell them how deep they are at any instant. If you ignore the gauge it is easy to go deeper than you intended.

"Second, you could have an accident, like a heart attack, and simply lose control of yourself. In that circumstance you are likely to sink and drown."

"Mr. Morgan, would you expect a heart attack in a twenty-year-old woman?"

"Objection," your honor," Kirkland interrupts. "Mr. Pearson is leading the witness. And the witness is not a medical expert."

"Overruled. Continued."

"I'll ask it again, Mr. Morgan. Would you expect a heart attack in a twenty-year-old woman?"

"Well, no, I wouldn't. I've never seen that or read about it. I would think someone would be in their forties or fifties, at least, to have a heart attack while diving."

"OK, what else would cause someone to sink?"

"Well they could get an air embolus."

"What's that?"

"It's like a clot in the blood system, but it's really a giant air bubble. It can go to your brain and cause a stroke or make you lose control."

"Is that common?"

"Common? No, it is uncommon, but it's one of the things that can happen."

"What else?"

"Well, they could simply become confused from nitrogen narcosis."

"I'm sorry, Mr. Morgan, could you spell that for us. Maybe you should write it on the poster." This has all been rehearsed, of course, but for the jury it is made to look spontaneous. Morgan writes 'NITROGEN NARCOSIS' on the poster, just above the scuba diver's head.

"What is that?"

"Nitrogen narcosis is a condition that comes from too much nitrogen in the blood and it can make you lose concern about what you are doing. We increase our nitrogen levels as we dive; the deeper we go the more nitrogen accumulates in our blood. This extra nitrogen can affect the body's central nervous system, the brain and spinal cord. Some people liken it to being inebriated, and call it the "martini effect." Sort of like having two or three martinis and then acting foolishly because you're not in control."

"So it's like being drunk?"

"Yes, that's really the best analogy. One diver suffering the martini effect might take his mouthpiece out and do a somersault, and next thing you know he drowns."

"But doesn't everyone who dives have a high nitrogen level?"

"Yes, it comes from breathing in air at greater than normal pressures. But nitrogen narcosis only occurs after certain depths are reached, and only to certain people."

"Well, how common is this nitrogen narcosis?"

"It's quite common actually. Lots of people report getting a little confused or addled at depth, but when they ascend the feeling goes away completely. That's the nice thing about nitrogen narcosis; it is cured by ascending."

"So would you say it happens half the time, or a quarter of the time?"

"Well, nitrogen narcosis is uncommon to non-existent on shallow dives. Probably never occurs at a depth of fifty feet or less. You begin to see it in some people at seventy-eighty feet, and it becomes really noticeable beyond one hundred feet."

"If someone was diving to eighty feet, then, and all of a sudden that person kept going deeper, could that be a nitrogen narcosis effect?"

Kirkland rose to object. "Objection, Your Honor. The witness has no basis for answering that question."

"Overruled. You may continue, counselor." The judge is listening intently. The witness is credible and – something often rare in the courtroom – he can nicely explain things to lay people.

"Well, yes. That certainly could be an explanation."

"Would that be the most likely explanation?"

"Well, it depends on the circumstances."

"Mr. Morgan. You have been called as an expert witness in this case, and as an expert, have you had a chance to review the records on Ms. Knowlton, specifically the records relating to her diving death on July 15, 2014?"

"Yes, I have."

"Have you reviewed the newspaper accounts?"

"Yes, I have."

"Have you reviewed the Cayman Island Coroner's report and the death certificate?"

"Yes."

"And have you reviewed the deposition transcripts taken of the people who dove with her that day, plus the depositions of Dr. Bergofsky and Dr. Martin?"

"Yes, I have."

"Having reviewed all this material, do you have an opinion with reasonable certainty, as to the likely, the most probable cause of her death?"

"Yes, I do."

Kirkland stood up, animated. "Objection, your Honor. Witness is not qualified to opine on the cause of death in this case. He was not on the scene, he was never asked to formally investigate, he has filed no medical report and, I might add, we already have a formal coroner's report. I move that last question be stricken."

"Your honor," replies Pearson in an even tone. "My witness has every right to an opinion. That's all I am asking him for. I am not asking him to file a formal report for the Cayman authorities, to alter the death certificate, or to create events that didn't occur. I am only asking him for his opinion. We are all entitled to our opinions. Mr. Morgan is an acknowledged expert in the field of scuba diving, and this court is legally entitled to hear his opinion of how Ms. Knowlton died."

"Overruled."

"Thank you. Now Mr. Morgan, what is your expert opinion as to just how Ms. Knowlton died on July 15, 2014?"

Morgan again turns to speak directly at the jury, just as he was coached to do for this question. But he is a professional and really doesn't need coaching.

"In my opinion she developed nitrogen narcosis at depth, and so became slightly confused, at least to the point that she did not check her depth gauge. If I can show this second poster," and he removes the first one to reveal a cross-sectional drawing showing a diver at various depths. There is suddenly a little tittering in the audience. Morgan turns around and sees people staring at the jury. Actually at just one juror, a man who is fast asleep, snoring.

"We'll take a ten-minute minute break," says the judge.

***

The Wall is available in as an ebook:
https://books2read.com/u/bPRYGr

Consenting Adults Only

Available in paperback and as ebook:
https://books2read.com/u/m2rO2G

The novel's protagonist is Las Vegas Emergency Medicine physician Dr. Joshua Luvkin, a nice, upstanding guy from the Midwest – with a few problems.

He falls in love with nurse Barbara Wilson, which leads to his breaking up with girlfriend Dr. Judy Berkowitz, also an emergency medicine physician. Barbara moves in. Judy shows up. What ensues is remindful of *Fatal Attraction*.

He meets Jack Strawn, an obese guy who enters quickie weight reduction contests, aka The Biggest Loser, but via a bathroom break and not from dieting. This somehow leads to his investment in a Las Vegas cable porn show...and more publicity than he ever wanted.

He is sued for malpractice, as if he didn't have enough trouble already. Will he settle? Go to trial?

Chapter 1

Believe me, I was not looking for a career change when Jack Strawn came to my Emergency Department. It just happened that way. You could say I was primed for it, by an unconscious desire to do something different than medicine, but that would be untrue. If Strawn had not shown up, I would have stayed happy in my job as a sin-city ED physician. After all, I was saving lives and making a good living. Not even a malpractice lawsuit hanging over my head marred my contentment. I even envisioned retiring in my early 50's.

Strawn, age thirty-eight, weighed 394 lbs. and stood 5'9". Super-morbidly obese, BMI of 58. Like others of this body habitus, he showed no neck, a massively protruding abdomen and large ankles with some brawny edema. He came to us around midnight, complaining of a "gout attack." I remember him as very personable, just in a lot of pain from his right big toe.

Las Vegas Memorial Hospital's Emergency Department is a busy place, with two doctors, two physician-assistants and a dozen nurses every shift. We are just off the Strip -- Las Vegas Blvd. -- and our 600 hospital beds and large array of specialists make us the go-to place for local trauma, most Strip ambulance runs and dozens of "walk-ins" daily.

The month was October and I was on the night shift. As you have no doubt heard, "Vegas never sleeps," which means Memorial's ED doesn't slow down much at night. Jack Strawn had a day job as manager of a small apartment building in Summerlin, but other interests brought him to our area at night.

"Let me see that toe."

Strawn sat in a big-boy wheel chair, one of several reserved for the largest patients. He extended his right foot. The toe was twice as large as normal, with some redness below the nail. I touched it lightly and he winced.

"Sorry about that." I turned to the nurse who took his vital signs and chief complaint. Barbara Wilson had been working at Memorial only a few weeks; this was our third shift together. Of medium height, about 130 lbs., she had a pretty face unadorned with very little makeup and nice medium-length wavy brown hair. I remember thinking when I first saw her:

lovely girl, nice body. After the second shift together, what I really wanted to do was get in bed with Barbara.

All heterosexual men fantasize when they meet a pretty woman, but I thought my fantasy had real possibility. I am only a few years older, in the same profession, and from a good family. Of course being a physician was a big plus. I had not yet asked her out but was getting close. I was hesitant in part because I had a girlfriend of sorts at the time, though she lived in Los Angeles and our relationship was intermittent and probably ending soon. I did not have a girlfriend in Las Vegas and felt a bit lonely.

That Barbara would be *this* patient's nurse on *this* night made me an instant convert to astrology, or whatever those alignments mean when things just happen to come together. *You will meet an unusual person who will facilitate a new love life.*

"Do you have his vital signs?"

Barbara handed me his clipboard and said in a sweet, submissive tone, "Yes, Dr. Luvkin, here they are." She had recently graduated nursing school and was still deferential to doctors. A more experienced nurse would say "Yep, here you go," hand me the clipboard and bop out of the exam room, with "call me if you need anything." But Barbara stood there, in a way I imagine nurses stood by fifty years ago, waiting for the doctor's orders. Lucky for me, since she got to hear my patient's story.

From his brief medical history I learned Mr. Strawn had suffered with gout for about two years, and had "always been heavy because I eat a lot." He was raised in Atlanta and spoke with a southern drawl. He came to us at midnight because "I was in the area and the pain felt real bad." He had run out of his medicine three days earlier and "was too busy to get it renewed."

I ordered some blood tests. "We'll treat it with colchicine," I said, and Barbara quickly retrieved the tablets from a nearby drug cart. She gave him one to swallow, and three more to use until he could get his prescription filled.

I always try to help out my patients with their lifestyle and so asked, "What are you doing about the weight?"

"What do you mean?" Strawn replied.

"It's obviously not healthy. You're only thirty-eight. Quite honestly, you might not make it to fifty with this weight. Have you ever considered bariatric surgery?"

"No, maybe later. I guess I have a few years to go. Hard to lose weight when you eat ten pounds of food a day."

"Wow, that's a lot." I thought of those times when I heard how many pounds of food a bear or elephant eats in a day. I don't remember the numbers, only that with big animals it was always at least two digits. I figure a normal-size human might eat maybe two-three pounds of food a day, if that.

"Well, you need to cut down, begin losing some weight," I said. This recommendation is one of medicine's clichés, so often ignored that -- while true -- it is useless. We say it anyway.

"Hard to do right now. Make money from my weight."

"How's that?" Was he in some sort of carnival act with elephants and bears, to see who could eat the most? Or perhaps on a Las Vegas Sumo wrestling team I knew nothing about? I had never heard of someone making 'money from my weight'. His answer would end up affecting my career at Memorial. Considerably.

"Shittin' contest. I'm one of the best. Can't do it without the food."

I winced and looked at Barbara. This caught Strawn's attention.

"Oh, I'm sorry, Miss," he said, "I shouldn't use that word in mixed company."

"No, that's OK," she replied, in a tone to suggest the patient is always right.

"Let's just call it an elimination contest," Strawn offered. "From front and back."

After two years in Memorial's ED I had seen many bizarre things and nothing really surprised me any longer. Most of the bizarreness was from consensual sexual acts with bad outcomes. A man with a dildo up his rectum, placed so far up we could not extract it in the ED; he went to the operating room for removal. A woman whose uterus suffered a rent from over-aggressive oral sex; she also went to the OR.

We have seen metal rings piercing genitals that led to inflammation or outright infections. And several cases of priapism from using erectile dysfunction drugs. There was one case of coprophagia (eating feces) in a psychiatric patient. I have not yet treated a man with severed penis caused by an angry lover, but have seen one lacerated by teeth marks. And once I saw a guy with a penile rash; he had an allergy to the peanut butter his girlfriend applied so she could lick it off. She came with him and when I offered the diagnosis she calmly said, "Jelly next time."

Strawn's answer intrigued me. What the hell did he mean?

"What do you mean?"

"You eat the food and it comes out the other end, right?"

"Got it," I said.

"Well, the more you eat, the more comes out."

"Makes sense to me." I was happy to play along, hoping of course for some light at the end of Jack's story.

"Well, he who eliminates the most wins the pot. And I win more often than not."

Wow! I thought. *That makes sense. This is Vegas. He who craps the most wins the pot.*

"They weigh it?"

"No, they don't weigh it. They weigh *you*. Before and after. Very clean."

"So it really is an elimination contest," I said.

"Right, just like I said. But those of us who compete, we like to use the s- word."

"And at which casino does this wager take place?" I asked.

"Ain't no casino. It's held at Joe's Plumbing Supplies, over on South Decatur."

I was not familiar with Joe's Plumbing, but it sounded like a legitimate business. "You use their bathroom?"

"He laughed. You never been to Joe's?"

"No, afraid not."

"They got *ten* bathrooms. Each contestant gets his own. Real nice. You got twenty minutes to get rid of your stuff, they you get re-weighed. People watch, people bet. I'm surprised you haven't heard of this. How long you been in Vegas, doc?"

"Is this legal?"

"You mean going to the bathroom? They gonna outlaw that too?"

"No, I mean the betting. Is that controlled by the Gaming Commission?"

"Hell, no. If people want to bet, that's their business. We never been raided, if that's what you mean. Say, you want to come watch one of our contests? We get lots of spectators. You don't have to bet, just come to watch."

"Sure." Why not? I asked myself. It should be interesting.

"OK, give me a piece of paper," he said. "I'll write down the address and date. It ain't gonna be posted on the internet."

I handed him the clip board with a piece of blank paper and he wrote down the date, time and address of Joe's Plumbing Supplies. A quick glance showed the next contest would take place just three days later. When finished, Strawn looked at Barbara and said, "You're invited too, Miss. Lots of women come. We watch our language there."

"Thank you." She blushed a little. At least she didn't recoil in disgust, or reject his invitation outright. I figured she was just being polite.

After Jack Strawn left I took out my phone and googled "Las Vegas elimination contests." I got one of those "disambiguation lists," showing links for boxing, golf, stock car racing and wrestling – popular Vegas sports where *contestants* were eliminated, not their bowels. Then I entered "Las Vegas shitting contest" -- 1.2 million results! All but one entry on the first two web pages was about "Vegas contests" of the more traditional variety. Didn't matter. The first one hit the jackpot, a link to Wikipedia. I clicked on it. The entry was brief, with one of those Wikipedia warnings for sketchy entries: "This article needs additional citations for verification. Please help improve this article by adding citations to reliable sources."

Excretion Contests – Las Vegas
From Wikipedia, the free encyclopedia

Contests whereby men, usually overweight or obese, compete with each other in how much body waste they can excrete over a short, preset time period. The contestant who loses the most body weight wins a pot of money. The money is provided by spectators who place bets – on who they think will win, what the amount of weight loss will be, and other metrics determined at the time of the contest.

It is a variation of The Biggest Loser contests popular on television, with the major difference being weight loss is over minutes, not weeks, and comes not from dieting but from bowel elimination.

These contests are known to occur in Las Vegas but have not been confirmed in other cities. Because the betting is not regulated by any agency, and may not conform to all state laws, no website exists that provides the location or date of the contests; communication of this information is usually by word of mouth or email. It is not known when these contests began in Las Vegas.

I caught up with Barbara at the nurse's station. Now I had an easy entry. "Look at this," I said, and showed her the Wikipedia text on my cell phone. To my delight, she didn't push me away but read it. Then she looked up at me and smiled, as if to say 'so what'?

"I think I'll go to his next contest," I said, in a casual sort of way, like 'I think I'll go to the next lecture'. To make my decision seem less voyeuristic, I added "professional curiosity, of course." Then I said, oh so casually, to make it sound like I wasn't really asking for a date, "Want to go with me? He said you're invited too."

She looked directly into my eyes but I could not read her emotion. Was she studying my face to see if she liked it? Or was she deciding how to say no without affecting our professional relationship? My heart raced.

"Yes," she said, "it should be interesting."

Chapter 2

I did some investigation. Turns out Joe's is well known among people in Vegas who shop for plumbing supplies. That meant just about everyone but me. There are three stores in the metro area, and Joe's Plumbing Supplies advertises on TV: "You need it. We got it." The store address Jack provided was three miles west of the hospital on South Decatur, in a strip shopping center. Jack advised arriving before the 10 pm contest time, to get a seat and check out the betting.

The commercial neighborhood could be anywhere USA but for the fact that several stores advertise "Play slots here!" It seemed reassuring that the store fronts were well-lit, and except for the fact that we were looking for a place where they hold elimination contests, nothing seemed out of the ordinary. I did envision getting mugged, with my parents forever commenting: "How could you have been so stupid to go to a plumbing store in the middle of the night? *What* kind of contest?"

"Barbara, are you sure you want to go in?" I asked after we parked.

If she had said no, let's leave, I would have stifled my curiosity and been out of there pronto. But she said, "Sure, we're here, why not?"

We exited the car and walked to Joe's Plumbing. Shades covered the large plate glass windows and a cardboard sign in front said "Store Closed. Private Showing." A heavy guy sat outside in a folding chair, wearing a baseball cap and a flowery, long-sleeved shirt. I wondered if he was one of the contestants.

"What are you looking for?" he asked.

I mumbled something about Jack Strawn inviting us and he opened the door. Pretty informal getting in. It certainly wasn't like the speakeasies of the 1930s, where some guy opens a four x four inch window in a bolted door and asks for a password. I think anyone off the street could have come in. Most likely Joe's door guy just wanted to keep out drunks, kids and anyone who seemed up to no good.

The store was much larger than I imagined from the outside, perhaps 200 feet deep. The front section had been cleared of showroom supplies, and instead held about fifty folding chairs.

We got there fifteen minutes early and already the place was dense with people, sitting or milling around. About a third were women.

Two rectangular card-type tables were arranged against one wall. On one table was lemonade and cookies, and copies of the night's "betting sheet." We heard one guy call it by another name that rhymes with betting, which made Barbara wince. Fortunately most of the patrons were not so crude.

A man sat behind another table and before him a short line of people stood waiting to place bets. They gave him cash, he filled out some slip of paper and stuffed the bills in a brown envelope with the contestant's name scribbled on front.

The people were cordial, and Barbara and I struck up conversation with another couple.

"Your first time?" the man asked.

"Yes, it is. How does it work?"

"The betting?"

"Well, yeah, but first, how do they get weighed?"

He pointed to two large scales situated in front of the chairs. "The men will come out, get weighed in boxer shorts, then go to one of Joe's bathrooms. About twenty minutes later they return to get weighed again. Pretty simple."

"And the betting?"

He showed me his sheet. "Lots of ways. You can bet who you think will win in each flight. There's three, based on body weight: between two and three hundred, three to four hundred, and over four hundred pounds. Or, you can bet on the amount of weight to be lost. Whoever gets closest wins that. Or, the order of winners. That gives the greatest odds."

"I see," I replied, "but how did all this get set up? We're new to Vegas and never heard of this before."

"For that you'll have to ask Joe himself. He's over there."

Joe Calabane looked to be about eighty, frail and slightly stooped. I decided not to query the owner and founder. I would get the information elsewhere, later.

"What about women contestants?" Barbara asked.

"No, honey," said the man's wife, "you don't want to go there. Joe's tried it with women a couple of times, but it got a little raucous. You ever see a fat broad in a thin bikini? Guys went nuts. We were there, right George?"

George nodded in agreement and elaborated. "Guys made catcalls, yelled to take their bikinis off, made offers to go sit with them in the bathrooms. One woman freaked out, crapped in front of the audience. Pretty gross. Joe won't deal with women again. Only men."

Within fifteen minutes Barbara and I gained a pretty good idea how things went at these contests. We did not bet, knowing zilch about anyone. The betting sheet showed the three contest flights based on weight, with five names in each. There was no distinction about height or BMI. There were handicapping odds, presumably based on previous wins and other factors unknown to us. Also, we noted only aliases. Jack Strawn's, we learned from asking, was SqueezeHard. Other names I remember were BrownNose, Buttercup, Rosewood and DumpTruck. Real names weren't necessary; these men had *reputations*.

We took a seat in the back, the better to make a quick exit. Could the place be raided? Could we be arrested if the cops showed up? I was thankful we had left no name or email address. At 10 pm the emcee for the evening appeared, a thin man about forty or so, clearly not one of the contestants.

"Ladies and gentlemen," he began, in showmanship fashion, "welcome to tonight's Biggest Loser contests. I trust all of you have placed your bets. After the men are weighed we'll check to see if there are any last minute wagers. The men who will be competing in flight one are, as you can see, behind me." He pointed to a large table about ten yards in back of the scales. Five large men sat in what appeared to be hospital gowns. They were drinking bottled water and eating fruit, in preparation for the contest. Each man wore a cardboard number around his neck: 1, 2, 3, 4 or 5.

"As is our custom, they will get behind one of the screens here, take off their robe and put on fresh, new boxer shorts. This action will be supervised by other contestants and two volunteers from our audience. In this way you will be assured that no contestant is wearing weights or leaded shorts or anything that might increase his body weight. After each contestant has retreated to his private bathroom, you may continue to place bets. Each contestant will have twenty minutes to return and be re-weighed. Any questions?"

A patron in front yelled out: "If a guy wants to get weighed naked, is that allowed?"

"Yes, under the rules, he doesn't have to wear the boxer shorts. The only requirement is the number sign around his neck. Thank you for that question. Any others?"

One by one the men came up, put on the new boxer shorts and got weighed. The process seemed transparent, literally open to inspection if you chose to look. Their weights recorded, the men retreated to the rear bathrooms. At that point two of Joe's minions circulated among the audience, taking more bets. They verbalized each wager to the bettor, then wrote a receipt. "Five point seven pounds." "Number five." "Number three." Barbara and I resisted betting out of sheer ignorance, but were nonetheless fascinated by the activity.

The couple we had spoken with earlier sat next to us.

"Any questions?" the man asked. "Pretty straightforward."

"Who'd you bet on?" I asked.

"Puffnose. Number four. He's our favorite. That guy can dump a lot."

"How much, if I may ask?"

"Just five. Hell, it's worth the price of admission." His wife nodded affirmation.

"And if you win, how much will you get?"

"Three to one odds, fifteen dollars. Minus ten percent for the house."

"The house?"

"Yeah, Joe's house. Right here," and he let out a chuckle.

The winner of Flight One lost 5.7 pounds in the bathroom. Puffnose came in second at 4.3 pounds, so my seatmate was out his five dollars.

Then came round two. More of the same, only heavier guys. Jack Strawn was easily recognized on the far right, contestant number five. He did not recognize us, reason being he didn't really make eye contact with the audience when he was weighed. On his return to the scale he had lost 7.8 lbs. and took first place in his flight. We did not wait for round three and left for the parking lot.

Chapter 3

In the car we had the same thought. "What is the attraction?"

"It's the Biggest Loser contest like they have on TV, with a few wrinkles," I said. "There, you diet to lose slowly. Here you eat to lose fast."

"Yes," agreed Barbara, "but the TV show isn't held at Joe's Plumbing. There's a reason for that."

We concluded it was sort of like illegal cockfighting carried out in many parts of the world: a populist approach to flouting authority while engaged in that universal human vice – betting. And like cockfighting, Joe's weight loss contests were grass roots in the extreme, with no chance of being co-opted by any casino. This was the people's betting parlor. We prided ourselves on our analysis and I toyed with the idea of adding text and fresh insight to the Wikipedia article.

Afterwards we went for coffee. I chose Melvin's Diner just off the Strip because it has large booths and is reasonably quiet; you can talk there without raising your voice. In half the restaurants in Las Vegas you almost have to lip read to carry on a conversation.

On the way Barbara and I had discussed little about each other, though I did get her to drop the "doctor" and call me Josh. Seated in a booth at Melvin's, we ordered coffee and a piece of pie to share.

"Excuse me, I've got to go the restroom," said Barbara.

"Me, too."

I washed my hands more thoroughly than usual.

Back in the booth I asked Barbara, "Did you feel dirty after Joe's?"

"A little, but the place itself wasn't actually dirty."

"So, what made you go to nursing school? I assume not right out of high school."

"Hardly. I went to college in Seattle, where I grew up. Majored in English, expecting to be a high school English teacher. Fell in love and got married my senior year."

"You're married?" *Am I wasting my time?*

"Not any more. Lasted two years. He was a graduate student at the time, a great guy I thought. That's a cliché' I suppose, for all the pricks who pose as great guys. He was a jerk, and we parted."

"So that drove you to nursing school?"

"No, it drove me to depression. Plus the fact I couldn't find a teaching job in or near Seattle. Spent all my time substituting. Seems every teacher from kindergarten to twelfth grade has a Masters, or seniority, or a friend in administration. I knew I should go back and get my Masters, but my heart wasn't in it."

I am so afraid of the next question, or rather her answer, but ask it anyway. "Any kids?"

"No. We didn't plan on it right away, and after the first year I realized it wasn't going to work out, and made sure I wouldn't get pregnant." I did not ask how, but wanted to: *Did you use the pill? Did you not sleep with him?*

"So I am having trouble connecting the dots between no teaching job in Seattle and becoming a nurse in Las Vegas. I need a little help here."

"Oh, Josh, it's so obvious." Her sarcasm was sweet, intelligent. "My best girlfriend whom I've known since high school was in Vegas, name's Irene. She's married now but back then she was single. She said I should move here, there were tons of opportunities for a girl with my talent."

"For teaching?"

"No, of course not. For pole dancing."

I was smitten already. She majored in English, recovered from the depression of a failed marriage, moved to Vegas to take up pole dancing, and was now a registered nurse in my ED. What more could I ask for? I just had one question.

"Huh?"

Barbara took a breath, brushed hair away from her forehead and continued. "My girlfriend worked the front desk at The Venetian, and had a second job as pole dancer at the Trader John Saloon. She said the money's great, and you meet all kinds of people."

"I can imagine."

"That's not what lured me here, Josh. Mainly the possibility of starting over, getting far away from my ex and maybe landing a teaching job here. I had no intention of becoming a pole dancer. I didn't even know what it was. So I came and stayed with her for a month, before finding my own place.

During that month I went with Irene to Trader John's, to watch her perform."

"And?"

"It's not what you think, or not what I thought. Their clientele includes a lot of couples, not just dirty old men, and every evening they invite women from the audience to perform. Their husbands or boyfriends think it's a hoot."

"Sorry," I said, "but what is *it*? For those of us from the Midwest, sounds like the first step toward sex for money. What we in old-fashioned land call the big P."

"I know, I know. But in the higher class places, that's not apparent. Believe it or not, they will kick out any customer who tries to hit on the girls, fondle or proposition them. It's one hundred percent looky-no touchy."

Our order arrived and we each took a bite of Melvin's delicious peanut butter chocolate pie.

"So where's the money come in? Girls don't do it for peanuts. If they did, I could see monkeys in that gig."

She did not laugh. Sometimes my jokes fall flat.

"You show your butt off, your boobs, one at a time, rarely if so inclined your crotch. Men throw money at you. You scoop it up."

"Is this the same as lap dancing?

"Hardly. They have that too, but that's more touchy-feely. Some girls go for that, but pole dancing is more of an art form. It's just you and a pole."

"Literally, a pole?"

"Literally, a pole. About this big around." She curved her thumb and index finger to show about three inches in diameter. "Goes from floor to ceiling."

"How did you know what to do with the pole?"

"Took a few lessons."

"Really? Some girls flunk?"

"No one flunks. Once they let you take the lessons you've more or less passed."

"You mean you've slept with the boss."

"Boy, you are cynical. It just means you've auditioned in a bikini."

She enjoyed the bantering and could take any question I asked. Each minute in that booth I grew more attracted to her.

"Something's not connecting here, Barbara, if I may be so blunt. You come from Seattle, recently divorced, hoping to be a school teacher. And within a month or so of being in Vegas you are auditioning for pole dancing?"

"Insane, isn't it?"

"I'll say."

"The truth is, I have the right figure and the money offered was more than I could make as a teacher. I felt confident from Irene that this was legitimate and nothing would be expected of me for sexual favors. I mean there's a pole dancer's union, for God sakes. So I tried it one night, enjoyed myself, and went on from there."

"So naturally this led to nursing."

"Of course."

"You're teasing me now, Barbara. How did you get from the dancing pole to the IV pole?"

"I did it for about a year. The novelty wore off. There were a couple of assholes who were a little frightening, but they were quickly bounced. So while the money was good, for not a whole lot of work, I saw there was no future."

She fondled her coffee cup in both hands, and I envisioned her fondling something else. "Well, I agree with that," I said.

"I began making inquiries about getting my Masters in education. Thought of going to UNLV, or doing it online through the University of Phoenix, or even moving to another city, though I really liked Vegas. But as I read about all the career opportunities, most of the jobs were for medicine, nursing, medical techs. Not so much for education, even with a Masters. I made a career change, almost instantly."

"So from teaching to nursing, in an instant. That's impressive."

"I wanted a career with a decent income, one where I can help people. I was accepted to UNLV's nursing school and three years later had my RN. Right away got the job at Memorial. It's really that simple."

I took another bite of pie. "How old are you, if I may ask?"

"You may ask. Twenty-seven. Getting up there. And you?"

"Thirty-three. Do you still pole dance?"

"I was afraid you were going to ask. I did it through nursing school, about once a week. That's how I paid for school, along with loans and some help from my parents. Now I'm going to quit. Soon."

"You don't sound so sure." She smiled, as I if had found out a deep secret.

"I'm sure, just not sure when. I can still make as much in two hours some nights as on a twelve-hour nursing shift."

I was going to ask about "relationships" since her move to Vegas, but she changed the subject.

"Enough about me," she said. "Tell me about yourself."

I am superb at taking a history – it's part of evaluating patients – but not so much at giving one. I did not want to bore her and just gave a telescoped summary. Grew up in Cleveland, Dad's an orthopedic surgeon, Mom's an OR nurse, older sister is a pediatrician with two kids. Parents wanted me to go to medical school, but I majored in liberal arts and playing the guitar. Wasn't attracted to medicine. After college spent several months in India. Then in Delhi one night decided I would, after all, go into medicine.

"Slow down, I'm dizzy," she said. "How did you end up in India?"

"So you don't like the Readers' Digest history?"

"Readers' Digest? You're more like the Twitter version."

This was good. She *was* interested.

"Did I mention Wendy?"

"She's your sister?"

"No, the girl I went to India with."

"I think you're having a little expressive aphasia right now. Not very coherent."

"Sorry, guess I'm just so afraid of boring you."

"So you mention an old girl friend? That's supposed to interest me?"

"She's why I went to India."

"So you're just giving me teasers about your past. Do you want me to ask twenty questions?"

"Go ahead."

"Did you marry Wendy?"

"No."

"Did you sleep with Wendy?"

"Yes."

"Then what happened?"

"Okay, I'm sorry, twenty questions won't do it. I'll tell you more, just promise to cut me off when it gets boring."

"Don't worry, I will."

"So in high school I had learned to play guitar reasonably well, even tried composing a couple of songs. When I got to college I met other like-minded wannabe Bob Dylans."

"You mean guys who write poetry but can't sing?"

"Well, yeah, if you want to look at it that way. There was a jam session almost every night in local coffee houses, and I learned most of the songs by heart. I took one science course, Biology, and got a B. Every time I went home Mom and Dad would ask, "Are you going to apply to medical school? What are you going to do with your life?" My answer was always the same. "Right now I'm learning a lot about the world." They thought it was BS, but that would back them off for a while."

"Okay," Barbara said. "I can relate to that. I was in liberal arts before I found nursing."

"Anyway, between my junior and senior year of college I worked at Yellowstone, at Old Faithful Inn, right across from the famous geyser. Ever been there?"

"No, it's on my list. I've been to Bryce and Zion, though."

"Yeah, me too. Magnificent. Anyway, those park lodge jobs tend to be menial but not easy to come by, so I was glad to get it. I cleaned rooms, worked as a waiter and busboy, did some lodge maintenance, all for the privilege of spending eight weeks in God's Country."

She looked at me doe-eyed. I was capturing her imagination and she was not bored. "On days off I hiked and got to visit most of the tourist sites. One in particular is called Artist's Point, which overlooks The Grand Canyon of the Yellowstone. It's an amazing vista. Let me show it to you." I pulled out my cell phone, googled the site and in less than a minute had a picture.

"Wow," she said. "Sort of reminds me of the canyon in Zion, except for the waterfall."

"Yeah, well it's even more impressive in person."

"So this is where you met Wendy?"

"Actually, yes. We had a thing going at Yellowstone. She was sort of hippie-like, and told me she was going to India after her college graduation in California. Her plan was to study at an ashram and she asked me to join her. I said yes, since I had no better plans after graduation. It seemed like a cool thing to do."

"And let me guess," said Barbara. "Your parents weren't happy."

"That's an understatement. They went ballistic, but in the end they really had no choice. I was prepared to pay my own way with savings from the summer job. That money would have run out in a few months. My father was afraid I'd end up destitute and sick in India. He agreed to fund the trip if I promised to take pre-med when I returned and consider medical school. That's a condensed version of a bitter struggle that lasted the better part of a week."

The waitress brought the check, and pointedly asked if we wanted anything else. The place was busy and I got the feeling she wanted the booth for new customers. I gave her my credit card.

"So please continue," Barbara said. "This is interesting."

"So do you know what an ashram is?"

"Sort of. A place of meditation. Guru and all."

"Exactly. Wendy found our ashram through a friend in California who had studied in India. It was located five miles outside Nagpur, a city south of Delhi. The ashram specialized in young Americans who wanted to 'find their way'. That sort of fit us."

"Not the Ritz Carlton, I take it."

"Hardly. For my taste it was downright Spartan. A couple of low slung buildings built of stucco, with mattresses on the floor for sleeping. Mostly vegetarian food, mostly no toilets or hot showers, and mostly meditation and study during the day, kind of boring. But there were two huge plusses."

"Wendy being one," she said. "What's the other?"

"Music. I was pleasantly surprised about the music. It was authentic Indian music. Do you play an instrument?"

"No, not really, but I used to sing in a choir."

"Well, Indian music is on a different scale system than in the west. The sitar is a distant cousin to our stringed instruments. It opened my eyes to Eastern melodies and intervals. Native Hindis played it in the evenings, and when I brought out my guitar to perform, they listened politely. My Western-style folk songs sounded strange to them, but as music is the universal language, there was mutual appreciation."

"So a jam session, Indian style."

"Sort of. Actually, the majority of the ashram visitors were from the states, so they joined in singalongs that reminded them of home. We played *The Sloop John B.* and *This Land Is Your Land* and a bunch of other American folk songs. The music opportunities were good, an unexpected bonus."

"But you broke up with Wendy?"

"Well, that's a short story. Want to hear it?"

"I'm all ears."

"Probably the only real requirement to survive in the Nagpur ashram was that you not disturb the peace. Our visit brought in needed income. I think we each paid about $200 a month to stay there. The head guru was one Dittyram Suburambian, who looked to be about sixty. His English was not very good but he understood American money, so we got alone fine."

"So let me guess. This Dittyram guy falls in love with Wendy and you lose her to his higher spirituality."

"Close. Not bad. You see, all along Wendy's goal was to quote find myself unquote. My goals were somewhat more prosaic. I remember making a list. Have sex with her. Learn about the culture of another country. Avoid my parents for a reasonable period. And decide what to do with my next fifty years or so. I succeeded on all counts but one."

"I can imagine which one. You learned about India. You avoided your parents. You have a long medical career ahead of you. That leaves..."

"Yeah, well, the more Wendy prayed, studied and meditated, the less inclined she was to sleep with me. Actually, there was communal sleeping, so there was no privacy at night. We had to go off a ways to do it, which was not that difficult. In any case, the teachings of this ashram did not exactly conform to my idea of sex. Do you know what she told me?"

"Something spiritual, I'm sure."

"Say, you're good. She said, 'Josh, we must love the spirit more than the body'. Can you believe that?"

"I mean you went with her to the ashram. Did you think it was going to be Club Med?"

"Who the hell knows? All I know is she was brainwashed. I was blunt. I told her "Yes, but I need you." And she said...?"

"You want me to guess?"

"Go ahead. You've nailed her pretty good so far."

"Okay, she said, 'Yes, Josh, but the needs are spiritual, not physical'."

"Dead on! That's exactly what she said! Do you know Wendy?"

"She's my sister."

For a half-second I believed her, but then she put a hand around my forearm and looked at me with twinkly eyes. "Oh, I'm just joshing with you, Josh. The way you tell this, her responses seem obvious. As you said, she was brainwashed."

"Yeah, well, it was a deal breaker, that's for sure. By the end of the first month sex was down to less once a week, and then with an embellishment. Guess again."

"She had the guru right there, praying for your soul."

"Good guess, but a little off this time. *She* prayed during the act, like she was screwing some god and not me. By the end of two months we were done. I left after the third month, and toured India with a guy I met in the ashram."

Just then the waitress brought over the credit card receipt, which I signed. "I think they want us out of here, to make room for other customers."

"Well, you have to tell me what happened with Wendy."

"God knows," I said. "About the time we broke up she became the close companion of the Guru's assistant, a young Hindi named Swami Gupta. I suspected she was doing it with him. Or doing *something* with him to give her the same kick as sex with me. I left her in India. That was twelve years ago. She's probably a Maharani by now."

Barbara laughed, a totally guileless laugh that made me feel I had conquered her soul. *She likes me.* I could have regaled her for another hour about my past. Seeing her genuine interest, however, I did suggest she and I were two like-minded vagabonds, each seeking a new beginning in Las Vegas.

"Seems that way," she agreed.

I would use the promise of *more Josh history* for another date. "India was fascinating, but I think it's best for another time."

Barbara pouted with her lips in a way to suggest she wanted more history – or just didn't want the date to end so soon. My thought as well. That night I discovered someone special: a woman with beauty, brains, determination and charm. I wanted her in my bed more than ever. I looked at my watch. An hour had gone by since we sat down and it was past midnight.

"Well, this has been fun."

"Yes, it has."

"I'll take you home" I said, which is not what I wanted to do. I decided to be bold. "Unless you want to come to my place. I live close by, in the Abington Tower." She knew what I meant, of course. *Unless you want to sleep with me tonight.*

"I don't know. Do you have a pole in your apartment?"

✶ ✶ ✶

Available in paperback and as ebook:
https://books2read.com/u/m2rO2G

Lawrence Martin

The Boy Who Dreamed Mount Everest

Available in paperback and as ebook:
https://books2read.com/u/bpEXdX

Eli is ten and lives in Chicago. He loves to rock climb in Bubba's indoor gym. He's never climbed any mountain, but is fascinated with Mount Everest, the tallest in the world. From reading he has learned the route to the top, and the dangers that can befall climbers.

Eli begins dreaming he's on a special Bubba's Kids Expedition to climb Everest. Night after night, his dreams take him higher up the mountain. Bad things happen, and sometimes his dreams turn into nightmares. During the day he argues with his little sister, worries his parents, daydreams in school, thinks about a cute girl in his class, and tries to figure out math problems. But at night, asleep, he continues to climb. Will Eli and his buddies reach the summit?

Come join the expedition! Along the way you will learn a lot about what it takes to climb Mount Everest.

 Note: Text indicating each of Eli's dreams is in bold-faced type and preceded by this graphic of a thought cloud.

Chapter 1

The rock wall was forty feet straight up, as high as a four-story building. Eli Walter looked up the length of the wall and gave a shudder. Sure, he'd climbed the wall before, but today in the gym he and four other boys were going to be timed! Speed, he knew, could lead to mistakes and he didn't want to fall.

Each boy had to wear a harness, and the floor was covered with thick mats. Still, Eli was nervous. Worse, he could sense his mother's anxiety at what was about to take place. She was standing to the side with the other parents, rubbing her hands together. Eli knew she did that only when nervous about something.

"Listen to the instructor, and don't do anything foolish." Mom's words on the drive to the gym echoed in his head. Eli loved to climb the rock wall, and of course would obey all instructions. He liked baseball and swimming also, but indoor rock climbing – always in Bubba's Gym in Chicago – was his favorite sport.

The group of five boys, all ten years old, gathered around the instructor, a young man just double their age, about twenty. "OK, boys, listen up. This morning I'm going to time you and see how long it takes each of you to reach the top grip. That's one of the big orange grips you see up there." The boys looked up. Four orange grips topped out the climbing wall.

"This is a challenging climb, but you've done it many times, so no big deal. Right?"

"Right," they echoed. Of course it *was* a big deal, being timed, but this was part of their training. Soon they would be competing against other boys in other gyms around Chicago.

"As soon as you grab any one of the orange handholds, you can come back down. By grab, I mean the palm of your hand has to grab onto the handhold."

The instructor walked to the wall to demonstrate on a lower handhold. "So, not the tips of your fingers. I want you to grab the handhold, even if it's for just a fraction of a second. Now, what's the most important thing when you climb?"

"Safety!" the boys yelled in unison. They had been well drilled.

"Right. It does no good to rush to the top if you miss a footing and fall. If you fall, the harness will catch you, but you'll lose valuable seconds. To win you've got to get to the top and grab the orange handhold. After that, no need to rush. Come down slowly. We're only timing your speed to the top. Any questions?"

There were none. "OK. We're going to go in alphabetical order. Michael Atwood, you're first."

Michael put on his harness. The instructor checked that it was secure, then took out his stopwatch. Michael applied chalk to his hands, rubbed them together and let the excess fall to the mat. He then faced the wall and announced, "I'm ready."

"Go!"

Michael began his climb. He was methodical, not missing a step. Right hand grip. Left foot step. Left hand grip. Right foot step. Up and up. He reached the top, grabbed the orange handhold and looked down. The kids clapped.

"Very good," the instructor called up. "Now come on down. Take your time."

As soon as Michael reached the floor he asked, "How'd I do?"

"One minute seven seconds," said the instructor. "Very good." Michael took off his harness and handed it to the next kid, Brian Gordon. It took Brian only a couple of minutes to put it on.

"Ready?" asked the instructor.

"Yes."

"OK, go."

Brian started his climb. He raced to the top. Grip. Step. Grip. Step. Up and up.

He's going too fast, thought Eli. Sure enough, a mere five feet from the top Brian lost his footing and fell. The boys on the ground jumped up, ready to catch him, but the harness held and he dangled off the side of the wall. Slowly Brian swayed back to the wall, grabbed one of the footholds and continued his climb. He had lost at least fifteen precious seconds.

Eli did not take pleasure in Brian's stumble; he knew it could happen to him, too. If anything, it made him even more nervous.

Brian climbed down and did not ask his time when he hit the mat.

"Nice recovery, Brian," said the instructor. "You clocked at one minute twenty. Don't worry, there will be plenty of other opportunities."

Next came Derek Richardson, Eli's closest friend in the group. If Eli couldn't win, he hoped Derek would. Up, up climbed Derek, sure-footed all the way. He did not look down even once. He grabbed the top orange handhold, at which point the kids applauded his successful climb. Then he began his slow descent, reaching the mat in a couple of minutes.

"Fifty-nine seconds, Derek. Excellent job."

Eli was next. As he put on the harness his mother crossed her fingers. Without raising her voice she said simply, "Good luck, Eli."

"Your son?" asked the woman next to her.

"Yes."

"Michael is my son. It's amazing what these kids can do."

"Yes it is," Eli's mom replied, keeping her eyes fixed on the wall.

Harness on, Eli began his climb. One hand over the other, feet expertly placed. Up, up, up. He forgot he was nervous and climbed like he'd done before. No missteps! He reached the top, grabbed the handhold and stayed for a few seconds, savoring what he felt was a fast climb, then climbed down. He had done well, but maybe not well enough. He wasn't sure.

"Fifty-seven seconds! Great job, Eli."

Eli unhooked his harness and ran to sit with the other boys. He turned briefly to look at Mom, who was smiling. She gave him a thumbs up. Now Eli thought he might have a chance. Just one more boy to climb, Charlie Zingale, whom he knew could be fast. Eli turned around to watch Charlie's effort. He just hoped and hoped.

Charlie scampered up and grabbed the handhold. "Click" went the stopwatch. Charlie's climb seemed fast to Eli, but there was no way to know if he was the fastest. The instructor wouldn't say until Charlie was safely back on the mat.

"Good job, Charlie. One minute exactly. OK, boys, we have a winner! Eli Walter, with a time of fifty-seven seconds. Congratulations, Eli."

Eli climbing rock wall inside Bubba's Gym

All the parents applauded. Eli felt flushed with excitement. This was his first climbing competition and he had won! He went up to receive a pin in the shape of a rock wall. It read "First Place. Junior Boys Division. Bubba's Rock Climbing Gym, Chicago, IL." He ran over and gave the pin to his mother, then rushed back to finish the session. There would be another half hour of practice before heading home.

On the drive home Eli's mom was full of praise. "That was amazing, Eli."

"Yeah, I thought Charlie would beat me. He's very fast some days."

"Well, you're pretty nimble."

"What's nimble?" Eli asked.

"It means you can move around rocks easily, get past obstacles."

"Mom, do you think I could climb Mount Everest one day?"

"Mount Everest? Wow! What made you bring that up?"

"I've been reading about it on the internet. It's the tallest mountain in the world. Kids have climbed it."

"Really? I don't think so. It's very dangerous up there."

"Well, I read that a thirteen-year-old boy did it. He was the youngest. His name is Jordan Romero."

"Eli, thirteen is hardly a kid. He was a teenager. You've just turned ten."

"I know, but still—"

"Eli, read all you want. But rock climbing in Bubba's Gym is not anything like climbing Mount Everest. Or any mountain for that matter."

"I know. I saw the pictures. It's really, really cold up there. Colder even than Chicago in winter!"

"Doesn't that sort of scare you?"

"Well…yes and no. I mean, they dress warmly. And they carry oxygen."

"How do you know that?"

"The internet. It shows pictures of climbers. Some died."

"Eli, can we change the subject?" She looked briefly at him, then returned her gaze to the street. "You're not climbing Mount Everest. It's halfway around the world and you're ten years old. Besides, you wouldn't want to leave your sister behind, would you?"

"Iris is only seven. That's too young."

"And what about ten?"

Eli did not respond. He thought of himself on top of the tallest mountain in the world. *And the youngest boy to ever climb Mount Everest is…Eli Walter.*

Chapter 2

At dinner the next night Dad brought up Mount Everest. "Mom told me your Everest books arrived. Have you begun reading any?"

"Finished two. They're mostly just picture books. But they have some good information."

"Learn anything you care to share with us?"

"Umm. Let me think." Eli briefly closed his eyes, then asked, "How high is Mount Everest?"

"You're asking me?"

"I know. It's a question."

"Let me guess," said Dad. "Five miles high."

"29,029 feet high. Above sea level."

"Well, that's almost five miles."

"I think it's more. I can go check."

"No, that's OK," said Dad. "Let me ask *you* a question. Who was the first person to climb Mount Everest?"

"That's *easy*! Edmund Hillary and Tenzing Norgay."

"That's two people."

"They did it together. Actually, I'm not sure which one got to the top first. The books didn't say."

"OK. What year?" his father asked.

Eli was stumped. He had certainly read about the first successful climb, but didn't remember the year. This bothered him a lot.

"Ummm…wait. I'll be right back." He ran to his room.

"He's really into this Everest thing," said his mother. "Once he reads all about it I'm sure he'll go on to something else. He doesn't like very cold weather."

"I hope he goes," said Iris, in a taunting manner. "Where is it? Is it in Michigan?"

"No, honey, it's far away, on the other side of the world."

Eli returned a few minutes later, plopped down in his chair and blurted out, "Nineteen fifty three. It was in May. That's the best month."

"Very good, Eli," said his father. "Very good. Now let's finish eating. We can talk more about Everest when you've finished the books. Two things I want you to check on, though."

"In the books?"

"Yes, in the books. How cold does it get at the top of Mount Everest, and how low is the oxygen level?"

"What do you mean how low? They use oxygen to get to the top."

"I know, but how much oxygen is there at the top? Just a little less than in Chicago, or a lot less? Think of fractions. Is it half as much, or only one-fourth as much when you get to the top?"

Eli was studying fractions in school so he understood the question. "OK, that's a good question."

"Eli, please eat your supper," said his mother. "It's getting cold."

That night Eli fell asleep with a book in his hands, *The Story of Mount Everest for Kids.* Just before closing his eyes he managed to shut off the flashlight. Sleep came quickly.

He dreamed.

Eli sat in the window seat and strained to look over the wing at the Himalayas. He was in Nepal! There were mountains in the distance, but no sign of Everest. Then he saw many rooftops and in a few minutes the plane landed safely in Kathmandu, the country's capital. After two very long plane rides from Chicago he was happy to get outside. The early April air felt chilly as he walked with his dad to the terminal building. They stood in line until it was their turn with the Nepalese customs agent.

"Passports and visas, sir."

Eli's father handed over two passports and visas.

"What is your purpose for visiting Nepal, sir?" the agent asked.

"Why, to climb Mount Everest, of course," said Eli, before his father could answer.

"You have your climbing permits?"

"My son is part of Bubba's Mt. Everest Expedition, out of Chicago," said his father. "All the kids are on this flight. We are meeting the guide here in Kathmandu. He has all the permits."

"Yes," said Eli. "We are all very good at rock climbing!"

The unsmiling gate agent studied the documents and stamped their passports. Then, looking at the line behind Eli and his father he yelled out, "Next."

Eli wondered why the agent did not seem much interested in Bubba's Expedition. Who wouldn't be interested in ten-year-olds climbing the world's highest mountain? *He must not think I am serious. That's it. Well, he'll see.*

Chapter 3

The next night Eli rushed through his homework, anxious to finish another book about Mount Everest. He crawled into bed, switched on the flashlight and began reading. After just a few minutes his eyes grew heavy and he felt sleep coming on. He hoped his dream would return.

"OK, boys," said the guide. "You're here for Bubba's Kids' Everest Expedition, being that you're all expert rock climbers." Eli didn't recognize the guide, but he appeared rugged, and had a beard. His name was Maxwell Burlington and he certainly looked important. The boys hung on his every word.

"Tomorrow we're going to fly from Kathmandu into the town of Lukla. We'll stay there three days and do day hikes, so you can get used to the higher altitude. How many of you have heard of Lukla?"

Eli raised his hand.

"What do you know about it, Eli?"

"It's where people can hike, if they want to, all the way to Everest Base Camp. But it takes two weeks, I think."

"Yes, that's right. Lukla's at 9383 feet altitude, much higher than Kathmandu. But we're not going to do the trek to Everest Base Camp. As you said, Eli, that takes about two weeks. We want you to save your energy for the climb up the mountain. Instead, we're going to take a helicopter to Base Camp."

"That's good!" said a couple of boys. Eli thought it was good, too. He had never been in a helicopter before.

"Base camp is over 17,000 feet above sea level, so you'll feel the altitude there. When we arrive you'll have to take it easy. Don't run around the first couple of days. We'll actually spend about three weeks at Base Camp getting used to the altitude. During that time we'll make several hikes up the Khumbu Icefall and return to Base Camp. We'll also hike to Camp One, spend the night there, and

300

return to Base Camp the next day. We do all this for acclimatization. That's an important part of climbing Mount Everest. Acclimatization. I want you all to say that word, acclimatization."

"Acclimatization," they all said, though not in unison. Some of them sounded like "Aclimb-a-zation."

"And what does it mean?" Maxwell asked.

"Getting used to the high altitude," said Eli.

"Right. Now, while at Base Camp we'll teach you how to use ice picks, use the ropes needed for the climb, and purify melted snow for drinking water. We'll have tents set up for sleeping, with four of you to a tent. Let's see..." Maxwell looked at his clipboard. "Eli and Brian, your fathers have elected to climb with you. So the four of you will share a tent at Base Camp. The Richardsons and Zingales will share a tent and I will be with Derek Richardson and his mother in another tent.

"Mr. Richardson, Mr. Zingale and Mrs. Atwood have no climbing experience, so they will remain at Base Camp while their sons are climbing the mountain." Eli wondered if his father did have climbing experience. That wasn't in his memory but he didn't question it.

"OK, that's about it," said Maxwell. "Any questions?"

Eli raised his hand. "When do we get the oxygen tanks?"

"Good question, Eli. You won't need the tanks at Base Camp, but while there we'll fit you for an oxygen mask and show you how to use the tanks. We'll start using oxygen when we reach Camp Three, which is at an altitude of about 23,500 feet. Any other questions?"

"Will Sherpas be with us?" asked Brian.

"Yes. Do you all know about Sherpas?"

Only Eli and Brian raised their hands. "OK," said Maxwell, "Sherpas are native Nepalese who specialize in helping people climb the mountain. They are very strong and are used to high altitudes. We have a lot of equipment to carry up the mountain. We've hired seven Sherpas to accompany us. So actually climbing the mountain, it'll be me as your guide, five kids and two adults – plus seven Sherpas. We'll meet the Sherpas at Base Camp."

"Have you climbed Mount Everest before?" asked Michael.

"Yes, this will be my third ascent," said Maxwell. Eli knew "ascent" meant going up the mountain.

The plane ride to Lukla was scary. Much scarier than flying into Midway Airport, which Eli had done several times on trips with his family. Unlike in Chicago, there were mountains to navigate, and the runway was very short; it ended at the edge of a steep cliff. Eli was very glad when they finally landed.

The higher altitude in Lukla didn't bother him, but his father felt a little lightheaded the first day. Eli was getting used to it. There were short day hikes to the surrounding mountains, only about three hours each, but important to help with acclimatization. On one hike they met some people trekking to Everest Base Camp. The trekkers were from California, and they each carried a heavy backpack. Eli's father asked one of them, "How long do you think it will take to walk to Base Camp?"

"We're giving it twelve days," the man replied. "We're from the Sierra Trekking Club, so we're all experienced hikers."

Eli was glad they would travel to Base Camp by helicopter. He had read that the distance from Lukla was only thirty-five miles, but it could take up to two weeks because the route included a lot of up-and-down and back-and-forth hiking. He wanted to climb the mountain, not hike for days just to get to the starting point.

After three days in Lukla they took off in a helicopter for the flight to Everest Base Camp. That was exciting. Everyone wore headphones because of the noise, so there was no conversation. But the views of the Himalayas were amazing. Jagged, snow-capped peaks, just like he'd seen in pictures, but this was real. He couldn't wait to climb.

Base Camp was just like the pictures he'd seen: a bunch of tents at the foot of the Khumbu Icefall. The Khumbu Icefall! Eli knew the Icefall itself was a giant moving glacier, full of cracks and hidden holes. So many bad things had happened there: avalanches and giant ice boulders that could dislodge at any time, and climbers sometimes falling into the ice cracks. *We have to climb it.*

Around the camp Eli noted several Nepalese shrines adorned with colorful prayer flags. He had read that the shrines bring good luck to climbers who walk around them.

Base Camp, Mount Everest

Eli and his father shared a tent with Brian and Mr. Gordon. Eli wished it would be with Derek, because Derek was his best friend on the trip. Maybe he and Derek could climb to the summit together, perhaps reach the top at the same moment. Isn't that what Hillary and Norgay did? He wasn't sure.

"Ugh!" said Brian, just back from the "bathroom."

"What's the matter?" asked Eli.

"It's gross. Disgusting. Just an open pit."

"We talked about this," said Mr. Gordon. "We warned you it's not going to be a picnic living at Base Camp. It's not a hotel, you know."

"Yeah, I read about that too," said Eli. "It's like camping out."

"That's the spirit, son," said Eli's father.

Still, Eli did not look forward to using the Base Camp's bathrooms.

✳ ✳ ✳

Available in paperback and as ebook:
https://books2read.com/u/bpEXdX

ABOUT THE AUTHOR

Lawrence Martin is a retired physician and author of over twenty books, plus numerous short stories. During his medical career as a pulmonologist in Cleveland, he wrote both textbooks for physicians (e.g., *Pulmonary Physiology in Clinical Practice*) and non-fiction works for a general audience (e.g., *Scuba Diving Explained: Questions and Answers on Physiology and Medical Aspects*). All of his books are listed at:

www.lakesidepress.com/books.html.

Near retirement, Dr. Martin began writing fiction, which he describes as "a whole different learning curve than non-fiction." Now fully retired, he lives in The Villages, Florida with his wife. They have three daughters and five grandchildren.

During 2017 Dr. Martin was president of the Writers League of The Villages, Florida. He remains active in several writing-related clubs. His short story "The Critique Group", though fictional, is based on experience gained in these groups.

You may contact the author at drlarry437@gmail.com.

Made in the USA
Columbia, SC
13 November 2021

48889245R00172